SAFE HARBOR

SAFE HARBOR

EUGENE IZZI

AVON BOOKS  NEW YORK

AVON BOOKS, INC.
1350 Avenue of the Americas
New York, New York 10019

Copyright © 1995 by Eugene Izzi
ISBN: 0-380-97343-X

Library of Congress Cataloging in Publication Data:
Izzi, Eugene.
Safe harbor / Eugene Izzi. —1st ed.
p. cm.
I. Title.
PS3559.Z9S24 1999   99-25042
813'.54—dc21   CIP

First Avon Books Printing: August 1999

AVON TRADEMARK REG. U.S. PAT. OFF. AND IN OTHER COUNTRIES, MARCA REGISTRADA,
HECHO EN U.S.A.

Printed in the U.S.A.

FIRST EDITION

QPM   10 9 8 7 6 5 4 3 2 1

www.avonbooks.com

Dedicated to Max Fitzpatrick—
Born into a safe harbor

SAFE HARBOR

HE'D GOTTEN A reputation early as a standup guy, back when his name had been Tommy Torelli and his life had been one of crime. He never said much then, even as a kid, but he knew how to show respect and his eyes were vacuum cleaners. always sweeping the street around him and never missing a trick.

It wasn't the sort of thing that wiseguys would neglect to notice.

He knew who they were; it was something you grew up with a total awareness of in Tommy's neighborhood in New York's Little Italy. He'd watch from the window of his tenement apartment building on Mulberry Street as they pulled their cars up to the curb in front of the candy store, young Tommy's eyes wide as the men double-parked on the narrow street, waving their keys to the uniformed cops if one happened to be around. Tourists in rented cars would sometimes honk at these violent men and they'd turn their massive bellies toward the sounds of the horns and glare until the car passed by. Sometimes they'd kick out at it as the car passed them, their faces expressing their rage at the insult, showing too their supreme confidence, an utter lack of fear which Tommy had admired. It was one of the reasons that he began to worship them; how easily and shamelessly they were allowed to express their anger, how they had nothing to fear because they themselves were fearsome.

He certainly wasn't ever allowed to show that he was upset. Tommy had learned to deal with it by living up in his head, staring out the window of the fifth floor walk-up apartment they rented in the filthy red brick building, imagining himself to be a man of respect. Tommy looking down through the rusted stairs of the fire escape that was attached to the front of his building, fantasizing, wanting to be like them. Right there outside his bedroom window, his father having put him there because the window faced the noisy street. His parents had a bedroom with a window that was six inches away from the building next door. Tommy knew that the residents with kids threw their diapers down that airshaft, and figured that he'd gotten the better of the deal. He wouldn't have minded the stink; this building *always* stunk. He thought he'd come out on top of the matter because he was able to look down at the wiseguys.

The candy store building itself was painted dark green, the paint slapped on haphazardly, streaks apparent in the finish. The store had not ever been meant to be a place where tourists were supposed to feel welcome. There were two large picture windows facing the streets, one on either side of the mostly always open door. Inside the window on the right was a statue of Jesus Christ, red blood painted onto the wounds of his hands and his feet. Christ was holding those hands out wide, showing the viewer how badly he'd been fucked over, a look of incredible pain on his face. Inside the window on the left stood a statue of Christ's mother, Holy Mary smiling benevolently, her hands, too, spread out wide, a rosary dangling from one of them. Beneath her feet was a brightly colored, long-fanged dying snake.

It was not the sort of window display that caused a passerby to wander into the store to see what they could buy. They weren't wanted inside, where the gangsters were. If some thick-headed tourist idiot still didn't get the hint, there were always two old and smelly men sitting at a table right inside the doorway, wearing colorless wrinkled suits, drinking coffee and glaring out at the sidewalk. It was the retirement plan for old buttonmen, those few who managed to get through their lives being neither whacked nor pinched and sent away for life.

Sometimes at night a group of them would be hanging out in front getting rowdy, and Tommy would watch, mimicking their movements, the inflections in their voices, until a tall, fat middle-aged man came over to the door and looked out at them with a passive face that told none of his many secrets. Tommy would study that face in the seconds it took for the man's presence to be felt by the gang, trying to see if the man was happy or sad, angry or pleased. It was a question that was never settled in his mind, not even years later, when the man became his friend. As soon as they saw him the wiseguys would fall silent, and Tommy would sit there, staring in awe.

Everyone in the neighborhood knew who those guys were, and most of the neighbors were in some way in their debt. They used the mob bookie, or they loaned money from the sharks; the local mob chief was the guy you saw when you needed a favor from the city or when you wanted to settle a beef.

Tommy's mother would buy meat and fish and vegetables from them, making her purchases off the back of the truck that would come around every Saturday morning, laden with goods that the neighborhood residents could purchase at a price that was better than the local markets.

The wiseguys were the only people Tommy knew who could do whatever they wanted, and nobody ever gave them a problem.

They'd be there in the smoke-filled back room of the candy store, those gangsters, paying Tommy fivers to run their errands for them and to park or wash their cars, Tommy working after school for them ever since he turned ten years old and one of them—a man who would die before Tommy turned eleven—for some reason took a liking to him. Legbreakers and bodyguards, buttonmen and killers, numbers bankers and payroll lawyers would be crowded around wooden tables, talking softly amongst themselves.

He'd wander into work in the back room of the Little Italy Candy Shop each day, often with his eyes blackened, his hair chopped into the shape of a bowl, his arms bruised orange and black, and there'd be four or five of them sitting around each of the five tables back there playing cards or waiting for Pete Papa to come out of his private office and tell them what to do. Their diamond pinky rings would shine in the light reflected from the overhead light, their hair would be shining, too, from the Brylcreme they used to slick it straight back. Their bellies would be hanging over their belts, the men lounging around and waiting for nightfall, waiting for their orders, waiting in the company of men they thought they could trust, drinking endless cups of espresso, throwing it back, Old Country style. And one of them would always feel the need to check him out, one of them would always have to ask, "Ey, Tommy, what da hell happened to youse?"

He'd never give them an answer. He figured that they knew

what happened—knew *precisely* what had happened—and were
only trying to see if he was sissy enough to complain.

His father had happened.

No matter how late it was that Tommy would wander in, the
postal clerk who'd fathered him would be awake and waiting,
belt in hand. And the later it was, the worse the beating, because
the old man would have had more time to pour cheap whiskey
down his throat and to work himself into a rage. For Tommy,
after a time, it became the price of doing business; the only thing
that mattered then was that his father never saw him cry.

When it was over—with Ma usually marked up or bleeding
from the beating she'd taken from the old man for coming to
Tommy's aid—the old man would tell him that the beating had
been for Tommy's own good. That Tommy couldn't just go to
school when he felt like showing up, that Tommy had to quit
running around with the goddamn animals down the street.

"You're turning into a bum!" he'd tell Tommy, "Hanging
around with them killers and thieves." At thirteen Tommy still
didn't have the nerve to tell the old man the truth: that the
killers and thieves paid him better than the postal service paid
his father. That every luxury—and some of the necessities—in
the house had been paid for with the money that Tommy brought
home and handed over to his mother. He was too young to
mention this then, still too afraid of his father's violent temper.
It was an emotional state of mind that hadn't lasted much longer.

He got the respect of the men of weight by showing them
what he could do, rather than by talking. Tommy knowing without being told when to hang around and when to fade, when to
grab some coffee and step outside to drink it. When Pete Papa
came out of his private office and into the crowded back room,
he knew enough to leave the room, to go check out the candy
store until somebody called him back in.

He'd watched the other young boys in the place, and learned
he had nothing in common with them. They didn't like him at
first, he suspected, because he didn't act the way they did.
Tommy never bragged on his exploits, never boasted about the
many fights he'd won, and he never walked with a swagger. It
didn't take long before most of the other kids moved on; into
the jails or into the cemeteries, and Tommy organized the rest,
and proved that he was an earner.

On 42nd Street he'd have three of them waiting; one to slice the pants pocket with a razor and grab the tourists' wallets, the other two to stop the mark from chasing the thief as he ran. The two accomplices would step in front of the victim and ask if he were all right, hold him as if he were about to fall down in fright, ensuring that their partner had adequate time for escape.

In the summer he would go into Chinatown and buy boxes of illegal fireworks, then head uptown and sell them at a 200% markup to the children of the privileged. He would spend weeks setting up a burglary, and they'd always go without a hitch, Tommy never cowboying, knowing his marks intimately; what they liked, what they hated, where they hung out and what nights they went out to dinner. Pete Papa would line up the crew, men he was certain could carry their own weight, and Tommy always took his advice and gave him a percentage of whatever he took down.

Always, always, he paid. Tribute to Pete Papa, percentages to doormen and security guards who would look the other way, and to cops who would come around after the score, knowing that Tommy had pulled it off and demanding payment in lieu of dropping their investigation.

He had a reputation for viciousness, but only if you stood in his way. First and foremost, he was a businessman, and in Tommy's business, his size and silence and his direct hard stare were the equivalent of the college degrees that other businessmen prized. They were his pedigrees; his qualifications to survive.

But there was one special feeling that set him apart from his peers, one emotion that he never discussed with anyone, because back then he was ashamed of even feeling it.

Tommy felt remorseful. Guilty about what he was doing. He would rationalize and justify and tell himself that everyone was doing it, but still, inside him, he knew that he was wrong, and always inside his head, a part of him wanted out.

Back then, however, he didn't let that stop him, saw it as the downside of being who and what he was.

The other young men did stupid and careless things, committed armed robberies and opportunistic, unplanned street muggings, and they'd be caught and sent away, but still, Tommy hung on, safe and making money, setting up scores and pulling them off on his own and letting the wiseguys in for a full quarter of all his hard-earned profits.

Things got better for him after his first arrest, due mostly to the fact that he'd kept his mouth shut. Not that running numbers was that important a crime in New York. He wouldn't have even gone down to detention if he hadn't punched the arresting officer square in the face. But he had, and he'd been arrested and sent to the legendary youth detention center at Spofford, off Bruckner Blvd. on Hunt's Point in the Bronx, and had battled a punk who'd tried to fuck him and had beaten the guy half to death, which made his reputation even larger in his circles. He'd sat in the hole for a month for his brutality, which won him further respect from the guys who hung out over at the candy store.

"You stood up," Pete Papa told him, high praise from the boss himself, from a guy who never wasted his time with the numbers runners and who only spoke to the men. "You grab a guy inna joint and you kick his ass for playing around, and yet you come in here every day with some new whip mark on your ass. You respect your father, and that's a good thing." Smart Pete Papa figuring things out for himself. A street shrink who'd finished third grade; Tommy didn't bother to tell the man how wrong his analysis was.

There were men inside the candy shop who offered to take care of his father, who said they would need to talk to him just one time and get him straightened out once and for all. But Tommy never took the bait, because he knew that then he'd owe them, and that wasn't something that he was ever willing to do. Even later, when he was sitting in the joint, he would never ask for favors.

At fourteen he'd been allowed to collect and pay off by himself, and at fifteen school had been history for Tommy. He was by then not only a numbers runner but a very experienced thief, and every day of his life on the street was for him a college degree.

Not that he was mentally deficient; he had far more than just the shrewdness that came to you when you hung out long enough on city pavement. Tommy read a lot of books and he had the wisdom of his elders, watched them constantly and paid strict attention to the things they said and to how they acted. The Silent One, they called him, and he never disagreed.

He would sit with them in bars as he grew older and he would slowly sip a beer and smoke his cigarettes, hearing about their lives and their families, their girlfriends and their money problems, Tommy with a benign and patient look on his face, wondering about them, thinking all the time, his mind always working and his mouth always shut.

"Look at the Silent One," Pete Papa would sometimes say, and the guards and the wiseguys would turn their attention over to Tommy.

Pete Papa would say proudly, "He's gonna go far, that boy, look at him, always scheming, but always paying his way. If I only had ten guys like him . . ."

But Tommy wasn't at those times scheming, he was often thinking of other things. He would sometimes be thinking of a better way of life, out of the rackets, but what was there for him?

One night on the Upper East Side he'd been having a beer in an outdoor cafe, casing the building across the street where he knew that an heiress kept jewels. Tommy wondering how hard it would be to get past the doorman and the closed circuit cameras. A group of French kids had sat down next to him, people around his age, but to Tommy, they were children. They laughed and spoke loudly, conversing in their beautiful tongue, and for the first time in his life, Tommy had felt jealousy, and from that day forward, he'd regularly daydreamed of another way of life, one where he could laugh openly and be carefree. One without crime and fear and danger, without death. It became a longing within him, a goal he wanted to attain.

At other times Tommy would be thinking about how dumb these wiseguys were, about what could be wrong with men who scored big money every day and who still somehow managed to have constant and pressing financial difficulties in their lives.

At twenty he didn't have any such problems, that was for sure. His cash was in safe deposit boxes, in his mother's brother's name. He had a phony driver's license which said that he was that man, buried inside a Baggie in the back yard of his and his mother's apartment building. His fortunes rose every time the men learned to trust him a little bit more, and by now he was nearly accepted as one of their own. His father had been ordered to leave a long time ago, and his mother and he lived in comfort, with their paths barely crossing.

He made his money, and as his savings grew to astronomical figures, Tommy began to seriously think about telling Pete Papa goodbye.

Two things had made him decide that he wanted to change his life: they'd been pressuring him to become a made man; and his girlfriend Janine—the daughter of Four-finger Jerry the thief—had had Tommy's child, given birth to a strapping son and they'd named him Mario, a child Tommy truly worshipped and couldn't see often enough.

He wanted no part of being brought into the mob, did not want the responsibility of being in someone's crew. As it stood at that point he could turn things down, and nobody ever got too upset, because he always paid them tribute on any money that he brought in. But once you had the button, you did what they told you to do or you died. They knew he was an earner, and they'd work him into his grave.

At night he would sit in the baby's bedroom and stare into the crib, wondering where little Mario's mother was and who she might be with. Jerry and his wife would be downstairs in the living room, barely speaking to Tommy these days but afraid to go up against him; it was no secret in the neighborhood that Tommy had Pete Papa's protection. Tommy came over and stayed with the child each night, played with him and fed him and bathed him and rocked him to sleep. There were times when he was glad that Jainine wasn't around, because he didn't want her to ever know about the tears that rolled down his cheeks when he watched that baby, gently sleeping.

Mama told him that Janine acted the way she did because Tommy refused to marry her, told Tommy that it was a pretty good idea for him to keep right on refusing. He never hit Janine when she finally did come home, and he never raised his voice, but he knew in his heart that he'd have to pay her off; get Mama to raise the bambino with him, the two of them could do it, it would be no problem at all.

Which was what he'd finally done, taken the baby home and given Janine the cash from one of the boxes, and was raising the kid alone when the score of his career came along, when the robbery that could put him on easy street forever nearly fell into his lap.

He took his idea to Pete Papa for help, and got backup for twenty-five points of the net score. Papa got him helpers that were outside of the mob, two boys that Papa said he could trust, and when things went bad, when he wound up getting caught the day after the score with the goods, and found himself all alone and behind prison bars, nobody came around to throw his bond or even to visit. The score had gone fine, but someone had dropped his name to the law, and they told him over and over again that if he would talk they would give him immunity.

Tommy ignored their pleas, and prepared himself to do serious time.

It wasn't a big arrest, as far as New York goes. A couple of lines in the daily papers, describing how the often-arrested Little Italy hoodlum with strong ties to the underworld had been arrested and charged with attempted murder and burglary. How authorities believed that they had finally caught the man who was single-handedly responsible for the reign of criminal terror that had been paralyzing upper Manhattan. When Tommy saw that, he knew the law was stacking the deck, and knew as well that there was nothing he could do about it, that there was no one he could turn to to bring him relief.

After the first visit by the FBI, a convict named LeBeaux came up to him in the Tombs—a jailhouse that had been aptly named—and asked him what his intentions were, and Tommy told him to go fuck himself, no one ever had to worry about him not doing what was right.

But there were people lined up waiting to speak to him, guys who made his life miserable. City cops and the FBI, the DEA and the Strike Force, trying to clear up cases now that they had him, pin things on him and clear their sheets. He never spoke a word to them, even though he had to see them, they wouldn't let him refuse, but it didn't mean he had to be friendly or even acknowledge their presence. The only sign of his nervousness that they'd ever seen was his chainsmoking, Tommy lighting a fresh cigarette with the butt of the other, smoking one after another until they told him that he could leave.

Every time they came to see him, the wiseguys grew more frightened, thinking that he was talking; it was a game the law liked to play, and one they couldn't lose.

Tommy didn't have a Social Security card, and he'd never had a driver's license that was in his legal name. He'd never paid a penny in tax and he'd never held a job.

They told him he was going down for life and he told them that was fine; they told him he could make it easy on himself and he asked them to leave him alone.

On the cell block one day LeBeaux had made things clear, told Tommy that too many serious people were curious, that they wondered what Tommy was saying. Tommy told him to tell them to come and pay him a visit, that he'd tell them to their faces what he was saying to the cops.

Yet no one came except the FBI, who spoke of safety and security and a brand new life. Tommy didn't even pay them a minute's attention.

Until the day that LeBeaux got hard, told Tommy that Pete Papa himself was growing gravely concerned. Told Tommy that the old man was starting to worry about Tommy, was so worried that he'd told Four-fingers to bring his grandson to the candy store. He said that the baby would be there every day, as Janine had given it up. Said that Tommy's mother was an old-fashioned woman, one who would not deny the baby's grandfather the right to visit with him. Said that if Pete Papa decided that Tommy was talking, even saying hello to the feds, he would take little Mario to a Jersey sausage factory, stick him in a hot dog stuffer to ensure that Tommy stayed silent.

Tommy looked at LeBeaux for a second, then wildly, fiercely, attacked the man without thought. He was out of solitary confinement before LeBeaux got out of the infirmary, and all he could think about for those long weeks that he was confined alone was his son, little Mario, being fed into a sausage machine.

When he got out of solitary, he did the only thing that he could do. He joined the Witness Protection Program, and he and Mario began new lives.

THE NAME THE killer was using these days was James Bracken. He liked the sound of it, the way the name rolled off the tongue. Nobody knew his real name, any family he'd once had was now long dead. He'd use this name until he got tired of it, or until too many people got used to it, until too many people he didn't want to know got to calling him by it, and then he'd change it again. He'd change the name, come up with something else, then change his appearance to match the new name. He was the Chameleon, he could be anyone he wanted. He tried to tell himself that, but tonight, his mind wasn't listening.

Tonight he was a young man again, in love, remembering back fourteen years, this night being the anniversary of an ugly, terrible death. Terri's.

Bracken stood sweating before a leather dummy in the private office of his expensive Greenwich Village home, his fingers held out before him, Bracken flexing them, as a pianist might do before beginning an especially difficult recital.

The dummy was on a stand in the middle of the room. It looked like a leather scarecrow, was built to human proportions. It was covered with slit marks, the frightening leather face was sliced nearly to ribbons. The dummy was attached to a strong round steel spring that was itself attached to a heavy, round metal stand that stood immovable in the center of the carpet. The dummy would move away when Bracken hit it, but not very far, then it would bounce back stiffly, ready to be struck again.

Bracken now began to circle the dummy, stripped to the waist, wearing only gray sweat shorts that were soaked dark, looking black. His shaved head glistened with sweat. His mind, as usual, was working over the details of his latest job, Bracken frightened, looking for perfection in a line of work that guaranteed mistakes.

There was a simple fact that explained his terror: in Bracken's line of work, mistakes could be fatal, and he wasn't getting any younger. Mistakes were happening far too often. What had once been so simple was beginning to become so complicated.

He tried to put it out of his mind, and there had been a time when that had been easy. Not anymore, though, not these past few years, and he couldn't blame his fears on tonight being the anniversary of Terri's death. He'd seen his life racing past him without delay, knew that he was now well beyond the mid-point. And still, he was ruled by the same compulsions that had owned him twenty years ago. Twenty-five, actually, now that he thought about it.

Bracken abruptly stopped moving and slashed out at the dummy with just the tips of the fingers of his right hand, saw several new slashes appear on the leather before the dummy flew back, and before it could settle itself upright he hit it again, three times with his left fist, sharp, rattlesnake jabs, then a heavy neck-breaking blow struck with the side of his right hand. Bracken danced away, letting the dummy bounce back and forth then settle straight up, Bracken breathing evenly, flexing his hands again.

There'd been a time when he'd thought that he'd never get to the kill, when he'd had to force himself to relax, to see things through to the end and not rush into it and maybe do something stupid. He prided himself on his attention to detail, on leaving no trail that could lead back to him. Or, almost as importantly, to whomever might be employing him at any given time.

He was the best, a legend now, spoken about in whispers in dark, seedy bars, and he knew that there were plenty of those who thought him merely an urban legend, not real, just smoke. A figment of overactive, paranoid imaginations. He let them think that, wanted them to think that. The people who needed to know about him knew that he was the best, and he hadn't gotten to be the best by acting on impulse or by bragging about his exploits.

But it was so difficult to take it slow sometimes, particularly when the end was in sight.

What if he killed the mark tonight? What if the mark died in a dark Manhattan alley? Would it make any difference to anyone, either way? Only to him, and he was the one that had to be pleased. Because he was the one who would die or go to prison if the job didn't go exactly, if he rushed it or made that one fatal error. Or maybe he'd even be dead tonight, join Terri in whatever was out there, after. There was always that possibility, on the anniversary night.

When he really wanted to rush things, Bracken would tell himself: this is New York! Nobody cares what you do or where you do it. He'd seen evidence of this with his own two eyes, women being brutally attacked on the street at rush-hour on Madison Avenue or 5th, with hordes of well-built men walking by, averting their eyes as they passed the gruesome muggings. Sometimes Bracken would stop and help, and sometimes he'd keep walking. It depended on how he'd feel at the moment, how much of an illusion of humanity he might at that time be trying to project.

He wasn't human, however, and he'd known that since he was little, knew that he was a unique species, and that he was the last of the breed.

He'd watched them, many years ago, those little ants who thought they were men, wrapped in their phony sense of security, thinking they were safe. Living in Manhattan and having things, while he himself had nothing. He hated them, despised them, them and the things that his sister had been forced to do for them in order to keep food on the table for the two of them and a roof over their heads, even if that roof was in alphabet city, even if that roof leaked. It was still better than the street or an orphanage, as she'd tell him when he complained. And far better than the home they'd run away from. A place he visited once again, just once, when he was twenty.

He'd hear them, those so-called *men*, in her bedroom at night with the door locked, but you couldn't lock out the sounds, there was no way that he could not hear the men grunting and cursing at her, telling his sister what to do. He'd hear his sister, too, acting as if she liked it. Later, he'd watched, humiliated and impotent, as she'd died of diseases that doctors were ashamed to speak of in polite company, his sister slowly deteriorating, losing her mind before anything else.

As a teenager he'd sometimes follow these men home, would hide in the alley behind his apartment house and wait for them to leave his house, then he'd be a spy, following slowly and unseen behind them as they went home to their wives, their kids, their families and their lives. He'd catch up to them right at their doorstep and show them some reality, end their lives for them, right there on the street.

That had been before he'd learned that there was a market out there willing to pay well for his particular talents. Before his sister had died, left him alone to fend for himself. Before he'd fallen in love with Terri, even, and long before he'd become the best that had ever lived, and well before the terror came to visit him with such regularity.

Bracken struck out at the dummy now with precise, economical movements, stabbed at its marble eyes with fingernails that were as sharp as razors, chopping it with the sides of his hands, attacking the neck, the eyes, kicking its groin with callused, trained feet. He hit it for minutes, without a lull, hit that dummy as hard and as often as he could, Bracken grimacing, trying not to think of Terri, but, as usual, unable to put the young, beautiful Terri out of his mind. Bracken was breathing through his nose, grunting as he punched and slashed and chopped and kicked, until he could hit it no more.

Then he stepped back, spent, tightened his thin muscles and tried to feel pleased with his work, but couldn't. Even though he was still faster than anyone he knew, he wasn't as fast as he used to be. Even though he was still stronger than any man of his size and weight, he was weakening, he knew, growing weaker with each passing year. Even though he'd hit the dummy for at least six or seven minutes, there had been a time when he would have hit it for ten. He was still the best, he tried to tell himself that, but in his mind, he wondered. Wondered if he was even very good any more.

He'd find out, soon, because—if he lived through the next two minutes—he'd be working tonight and tomorrow, Monday. Maybe this time he'd get lucky. Maybe this time, he'd perform the perfect killing.

Bracken turned his back on the dummy and went over to his office door and made sure that he had locked it. He went to his desk, sat down behind it, breathing heavily, out of fear more than from the workout. He unlocked his desk drawer and took out a color picture, stood the frame in the middle of the desk, and looked at a picture of himself and Terri, the two of them happy, so much in love back then. Absently, he took a .38 revolver out of the desk, and dumped the bullets next to the picture.

An ocean of sweat was pouring down Bracken's face now, his lips twisted, teeth clenched tight together, so tightly that it hurt his jaw. He put one bullet into the pistol, spun the chamber and slammed it shut, about to perform the ritual that he had performed thirteen times before, on this date in April, the date of Terri's death.

Bracken stared at the picture, brought the pistol to his head, grimaced, shouted, and pulled the trigger.

Click.

He reloaded the pistol and dropped it back into the drawer, placed the picture carefully next to it. The picture he would need to look at again, many times in the next year, for strength. The weapon he would ignore, until next year at this time.

"I miss you, Terri," Bracken said, took a deep breath and rose.

He unlocked his office door, stepped out into the hallway and walked to his staircase, heading up to take a shower and dress, to smoke countless cigarettes as he waited for the appointed hour to arrive. Tawny wasn't in tonight. He had no idea where Tawny might be. But it was good, he didn't need to see Tawny right now, didn't need to be asked any questions, not when he was so close to the end. If Tawny asked the wrong thing, as Bracken felt right now, this minute, he might strike out in anger, and Tawny was good to him, too very good to kill. Yet.

Bracken mounted the stairs, steeped in doubt, fighting to keep those doubts out of his mind but losing. They'd go away tomorrow, he knew, after he completed the kill.

LLOYD TOMCZAK STOOD in his upstairs bedroom window, binoculars trained on the house next door. Loose manuscript pages littered the bed behind him, his little Yorkie galavanting around them, sniffing them, checking them out. Tomczak's life work being rewritten in the evenings, Meeky getting ready to take a piss on it. She might as well join the club, everyone else seemed to piss on it, too.

Expensive photographic equipment hung from spikes that had been pounded directly into the wall studs. The equipment was a present from his mother, who recognized his talent. His mother maybe the only person alive beside himself who was aware of his potential, or, at least, who had once believed in him. These days Tomczak wasn't sure what she believed anymore. His mother had paid for the binoculars, too. The fact was, nearly everything Lloyd owned was a present, a gift from his mother, and she did her best, even now that she was in a wheelchair and losing her mind, to make sure that Lloyd never forgot what he owed her.

The one thing she hadn't given him was stuck down the waistband of Lloyd Tomczak's pants. A pistol, a .38 Colt auto that looked like a .45 and held seventeen bullets if you counted the one in the chamber. It had been inherited, the only thing that Tomczak's father had not left to his wife. All the good stuff, all the money, all the property, all the stocks and bonds and insurance stuff, had been left to Tomczak's mother. Tomczak did not know if she would leave it to him when she died. The crazy old bat, she'd probably leave it to Tomczak's wife, even though Mother had spent the past twenty years professing to hate the woman, changing her tune now that she was helpless; Aiko suddenly had become her best friend and companion. But it was the sort of thing she'd do—leave the money to Aiko—to make sure that he spent his entire life beholden to some woman.

There was a full-length mirror attached to the closet door, and Tomczak would sometimes stand before it with the pistol sticking out of his waistband, the butt depressing his roll of fat. He'd have his hands on his hips, would be sneering at the mirror.

15

"Fuck you," Tomczak would say. Depending on his mood, he would be speaking to his boss, to his mother, or to the man next door, Torrence. He'd draw the pistol and point it at his image, putting even more of a badass look on his face, the pistol held in both hands. At other times he would take it with him when he got one of his frequent evening callouts to cover a story for the *Leader*. Have it in his pants, facing the jigs who always gathered around the scene of a crime, looking for trouble. He hadn't had to use it yet, or even pull it out. Just knowing it was there was enough for him.

Now he felt the pistol's cool comfort on his belly, under the sweatshirt, as he watched his neighbors through the binoculars, the snobs who lived next door.

How long had these people lived in Chicago? he wondered. How long had they survived being this lax about their home security? Tomczak didn't know, but he was grateful that they were so casual, that they usually left the blinds up or the drapes open, at least downstairs. He could see them better this way, watch them and maybe figure out what their problem was. If he was lucky, he might even find evidence that the guy, Mark Torrence, had stolen his photographs.

They had a problem with him, there was no fucking doubt about that. But then again, most people usually did, sooner or later, once they got to know him. Most of the time, throughout his life, Tomczak wound up shunned.

Next to him, on the floor, a police scanner chattered away, bored voices telling him what was going on all over the district. He'd hear a good one and grab a camera and his notebook and head off into the night, his press pass stapled to his car's sun visor. He'd become adept at tuning the usual calls out, only came alert when a hot call went out.

He heard his wife knock softly, then open the door to his bedroom, then she asked him shyly if he was ready to come down and eat. He ignored her, ignored her chink ass, he wished he'd never met her.

"Your mother is eating already, in her room, I wheeled her in there," he heard her say, and he didn't even bother to take his eyes off the Torrence family. Her voice was shaky, as usual these days, whenever she spoke to him. He knew that she was aware of the pistol in his waistband. Sometimes, when he was feeling particularly friendly, he'd tell her that he was working undercover for the CIA.

Tomczak said, "Yo mutha is eeeting aweady, in hur loom, I eeled hur in thahr" making fun of the Japanese accent that she's never tried to lose. He heard her close the door quietly, hurtfully, behind herself as she left the room. Now she'd go and cry, feel all hurt and homesick, which Tomczak appreciated. Maybe, if she suffered enough, she'd get her ass on a plane back home to the land of the rising sun. He couldn't wait for that day to come.

His mother had cursed the marriage from the start, and she'd been right, the exact words that she'd spoken from thousands of miles away still rang in his mind often, words Mother had said with derision, when he'd called her to break the news: "First piece of ass you ever get, you gotta go and marry it," Mother had said, and she'd been right, but back then Tomczak didn't know it. Back then, he'd thought that he'd been in love.

He knew better now, though, knew that Mother had been right. Now that he'd come to agree with her though, she herself had had a sudden change of heart. But what could he do about it? Divorce the bitch? Mother would disown him. Aiko had become Mother's own personal slave, and Mother held the pursestrings, bought the food, bought the equipment that Tomczak needed for his career, she had even paid for this house, moved right in although she'd never see the outside of it again.

Poor Mother, in her wheelchair, crippled and not knowing who she was half the time. These days she loved Aiko, and Tomczak blamed it on her rapidly deteriorating mental condition. How could anyone love someone like Aiko, a woman nearly twenty years older than Tomczak, a woman who'd jumped on the bandwagon with a poor sailor boy who didn't know what he was getting into twenty-two years ago when he'd been seventeen and very lonely? Stationed in Japan, meeting Aiko in a bar, Aiko, who'd thought that the American streets were paved with gold.

Well, he'd proved to her that they were, shown her the price tag that there was on those streets, too. Maybe he'd dump her after Mother died, when everything came to him. He could lose her and hide all his inherited money, see what she could get out of him with some dipshit Japanese lawyer.

Tomczak watched the Torrence family as they played a board game, squinting, adjusting the focus on the glasses for close ups, taking good long looks at the woman next door's breasts. They were bigger than Aiko's, that was for sure. Beestings were bigger than his wife Aiko's breasts.

He saw the two little kids next door look to be fighting, and he smiled. It showed that the family was dysfunctional, that he hadn't been wrong about them.

His dog rubbed its muzzle against Tomczak's leg, and he held the glasses with one hand and leaned down and petted her. "Good Meeky, that's a *good* girl," Tomczak said.

Meeky had started the trouble between them, between Tomczak and the man who lived next door. He'd turned out to be a speciesist, a meat-eating son of a bitch like so many people that Tomczak knew, looking down his nose at Tomczak when Lloyd had told him how much he loved little Meeky.

That had been the start of it, but it hadn't been the last. For the two months that they'd lived there, it seemed, all they had done was argue. The man, Torrence, didn't care that Tomczak was a photojournalist, got mad at him when he tried to take his picture, just expressing his First Amendment right.

Friday, though, Tomczak had learned that the man was also a thief. An entire roll of pictures that he'd taken of Torrence had disappeared from his desk over at the *Weekly Leader*, the newspaper where Tomczak worked, freelance. Two dozen 8 × 12s, stolen from out of his desk. Nobody at work would do such a thing, they all knew better than to bother Lloyd Tomczak. If they did the tires of their cars would get slashed, sugar would get poured into their gastanks. People always learned not to bother Tomczak, not to try and push him around. Everyone except this bastard next door, and sometime soon, he'd learn too.

He wondered if his reputation had preceded him in the artistic community, if word had gotten around that he was a man who took revenge when he had to. It must have, with his genius, with his talent, what else could be holding him back? He couldn't find a job anywhere else, not what he wanted, a job where he could express his strong creative abilities.

There was a small steel table beside the window, what Tomczak called his desk, the way he called this bedroom his office. The table had a portable Smith Corona typewriter sitting on top. There wasn't room for anything else atop the table; a ream of clean paper was on the floor, a single sheet had been rolled into the typewriter, still blank. Since moving out of the bedroom that he'd once shared with his wife, back when they were still living at the old house, since becoming celibate a year ago, Tomczak had written three screenplays that had never sold to Hollywood. He'd written an entire novel that no publisher had shown any interest in. He couldn't even find an agent willing to push any of his work, all of that work having been written at the old house, before they'd moved in here. In the months that he'd lived here, he hadn't been able to make a single page come alive. He thought that was because of the man next door, Torrence, because of the bad vibes that the man constantly sent his way. All they'd ever done, from the beginning, was fight.

"Fuckin' thief bastard," Tomczak muttered, nasty words for a soft man, with no muscle to speak of, spoken in a high, nasally whiny voice that everyone used to make fun of when he'd been just a kid. Nobody made fun of him anymore, though, that was for sure. Her always got even, and he would with this guy Torrence, too.

He'd tried to confront Torrence about the missing pictures, man to man the other day, Friday afternoon as the guy came home from work. The man would never know how hard it had been for Tomczak to screw up the courage to confront him, how scared he'd been inside, fear being Tomczak's normal mental state. He knew that he sometimes compensated for that fear by being pushy, but still, it had taken a lot, to step outside and confront him as he'd done, a man the size of his neighbor. And what had the bastard done? He'd snubbed him, that's what. Said something insulting then laughed at Lloyd Tomczak. He'd learn not to do that. Tomczak would teach him the hard way.

All he had to do was find out how Torrence had gotten into Tomczak's desk, find evidence that Torrence indeed had the pictures, then his editor would let him write the entire expose and would publish it, front page of the *Leader*, with color pictures showing the type of man this Torrence was. And write it he would, he'd destroy this son of a bitch. Destroy anyone who got in the way of Lloyd Tomczak, Jr.

His editor was also his publisher, a man with strong mob connections who never let anyone doubt them. "You want your fuckin' knees busted?" he'd ask, always in an outfit tone of voice, the words spoken in a manner which told whomever he was talking to that all it would take to have it done would be a simple phone call. The publisher-editor would nuke all *Leader* stories on organized crime, unless it was one that made a stool pigeon look like a liar. Would terrorize the women in the office, try to get them into a sleazy motel room. He was a low-life, miserable, bully of a man, but the only man in Chicago who would pay Tomczak for his writing. And he'd already agreed to print the Torrence story, if Tomczak could come up with proof.

It looked as if he wasn't going to learn much tonight, though. The family all sitting there playing some stupid game, that teen-age punk of theirs home, on a weekend night. he was probably a queer; Tomczak thought he could smell them a mile away.

He needed a bath, some warm milk, and a vegetarian meal to eat. Aiko was great at making fishballs, but she couldn't make a salad to save her life, even after a generation in the States. He'd go see what she'd prepared, and if the food was cold, he would have an excuse to yell at Aiko. He liked yelling at Aiko. She never fought back. He had to keep calm today, though, because he had a job interview in the morning, and if he got the job at the ad agency, he could stop writing the weekly column for the *Leader*, could stop chasing ambulances with his camera and his notebook. He'd get the job, he was sure of it, he had some ideas that would knock them on their asses.

He put the glasses down and turned off the scanner, patted Meeky again, looked down at the dog and smiled. *"Good* dog, Meeky's a *good girl!"* He let the dog lick his hand for a minute, then made sure that his sweatshirt covered the pistol butt. He would go and see if Mother needed any help eating her dinner; it would give him an excuse to see what sort of garbage Aiko had cooked up tonight, then for some reason called it dinner.

HE'D JOINED THE Federal Witness Protection Program over fifteen years ago, but his past still sometimes weighed heavily on his mind. Today his name was Mark Torrence, and on occasion he would still think about it, and the thought never failed to make him shiver with fear. Until just recently entire months used to go by without his having a thought of his past, but then it would descend upon him with a vengeance, and he would have to watch his step. These days, since the last Christmas holidays, though, the thought of what he used to be was never very far from his mind.

Like now, on a Sunday night in the middle of April, at the

end of a rare weekend where he and his wife hadn't had one major argument, and there hadn't been a single emergency call for either one of them, the family all present and accounted for, Mark playing Uno at the kitchen table with his tribe and *wham,* it nailed him hard, the thoughts of what he'd been.

He knew what had brought it on these past four months, knew why the past was always on his mind these days. There were, really, two reasons. First, his wife, Caroline, was all of a sudden on his ass, wanting answers to questions that he wasn't willing to give. Second, and maybe just as importantly, a new neighbor had moved into the house next door, and from the first day, he and the guy had never gotten along, although Mark had tried.

The guy had a problem, and he had a bad attitude. He was a short, bald guy who didn't seem to mind being thirty pounds overweight while still under forty years of age, and he had a pushy way about him, he was the kind of jerk who let his dog run free to shit wherever it pleased. When Mark's daughter Elaine had brought some of it into the house on her shoe, and from there onto the carpet, Mark had gone over to talk to the guy and the man had gotten snippy, had informed Mark in a superior tone that he was what he called an "activist."

"I love my dog the same as you love your kids."

"Don't say that," Mark had warned him, softly. He'd felt blind anger rising, and he fought to keep himself under control. Still, he'd added, "Don't you *ever* say that to me."

"Well, it's *true,*" the jerk had said.

It had been in Mark's mind, right there: slap this guy, one time in the face. But he hadn't, had fought himself instead, fought his temper at the man's ignorance, told himself it wasn't his problem.

"I'm sorry you feel that way," Mark had said. "Disappointed, too." And then he left, and the dog, Meeky, had been running loose ever since.

So what was he supposed to do, shoot the dog because its owner was an asshole? He couldn't bring himself to do it, it wasn't the *dog's* fault. And the cops, even the ones who owed Mark favors, had better things to do than chase around enforcing the leash laws. Mark couldn't even bring himself to ask them; it wasn't the way he was.

The poor relationship with the neighbor only seemed to exacerbate it, Mark's slowly growing discontent. In the few weeks that the neighbors, the Tomczaks, had been in the neighborhood, there'd been four or five small confrontations, over mostly stupid things. With the man, though, Lloyd; there was never a problem with the wife, if they were even married. The woman who lived next door with him was a tiny Japanese woman, who appeared almost stereotypical, servile and submissive. She'd come out into the yard sometimes when Mark was outside, and he'd hear Lloyd order her around like she was his dog.

No, that wasn't true, Tomczak treated his dog with more respect. Caroline would hear the man and her face would turn red with anger. All the woman needed was to live here for a year or two, Caroline would straighten her out, teach her how to act. Then again, you never could tell, an idiot like Tomczak might have paid for the woman through mail-order, might still be paying her to act like his slave. When his money ran out, maybe she'd leave. Or maybe, if Mark was lucky, Tomczak himself would leave.

Tomczak didn't like Mark's privacy fence, wanted to know what Mark had to hide. Tomczak wanted to know if Mark intended to paint the fence, suggested that it would be better if Mark painted it to match the house. Tomczak complained that Mark's son, Mario, played the car radio too loud when he came in late on weekends. Tomczak had decided to cut his grass, these past couple weeks that the weather had been nice, at six a.m., two Saturdays in a row.

Tomczak claimed to earn his living as a free-lance journalist who wrote cutesy, sarcastic columns about urban living for the *Leader*. The wife must have come from money or have a good job herself, because Mark knew enough about journalism to know that it didn't pay well enough to pay for a house like the one Tomczak had bought. The guy had to be maybe the only writer for that rag who lived south of Van Buren. Mark had spotted himself in some columns, thinly disguised, in articles about the problems of urban living today, and he wasn't too happy about it, had made his feelings known to Tomczak. The worst part of it was, the guy was always taking pictures of everything, including him, and Mark didn't care for that, knew that it was probably harmless but still, pictures were pictures, and he didn't allow them to be taken of him, ever. He'd mentioned it to the guy respectfully, gone out of his way to not let his true feelings for the man show as he spoke to him, kindly.

Only with this asshole, courtesy didn't work.

It's the First Amendment, Tomczak would tell him. He had a right to shoot whatever he wanted to on a public street. Mark wanted to choke him. He hated when people did that, pried into your life thinking they had some God-given right to do so. He'd taken to covering up his face whenever he saw the idiot with his camera, or giving him the finger. Put *that* in the *Leader*, you busybody little shit.

This past Friday, as Mark had pulled his car to the curb after work, Tomczak had been waiting, had come running out of his house wearing a pair of Bermuda shorts and nothing else. He had a very hairy chest that had no muscle tone to it, the chest sunken, with a soft little round paunch belly under it, the gut straining at the waist of the shorts, hanging over it, jiggling, hairy and pulpy.

"I want to talk to you, Torrence," the little shit said, menacingly, and Mark looked at him without expression and walked right by him, caught a glimpse of the red face and the morally righteous burning eyes, saw Tomczak putting his hands on his hips, without any doubt in his mind that Mark would halt in his tracks at the sight of him.

"Lots of people want to talk to me," Mark said as he passed. "I'll tell you like I tell them: I don't have time."

"Well you'd better *make* time, buddy!" Tomczak had shouted at him, at Mark's back.

Mark had fought his anger, and had turned and walked backwards so Tomczak would understand his words, see the smirk on Mark's face.

"Don't overrate your sense of self-importance, little man," Mark said, and laughed. Then turned and walked through his gate.

The remark had gotten its intended reaction, Tomczak had become enraged.

"You don't walk away from *me*, mister! You don't know who you're fucking with!" Mark had shaken his head, laughing, keeping his own rage bottled up inside.

He hadn't cared about whatever it was Tomczak had wanted to talk about. Mark didn't care about him, about his dog, about his entire fucking existence . . .

23

That meeting had been on his mind, though, all weekend, bugging him, the way he'd wanted to punch the guy, hurt him bad, physically. He wasn't like that anymore . . .

. . . Or was he?

Mark spent every day of his life dealing with people who lived in denial, people who rationalized away all sorts of behavior, who blamed everyone but themselves for the problems they were having. Was he capable of such action? Maybe he was doing it now.

Living so happily for most of these past ten years, he'd built a self-image of himself that was now in sudden doubt. Maybe he wasn't the calm, cool character he'd thought himself to be. Maybe the animal was right under the surface, hibernating. Waiting for the wrong word to be said to the host human before leaping out from cover and chewing into somebody's neck. Tall, lanky gangbangers with attitudes that would anger Christ didn't bother Mark, they were his meat, he ate them up and spit them out, using words these days instead of his fists, over at the youth center that he ran, and nobody ever got hurt.

So why did this silly little man next door get under his skin the way he did? What was there about him that made Mark want to hurt him? Mark wasn't sure.

His older son, Mario, noticed the change in his father first, and looked at him funny, his forehead lined with worry, but the kid didn't say anything. Did he remember anything? He had to.

Somewhere in his mind there would be memories of a time when the only other relatives he had besides his father were an "aunt" and "uncle," Dan and Andrea Bella, who were in reality a United States federal marshal and his kindly, wonderful wife. Mark hoped that there were no conscious memories; that his son could look back and see his childhood as normal. And if it hadn't been exactly so for the first six years of his life, then it surely was today.

At least as normal as life ever got around this household.

It used to be wonderful around here, up until last Christmas. Before the stony, hurt silences began, the prolonged pouting, Mark and Caroline ignoring each other. Before things began to go bad. He put those thoughts out of his mind, was forced to when his daughter spoke to him in exasperation.

"Green six to *you*, Daddy," his daughter Elaine said, aggravated. "You're not paying attention."

"Sure I am," Mark told her, smiling. "How could anyone not pay attention when a princess talks, Elaine?"

Was he paranoid, or was Caroline looking at him funny, now, too? She'd been so pushy lately, they had hardly gotten along since late fall, the beginning of winter. He had to be careful around her, she had the instincts of a cop. But she had never asked him many questions, until the last few months. He'd married a woman who believed in confidentiality, and although he'd told her plenty of his secrets, he'd never told them all. Now, it seemed, she was bound and determined to hear them all. She was always on him lately, wanting to know. What was Mario's mother like? Where had he grown up? Things that she had never bothered asking him about before were now of great importance to her, and when he evaded, when he told her to leave it lie, she'd grow cold and distant. It was only when they were together with the kids that he felt they were together at all.

Their sex life sure had changed. There'd been so many years of happy, carefree lust, and now they barely touched each other, neither of them wanting to reach out, as if doing so would be giving in.

Mark played a red six, changing the color of the deck. His nine-year-old son, Kenny, sitting beside him, threw in his last card. "I'm out," Kenny said.

Elaine went nuclear. "You didn't call Uno, you have to pick up two cards!"

"I don't have to pick up *nothing* if you don't catch me before the next player draws."

"He's right, Elaine," Caroline said, then, to their son, "It's anything."

"What?"

"I don't have to pick up *any*thing, Kenny, you said *no*thing."

"Oh."

MARK WOULD TALK to his colleagues at work, listen to them—he was very good at listening—and sit in awe that never showed on his face at some of the stories he'd hear. About "parenting burnout" and "sibling rivalries." About needing to get away, and vacationing without the kids.

He couldn't imagine himself spending a night away from his

children, never got too angry at their bickering or arguing, even sometimes enjoyed it when they fought amongst themselves. He'd sit back, as he did now, large, powerful shoulders threatening to break the wooden back of the kitchen chair, his face a blank, watching them go at it. Secure enough in their personalities and in their parents' love to express their anger toward each other without fearing that they'd catch a beating. A nine-year-old son and an eight-year-old daughter, arguing over the rules, over what was and wasn't fair.

Christ, the things that he could tell them about fair.

But he wouldn't; they could never know. And Caroline couldn't, either. Although they'd had a rough few months, she was still the love of his life today, his entire reason for sanity, and he was in too deep to lose her now, as he surely would if she were to learn the truth about his past.

So why did she have to bug him about it? Why, suddenly, the cold silences after he'd evaded questions about his past life? Why did she feel she had to know? And why was she being such a bitch about it, harping about it, even after they'd been getting along for a time and he thought the argument was over? She'd pester him again, and he'd become unresponsive, to the point of insulting her. Why the hell did she feel the sudden urge to know everything about his life? She'd only leave him if he told her the truth.

Which wasn't a fair thought to have. Even in these troubled times, he believed that his wife loved him as much as he loved her, and somewhere in his mind he thought that she would probably understand. Even now, after a months-long argument, he knew that she loved him, could feel it when she was near him. But he'd trained himself early on to always expect the worst and to never tell anyone anything that could later be used to hurt you.

He wondered about it now, though. What would Caroline do? What would she do if she found out what he'd been? It was something he often thought about, because he'd flirted with telling her a great many times. It would shut her up, that was for sure, one way or the other. Telling her about his past would either end the rift in their marriage or end the marriage altogether.

Would it? He wondered about that now.

After a family weekend like this, with games and movies and

a Pay-TV cable boxing match on Saturday night that they'd watched together as a family, he felt that she might understand, might forgive him if he told her, that it might even make their marriage stronger. The thing that kept him from telling her was that he also suspected that it wouldn't, that his deception and ugly secret would be the end of their marriage. And he'd rather die than live without her.

He'd tried reasoning with her, but it just hadn't worked.

"You don't trust me enough to leave it alone," he'd tell her, and she'd tell him that he didn't trust her enough to tell her. He'd tell her that she'd never asked before and she'd tell him that it hadn't been important to her before. He couldn't win an argument with her, she was too well educated, too smart for him.

She was a shrink who hated it when he called her by that term. Her patients were adolescents, who were told to call her Caroline; their parents called her Doctor Janeway and she never told them not to. A clinical psychologist is what she truly was, and whenever she tried to analyze him—like she'd been doing for the last four months or so—he'd call her a shrink just to piss her off, tell her that he wasn't one of her patients, and then she'd get mad, and once again the cold, painful silence would settle in.

Ten years of marriage, and she'd rarely raised her voice until just recently. How controlled did you have to be to be able to pull that off? But he'd rather she'd yell and scream than ignore him. The silence, the silent suffering, it was starting to drive him crazy.

Not that she was retentive or repressed—terms he'd learned in college. In bed, back before these problems had begun, she'd been a wild woman, and he had to admit that they'd sometimes played games that he wouldn't want his kids to learn. He loved her more than life itself, there was no contest there for discussion. If it came right down to one of them dying, he'd raise his hand and volunteer without even a second of doubt or hesitation. She could do more for the world than he ever could, with her education and her ways with kids, and besides, their own kids needed her more than they needed him, even his Mario, who had early on in the marriage begun to call her mom.

And what about that? How did he truly feel about the way that Mario loved her? A little jealous, for sure, about their closeness, a slight resentment over the fact that Mario had bonded so closely with Mark's wife.

But still, he wondered, what would she do if she ever learned the truth? Learned that her husband wasn't what she'd been led to believe, learned that the man she thought she knew was really a dropout from federal protection?

It wasn't the time to think of it; he was feeling paranoid enough.

Today he had a college degree that had taken him six years to get, going to school at night. Today he worked with gang youth, taught them how to box, how to handle life's disappointments and stresses without having to shoot someone over anger or ego. Talked with them and, more importantly, listened to them, opened himself up to them and helped them with their problems. Today he pulled in twenty-eight a year and his wife more than tripled that, but neither of them ever discussed it and she didn't let it become an issue, not even now, not even when she was mad at him. Today, her income did not bother him, didn't cause him to have any insecure male jealousies. Today he was an entirely different man from the one he'd been. Today he was making a difference, he thought, doing something for others who needed him. Ten years ago, when they'd married, he hadn't been hurt when she'd decided to keep her maiden name instead of taking his; today her being called Doctor Caroline Janeway instead of Torrence did not bother him. Today he could live in a house that had been given to her by her father after her mother had died. Today, there was no false pride there, wanting her to have his name, wanting to pay for a house himself or at least have his name on the papers.

All these things were a part of Mark Torrence; things that would have driven Tommy Torelli insane didn't bother Mark Torrence, not today.

On the other hand, though, today he still had most of the money he'd locked away all those years ago. Today, he was still afraid to have anyone else know that he had it. Caroline didn't know about it, did not have a key to the lockboxes, her signature could not break him. Didn't that prove her point, that he didn't trust her? He wasn't willing to let her walk away with his fortune.

So maybe he wasn't the man he thought he was. Maybe there were links to the past that Mark would never break. Still, for the most part, he'd broken away from it, from what he'd been. The mental and emotional make-ups were different, there was no dispute about that.

But his eyes were still vacuum cleaners, and he still never missed a trick.

Like now, noticing the look of concern on young Mario's face, the kid was still worried about him, saw something in the way that his father was sitting there. Mark looked at his son, a tall, muscular young man, a mirror image of himself when he had been Mario's age. A kid who'd never had a parental hand lain upon him in anger. Dear God, don't let him be like me. Don't let him become a loser.

Softly, in a barely audible voice, Mario asked, "You cool?" and Mark nodded, slowly, his lower lip turned down. He could feel Caroline's eyes burning into the side of his face.

Elaine, ignoring the interchange said, "I don't want to play with a cheater!"

Kenny knew that he had her goat, and was smiling as he said, "I don't want to play with a baby!"

"Had enough Uno for one night?" Caroline spoke to Mark and she was half-smiling now, ignoring the kids as they argued. The smile felt good, it was genuine and warm. So often these days when she spoke to him, it was with a sadness in her voice that would make him want to cry.

He smiled back at her while the little ones battled, with Mario remaining above the battle, just playing the game in the first place to be doing something with his dad. Sixteen now, a big guy, almost as big as his father. Mario now a junior in high school, soon to be a senior, with a part-time after-school job and a pretty girlfriend who lived right down the street. Mark and Mario didn't spend the sort of time together that they once had. Where had the years gone to? Mark didn't know. All he knew was that they'd been safe years, and safety was all that mattered. He'd spent the past fifteen years searching for that safety, and now Mark figured that he was as close as he'd come to finding it. At least he'd felt that way until recently, until the past few fucking months . . .

"I think I could give it up," he said, still smiling at his wife. She dropped her smile, just looked at Mark, sadly.

"I won," Kenny said, and Elaine told him that he was a cheater.

*   *   *

HE HAD KIDS with well-honed survival instincts, who knew how to last on the street. They would never allow strangers into the house, knew how to handle it when approached by them on the street, how to ask questions of them over the telephone, instead of giving answers. His firm hand and guidance, coupled with their mother's wisdom and understanding—her total goddamn charm—had made their children somehow become, so far, much more than he'd expected.

Although he'd never let them know that. He always praised them, no matter what they did, as long as their actions were even partly good. Mario had once brought home a report card with as many Fs as As, and before his father was through with him, the kid had believed that he was a genius. And the next report card had shown a vast improvement. It was one of the things he was expert at, motivating others through consistent positive input.

His problem had been that he'd thought it was in their blood; that they were destined to become the monster he had once been simply through their genetic makeup. He could look at them now, especially his firstborn son, and see how wrong he'd been.

He worked at the South Loop Youth Rehabilitation Center, evaluating and counseling the younger but still violent gang teenagers of the region who were sent there by judges or brought in by the Gang Crimes cops; Mark, their last chance before they were tossed out of school and from there sent to the penitentiary. He'd gone in as an administrative assistant and within four years was made chief of the department. He never talked to the reporters when they came around, always shunted them off to his deputy or to one of the other four people who ran the place, all of whom accepted the chance to talk and appreciated the exposure and never asked Mark why he'd refused the interviews. They were the sort of men who liked to read about themselves in the newspapers.

Mark had a reputation for being very good at what he did. The word was around in the building that things happened to a kid after a closed-door session with Mark Torrence. And Mark wasn't telling anybody what his secret was; what was said behind those doors. It was nobody's business but his and the kid's.

His wife was a boss, too. Her own, in private practice. A fancy downtown office, though, wasn't in Caroline's makeup. She worked in the neighborhood in which she'd been raised and where the family now lived; on Avenue B on the far Southeast Side of the city of Chicago, Caroline's office being over on Ewing Avenue, just a mile from their home. She'd get the tough ones, kids with emotional problems, the abused and neglected, those who'd been forgotten. The children were sometimes referred to her by the juvenile court system too; it was the way they'd met, when she was still working on her doctorate and he'd been working toward his degree, the two of them in a courtroom, trying to help young kids.

Something Caroline had learned to do at the knee of her parents, her mother having been a city social worker, her father an assistant chief of police who'd been decades ahead of his time in implementing special programs for troubled youth. He'd retired as a relatively young man, twenty years on the job and out, her father now running his own security firm in Phoenix, Arizona, her mother dead for a long time now; Mark had only met her a couple of times, she'd died before the wedding. The house had been a present to his daughter, was in her name. Mark respected the man for that, it showed his character and strength, and his lack of insecurities. It was the sort of thing he could see Caroline doing someday with Elaine, ensuring that the family home stayed within the family, no matter what happened to the marriage.

The old man would come out for Christmas and sit comfortably in the house he'd owned so long, and stare at Mark in ways he didn't care for when the two of them were alone, near the fireplace. But even at those times he never got nosy, never asked Mark any personal questions, and Mark appreciated that. He wished that the old man's discretionary habits had rubbed off more on the daughter he'd raised.

In her work Caroline had to make hard choices that Mark fortunately never had to consider. She was allowed to bill the state a fast twenty-an-hour for each child she evaluated, and she usually underbilled, Caroline in her anger at the system working overtime to save them from leading the same kinds of desperate lives that their parents had led and often were still living. Sometimes she could make some progress, sometimes she could see no hope. She never lied or pulled any punches and her reputation was impeccable. She'd charge the private cases as much as their parents could afford, and soaked the rich who brought their children long distances because they'd heard how good she was with children.

But her heart was with the disaffected, the throwaways of the city. She kept pictures of those whom she'd helped turn their lives around, was godmother to the children of adults who'd once been considered nearly hopeless by the courts. How many young daughters had been named after her? An award-winning novel written by one of her ex-patients had been dedicated to Caroline, her copy of the book was leaning on a stone over their fireplace.

She was three years older than he was, forty-two now, and her long brown hair was streaked with gray. He'd watch her from the doorway of her upstairs study, Caroline wearing reading half-glasses, Caroline bent over her desk, her lips pursed in concentration, one hand holding up her head as she read in the soft glow of the light of the banker's lamp on the small wooden desk. Her fingers would be absently running through that thick head of hair, twirling the ends.

And at those moments he'd want to tell her. Believed in his heart at such times that she'd understand.

But would she really? Dear God. It was a heavy rock to carry.

And what if he didn't tell her? How long would this argument last? She'd have enough sooner or later; she'd either learn to accept his silence or she'd leave him. Even as angry as he'd been with her lately, even as much as her prying had hurt him, he couldn't imagine living without her, having to start over, seeing Kenny and Elaine only on the weekends . . .

"I'm gonna go out for a while, if you don't mind . . . ?" Half a question from his eldest son, wanting the keys to the car. Mark looked quickly at his wife and saw her smile.

Caroline said, "You seeing Diane down the street? On a school night?" and Mario blushed.

"There's school tomorrow," Mark said. "And Diane's grades are slipping. Her dad mentioned it to me, just in passing."

"I know, but there's only a few weeks left, and I'm helping her with her studies, and you don't have to be sarcastic, Mom."

"A few weeks left in school?" Caroline was smiling again now. "It's mid-April, Mario."

"Ma, I got it aced." He looked at his father. "She will, too, believe me."

"Lots of studying planned for tonight, is there?" Mario did not answer, and his father laughed softly.

"Be home by eleven." The second Mark spoke, his son was out of the chair, heading for the back door, grabbing the keys off the nail hanging next to the door.

Mario driving. A four-year-old Ford that Mark had bought new. Caroline had her own Ford Probe, new and sporty, while Mark drove a Crown Victoria. What had he driven back when he had been sixteen years old? Hot Cadillacs and Lincolns, usually. Christ, what was wrong with him, thinking so much about the past these days?

"Not one minute later," Caroline said, and Mario nodded as he ran out the door.

Before it closed behind him, Elaine said, "Mommy?"

"Yes, Elaine?"

"How come Mario gets to stay out so late and I have to go to bed at eight-thirty?"

"Mario's much older than you are."

"Do older people need less sleep?"

"Well, younger people need more, Elaine."

"I'm gonna go take a bath now."

"Without being told?" Mark the motivator, jumping right in. "That's a sign of maturity!"

"If I'm mature, can I stay up until nine, then?"

"I was going to take a bath, first!" Kenny said.

"Kenny, if you let Elaine take her bath first, you can come down into the basement with me and spot the weights, all right?"

"Can I?"

He'd been talking to Kenny and hadn't noticed Elaine walking around the table toward him. She put her arms as far around his chest as they would go and climbed up into his lap, snuggled her head into his neck then quickly pecked his cheek. Kenny rolled his eyes and went down into the basement to wait to help his father lift weights.

In two hours, both younger kids would be asleep. He suddenly decided that he'd then tell Caroline everything.

"I love you Daddy," Mark's daughter said, and after the thoughts that he'd been having about his past, it was all Mark could do to not break down and cry. He needed to be loved today, needed the feelings he'd spent the first part of his life running away from.

He needed more than this child's love, though, he needed Caroline's, too. He nodded his head. He'd tell her, tonight.

"I love *you*, Elaine," Mark said, then swallowed the lump that was growing in his throat, threatening him, disturbing him. He softly hugged her to him, rubbed her back, smelled her hair, thinking of how much he would have liked to have been able to do that as a kid, just one time. Climb up into his father's lap, kiss him and hug him and tell him he loved him . . .

Stop it!

Mark caught himself before he did something stupid, like sob out loud and then have Caroline diagnose him. There'd been enough of that going on around here lately. He gently helped Elaine down off his lap, then watched her walk out of the room, heading for the stairs, to go upstairs and take her bath, so young, so innocent, thinking the world was a good, safe place.

Mark turned back to the table, uncomfortable with the children gone. It meant that he and Caroline were alone. Should he start now, or wait for the kids to be in bed? He'd wait. He was too nervous now to tell her, he'd think of a way to start the conversation when he was downstairs working out.

Caroline was looking at him, holding her head in her hand as she did when she studied, with the same intent look on her face, the same sort of rapt concentration. Her face, though, was hard, Caroline's eyes telling him things that he didn't really need to know.

"I've always been so goddamned glad I married you," Mark Torrence's wife said to him.

"*You're* glad," Mark said. He'd start the healing, right now. He reached over and took her free hand. "Without you, I'd just be drifting."

"I'm not so glad anymore. There are things, Mark, we have to discuss."

Mark was suddenly angry. Not so glad anymore? Just when he was about to tell her everything? Maybe thinking he should do that was a mistake. He'd play it by ear, let Caroline take the lead. He let her hand drop.

"Thanks," Mark said. "Thanks a lot, Caroline." The resentment was stirring around, she'd cut him. "That's the way to wrap up a good weekend."

He could feel her eyes burning into him again, like the sun, right through his eyes and deep into his brain. He winced and looked away.

He said, "Not right now, Caroline, all right? For Christ's sake, what's the problem?"

"The problem is we've been married ten years and I don't know you, nothing about your life."

"My life began when we met."

"That was fine, Mark, before. A nice, romantic response. But it's not true, your life started somewhere else, what formed you happened elsewhere. And you feel that what made you what you are is not supposed to be my business."

"What's wrong with the way I am?" Mark shrugged. "It doesn't matter anymore." When she got like this he felt a lot less like opening up. She was making it an either-or scenario, giving him an ultimatum. If she'd let it flow naturally, he'd take her by the hand and tell her; but she wouldn't. He'd reached for her hand and she hadn't even responded. He thought it might be a power thing, Caroline seeing if she could control him, get him to do things that were against his nature.

"It matters to me."

"I don't pry. I don't ask you about your childhood, Caroline."

"Go ahead. Ask away. I'll tell you anything that you want."

"That's not fair."

"Now you sound like Elaine." Caroline sighed, exasperated, and when she spoke now, her voice was dead, without emotion. As if she'd given up on it, on prying into his past.

"You'd better go down there and pump your silly fucking weights, before your son gets bored waiting and comes up here and makes me crazy."

"Silly fucking weights?" Mark looked at her, what was she saying? "What do you want, an old man with a pot belly and a sunken chest? You like the benefits enough. Or you *used* to, anyway. Before this fifth degree shit started. I ought to tell you what you want to know, just to get laid again."

She was watching him in that shrink way that made him crazy, aloof, outside of their relationship now, a damn shrink studying a patient, wondering what made him tick. His weak attempt at humor hadn't had much affect on her, Caroline was analyzing him, without love, without warmth.

"A bit defensive, aren't we?"

"I don't know about *you*," Mark said, "but *I'm* feeling a little defensive tonight, now that you mention it. And for a few months now."

He reached out and squeezed her hand and let it go and rose from the table, wondering if she had any idea how honest his last statement had been. She hadn't squeezed his hand back, had allowed her hand to lie there. He shouldn't have taken the goddamned emotional risk. He looked at her, hurt, but Caroline just sat there staring at him, and now her gaze was once again sad.

AS MARK ANGRILY worked out in his well-equipped basement gymnasium on the East Side of Chicago, a man who was known to very few people as James Bracken was kissing his girlfriend goodnight, eight hundred miles and a lifetime away. Leehanna had snuck out of a restaurant to meet him in the alley, and Bracken was acting angry about that, although it was exactly as he wanted it. He knew that she was turned on by the excitement of sneaking around, knew that it aroused her. There was so much that Bracken knew that Leehanna often told him that he had to be some kind of a mind reader.

He leaned into her as he gently kissed her, barely brushing her lips with his tongue. She did not know it, but Bracken was not turned on by the sensual kiss. She did not know it, but in his mind, he was totally disgusted.

Still, he smiled softly as the two of them pulled apart. Bracken looking sheepish, glancing down at the sidewalk as they parted, seeing the pumps on her feet, the cuffs of a pair of six hundred dollar slacks. Leehanna's idea of dressing down was only wearing five grand on her back and not meeting with her cosmetologist or hairstylist for the day.

"It won't be long now, darling," the woman, Leehanna, told him. She spoke with authority and in a superior manner, the traditional roles reversed; Leehanna taking the initiative and bringing Bracken out of himself. Being strong for him, for the boyfriend who felt so isolated and alone. She spoke now in a whisper, leaning into him and saying urgently, "I want you so damn *bad*ly."

She actually talked like that, and Bracken never made a negative comment about her style of speech, although he had to fight to not laugh—she was such a silly bitch. She'd been raised properly and had lived most of her adult life within the constraint of what was, on her part at least, a monogamous marriage, and her life experience of infidelities would be based on what she'd seen on the afternoon soap operas and what she'd read in romance novels.

Bracken looked up, bashfully. "Me, too." Then said, shyly, "But is it right? Leehanna, you're still married . . ."

"I won't be for long."

They were standing in the shadows in the alley behind an extremely trendy restaurant where she and her group had eaten, on the Upper East Side, Leehanna's limo idling discreetly, around the corner and a block away.

"He'll find out sooner or later, Leehanna, no matter how careful we are. You have to be prepared for that."

"My lawyer says the prenup's worthless; as soon as I get a fair offer from Ronald, William, I'm gone."

"Still, Leehanna. Sneaking around like this, meeting in alleys, at art galleries." Bracken looked up, directly into her eyes. "It has to end one way or the other, and soon. I can't keep going like this. We'll get *caught*, Leehanna, and if that happens, you'll be begging your lawyer to get you what was promised in the same prenuptial agreement you're trying to hard to break." Bracken paused and sighed, deeply. When he spoke again, he projected acute exasperation and pain. It was just one of the things he was expert at, had worked at throughout his life.

"I'm always thinking about you, wanting you, and I can never see you anyplace in public, I always have to meet you in out of the way places like this, or 'chance' meetings somewhere with your driver just outside the door of some bar, acting as if there's nothing wrong with a woman of your position walking out of places alone and disappearing for fifteen minutes. You think anyone in that restaurant didn't recognize you? By now, everyone in New York City knows who you are. My God, you've been on the cover of the tabloids since your husband started cheating on you. *He* gets to jet all over the country with his little golddigger piece of ass, and *we* have to meet like this, in alleys. As if we're cheap, as if we're doing something wrong."

Bracken spoke forcefully, yet humbly, gazing into her eyes, holding her upper arms.

"But it *can't* be wrong, Leehanna, it's what I've been waiting for my entire life." He swallowed and put everything he had into his look, into his next words. If she didn't believe him without a doubt, he could, at the very least, lose a half a million hard-earned dollars. At the most—the unthinkable—he could spend the rest of his life in Attica.

"I can't give you what Ronald has, Leehanna, but I can love you, I can do that."

He saw the tears forming in her eyes and knew that his words, his sincerity, had touched her. Quickly, she drew him to her and hugged him tightly, burying her head in his neck, Leehanna squeezing, breathing shallowly. Bracken smelled the overly applied Obsession perfume, the scent overpowering him, nauseating him, but he didn't let his distaste show on his face or in his tone of voice.

"I can love you, Leehanna," he said again, matching her urgent whisper.

"Oh, William, I do love you so."

She pulled back and stared at him, a middle-aged woman who'd been well served by surgery. Her hair was dyed blond, her makeup expertly applied; in the soft light of the alley lamp she could pass for forty, easily. A soft forty, without a lot of hard miles. The problem being that to her spouse, the billionaire husband she'd been married to for fifteen years, that age was now twice the acceptable limit.

"And tomorrow, I'll prove it," Leehanna half-growled. "I'm so excited, thinking about it, I don't know if I'll last."

"Noon tomorrow, Leehanna. You know where, and you have to lose the driver."

"Stan is so loyal to me—"

"Ronald pays his wages." He saw the hesitation in her eyes, the fear there, too. Socialites of Leehanna's stature were terrified and completely lost in Manhattan without their driver/bodyguards, but it was absolutely imperative that no one know where she was going, know whom she was meeting, or ever be allowed to find out why.

"I'm a lawyer, Leehanna," Bracken said, although he was no such thing. "A tax lawyer, sure, but I know about these sort of divorces, I know how ugly they can get. If Stan so much as suspected me of being a part of your life, Ronald would have his hook, his way to leave you with nothing. That or he'd have his reps smear you in the papers, call you a tramp and a whore, say that you and I were cheating first and he was too much of a gentleman to bring it to the attention of the public." Bracken shook his head in loving admiration of her childish naivete.

Bracken said, "The guy's a master at public relations, you of all people know that. The public's with you right now, Leehanna, but that will change in a minute if you and I are seen together. And if Ronald were to find out about what we're going to do tomorrow, my God, you'd definitely lose it all." He smiled at her, his special trick, a smile calculated to melt her, the smile as calculated as his next words were, and just as artificial.

"Now *I* could live with that, Leehanna, in fact, I would prefer it, but you've given him fifteen years of your life . . ." He let the sentence trail off, knowing that Leehanna would finish it; before he'd even met her, Bracken had known Leehanna far better than Leehanna would ever know herself.

"Those years are worth *some*thing," Leehanna said, and smiled. "All right, counselor, you win. Stan stays home, but don't you be late!"

"For you, Leehanna, I'll get there an hour early."

"Tomorrow we lose our secrets." Leehanna was looking down at the soft thin white gloves that Bracken always wore. He put a resigned expression on his face, one of almost pain. As if Leehanna would leave him if she ever saw his hands.

"They'll come off tomorrow," Bracken winked. "Along with everything else."

She giggled, like a schoolgirl, and Bracken smiled, charmingly, although he wanted to slap her. "I must go, William."

"Tomorrow, Leehanna," Bracken said.

As she backed to the corner, Leehanna said, "I love you William Reynolds," and James Bracken grabbed at the kiss she threw him, and held it before him in one clenched gloved fist until she was out of sight.

The second she turned the corner, his smile twisted into a grimace and he said, "I know you do, you shabby little cow."

CABS WERE EVERYWHERE this Sunday night, the economy was bad, and they fought each other to get to you. Still, Bracken walked, preferring to be alone. There were things he still had to sort out inside his head, details to be checked and then checked once again. The unseasonal warmth had brought the tourists to town, and although the streets were mostly empty, there were several people, mostly couples, walking and visible on both sides of Fifth

Avenue. Even in his wimp costume, Bracken felt completely secure.

He stayed in full character, walked a little hunched over, rather meekly, his eyes staring straight ahead, Bracken walking quickly. A native New Yorker who was well aware of the dangers of the night. All of his insecurities were gone. Now that he was working, away from his home, Terri was not on his mind.

A cloud of exhaust fumes descended onto the street, Bracken could see it, reflected in the streetlights, poison fumes gently settling. He walked halfway between the storefronts and the street, able to step aside quickly and keep the beggars at bay, yet far enough away from the trolling cabbies so that they couldn't run him over in their hurry to get a fare. That would be all he needed, this late in the operation, to get run over and killed by some over-zealous Pakistani, wanting to feed his babies and coming a little too close to the curb in his haste to get Bracken into the backseat of his cab. It was tempting, to get into a cab and drive away from this, from the hellhole of the earth that Manhattan had become.

Around him, on the sidewalk, little brown men in green coveralls carrying shortened brooms and dustpans on sticks swept up outside their own individual buildings on 5th, ignoring the filth accumulated on the sidewalks that was past the corners of their own little pieces of real estate.

Bracken felt as if he was walking on a layer of scum. Beggars with paper cups approached every few yards, their territory carefully staked out, ready to do battle if some other beggar encroached on their turf. There was a black woman wrapped in a multi-colored quilt sitting in a wheelchair smack in the middle of the street between 54th and 53rd, holding a paperback book in her hand and reading it raptly, oblivious to the blaring horns and curses shouted at her as traffic whizzed by, inches away from her chair. Maybe the light was better for reading there in the middle of the street, who knew? And besides, what in the name of Christ could she possibly have to lose?

Bracken walked on, watching, always watching.

An emaciated man in filthy, tattered clothing lay directly in the middle of the sidewalk on the corner of 46th St. huddled with something that might have once been a blanket pulled tight around his chest. Bracken could almost see the bugs leaping off his skin, parasites deserting him, knowing the man was dying.

His cheeks were sunken and his hair was matted, the heavily-lined, dirt-streaked face blank and without expression. A hand-written sign on his chest told Bracken that he was homeless and dying of AIDS, the sign imploring passersby to help his pitiful ass, in the name of compassion, God bless and thank you. Bracken walked around the man, as if he wasn't there. He had to fight the urge to lash out at him. Bracken would only have to kick him once to put him out of his misery, once and forever.

In any event, Bracken did not think that the man would last the night. Out there in the open, he'd be fair game for the mutant scum who'd come over the bridges after the pedestrian traffic cleared off the sidewalks for the night, hunting for easy prey such as this to amuse themselves. He would be safe from the animals who would wander down from Harlem—they would be looking to score some cash, and beggars with AIDS were ignored. But the toughs from Brooklyn and Queens would eat him up; it was survival of the fittest after midnight in Manhattan.

Most of the violent trouble these days had an early warning system; the blaring, driving bass of rap music signaled its arrival from several blocks away. When Bracken heard it at night he'd step inside the nearest building and admire the window display, watch in the glass as the Jeep Cherokee or highly-polished Toyota passed. The young men inside would prey on the weak and enjoy it, and few nights went by when death didn't visit some bum.

But the bums weren't Bracken's problem, nor was New York's decline. Leehanna was his problem, and he'd have that problem solved by this time tomorrow. He couldn't wait for tomorrow to come, so he could get it over with. He had wanted to do it in the morning, but she had a charity thing at one of the hotels her husband owned, and she couldn't get out of it, it would look too suspicious. One had to keep one's upper lip stiff, especially in times of suffering. The press didn't like sore losers, it wanted and loved the gloriously and bravely afflicted.

So it would take a couple of more hours, that's all. It would give him time to plan. This one, he knew, would be absolutely perfect. Bracken did not dare to hope that it would be so. Because, if it was perfect, he would finally be able to quit.

If she'd hired private detectives they would have told her that:

William Reynolds was forty-four, and a successful tax lawyer with a Wall Street firm. Computers would spit out his work records, his loyal years of service and the fact that he'd never taken

41

a sick day during his seventeen years with the firm. They would find that he'd worked his way up to junior partner, and that he'd made six figures for most of his career, and then mid-six figures in the past two years, and that he had a net worth of close to 3 million dollars.

Phone calls to sources within the IRS would have found that his own taxes were paid on time and quarterly, and that he lived with his elderly mother, who was now aged and ailing.

Perusal of the obituaries would discover that his wife had died at thirty-two, leaving him childless and alone. Personal references would happily disclose that William Reynolds loved the opera and art galleries, and that he found Manhattan exciting and invigorating, in spite of the increase in violent crime. The words he used to describe New York to his friends were "energetic" and "dynamic."

They would learn that he donated his services to liberal causes and that he served food in a homeless shelter one night each month. That he was active in the animal rights movement, although in a passive way. He would never throw blood on a woman's fur coat, or even holler at a woman who chose to wear the skin of dead animals upon her back. He would see it as her choice.

They would find that he had served in Vietnam and that he'd been decorated and discharged honorably, that he had several service medals which he never bragged about. That he had never been arrested and had lived a life that was completely above reproach. That he was kind, gentle and very hard-working, that he shunned the spotlight and was known for his humility, and that he never argued much when someone told him what to do.

William Reynolds was all the things that Leehanna Staples loved.

It had cost James Bracken over a hundred thousand dollars to become that man, to earn her love and trust, to set up the network that had made him what he was.

James Bracken, on the other hand, was an entirely different story. But she didn't have to know about him, would never learn who he truly was. Nobody would, could ever get to know him, they'd only get to see the things that he wanted to show.

Maybe, given enough time, money and effort, the private detectives would have caught onto a rumor that things weren't exactly right with this William Reynolds guy. But time would not be what they would have. Bracken knew how those guys operated, and it wasn't like in the movies. They'd have taken her money and run a few printouts, made a few calls to justify their fee, and turned their reports over without a second's doubt, and William Reynolds would never be linked to James Bracken in this lifetime.

And after she died, they'd destroy any records that they might have, would want no tie or link between themselves and the dead woman. Her husband was so powerful and feared in this town, that even the slightest hint of impropriety on their parts would cause his wrath to descend upon them, and that would not be something that any smart private detective would want, not if he wanted to keep his license.

What a phony little sneak Leehanna truly was. Looking down at his gloves and acting as if she were curious. As if her private detectives hadn't snuck looks into the computer hacker-planted records of the VA hospitals. As if she didn't know that Reynolds had been disfigured in the war. Well, she'd get to see those fingers tomorrow, Leehanna would. Just once, he'd show them to her. It would be her dying wish, before William Reynolds let her see who he truly was.

Monday afternoon the tie to the sensitive, lonely lawyer would be cut forever, and Bracken the chameleon would crawl back into his jungle for a time. Every record would be destroyed, every planted bit of information would be erased. Every character reference—who'd never met him in the first place—would deny that they'd ever heard his name in the unlikely event that they were asked. William Reynolds would drop off the face of the earth, the man would have never existed.

But tonight he would worry, and would drink and smoke too much, thinking about things that might go wrong, worrying about things he would have laughed at twenty years ago.

But twenty years ago he'd only one thing to lose, and after he'd lost it, after he had been forced to kill it, he'd almost lost his mind right along with that so deeply loved human being.

These days there were no people he loved, it was a luxury he could no longer allow himself to indulge in. But he did have things he enjoyed, and he was noticing the ever more rapid passage of time. Saw middle age attacking him, making him slow and afraid. He needed the time to enjoy the things he had, to spend his money, to savor the possessions he'd earned. And he would have that time someday, he vowed, when all this was a memory. When he didn't have to kill people in order to make his fortune.

Would that day ever come? Bracken wondered, then shook his head at the thought. Maybe not. Maybe never. Maybe tomorrow. There was only one way that time would ever come, and if it was ever going to, tomorrow was a perfect time for it to happen.

There had been a time when he'd thought that each one would be his last, a time when the release he'd feel from killing had made him spent. As he'd felt after sex, the compulsion gone, satisfied. But, as with the sex drive, it would come back after a time.

He'd decided years ago that the compulsion wouldn't leave him until the moment that he'd committed the absolutely perfect murder, until he'd left no loose ends and it had gone exactly as he planned.

To date, that day had never come, but he thought that it might, tomorrow.

And when he was near the end of a project, such as now, the sex drive would leave him entirely, whomever he might be living with would be moved into a separate bedroom, replaced by the unbearable excitement of knowing that the end of life for another human being—an ending at his hands—was near.

He crossed a street and looked up at the sign absently, saw that he was in the 20s. Dear Lord, he'd walked forever, and it was getting pretty late. Bracken stepped around the huge plastic bags filled with trash and stood on the curb, lifted his hand, and waited until the cab had come to a complete stop before reaching for the door handle.

EDDIE DOLAN SAT in a small dark room across the hall from the main interrogation room, talking to the kid who'd been telling him that he was only a juvenile and taking a real attitude about it.

"What the worst you gonna do to me, shit, ninety days in St. Charles." He gave Eddie a look of pure superior ignorance, a look Eddie saw all the time with these young kids, and had been seeing for most of the twenty minutes that he'd been talking to this one.

Which was why the other detectives had asked him to take a shot at talking to him. They were getting tired of it, and knew better than to show their anger when they had a large advantage that the suspect wasn't aware of.

Dolan was handsome, young looking, thirty-four years old and he looked around twenty-five. He had blond hair and bright blue eyes that shined with sincerity, eyes that served him well in his daily duties in the youth department. He could smile, nod, spray some sincerity at you while lying on your mother at the very same time.

He showed that bright smile to the boy sitting in front of him now, the punk who was so incredibly secure in his knowledge of the law; a fifth grade dropout who fancied himself to be F. Lee Bailey.

"Why for I should tell you shit?" the boy said, and crossed his arms. "Fact is, I was a white boy, we wouldn't even be here in this room. You'd'a let me go a long time ago." He nodded his head, Jonah in full agreement with himself.

"All of you cops is like this, even the slave men-tal-ity niggers on your force. Don't wanna do nothin' but keep the black man down."

Eddie Dolan smiled indulgently. He did that well, too. Could play big brother with the best of them. What did slightly bother him was the honest belief in the young man's voice, there was no doubt in the kid's mind that what he'd said was true. This, too, he heard all the time. And wasn't truly certain that the speakers weren't correct.

The room they were in was smaller than the interrogation room, was used mostly for quick consultations with lawyers who carried busy workloads. A small table with a steel folding chair on each end took up most of the available room space. A single low-watt light bulb hung unprotected above their heads. The four walls were painted dull green, a color now darkened by hundreds of quickly smoked, deeply inhaled cigarettes.

Eddie had left the door open, so that Jonah could see all the happy detectives walking in and out of the interrogation room, where this kid's rap partner was sitting, his jherri-curled head up against the white wall, leaving stains. The kid in there wasn't saying anything, other than asking to use the bathroom around every five minutes. The cops weren't letting him go. He would look at them, with over-acted quizzical drama, as they sauntered in and out of the room. He didn't understand what the hell was going on, wanted them to know that he saw them as stupid.

But to Jonah's inexperienced eye, it would appear that a lot of action was going on in there.

"If that's all you're looking at, ninety lousy days juvie," Dolan told him, "then you ought to just tell me the truth. You can do ninety days and be back on the street for August."

"Now your homie in there," Dolan tossed his head toward the interrogation room, "is gonna cop if you don't. From all the movement in and out, I'd say he's giving a detailed statement right now. *He's* eighteen, Jonah, *he's* looking at serious time in the pen. He puts it all on you, man, and it might not be just ninety days in Charlie. You might get charged as an adult. You might wind up at the youth facility at Joliet, until you're twenty-one, and then they'll send you across the river to the big house. That's what happens when you're only a juvenile and you get charged as an adult." The boy still glared at Eddie—it was the major part of his self-image—but Dolan could see that the kid was wavering, having trouble understanding what he'd just been told.

It had been warm for a Chicago April, but the evenings still got chilly. It was maybe fifty degrees out there and Jonah was already wearing his standard summer uniform, a tank top—to show off skinny, ropy muscles—with super baggy knee-length shorts with pictures of grinning cartoon pit bulls on either knee. He had black Air Jordans on his feet, without any stockings.

There were several jailhouse tattoos on his arms, blue ink applied with a sterilized straight pin onto dark brown skin. One of the tattoos was of a woman's name that had been half-cut off with a razor. Eddie could see a C-L-A, then scar tissue covered the rest of the letters that had once been printed on the boy's right bicep. He'd had a street divorce, quick and easy, but slightly painful. Jonah had a haircut like Dominique Wilkins.

He was only seventeen years old, but already there were several heavy knife scars on his face. One of them ran all the way down the left side, from the top of Jonah's forehead, crossing the top and bottom of the eye, and curving all the way down to the jawbone, making Jonah's left eye look half-shut all the time and giving his mouth the appearance of a permanent sneer.

Jonah, seeking information but trying to be casual about it, said, "I hear some shit about that Jo-liet place, that center, where they send you when you convicted as an *a*-dult."

"Aggravated arson and murder, you could be tried that way, that's for sure, Jonah." Eddie waved a yellow folder in the air, dropped it onto the desk.

"Ain't no murder in there, man, that's bullshit, you know there weren't no murder."

"There was a likelihood that people would be home at the time that the fire was set, Jonah, that qualifies it as first degree murder." Dolan tapped the folder with his hand.

"Take a look at this shit, man, go ahead, it's your juvenile record. You been arrested more times than I had birthdays." Jonah shrugged, proud yet humble.

"Judge takes a look at this, Jonah, you're going down, especially with your homie across the hall in there talking against you worse than a dog. Some neighbors are giving statements, too, I hear, want you both out of the neighborhood for as long as we can lock you up."

Nervously, Jonah said, "G-Dog-Killer don't bust out on no motherfucker, he won't dime me out, baby. I his homeboy." The words hung hollow in the air, Jonah whistling past the graveyard. Dolan let them hang for a few seconds, staring hard at the kid, not smiling now.

"You willing to place twenty years of your life on that bet?" Eddie began to act exasperated, but spoke in a simple, reasonable tone of voice, as if Jonah was too stupid to understand what he was trying to say and it was his life's work to make the kid understand his true position.

"Why d'you think they sent *me* in here? I'm a *youth* officer, for Christ's sake. They don't want to see *you* go down, they want the badass, hardcore, adult gangster in *there* to do the time. They want me to talk some sense into you, that's why *I'm* in here instead of some gorilla homicide asshole who'd be yelling into your face by now."

The kid seemed even more nervous, squirming in his chair, wondering what kind of game Eddie was running down.

"You got a square?"

Eddie said, "Nobody's allowed to smoke in the stations anymore, it's the new law around here. Cruel and unusual punishment." He sighed, heavily. Reached into his jacket pocket. "These are yours." He tossed a pack of Kools on the desk. They'd been opened on the bottom. "Put the ashes on the floor, I'll clean them up later."

Jonah looked at him suspiciously, then grabbed at the pack, turned it upside down and pulled out a cigarette that had itself been turned upside down and placed back in the pack, filter side showing.

"This my lucky square. Guess I need it now."

"You don't need luck, Jonah." Eddie waited until the kid had lit the smoke and stuffed the book of matches back into the cellophane and looked up at him. "You need a friend, and right now, from what I can see, I'm the only friend you've got in this world right now."

"Dogg wit' me."

"Hold your breath to see how that comes out." Eddie shook his head.

"You need someone to get you through this, Jonah. Someone with enough sense to keep you out of the pen. You want a lawyer, I'll get you one, but I'll tell you straight up, Jonah, once I call one, you're fucked. All they want is money, and if you can't afford one, the stiff appointed to you will be straight out of law school, trying to get enough trial experience and bucks together to buy a three-piece suit and head off to private practice. They'll sell you down the river, and Jonah, I got to be straight with you here, somebody died tonight, and you really will be charged as an adult if we charge you at all. Christ, kid, if it was an accident, like we think, you won't do any time. When was the last time you heard of anyone going to the pen because of an accident?"

Jonah was getting scared, Eddie could tell. He'd been counting on his youth to get him out of trouble all of his life, and now he was looking at a serious sentence for the first time and did not know how to act. Eddie played to it, put his elbows on the table and placed his chin on his forearms, nodding his head a couple of times before he spoke.

"I can help you."

"How *you* gonna help me? You the man."

Dolan said, "You tell me what happened. We already know most of it, from investigating it, how it happened, but what we don't know is *why* it happened.

"Now, what we got here, see, Jonah, is a race. But it can have a happy ending for you. Those guys in there, they don't give a shit about G-Dogg. They'll get him to cop and lock him up and throw away the key, and you with him, if they can. But, if you tell me the truth before he tells *them* the truth, I take care of you."

"I go home?"

"You'll be doing the right thing, why shouldn't you go home? Worst you'll be looking at is like you said before, maybe six months in Charlie. You can handle that, right?"

"Man, shit, it was an *acc*-i-dent," Jonah said, and crossed his arms, his brow creased in deep concentration.

An older, beefy, plain clothes officer walked up to the interrogation door just then, holding a bunch of official looking papers in his hand. He had gray hair and a lined red face. He looked more like a doting grandfather than a homicide cop. Dolan watched him, knowing Procter well. Procter was the kind of cop who could find an old-time song to sing that celebrated every ghoulish occasion. Procter had gotten suspended once at the scene of a Metra commuter train fatality when, after viewing the assorted body parts of the two victims who'd been in the car—trying to go around the crossing gates before the train arrived—he began to sing, "I Fall to Pieces," with all the Patsy Cline sincerity he could muster up. His mistake had been doing it in front of dozens of humorless civilians.

Before entering the interrogation room Procter looked over, saw Eddie talking to Jonah, shook his head and smiled.

"Don't waste your time, Dolan," the cop said. "We got the Dogg-man in here singing like a birdie. Just lock that punk down, and not in juvie. He'll be tried as an adult. Put him in back, in the cage, we'll process him later." Procter shook his head in revulsion. "You'll want to hear what this cat in here's saying, anyway, the way he's laying it on that punk. You'll be sorry you ever were nice to the bastard." He didn't wait for Dolan's answer, just walked into the interrogation room, carrying the papers, whistling.

Eddie got up and closed the door. Then sat down again and looked at Jonah, severely.

"It's over, you heard the man. Have another smoke to last you through the night and let's go. I got to lock you up, Jonah, you don't leave me any choice."

Jonah was near tears now, frustrated, angry, despairing. He lit the cigarette and took a deep drag, put his elbows on his knees and hung his head between his arms, shook it from side to side, suddenly comprehending his plight.

Dolan said, "Come on, talk to me. I won't hate you, no matter what the other detectives or your friend in there says. You think I don't know what it's like out there because I'm white? You think I never thought of doing what you did? I can't tell you how many times I wanted to do that, to throw gas on some prick's house and toss a match on it. Sometimes, Jonah, some people got that coming."

"I is only seventeen."

"You could be fifteen, sixteen, it doesn't matter." Eddie had him now, he knew, and he had to play it smart. Punks like this could sense fear, could tell if you weren't secure in your position.

"Talk to me, man, now, it's your last shot."

"I ain't goin' to the County?"

"You forget about the lawyer, sign the waiver of rights, make your statement in front of a witness, and then you're with me, Jonah, and I look out for my people. The worst that I'll let happen is you go to the Audie home until you testify. You're seventeen, remember. You'll run that joint, with all the punks in there," Eddie Dolan said. He watched Jonah's eyes widen at the idea, himself in charge or close to the top at Audie, a gang-leader at last.

Jonah looked at him and smiled.

"I was just kind of along with G-Dog-Killer—"

"What's his real name?"

"Billy Gonzales. But he ain't no Meskin, he a brother—"

"And what happened, what did you and Billy do?" the woman on call from the state's attorney's office wanted to know. The room was suddenly way too small, what with her, Jonah, Dolan and a stenographer. Procter was also in the room, leaning against the wall, lighting Jonah's menthol cigarettes for him with his mini-Bic, one after another. Dolan could hear the tape recorder humming in the long silences before Jonah answered questions.

"Well, see, there was Tyree, old man down the street? Owed me three-honnert-seventy dollar for painting the outside of his house . . ."

Which Tyree had never paid, and which Jonah had, for two good reasons, forgiven. The old man said he was broke and you didn't get blood from a turnip, his mama had always told him that, and how much face can you save by beating an old man to death, unless you do it when you're robbing him, and Tyree had nothing to rob. Besides, Jonah couldn't let the other people in the neighborhood know that Tyree had held out on him, they'd all take a piece of him then, and in Jonah's neighborhood, the pieces that they took were literally cut out of your flesh.

But less than a week later, old Tyree had shown up driving a brand spanking new custom-made Plymouth van, and that had done it, had been a slap at Jonah's manhood.

"I is a man of action," Jonah told Dolan, Procter, the assistant state's attorney, the stenographer and the willing tape recorder.

A man of action who'd gone and bought a half-gallon of gas at the Clark station, putting it into a plastic one-gallon milk carton. A man who'd had G-Dogg-Killer stand watch, and who spent two hours trying to convince them otherwise, trying to tell them that G-Dogg-Killer had done the crime, not giving in until after a small, private consultation with his friend Dolan he finally copped that he'd poured the gas on the house himself, with Billy Gonzales playing lookout for him.

"I didn't know that anyone was home."

Which, he thought, made it all a mistake, and you didn't do time behind a dumbass mistake.

Or so Jonah had been told once again during the private conference with his new best friend, Eddie Dolan.

"That's all," the assistant state's attorney finally said, and pushed herself away from the wall. She thanked the officers and the stenographer, and left the two cops to help Jonah write out his confession in his own hand and of his own free will. The stenographer would have it typed up by morning, and if by then Jonah decided not to sign it, they would always have the tape recorded confession, on which Jonah had been assured throughout the meeting that he could stop at any time and seek the advice and counsel of an attorney that would be appointed to him by the courts. Jonah had steadfastly declined the generous offer, and he'd spoken in a casual voice, the tape would pick up bursts of the boy's laughter.

But the tape recorder would never pick up the many winks and knowing, insider smiles that passed between Jonah and Eddie Dolan.

Dolan could still smell the woman's perfume, long after she

was gone, the Tabu mingling in with the smell of Jonah's fear sweat, with the smell of stale cigarette smoke.

He had Jonah sign the confession, stopping during the writing of it twice in order to help ease the boy's sudden fears, to calm him, pat his back, whisper reassuring words. Procter witnessed the signature, and Dolan, as the investigating officer, put his name at the bottom, too.

Then, before the ink dried, Procter became Elvis Presley, drawling soulfully, "Ah-ah fought the law—and the law won, Ah fought the law-aw and the—law won." Jonah looked up, the sympathetic, somber mood of the room destroyed. He was a killer who was now morally offended at the behavior of a policeman.

"Why you singin', man, this shit ain't funny."

Procter chuckled and said, "You want to tell him or you want me to?"

Dolan rose, looking down at Jonah.

"Come on, son, we've got to go now."

"You taking me home, right, like you say you do before? I ain't got to go to the Audie even, I bet." Jonah shot a victorious look at Procter, the outsider. The hope in Jonah's voice was almost painful to Dolan, he had to remind himself that this was just another killer, begging for his freedom.

"Sure, you're going home," Dolan said.

Procter finished the statement for him.

"To your new home, over at Twenty-sixth and California. You'll be there until you go to court, Jonah." Jonah began to understand. His eyes got wild, anger mixed with terror. Spittle flew from his lips when he spoke.

"You tole me when we was alone that if I told the truth you'd take me home! Tole me you give me your word on that if I told you the truth and it was an accident. Why I got to go to County? It was an accident! What about Audie, man?"

"Thank God you fuckers are stupid," Procter said. "Or we'd be overwhelmed with unsolved crimes."

Jonah looked at Dolan, pleadingly. "You bullshitting, right, I ain't going nowhere!"

"I got to lock you up now, Jonah. You confessed in front of God and everyone."

"I take it back, I was lied to!"

"Too late." Dolan lifted Jonah up, half-wrestled him facedown on the table, began fastening cuffs to the boy's wrists from behind. Jonah fought it.

The boy screamed, "Fucks you, you lied to me! I takes it all back, I'm just a juvenile! You can't takes me to no County Jail!"

"Not in this state, kid," Dolan corrected him. "You're seventeen in Illinois, Jonah, and you're a man. Your days at the Audie Home end as of now."

"Look at it this way," Procter told him. "You went from being an eighth-grade bully to a freshman in high school gotta take shit from the upper classmen for a while." Procter rubbed Jonah's head and shrugged. "Don't take it too hard, kid. Before you know it, you'll be a senior."

THE FACT THAT he'd outslicked the ignorant ghetto punk was of little consolation to Dolan, even though he shook the other officers' hands and accepted their congratulations on a job well done. They could see it as a masterstroke of interrogation if they chose to, but Dolan saw it for what it was; a con on a kid who'd dropped out of school before they got around to teaching you how to write more than your name.

He sat in his small office now, his feet up on his desk, paging through a copy of Jonah's detailed confession. Looking at the blatant misspellings and phonetically written mistakes. "Me and me's homeboyz," Jesus. Dolan and Procter had had to spell most of the words out for him, nice and slow. The confession would stand up in court, though, and that was all that really mattered.

The words Jonah had shouted after him still rang in his ear, the kid cursing him, crying bitter tears, shouting in the tank, yelling over the angry or laughing objections of the other men inside the cell. They'd quiet him up, Eddie knew, the second they heard the outer door clang shut behind Dolan.

Jonah had screamed in frustration, believing himself to still be a juvenile. He'd first started to get scared when Dolan had mentioned the juvenile home over in Joliet. Wait until he got a load of the County tomorrow, after his bond hearing. It made the juvenile detention center look like an eighth grade field trip, what with eight thousand detainees in there at any given time.

He wondered if he should check up on the kid now, make sure he wasn't being raped. Eddie decided not to. Accident or not, the kid was a killer. A killer who'd started out wanting nothing more than to be paid for the paint job he'd performed on some guy's house. The justice of the street had seduced another one, made him forget that the laws applied to everyone, even himself, no matter how many crimes he'd gotten away with in the past, or how many times he'd walked out of a juvenile courtroom, smiling. Something like this happened to all of them, sooner or later, after they became adults, after they got away with too much for too long.

Rather than feeling sorry for Jonah, Dolan should be weighing what had happened earlier that night, without regard toward the kid's intent. Mr. Tyree had run out of the house, had escaped the fire with most of his family. His grandson, though, hadn't been so lucky. A seven-year-old life had been snuffed out before it had even really had much of a chance to begin. The child had been found huddled in a closet, clutching a stuffed toy to him, as if the toy might bring him safety. His plan hadn't worked. The child had been dead of smoke inhalation before the flames ever reached him.

Blessings in disguise, the little things that Dolan clung to in order to stay sane in this job.

Dolan did not want to think about it anymore. Nor did he want to think about his wife, who she might be with tonight, or who she might have left the kids with when she'd gone out with the son of a bitch. The kids would tell him on the weekend, next Saturday, when he saw them again. The fly in that ointment being that today was only Sunday. He had a whole week to go before he could see them again, and then, he'd have to kiss them goodbye early in order to go to work.

He'd be off tomorrow and Tuesday, but he knew she wouldn't let him see them on his days off. The agreement expressly stated Saturdays, every week, more than that during the summer, and summer was still six weeks away. She'd tried to deny him any custody at all, had her lawyer point out Dolan's defects to the judge, but Dolan's own lawyer had responded that Dolan was working hard to change, had gone into a rehab center and given up alcohol, given up pills. Back then, it had been nearly the truth. Today, though, he was clean, even though he sometimes regretted that fact.

Look at him, what he'd gone ahead and done, again. Tried to take his mind off of what he'd done to Jonah, and got to thinking

about his kids, about the death of his marriage. Far more dangerous topics, topics that he tried to stay away from but never
really could.

They were on his mind all the time, lately, his kids more than
his wife. Far more than they ever were when they were living
together as a family. Even though Marsha had radically changed,
even though he didn't love her, the things she'd said to Dolan,
the things she still believed about him, haunted him worse than
anything Jonah could ever dream of saying. Because she knew
him far better, had more insight into him than maybe he did
himself. And because he suspected that she'd been right.

If he were going to be happy with himself, he would have to
keep analyzing what Marsha thought, rather than rejecting it
out of hand as the rambling of a hateful, miserable, soon to be
ex-spouse.

Dolan took his feet off the desk and spun around in his chair,
looked out the window at the darkness of South State Street.
There always seemed to be something going on out there, no
matter what time of day. State Street never seemed quiet to him.

To his left, he could see the L tracks; across the street was
yuppie housing, people paying a fortune to live in those units
and believing themselves to be safe because they were across the
street from a police station. But the high wall that protected their
apartments from State Street gave lie to their beliefs. He wondered if any of them knew why that wall was there, or if they
thought that it was just to break the sound of sirens.

He should have been out of here hours ago, after making the
last of his Sunday house calls, surprise visits that were somehow
usually expected by the client and the family, Dolan supposedly
checking up and making sure that the kids that he supervised
were home, had gone to church or had otherwise spent the day
with their families, doing whatever the families had done.

It was honorable methodology, from the standpoint of the
judge, checking to make sure that families were together on Sunday, that the prodigal children were getting another chance to
become a member of the clan. It was too bad that the families
he dealt with didn't live up to some judge's image of what life
should be like for them.

Dolan's clients weren't out of a sitcom or a movie, did not
live the life portrayed in *My Three Sons* or *Boys Town*. They were
for the most part youngsters whose life paths had already been

mapped, maps which stopped at dead end streets that would usually be violent, ugly and senseless. Some of them would be shooting victims, others would be stabbing victims, and still others would be just plain beaten to death. Some would become suicides, while others would die from drug overdoses or car accidents, from the devastating effects of long term abuse of alcohol, or from heart attacks or lung cancer from chainsmoking Kools since they were old enough to want to emulate their elders.

You could see it in their eyes, the knowledge that their lives would be short. Kids would talk to him about their hopes, their dreams, and they would always speak with a near pathetic longing, because even at the age of ten they were aware that those dreams weren't likely to ever come true. There was only one Michael Jordan, and who knew how long rap would last?

His clients never spoke to him of future careers in science or as teachers or even working on the assembly line at the Ford plant over in Hegewisch. Their dreams, their futures were tied to joining rap groups or a professional sports team, in acting in or directing films.

Those who had not yet learned to lie to the Man told him straight out that their goal in life was to deal drugs so they could live in big houses and have a lot of girlfriends.

Their local role models were males who drove the fancy cars or had the nicest clothes, the loudest radio or the most kills under their belts. Those men with rings that spelled out their street names in heavy gold, rings so big that they had to be worn across four fingers, like highly expensive brass knuckles. The police were the enemy, the Man, the occupying force that they had to deal with to survive. The police were resented, hated, objects of scorn and derision.

The female clients were even worse, they had no fear or respect for the police. They would scream and sometimes assault you, and you could never be with them in a room, alone. They showed no mercy when it came down to a fight, and their goal was to have more babies, to become more of a woman through steady procreation.

Dolan always told himself that it was easy for some cops to respond negatively to the feelings of the street, to see the ghetto dwellers of the West and South sides as inferior, as objects of contempt and loathing. It made him feel better about the way he sometimes felt, about the things he sometimes said when he was full of frustration and anger.

Marsha had heard him vent that frustration, had seen what it had done to him, how he'd staggered home most nights, drunk and flying on diet pills. High, he would allow himself to drunkenly discuss what he felt, how he was, the things that were inside of him. Marsha had then formed her negative opinions of him, based on what she'd observed, after years of taking it in, listening to it without comment.

Because he didn't have to live out there with them it was easy for him to sometimes look down upon them. Some cops fell into that trap, and Dolan often would feel the urge to, back when he was riding a squad car. He had feelings too, even though the people he'd sworn to protect thought otherwise, would like to see him as just another symbol of the white man keeping them down.

Those feelings got hurt even more quickly when you felt a natural superiority over those you served, those hard feelings exacerbated by the fact that the people you thought you were protecting were calling you filthy, vile names, and trying to goad you into fights so they could sue the city and make their fortune. Feelings that were already on your sleeve could explode when you had the supersensitivity of the active drunk, when you felt that you had the strength of superman from the speed racing through your system.

What was it coming down to? Eddie wished he knew. His attitude had changed since he'd been in Youth, and he thought that was mainly because he wasn't hated all day long, day in, day out, that hatred being part of what he had to put up with for his six hundred and fifty dollar weekly take-home pay. It still made him shiver, the memory of the way they'd look at you as you drove the squadcar by . . . it was the reason that he'd started drinking, the way they hated him out there.

At first he'd tried to be friendly and compassionate, had come onto the force with high ideals, but Christ, it wasn't easy, not working the streets of Chicago. His idealism and lofty goals had been slapped out of him quickly, such things never lasted long when you faced death, cold and real. When you tried to be polite to someone who'd just spit upon you in brutal contempt as you'd responded to a call they'd made, as you tried to help them out. They had to take it out on someone, and the cops were elected.

They were out there, tokens of the communities' disrespect. The cops, maybe the only people they could take their anger out upon with the assurance that they wouldn't be shot dead by them for openly expressing themselves. A street gang with blue colors, but a street gang without teeth. And how did you please such people, when your common enemy had more in common with them than you ever would?

There were kids out there today with weapons out of a sci-fi movie, laser-sighted automatic weapons in the pockets of twelve-year-old children. There were teenage girls who would gladly kill you if given half a chance, it wasn't just wild-eyed, doped up males anymore, everyone you met had the potentiality of becoming your assassin.

Dolan had been raised in a white enclave on the Northwest Side, had never interacted with a black person until high school, and he'd noticed right away that they weren't like the blacks he'd seen on the news, with their coats over their heads, held there by cuffed wrists. These were decent people, kids who only wanted to fit in, to play on the teams, to date the prettiest cheerleaders.

Yet every day, these people paid the price of integration. Dolan would hear the mutterings, the curses leveled at those black kids then, and he would explode with rage, attack in their defense. It made him feel good to do that, back then, when he was too young to know that they didn't want his help. Back then he'd seen everyone as brothers; it would be a while before he met people who would shame him if they were related.

It was different, on the street, especially if you wore a badge.

A newspaper writer riding along one night had told Dolan that the residents of the community feared him, viewed his badge and gun and handcuffs as symbols of his power, that power being a sign of oppression rather than a symbol of authority. The writer had told Dolan that he believed that his views of the neighborhood were slanted, prejudiced by all the pain and suffering that he witnessed every day. Told Dolan that he was honestly more afraid in the car with Dolan that night than he ever was when he walked those streets alone. There was more of a chance of a violent confrontation with a cop next to him than there was when he was by himself.

All Dolan could think of to say was, "You walk down here *alone?*" At the time he'd seen the guy as a bleeding heart liberal asshole, and had stopped just short of telling him so. But later, after he thought about it—after he'd gotten over his resentment at having the guy with him, after all, when he had a ride-a-long, he couldn't get a bottle—he came to believe that the guy might have been right.

When you have cop experiences, when you see what cops have to look at every day, you run the risk of becoming jaded. Maybe even bigoted.

Some nights back then he'd felt like nothing more than a walking bull's-eye. A night rarely went by where something soft and rotten hadn't been tossed onto the hood or roof of the squadcar, fruit or vegetables gone bad or sometimes dirty diapers, aimed at him from high-rise windows.

It had gotten so that he'd grown used to it, didn't even jump when the squad was attacked. The only time he noticed it was when he'd have ride-a-longs, someone like the writer who had been approved by the brass to go with a cop on an eight-hour tour. Good public relations, the street cops were told. As if someone could learn what it was like to be a cop by spending eight hours in a squad car with one. But *they'd* sure jump when a tomato hit the roof, that reporter certainly had; he'd thought they were under fire.

What Dolan had to figure out was: had he really buried his prejudices? Put them away in the back of his mind, where such ugly thoughts belonged? He wanted to be a good man, a good person, a good cop. But he didn't know if he had what it took to be objective anymore, didn't know if he was part of the problem rather than what he truly wanted to be, which was part of the solution.

He wished that he could go and talk to somebody about it, somebody who was trained to help you figure out that sort of thing, but he couldn't, even though the department encouraged it and paid for it when an officer sought out assistance. Dolan was a principal on the Barricade and Hostage Negotiating Team, and you had to be slick for that, above any hint of reproach. A high-profile, premiere unit like that would cut you out in a minute, all they needed was some psycho to blow a negotiation, in front of all those TV cameras . . . Talk about bad public relations? Christ.

It wasn't a risk he was willing to take. He couldn't even give the impression of not being in total control of himself. He wouldn't be on the team at all, if the department didn't have a strict policy that protected the anonymity of an officer who'd gone through rehab. His past sickness could not be used against him. Word could get out about that, and nobody would even bother to think twice. There were as many alcoholic cops these days as there were cops who were divorced. As for Marsha's accusations in divorce court, those were merely seen as the vicious revenge of a scorned and brutal woman. With what he had to lose, and mindful of what he'd already lost, seeking help was out. Eddie would have to do it himself, would have to look at himself and analyze what he saw.

He'd felt a sense of superiority dealing with Jonah, there was no doubt about that. He wanted to believe he'd felt it because he'd been getting one over on a killer, but now, alone with his thoughts, he wasn't so sure anymore.

One of the reasons his wife thought that their marriage had broken up was her perceptions of what she thought to be his bigotry toward minorities. She certainly didn't believe in pulling punches, that was for sure, Marsha always going for the jugular, or lower, swiping at his balls. And she never cared how drunk he was, in fact, she seemed to enjoy her tirades more when she caught him in his cups.

"You're nothing but a drunken racist pig!" She'd scream it when the weather was nice, with all the doors and windows open, for all the neighbors to hear. Marsha didn't care. She probably enjoyed playing to the crowd.

"That job turned you into a Nazi." Other times, she'd be less kind, tell him that she was going to have an affair with a black man, just to see how he'd deal with that. All of this was said in front of the kids. No wonder they were having so much trouble in school.

The strangest reactions, though, came from their Hyde Park neighbors. Some would buy him a shot and a beer down at the corner tavern and feel safe in expressing their hatred of blacks, convey to him their anger at how the niggers had destroyed the city. Others wouldn't speak to him at all, and he could never figure out if it was because he was a cop, or because they believed what Marsha was always saying about him.

There had surely been a hint of truth to what she'd said, but he didn't think that it had ever been as bad as Marsha would have liked to believe. Marsha the college student, who at 29 had felt the urge to go back to school and find herself. Marsha, who wore low-cut blouses and tight jeans to school, acting like a teenager again because she'd wasted the latter part of those years being somebody's wife. She was highly attractive even into her thirties and enjoyed the attention she got, Marsha talking on the phone with guys from school, Marsha having coffee with them after class, talking about their studies, or so she'd tried to tell him at first . . .

Dolan was getting depressed. She'd told him, when she'd thrown him out, that she was tried of his living in denial. He told her that he didn't need to go to school for four years to learn fancy words to say things that were really a lot more simple to verbalize. Called her a bitch, just to prove his point.

He'd spent weeks, alone in his new North Side efficiency apartment, a year and six months without a drink and having to look at reality for a change, thinking about the things that she'd said to him. They'd grown apart, he'd seen it coming, and the breakup hadn't destroyed him. He'd thought that it would, though, back when he'd been drinking, thought that without her, he would dry up and blow away. Maybe being sober for a time had given him the confidence to live without her. Maybe he didn't see himself as a man that no other woman could love. He missed the constancy at first, the normality of being a part of a family, but even in his darkest hour, he hadn't missed Marsha all that much.

She'd changed into someone that he no longer loved, had gone from a loving, caring partner to a superior intellectual, always criticizing, constantly finding fault in him. He could only imagine what the "kids" at school had said to her when they'd learned that she was married to a cop. They didn't have many parties after her first semester at the university. And the invitations she received never included him. She'd told him that was because her crowd didn't have much use for alcoholics.

But still, even knowing what she was, he looked into himself, tried to see what Marsha saw.

He saw a man with weaknesses, a drunk and a druggie, but certainly not a bigot. He didn't hate blacks, or anyone else for that matter. What he hated was what some of them could become, and he wanted, these days *needed* to believe, that he hated that same part of white people, the part that made them kill each other for the change that they had in their pockets.

He had to admit, though, that for a while, when he was still in the squad, he'd been different. And Marsha had been there with him through that, had seen and heard him discuss the worst of it.

He hadn't had the proper distance or objectivity that he would have needed then to see things as they were, Dolan seeing only what was right there in front of him, without wondering *why* it was there, its causes. He'd spent his days responding in kind with anger at people who thought they had reason to hate him. For a time, he'd played into it, had been rude, surly, short tempered and even violent. But then he'd finally understood that for most of them there was no way out, and they realized it and hated what they thought had put them there.

Since he'd been clean and in the youth division, Dolan had walked the streets and talked to plenty of people who lived in the communities, and had found out that, apart from cultural distinctions, most of them were actually not much different from himself. And he'd done that *before* he and Marsha had split up.

Dolan dealt with parents who loved and nurtured their children, with folks who would hang their heads in shame when they brought their kids in for their monthly visits. These were people who were so depressed by the problems surrounding them that they didn't know where to turn, people who lived in mortal terror of the gangs, because they saw proof every day of what happened to those who stood up to them. They often went to the wakes and the funerals of the few brave people who dared to defy the gangs. It was easier to see them as people, too, when you weren't looking at them through the eyes of a hate-filled lush.

These days Dolan would go out on his home visits and would be offered dinner and drinks, and coffee would be made, the parents, usually single females, trying their best to give the visit the appearance and propriety of a social occasion.

But with other parents, though, things would be radically different. He would be cursed, or refused entry to the home, even though he had a legal right to enter without permission. He never pushed it and rarely argued with such parents though, didn't want to cause a scene. He would let them believe that they knew their rights, and would speak to the youth out on the stoop, or sitting in the car with the doors open wide so no one could accuse him of molesting the kid.

There were all kinds of people in the world, and color wasn't what made you what you were.

Dolan used to believe it was all in how you were raised, but now he wasn't so sure of that, now that he'd seen the pressures that some of these kids had to live with, day in and day out. Join a gang or don't even think about crossing their turf so you could go to school. If you studied, you were a freak. Pay me to use this washroom, motherfucker.

A third of the kids in this city carried weapons to school at one time or another, some of them for protection, others for reasons less worthy. All of them, from Dolan's area at least, knew plenty of people who had died young and brutally.

It was expecting too much of them to want them to be surgeons, to grow up without scars, and yet, society—white society—demanded that of them. The same white society would flaunt the so-called odds-beaters in front of them whenever the issue of racism arose, cite chapter and verse as to what they had to do in order to escape an environment that was eating them up alive.

The problem with that was, most of the people telling them how to do that did not choose to live in the community to which they preached.

There was no longer a highly visible black man preaching love and peace and civil disobedience; now it was, "Take back the streets," and the leaders of the separatist movements were being carefully listened to. Many of Dolan's clients had names from ancient Africa, many of those who did have fathers had the type who had been politicized in a penitentiary, who would not even deign to speak to Dolan when he came calling.

The division was getting wider, and there was no cohesive dialogue being established to bring it back together.

Where would it all wind up, he wondered, how many would have to die before society realized that changes had to be made?

Dolan often wondered if he himself would die out there, a usually unarmed youth officer, gunned down by some wild psychotic who hated him for the brightness of his skin.

Too much to think about, with his weekend just beginning.

Dolan filled out his overtime card and stuck it in the lieutenant's box on his way out to the parking lot. He never did bother to go back and check on the young boy who'd started a fire and taken a life to seek revenge over a few lousy dollars that he'd now never in his lifetime see.

MARK WAS PUSHING the weights hard tonight, not being very friendly, and it was obvious that Kenny wanted to go upstairs and play. Usually, when they were down here, Mark talked to him, father to son, without mom or the other kids around. Tonight, Mark was distracted, into his own head.

He had two-forty on the bar, was straining to lift it up. Got his arms straight and dropped the bar into the sleeves of the weight bench, blowing out a grateful breath as the bar clanged into the slots.

What was wrong with his wife? What had driven her to become so possessive? Who the hell knew anymore, what anyone was thinking. He'd figured out back when he was just a kid that nobody ever really knew anyone.

"That was only six reps, Dad."

"I did three sets earlier, of eight reps each."

"Not that heavy, nobody was down here spotting for you, you wouldn't lift that kind of weight alone, would you?" Kenny's voice was anxious, the boy was scared, imagining his dad with an eighth of a ton on his chest, crushed to death, trying to call out to his son for help.

"Never over two hundred when I'm down here by myself."

"I can't wait until I'm old enough to work out like you."

"That's what Mario used to say, until he was old enough to do it. Then he sort of lost interest."

"*I* won't lose interest."

"I'll bet you won't."

Mark was lying on the padded vinyl bench, catching his breath, trying to be a dad and solve his problems at the same time. He heard the kitchen door open, heard footfalls on the stairs. That would be Caroline; the steps were too graceful for it to be Elaine. Mario was out with Diane, and Elaine would clomp down, awkwardly. Caroline walked as lightly as a bird. She'd be coming down here, to his inner sanctum, to give him some more hard time. Shit.

"One more set."

Around them were free weights, loose iron plates and cast

SAFE HARBOR

iron dumbbells. A slant board leaning against the concrete wall. As Mark reached up to grab the bar, headlights suddenly lit up the south basement block window at the same time that the neighbor's car roared to life in his driveway. The car had no muffler. Mark watched the headlights recede across the wall, heard rubber squeal on the street out front as the car backed quickly out, then peal for a long time once again as the car shot forward, careening down the street.

"There goes the next Walter Jacobson, off to another fast breaking news story. At least it's something to throw back at him, the next time he complains about Mario playing the radio too loudly."

Caroline was wearing a sweater to ward off the basement's cold. She stood with her arms crossed, looking at the window, distracted, and said, "He does it all the time. Drives around here like it's a racetrack." She walked up behind Kenny and rubbed his head, then patted it.

"Honey, run along upstairs now. Go take your bath. I'll spot for your dad." If she'd been expecting an argument, she was disappointed. Kenny couldn't wait to get up those stairs tonight. Mark sat up, heard the upstairs door slam.

"Caroline, goddamnit, don't start with me again, please." He leaned his back against the bar, felt the cold hardness there, his sweat dripping down onto it, tickling as it dripped off his back. Caroline stood there, one foot in front of the other, that sad, sorry look on her face . . .

"I didn't come down here to 'start with you.' " She wasn't in her professional role now, was Caroline again, his wife again, standing there looking hurt.

She said, "How many times do you expect me to reach out to you? My God, Mark, you don't tell me to wait, you don't say you aren't ready to discuss it. You just slam the door, it's simply none of my business. It's a closed topic for you, Mark, you've already made up your mind that you'll never be able to trust me enough to tell me the truth."

Mark shot forward, stood quickly and stormed over to the washing machine, grabbed a towel off a pile that was stacked in a basket next to it. He rubbed his face hard, kneading his eyes with the fabric.

"You'll never be able to discuss it with me, will you, Mark?"

Should he tell her that he'd wanted to, that he'd decided to

65

tell her tonight before she'd hurt him, before she'd insulted him? No, it was better to wait. If this was a worst-case deal, if she had another man or something equally as bad, he wouldn't give her that ammunition, would not give her anything she could use to hurt him with later.

Mark said, "Will you for Christ's sake get off my back?" more than a little heatedly.

Caroline walked over to him, grabbed a folded pair of Mario's blue jeans out of a different basket. She reached into a back pocket and removed a small, square package. "Look, Mark, what Mario's carrying around."

She held a single wrapped condom out toward her husband.

"I left it in the pocket so he wouldn't know that we know. If he wants to tell us, it's up to him. But thank God he's using them, with what's out there these days." She stared at him now, sizing him up.

Caroline said, "He never talked to you about it, though, did he, Mark? I can tell by the shock on your face, he never went to his father to discuss it, when he started having sex." When she spoke now her voice was accusatory.

"And the two of you used to be so close."

"Using them!" Mark was outraged. "*Using* them! He should consider sneaking a kiss getting lucky, at his age!"

"They grow up fast, Mark. They don't stay kids long anymore."

She looked so damned sorrowful, standing there, looking down at the rubber. Mark reached out to her and she stiffened up, backed away from him.

"I've noticed that it's not just me that you're pushing away."

"What? Who's pushing *who* away, Caroline? Every time I reach for you, you pull away. Every time I touch you, you cringe, like I disgust you."

"I have my reasons. But I mean the kids, Mark, particularly Mario, you're not as close as you used to be with him, you can't deny that."

Mario? The kids? Pushing them away? What the hell was she talking about? He tried to keep his voice calm, he didn't want her to know that she'd hurt him again.

"He's a big kid now, he has his own issues. He has a driver's license now, Caroline, how much time will he want to spend hanging out with his old man?"

"It's not just that. Not even just your silence, or not talking about your life with me. It's a lot of different things. Even when you're here with us, you're really not *here* anymore." She crossed her arms and turned away from him, as if thinking. She turned back toward him, saw the look on his face, and when she spoke, her voice was gentle.

"Mark, you're downtown more than you're here. Eight hours a day is enough for most people, ten is pushing it, but not for you."

"The whole weekend—"

"Yes, and wasn't it great? For the kids, sure, they had their dad around. Even Mario hung around more than he usually does. But what about me? How long do you think I'm going to wait for you to start treating me as your friend instead of just your wife? You're never here for me, not anymore."

"You get your share of emergencies, you take off a lot, too."

"I know what you are but what am I?" Caroline was making fun of him. Mark felt his face harden.

"It's not a joke, Caroline. How much have you been here for me, lately? Like since the beginning of the fucking year?"

"You don't think there are reasons for that? You don't think that you know those reasons?" Caroline's voice was now rigid and severe: it matched the look on her face. She was no longer caring or friendly, not a psychologist any longer, now she was an angry woman striking out at what had hurt her.

"There are some things I have to say to you, Mark, that I've been thinking about for a long time." She looked up at him, determined. "Don't say a word until I'm finished, all right? Give me that much?"

In her sweater pocket, her beeper went off. She made no move to check it. Upstairs, he could hear small feet running, more than just one pair. Kenny and Elaine might be fighting.

She would ask him for a divorce, he could feel it. Panic hit him, hard. Mark threw both hands up to his shoulders, palms outward.

"Wait," Mark said. Even to his own ears, he sounded as if he were begging. He didn't care. He said, "Please, Caroline, wait."

Caroline slowly reached into her sweater pocket and pulled her beeper out, held it to the light and squinted at the readout. When she spoke her voice was dead, without feeling or emotion.

"I've waited too long already, I think."

Hiding that exploding fear behind a fraction of a smile, Mark said, "It's waited this long, it can wait until you see who's calling you at this time of night."

A quick call informed Caroline that one of her young female clients had tried to commit suicide. Without even kissing the kids goodnight, Caroline grabbed a light jacket and ran out the door. Mark watched her as she started her car and took off from the curb, fast enough to make Tomczak next door turn green with jealousy.

Thank God, Mark thought, then stood there at the living room door, stunned by what he'd been thinking. He'd been thanking God that some adolescent child had slashed her wrists, wanting to die.

WHENEVER BELLA THOUGHT of federal marshals, even after twenty-two years in the service himself, he would think of Matt Dillon and Pat Garrett, true lawmen of the wild West. Today Dan Bella carried the badge and the photo ID, but he never thought of himself as a federal marshal anymore, although he used to, a long time ago. Before he'd gotten his eyes opened to what the job was really all about these days.

Politics and ladder climbing, kissing ass and taking orders and never questioning your superiors, that's how a good marshal was supposed to act. Dan had never been good at performing such acts, and neither had his wife. For her, though, the transition to being a person of solid morals had to have been more difficult than it had been for him. In fact, in Andi's life, being a political animal should have come easy.

Raised by a headstrong government lawyer with political aspirations and strong ties to the Republican party, Andrea had rebelled early, had refused to fit their mold. When she'd married him, it had been a major disappointment to what was left of her family. Her mother and father had already been dead, but the uncle who'd raised her—at the time an aide to the governor of Virginia—had come close to disowning her, until he saw for himself how happy his baby was with Daniel Bella. Then he'd given them his blessing, but guardedly. Bella had never given him reason to revoke that blessing in all the years since that time.

And it was a good thing, too. Because the guy who'd once

been a political aide was now himself a senator. Without his clout, Bella knew, he'd have been out of the service many years ago.

As for himself, he believed that at one time in his life he would have made an expert ass kisser and political animal, could have soared to the top of his profession without a whole lot of difficulty. But then he'd met her, met his Andi, and his priorities had unexpectedly changed.

After meeting her, after falling in love, he could never bring himself to do anything that would cause his darling to look at him with anything less than pride. He'd sooner die than to have her ashamed of his actions or behavior. His need for her approval had nearly cost him his job thirteen years ago, but it had been worth it, to see that look, that look of pride she'd given him when he'd done the right thing.

His wife. Andi. He looked at her now, his darling lying on what might well be her deathbed, Dan's face showing his torment as truly as Andi's showed her own.

Andrea was ill, and the doctors thought that she would die.

It was not a word they ever used around the house, one that was left completely unspoken, but still, in their house and in Dan's mind, death loomed over Andrea's frail shoulder, waiting for the chance to make his move.

Lots of luck to that. If death was waiting for a weak moment, or for Andrea to give up the struggle, he'd be hanging around for a long time, suffering the disappointment. Although you could tell just by looking at her; Andrea was suffering.

Her once rich black hair was now very weak and thin, and most of it was gone, a side effect of the chemotherapy treatments. Dan could see the scalp right through what was left, her hair was now stringy and lifeless, still falling out in clumps. When she went out into the world, something she tried to do as often as possible between chemotherapy treatments, Andi would wear a bright red scarf to cover her skull, to protect it from the harsh rays of the sun. Huge wraparound sunglasses with pitch black lenses would protect her super-sensitive eyes. But the pale, doughy face could no longer be brought back to life with makeup, the terrible bloating she'd experienced gave her the appearance of a woman with a thyroid gone mad.

She groaned now, in her sleep, pain never far away from her. The bucket was by the side of the bed and Dan reached for it, thinking that she might be about to vomit again. Sometimes, when that happened, a tooth would wind up in the bucket.

There were no pills strong enough to stop her agony, no liquid that he could inject into her veins that would stop the torment, stop the disorder from eating her alive. Even as she slept, the suffering was with her.

What did she dream about? Did she have cruel dreams, remembering herself as youthful and slender? Did she dream of the happiness they'd once shared, before ugly reality had reared its head? Did she dream of what it had been like when they'd still been a real family, when they had a future that they didn't know would be filled with heartbreak and tragedy? How terrible it would be, to awaken from those dreams and realize your full reality, what was happening to your body, what your disease was doing not only to you, but to your family.

Family, what a word it was, one that meant the world to the Bellas. The family consisted of them and only the two daughters now—their baby, their son, had died at the age of two, a victim of the very same disease that was now slowly strangling Andrea. He'd been born in bad shape, and they'd been prepared for the worst, but still, when the end came, it wasn't a blessing for them as it was for some. Danny was supposed to beat it, he'd always been so cheerful . . .

Dan could remember his son smiling at them, while the baby was hooked up to tubes and machines, his tiny bald head shining. The boy gurgling and stretching his back at their touch, undersized Danny touching his lips to their cheeks goodnight. The child who'd never known anything but misery.

He'd wasted away to nothing and he'd died, having never even learned to walk; his entire world had been beds and needles and the endless torment, the unrelenting suffering that had been his pitiful fortune.

Dan would still go to the cemetery when he could, out in Virginia, where they'd been living when the boy had died. When it had been time to move on, Andi had lived up to the decision she'd made when little Danny had been born sickly. She'd ignored the pleadings of her uncle the senator, she'd argued with Dan's bosses, but she'd stuck to her guns. She'd quit mothering the children of protected witnesses. She'd go with her husband wherever he was transferred, stay with him and stand beside him, but she wanted no part of a career where the children she looked after—the children of subhuman, conscienceless animals—were shown more compassion by the government than her own son had ever been granted.

After the baby's death, Andrea realized what she had given up, how much of their daughters' lives she'd missed, on special payroll assignment, looking after other people's children while their own stayed with Dan's loving parents. Even after she'd stopped traveling with him, when baby Danny was sick, she still hadn't had a lot of time to give the girls, every minute of her life, it seemed, revolved around the baby. After Danny's death, she'd become a full-time mother, had been there every day for their surviving daughters throughout the rest of their childhood, until they went out on their own.

It had been a good decision; their daughters had been raised well. At least she'd been able to see that much, at least Andi could go to her grave knowing that she'd done her best, and it had been good enough. She had her religion, her god, too, that seemed to give her strength.

If only Dan could feel the same, if only he could save her, if only he could believe in something that he couldn't see, feel, or touch. What a blessing it would be to be able to pray, to petition a power greater than yourself for help to relieve her torment. He tried, oh, how he tried, but the words seemed to fall from his lips and drop to the floor and lie there. There had never been one time when he'd believed that some god had been listening to him.

The best they could hope for now, for Andi, was some sort of rare remission. When it was in your bloodstream, they all were aware, it could never fully go away.

But still, there were stories, some others had recovered, gone into remission for up to years at a time. And the fact remained that, contrary to all the canon of modern medical science, a small percentage of people with this sort of disorder for some reason completely healed, the disease just . . . went away.

Some called it spontaneous remission, others called it a miracle. The doctors had told them not to count on such a thing, but Andi and Dan clung to the belief wholeheartedly, she prayed that it would happen for her, that she would be somehow blessed.

She'd tell him what she'd do, if such an event were to occur. How she'd witness every day for the rest of her life, testifying of God's love and power, tell the world what He'd done for her and let the believers be damned. Dan would listen to her, holding her, wishing that he could believe. That he himself could ask her god for the help she'd need to survive.

He'd take her to the hospital for treatment every Sunday, right after church, once a week and while he waited he'd see the sick children, and Dan would feel guilty. He would remember their son, and feel resentment that he had died, then look at those poor dying youngsters and wonder how many of them would be cured, wonder why Andrea couldn't have their chance for success, why Danny hadn't had the opportunity that they did.

Things had been different seven years ago, science had come a long way since Danny's death. Still, though, where was God for these little kids? Where had He been for Danny? If He was there, did He hate these children for some reason, did He know that if they grew up they would become monsters?

No, that couldn't be the case, there were too many monsters that had been allowed to live in health. People like John Gacy could live into their seventies, and these poor little kids would die, as his Danny had died.

He'd fight those feelings, battle those guilty, jealous, sick, self-pitying thoughts. He'd tell himself that his wife had had over forty years on earth, that his wife at least had had the chance to live. But in his secret heart he knew that he'd willingly sacrifice all of those young kids, if only he could have Andrea, his Andi back, as she'd once been.

Young and full of life, always happy, hiding her rare depressions. Even after the death of their son, she'd thrown herself back into her life, her church, counting on her belief in God, telling him that their Danny had been taken to a better place, a place where there was no pain, a place full of joy and laughter and happy, dancing children.

He'd wondered where she'd gotten it, that sort of belief in an afterlife. She'd speak as if she truly believed it, as if it was a foregone conclusion that she had evidence to support.

But if she felt that way, why was she clinging so tenaciously to life? What was she so terrified of? He did not know and would never think to ask, he could only be glad that she was doing it.

Andrea had watched as both of her parents died—slowly and painfully—in their thirties. Andrea believed that every day was a gift. Andrea believed that God was love and that life was precious. Andrea did not want to ever admit that what had happened to

SAFE HARBOR

her parents at such an early age might be hereditary, that she might one day die herself due to a bloodstream that decided to mutate on its own, into something that would poison her, feed upon her flesh.

Dan had learned in the past year how to care for her, what to do to make her life as comfortable as it could be. They could not afford a live-in-nurse, and he would not let this horror happen to her in a hospital, alone. He had to be a part of it, whichever way it went. If she lived, he vowed that he would go to church every day, give thanks to Andrea's god for the miracle of her life. It wouldn't matter if that god could hear him or not, Dan would fall on his knees and sing that god's praises.

If she died—there it was again, that word, always in his mind—he would curse whatever gods there were, go about the rest of his life simply waiting for death to come.

He could still not bring himself to think about life without her. Although he would constantly think of her death, he would never go beyond it, to what might happen to him after she was gone. Those thoughts crept in now, unbidden, and, like all filthy thoughts, it was impossible to drive them from his mind without at least a peek at what they had to offer.

Who would there be for him to laugh with? Who could he possibly speak to as freely as he'd always spoken to Andi? Even today she would try to laugh, even though she often fell short, Andi having to force a smile at him in moments of lucidity, smiling and grimacing at the same time, through her torment. She could bring herself to answer the phone as if she were her old self, force cheerfulness into her tone, say "Hello" as brightly as any secretary at a corporation. She could not sustain the charade for long, the pain would overcome her in a matter of minutes, but their daughters and her uncle found hope in the way she said hello, people who loved her clinging to tiny islands of reason, using that to reinforce their denial, to convince themselves that she'd recover.

Only their elder daughter had had the courage to ask: Dad, will it happen to *me?* Will *I* die the same way? She was twenty now, the oldest, and they would both be home soon from college. She and her younger sister would be by their mother's side, there to help, there to love, and what would those two girls see? Themselves, in twenty-five years? Lying dying on a bed, with no one on earth to relieve their suffering?

73

He'd been thinking other thoughts lately, too, some he was ashamed to admit, even to himself. It wasn't too bad when he was at work, at the office he could even laugh and joke around with his comrades.

But here, alone, in the dark of the night with his darling dying in front of him on the bed, the thoughts crept in unbidden, real and logical to Dan.

The costs, the expenses, were tearing at their lives. He'd taken a second mortgage loan out on their nearly-paid-for modest Northern Indiana home. The girls might have to be told that this year in school would be their last. There was nothing left in the savings account, he wouldn't be able to earn enough to keep their heads above water throughout the coming summer. Before September, even cutting it close, the Bellas would be broke. And what would they do then?

He looked at what was left of his woman, heard her ragged, wheezing breathing. Saw her flattened breasts through the fabric of the nightgown, lying on her belly. It was as if the disease had depleted them, as if her body had sapped their roundness, their health.

Dan looked at what was left of his wife's breasts and shuddered as he thought of the only way his daughters would be able to continue their lives.

He could take his service pistol and kill her, put her out of her suffering. Then himself, done quickly, before Andi's body stopped its death shake. The life insurance policies had been in force for well over two years, even the second mortgage would be paid off in the event of his death. The girls would suffer, but they might someday understand, and they'd inherit, what, well over a half million dollars. They could get their education, they could have a start in life.

If he lived, if Andi got worse or stayed the same, he wouldn't be able to give them anything. Worse yet, if she died after August, he would not even be able to bury her.

Compassionate murder and suicide. Something to think about. Something to consider. He'd disgrace himself and his memory forever, would be seen as weak by his colleagues and as a psychotic by his family, but what would it matter, after he was gone, what anyone might think of him, of what he'd done? He would do what had to be done for the most noble of reasons, for his darlings, for his daughters.

Late night thoughts that must never be discussed, an intellectual exercise that could never be set into practical motion.

But it's what it had all come down to, it was maybe the only way out. Something to think about when nobody else was around, on the night that his wife was suffering the effects of that afternoon's chemotherapy.

He'd think better of things tomorrow, he knew, when Andi could sit up in bed again. By Tuesday she'd be kidding him, making fun of his full head of hair, pretending to be jealous. On Wednesday she's want to cook and he'd let her, would not try to stop her from doing anything that she wanted. And by Saturday, with a wig and makeup on, she'd look like an overweight Andi Bella.

Then Sunday would come and it would start all over again. Please God, Bella thought, let her get well.

He felt as if he was speaking to a wall, singing in his car on the way to work. There was nothing there, Andi had been wrong. When you died, you died, and there was nothing left, nowhere to go but into a filthy hole in the ground.

It was cold out tonight, but still not too bad, for April. Dan Bella pulled the blankets up to his wife's chin and sat in his chair and watched her sleep until, near dawn, he fell asleep himself.

MORNING CAME, AND he was alone, Mark knew that before he was even fully awake. Caroline's side of the bed hadn't even been disturbed. He could feel her absence, could feel the loneliness in the bed. A roving hand confirmed his suspicions. So where was she? Where had she spent the night? He hadn't heard her come into the house, which didn't mean much, he slept well these days. He'd waited up until Mario came home last night, and then he'd lain in bed worrying, thinking, wondering which way to play things today, what he could possibly do to get things back to the way they'd once been. He'd fallen asleep without coming to any major conclusions.

Mark sensed that it was time to get up before he'd even opened his eyes. He guessed that it was seven, then opened his eyes and looked at the clock. 6:54. He was never far off.

Although he had slept undisturbed for nearly seven hours, Mark didn't feel very rested, had vague memories of nightmares.

Someone chasing him, Mark naked, running for his life and abandoning—who? His kids? Was he that much of a coward that he'd leave his children to the wolves, let them die horrible deaths, as long as he himself escaped? It was only a dream, he told himself, and tried to put it out of his mind.

Yet he remembered being ashamed, in the dream. Ashamed of what he was doing but powerless to stop himself from running, from trying to escape.

Caroline would be able to tell him what it meant, if he could only bring himself to explain things to her. It didn't take an analyst to figure out that what he was dreaming had been, in a symbolic way, the story of his life. Or at least the only part of his life that had been worth living.

Always on the run, always thinking, planning, trying to stay ahead of the game. For most of his years as Mark Torrence, he hadn't worried about them, hadn't given the wiseguys much thought. Now, it seemed, it was all he ever thought about anymore.

Mark got out of bed and staggered out into the hall, made sure the kids were up, and then went back into his bedroom. He'd glimpsed his wife downstairs as he'd passed the second floor railing, fully dressed and messing around in the kitchen. Mario, too, was down there, he had to be. He hadn't been in his bedroom, and his bed had already been made.

By the time Mark was showered and dressed it was 7:30, nearly time to go. He'd have a cup of coffee and then drop Kenny and Elaine off at school as he always did on his way to work. Then he'd sit in the car and watch them, make sure they went through the doors, and that the doors closed firmly behind them. He'd watch for a time, to make sure no swarthy types followed his children through those doors.

It was a habit he'd acquired back when Mario had been in kindergarten. A habit that he had renewed lately, and one that was now impossible for Mark to even consider giving up.

Caroline was reading the paper and sipping coffee at the kitchen table, solemn. It was her usual morning state of mind, but somehow today, her normal morning mood seemed ominous. She was wearing different clothing than she'd had on when she'd left last night, must have grabbed them off the drying line in the basement, and ironed them before anyone had awakened. She couldn't have gotten to the bedroom closet without waking him, he knew. She looked tired, burned out. And, as usual lately, unhappy.

She would have slept on the sofa in her study, either not wanting to disturb his sleep, or not wanting to be in the same room with him. Mark wished he knew which it was. It would make it easier for him to make up his mind about what he wanted to say to her this morning. He walked into the kitchen cautiously, acting happy, not wanting to upset the children.

Caroline didn't look up at him. She said casually, while looking at the paper, "You'd better hurry Mario, he'll be late for school again."

"I thought he was down here . . ."

"He didn't come down here." Caroline turned to the younger children. "Did you see your brother while I was downstairs ironing my blouse?" They barely looked up from their cereal bowls, shook their heads. Night people. Like him. They'd never enjoyed the mornings.

Mark felt his face fall, felt an icy terror in his belly, his spine. He immediately knew why his history had been haunting him so much lately. In a fraction of a second a dozen thoughts ran through his mind, and he knew what had been troubling him, knew why he'd been dwelling so much on the past.

They were on to him.

He'd been having a premonition. His instincts had warned him, sent him an omen that his nice, safe urban existence was about to come to an end. And this was exactly how they'd do it: they would come at him through his son.

Without thinking he ran to the stairs, took them three at a time and barged through Mario's door, stood staring at the carefully made bed, beginning to tremble.

They'd take Mario somewhere and torture him, put him up on a meathook, stick it right through the flesh of his back and he'd hang there while they made the child suffer for the sins of the father.

Why hadn't he changed Mario's first name, the way the government had wanted him to? Why had he thought it so important that the kid keep at least that much of his identity? It was the only way they could have found him, through school records, somehow.

Jesus Christ, where are you, Mario?

"Mario!" Mark screamed the name in anguish, then ran to

the small half-bath that connected to Mario's bedroom, turned the knob, his heart racing, and threw the door open, hard.

The door banged into Mario, who'd been reaching for the knob from inside.

The door smacked Mario in the forehead and he lurched back and almost fell into the tiny shower stall. Mark stood and looked at him, his own chest pounding, his relief so great that for a moment he couldn't speak.

Mario's face was bright red; the smell of a strong antiseptic cleansing agent filled the small room. There was now a single spot that was even redder than the rest of Mario's face, right in the center of the forehead, where the wooden door had smacked him.

"Goddamnit, Dad!" Mario said, holding his head with his palm, the other arm reaching out to steady himself. He regained his balance and stood there, looking at his father, then turned to the mirror.

Mark stammered, "What the hell were you doing in here so long?"

"What?" Mario looked into the mirror, touched the skin around the swollen area, caught his father's eye. "What's *wrong* with you lately? Jesus, my head!"

"Did you split the skin?" Mark walked toward his son, taking deep breaths. He put a tentative hand on Mario's shoulder, looked into the mirror at his son's angry face, saw the red welt forming, a small swelling growing even as he looked at it. There was no blood, the skin hadn't been broken. Nothing much, Mario had gotten banged up worse on any given schoolyard fight back when he'd still believed such behavior to be somehow manly.

"I was washing my face with Noxzema. I've been getting zits." The boy was angry at having to give up his personal secrets. Mark squeezed his shoulder as Mario pressed his fingers around the swollen spot. "Damn."

"Mario, watch your mouth, I'm telling you."

"Watch my *mouth?* Why don't you worry less about my language and more about my privacy?" Oh, was he pissed. Mark was too relieved at the sight of his son, standing there safe, to get upset at his impertinence.

He said, softly, "I'm sorry. You weren't downstairs, and you weren't in here when I came to wake you."

"Pretty lame, Dad. I was in the shower, you know, earlier.

Then I shaved, then I brushed my teeth, is that all right with
you? Then I got dressed. Then I scrubbed my face with Noxzema,
Dad." The sarcasm wasn't lost on Mark.

Mario said, "You want a written record from now on, a jour-
nal of my daily rituals?" Mario looked away from the mirror,
turned to glare at his father. Mark's hand fell off the boy's
shoulder.

"I thought nobody was supposed to walk in on anyone else
without knocking."

Mark thought he got it then, why his son was outraged. And
knew it had nothing to do with a slight knock on the forehead.
He was far too embarrassed and offended than the occasion called
for. Mark decided to cover it up, to act as if he hadn't figured
Mario out, but it was obvious that the boy had certain desires
that carrying a rubber in his pocket didn't necessarily fill.

"I'm sorry, Mario, I didn't mean to upset you. I didn't see
you, your mother didn't see you, I got worried."

"Why?" Mario walked past him, somewhat mollified, into the
bedroom, and grabbed a bunch of books off his small study desk;
a school jacket off a hook in the closet. "Did you think I snuck
out on you? Stole the car and went joyriding? First I have no
privacy, then I can't be trusted. You're getting strange in your
old age, Dad."

"Mario?"

The boy turned, looked at Mark, and Mark swallowed his
pride. He spent every working day looking at kids younger than
his son, kids who dealt crack out of burned out West Side buildings. He trusted this kid, and Mario had a right to know it.

"I'm sorry, all right? I just got scared. It was never a matter
of trust. You're the only person in the entire world that I *do*
fully trust."

Mario seemed embarrassed, and looked away.

"Yeah, right, no problem." He still seemed a little sarcastic.

Mark said, "But watch your mouth, Mario. I'm still your
old man."

Mario nodded at the doorway behind Mark. "Better check
with her and make sure before you make bold statements like
that, buddy."

Mario was smiling and Mark turned, saw Caroline standing
in the doorway, a look of disturbed curiosity on her face.

"He's your father," Caroline said wryly. "You doubt it, just look in the mirror. You're his spitting image, only his forehead isn't swollen."

"It's a birthmark," Mario said. "Like being born as a seventh son? I was born with a father that can't mind his own business. It leaves a mark on you, like in Revelations, the mark of the busybody."

"Mario . . ." Mark said it warningly, turning away from Caroline, not wanting to face that glare.

"I know, I know, you're still my father." But now the boy was half-smiling, uncomfortable with the attention and knowing that Caroline had heard his father's remark about trust. And that lighthearted remark about checking with Caroline before making statements about Mario's paternity. Did he love the woman so much that he had convinced himself that she had given him birth?

"Lighten up, will you? I was only kidding, Dad."

Lighten up? Didn't he wish that he could. He tried, now that he knew Mario was safe. That he'd only been overreacting. Getting paranoid in his middle years. Life had been too good.

Mark followed his son out of the bedroom, past Caroline, who stepped aside a few inches to let him pass, her arms folded across her chest, and he could feel her eyes following him, all the way to the bottom of the stairs.

Later, in the kitchen, after Mario had left and Kenny and Elaine had kissed her goodbye, Mark screwed up his courage and stood before her, all alone.

"Tonight, we'll talk, all right? Please. Without any recriminations, without any hard feelings. I promise you, I'll tell you whatever you want to know. And if you still want a divorce, I won't try and fight it."

Caroline seemed taken aback, but still angry.

"You're going to *trust* me now? And when did I say anything about a divorce?"

"You didn't have to," Mark told her, and walked to the door, looking down. He turned then and looked at her, trying to hide his pain.

"It's in your eyes, in the way you look at me. In the way you pull back when I reach out for you at night. Something's wrong, you said last night, you didn't love me the way you used to . . ."

"I never said I didn't love you, never said I wanted a divorce."

"Then what was last night about? What was all that, 'Let me say this and don't interrupt' shit about? About not being glad that you were married to me anymore?"

Caroline looked hurt, and Mark felt his hopes rise. Maybe she *hadn't* been thinking of divorce. Maybe all she wanted to do was chew him out for being so silent, giving him hell for all his shortcomings.

He'd change them, get rid of them, tell her whatever she wanted to know, oh God, just let her stay.

He wanted to tell her these things right now, to reach out to her and hold her and say what was in his heart, but he couldn't. She'd only pull away from him, only reject him again as she'd done so many times before.

Caroline said, "We'll talk tonight," and turned her back, and leaned against the table. She put her palms down flat and hung her head.

Should he go to her? Should he comfort her? Would she see it as manipulation, or would she respond with affection?

Outside, the car horn honked. That would be Elaine, it was her turn to ride in the front seat today, and she was impatient. Kenny didn't care if they ever got to school.

Mark stood staring at his grieving wife, torn. He was taking a tentative step toward her when the horn blasted again.

"Just go," Caroline said, without turning. He could hear the tears in her voice. "Mark, just please go." She turned to him now, and the tears were gone. Her strength had returned, more powerful than ever.

Mark had the strange impression that he was looking at a stranger. At Caroline's twin, someone he thought he knew intimately but had never really met.

"We'll talk tonight," Caroline said.

But judging from the tone of her voice, Mark wasn't sure that he believed her.

THE YOUTH CENTER was on South Wabash Street, on the top two floors of an old dilapidated six-story building that wasn't getting a lot of upkeep. There were three artists lofts on the third and fourth floors, the second floor was rented by a walk-in church, and the first floor was occupied by an acting troupe that couldn't afford valuable theater district space.

There was life south of Randolph, though, no matter what some North Siders thought.

It was a cool morning, with a slight mist in the air. Mark parked his car in the back of the building, in the small loading zone that was never used by trucks anymore, the loading zone a remainder from the time when the building had been filled with a far different clientele, the type who brought things in to work with, instead of the kind they had now, who created things for sale. He put his visor down so the parking access sticker could be clearly seen. Lincoln Towing had enough money without any donations from him.

Mark walked around front with his keys in his hand, past the two buildings before him, dodging two filthy black men who were pitching pennies on the sidewalk in front of his building, tossing the pennies onto a crack in front of the grocery store beside it. The men paid no attention to him, their total concentration was on their game. One of them had one eye closed, so he wouldn't see two cracks in the sidewalk in front of him. He was already drunk. The owner of the grocery store would be out as soon as he spotted them, and chase them away with threats and warnings. He'd sell them their beer and whiskey, but he didn't want them hanging around.

Mark's shoulders hunched involuntarily, and he stopped before entering the building, looked at the security intercom, then at the dirty, streaked glass of the large window entrance to his building.

He felt a sense of paranoia, of someone watching his back. He tried to fight it, he'd been having too many weird feelings lately to take any one of them seriously anymore. Still, he couldn't dismiss it. Mark turned, casually, and checked the street around him.

The block across the street was dominated by the St. James Hotel, a seven-story relic of grander times. The old hotel was just a block from Michigan Avenue, but light years separated the St. James from the regal hotels that fronted the city's most renowned boulevard.

The front facade was now light red brick, which was a relatively recent addition, the benefit of a facelift performed sometime in the past twenty years. The place had at one time been a classy brownstone hotel; the side of the building that Mark could see still had the original brick, which was now patched in places with concrete, with a huge top corner of it pervertedly marked over with a large hand-painted sign that was black and orange with white lettering and an arrow of varying shades of blue that pointed toward the entrance, the white lettering pronouncing the place to be: THE ST. JAMES HOTEL.

At one time the St. James had been quite a building, you could see that if you looked closely, beyond what it was today. There was still a slight remnant of the old cement masonry on the front of the building, a remnant that was now shot; what was left was now weatherbeaten and dull, had been allowed to go to hell. There was a small, circular, filthy green canopy over the door that looked to be made of canvas, it appeared to be many years old, had torn pieces that hung down dismally and flapped loudly in the wind.

Some of the hotel's windows had been shot out, some had blown out during storms, some had been busted out by angry tenants; the fact was that most of the windows were simply no longer there. Those that remained were filthy and locked into a closed position.

Cheap, secondhand air-conditioning units half-hung out of some of the windows. There were no regular curtains to be seen, the empty spaces that had once been windows were now covered by either flattened cardboard boxes or thick plastic or aluminum foil that had been taped to the walls surrounding the frames. A piece of wood covered one of the glassless top floor windowframes, with a slim pipe protruding out of the wood that curved all the way up to the roof. Some enterprising pimp had installed a woodburning stove, probably thinking that it gave the room class, or maybe a sense of ambience. Or perhaps the pensioned senior citizen who rented the room just needed the extra heat in the winter.

There were a lot of senior citizens living in the St. James Hotel. And single mothers, and day laborers whom Mark would see each morning, waiting on the corner for the truck to come and pick them up and take them off to their jobs. The labor company would pay them minimum wage if they were lucky, then pocket any other dough that the companies might lay out. The St. James had more than its share of hookers, pimps, thieves and junkies.

Mark looked past the double-parked cars on the street, his eyes roaming, trying to see if anyone was watching him.

Despite the morning chill, a black man wearing only a sleeveless undershirt over his skinny chest was carrying on an animated conversation over a portable cordless phone, leaning way out of his front fourth-window to look down on the street below him. Mark could hear him cursing at someone, loudly. A foul-mouthed man who felt that he needed a cordless phone to communicate in a fifteen by twenty, ten-buck-a-night flophouse. Mark could only believe that the phone made the man feel like he was somehow still a player, or still had a shot at being one, or perhaps he had just gotten the phone at a discount from one of the neighborhood junkies.

There were three of them out in front of the hotel, all using the same single crutch as a dodge, taking turns with it, hobbling around and begging for money from the few people who passed them—and ignored them—on the busy morning street. The men were laughing, joking around with each other, not taking the scam, if it was one, seriously.

Mark tried to figure out if all three were crippled, or if only one of them was, or if none of them was, if they were just looking for sympathy or amusement from their artless con.

Crackheads nodded in the alley under the L tracks behind the hotel, disregarding the fact that Police Headquarters was only a few yards away. As soon as nighttime came, the hookers would be lined up on Roosevelt Road, 12th St., females that could be aged anywhere from fifteen to fifty, not downtown hookers, but rather where the downtown hookers wound up if they didn't catch an early break, or if a heartless pimp happened to have caught them coming out of the bus station before they could hit the downtown stroll. They burned up quick down here. Mark didn't know where they were buried when they died.

If you stood there long enough you could smell the pain in the air.

At night, the sounds of angry black voices could be heard coming out of the hotel's windows. But sometimes the voices were joyous. Screams of terror, pain or ecstasy would bounce off the asphalt of Wabash Avenue, throughout the night and into the early morning hours. Every two weeks, when the welfare checks came in, the street would be busy for a couple of days, lined with either skeletal or grossly overweight people, newly lush, rushing headily out into their biweekly feeding frenzy. Two days later, the money gone, their anger would return, and they'd be leaning out their windows, staring at nothing, dreaming of what they'd do when the next check came. Drinking on credit and hardly eating at all.

It was a place of utter desperation; of loneliness and isolation, of ten-minute lovers and five-dollar thirty-second highs, of furtively smoked rocks in a can that were far more expensive than their price tags could infer, highs that soon left you empty, with an ever deepening, stronger craving within. A place of surreptitious drug deals performed in broad daylight right out on the street, the rock cocaine held under a coat in a tightly clenched fist until an Abraham Lincoln crossed the other palm.

Attached to the St. James was a hot dog place that Mark suspected was used for purposes other than selling red hots. There was a parking lot next door to that, and across 12th St., on the same side of the street as the St. James, was a liquor store whose neon lights beckoned the St. James's residents for 24 hours each day. You couldn't even call it temptation around here. The liquor store was attached to the Roosevelt Hotel, which, despite being freshly painted in a gaudy shade of red, was still a step down from the St. James.

Once every month or so one of the art galleries in Mark's building would have a well-advertised, large Friday or Saturday night opening, and BMWs and Jaguars and Mercedes would line the filthy street, their owners offered the opportunity to have their cars guarded if you let the guy who offered to guard it hold onto five of your dollars. Those who didn't know better and passed the offer by came down from the art galleries to find their radios gone, their mirror-polished paint jobs scratched deep and often, their windows smashed and their grilles destroyed. Mark knew that one of the artistic gallery owners paid some of the local kids to hunt down and destroy the cars of people who reneged on deals, who showed off in front of their friends and said they'd buy a painting then would call the next day, having changed their minds. The red sticker would come off the frame and the artist, Tony Fitzpatrick, would call one of the local boys to his loft to talk business. It was the sort of neighborhood that it was, and there was no escaping it, it was South Loop reality.

In all the years that Mark had been working here, he'd never seen a politician walking or working these streets, pressing the flesh, and the only time he saw uniformed cops was when they got a call of trouble or rousted the hookers at the St. James. Even with the station only a block away, this street wasn't on their usual route to drive through, not part of their sworn duty to serve or protect.

Other cops came by, though, the type that wore street clothes.

Mark had hated them for most of his life, had a lifelong distrust of anyone who carried a badge. And like most of his past beliefs, this one, too, had been proven false. His feelings about them were these days mostly dependent upon the individual who was carrying the badge.

Some of the gang crimes cops were crude, bigoted and hated everyone who wasn't just like them; others brought in troubled youths to the center and you could see the pain in their eyes, their longing for this one to get what he needed to stay out of the penitentiaries, to stay off the one-way streets. Even then, knowing that some were good, Mark still watched what he said to them, and he never went for a beer with them or pretended that they were his friends.

Was one of those cops out there now? Mark wondered. Who was watching him? Why was he feeling so observed?

Across the street to Mark's left and across 13th St. was a large brown and red stone building that he could tell had once been something to see, with bay windows and a solid stone front, the place now nothing more than a white trash tenement that had been cut up into "apartments." Several suspicious white faces stared out at him through cracked, broken windows. Mark could see the firmly set jaws; their opinions of him had already been formed. He let his gaze wander past them, looked up the street. You never knew anymore when just a casual glance, taken the wrong way, would cause a bullet to explode toward you from the darkness of a rented room. So many people filled with resentment, so many unfulfilled dreams caused some people not to care . . .

There were wasted lives on this street, but behind him, inside, were people who worked every day of their lives to ensure that still-young lives have a sense of purpose. Mark turned his back on S. Wabash and unlocked the door to the building, hurried inside and started walking up the stairs before the plight of those who lived on Wabash Street could get to him too badly. He had enough on his mind, enough worries of his own, without taking on the troubles of everybody on the street.

TODAY THEY WILL hunt me down and kill me.

It was the first thing that Bracken thought every morning when he awoke.

He lay half-asleep in the king-size bed, his brain registering the fact that coffee was brewing downstairs in the kitchen, Bracken thinking that today was really and truly the day that he would die.

His head was foggy from the wine he'd drunk last night, and his chest hurt from smoking too many cigarettes the night before. These days he was always a little nauseous in the mornings, and he knew that he would be that way until he got some fruit or cereal in his stomach, drank some coffee and had his first few cigarettes.

Today they will catch me and lock me away forever.

The second thing he always thought.

The thoughts kept him on his toes, even as they terrified him. He stared at the white ceiling and thought about these two things, let his mind roam free and unfettered his darkest fantasies.

Bracken saw the feds closing in—it would have to be the feds, no New York cops would ever be smart enough to catch him—saw them surrounding him, forty or fifty of them in unmarked cars pulling to the side of him, giving him no opportunity for escape. They'd announce themselves as the FBI and then they'd open fire, riddle his body with bullets, firing into him long after he was dead . . .

Or else, if there was a camera crew along, "20/20" or "60 Minutes," filming the heroes in action so the public could see their tax dollars at work, they'd want to take him alive. Which meant they'd have the goods on him, as Bracken knew how they worked. They'd have enough to hang him for ten lifetimes or they'd never risk letting a man like Bracken live. Simply because there *were* no other men like Bracken, they'd want him out of the picture forever. So in order to take him alive, they'd have to have the goods, and they'd take him down without firing a shot, lock him downtown in the MCC for a year and when his trial came up he'd be down for the count, Bracken wearing orange jumpsuits and laceless white tennis shoes for the rest of his natural life.

It would be quite a change from the way things were in his life today.

Unpleasant morning thoughts for a man who was still sleep foggy and fiercely craving a cigarette, but necessary thoughts, thoughts that he forced himself to have every morning of his life. They kept him alert and alive, and stopped him from making mistakes or rushing into things, no matter how much it might cost him to wait.

Bracken rolled over and put his feet on the floor, wriggled his toes in the thick shag carpet. Downstairs, Tawny would be fussing around in the kitchen. Bracken couldn't smile yet, but he nodded his head at the thought of Tawny. It had been a good move, for a while at least, bringing Tawny in. Tawny was bright and obedient and, until recently, never questioned orders. He wondered about Tawny, about if there was a problem. If there was, it would not be one for very long. Bracken had no tolerance for his lovers, for his helpers who got too nosy.

There was a pack of cigarettes on the nightstand next to him, and Bracken didn't have to think about it long before he reached out and grabbed one. He'd turned forty-four years old last month; if the filthy weeds hadn't killed him yet, he didn't think that they were likely to. With the torturous things he did to keep himself in shape, to stay at the top of his game, good God, wasn't he entitled to one little vice? With the way he'd been drinking the booze lately, maybe there were two vices. But both of them were under control, he didn't let either one of them run his life or let him make mistakes.

He sucked in a deep drag of the non-filtered English Oval, coughed the smoke out and shook his head, his muscles tight, oxygen starved. He took a smaller drag when he was back in control, then blew the smoke out quickly. He was thinking about his early warning systems, his morning thoughts that kept him alert. Thinking of being shot down like a dog on the street, or worse yet, arrested, put down in the joint for life.

"Today they will hunt me down and kill me." His voice was deep and slightly raspy from thirty years of chain-smoking. The words seemed to have a more chilling effect when he heard them spoken aloud. He didn't fear death, and he didn't think that he ever had. He only feared being killed by them, by the law, dying dishonorably and alone.

"Today they will catch me and lock me away forever."

He *did* fear prison. Bracken shivered. Naked, thin, tight muscles jumped in his chest, in his arms, as he did so. He looked down at the hand that held the cigarette, at the sharp veins protruding out of the back and up into the wrist, all the way up into his bicep, defined and brutally disciplined. He looked at the manicured nails.

He had hard hands, with thin fingers, hands that could kill instinctively when they had to. There was a ridge of callous around the edges of those hands, and he had those ridges filed regularly when he went to the barber for his haircut and manicure. They were long-nailed hands, the nails sharp as knives. He could shove them through an eyeball without a moment's hesitation. Into the brain and walk away, wiping the goo from his fingers with his handkerchief before the body behind him had even hit the ground.

Bracken's legs were like pistons, he could shoot a booted foot out and break a kneecap with impunity. His fake credit cards had been carefully filed down, until they were single-edged plastic razors. A pen, in Bracken's hands, was more dangerous than a switchblade. You knew a switchblade was designed to cut you; Bracken would kill you while he was signing a check, stick the pen right into your heart and then finish writing his name.

Magazines and paperback books, he'd used them both at times, knew how to roll them properly and how to twist them as he struck, doing more damage with them than most killers could do with an Uzi. He never carried guns or knives, and he spat upon explosives. Bracken did his killing up close, looking his victim in the eyes when he could.

He'd stopped counting when he'd still been in his twenties, no longer needing to notch his belt. To Bracken, it was a job, it was the way he'd made his living. If he thought about it, though, he'd have to admit that he'd probably killed more than fifty people.

Sometimes for the mob, which he liked to work for on a freelance basis. They were pros and didn't come on too strong, and with the exception of Pete Papa, who'd known him since the time Bracken had been a child, most of them never pretended to be his friends, the way some other people who hired him sometimes did. Some of them, like Leehanna's husband, were even funny about it, as if you had to establish a civilized, cordial interpersonal relationship with the killer you'd hired to brutally murder your wife.

But the mob never played those games, not even Pete Papa. They knew that there was a difference between business and social activities.

With the mob, a large amount of money would change hands, and a couple of weeks or a month later the job would be done and a disguised Bracken would enter a Little Italy social club, and would leave with the rest of his payment, and with a bellyful of spaghetti.

Other times, he worked for civilians, using people who knew how to find him. A select few could reach out to Bracken, and when they heard about the right type of person who needed his services, they'd get in touch, and Bracken would open a file on the person who was looking for him, make his decision to work for them based on what he found. If there was even a single week of the person's adult life that couldn't be accounted for, Bracken would blow the whole thing off, rather than take the chance that the potential employer was an undercover cop.

A couple of times he'd seen the fruit of such caution, read about the mark in the paper, having been arrested for killing their enemy themselves, or for hiring cops who'd been posing as hit men. When he'd come across such items, Bracken would be disappointed. There'd been a hell of a lot of money lost, because he'd been suspicious.

He'd never done any prison time, although he'd twice come close. And he didn't intend to do time now, not this close to retirement.

Fifty, that would be it, or when he performed the perfect murder. Even six more years was more than he could reasonably expect from himself. By then he'd be fighting a losing battle, hell, he was feeling old now. Six more years and then retire to Paris, he and Tawny, or most likely somebody else. He didn't see Tawny being with him, six years down the road.

Would he be able to do it? Yes, by then he'd have to. It would be that or get caught, the odds would have to catch up with him if he stayed at it any longer than that.

It was his contingency plan, in case he never did it right. In case a murder never came off with every planned detail performed. If, of course, things went exactly right today, then he could stop now, and leave tomorrow, after the rest of the money was transferred to his account.

He believed in his heart, Bracken did, that he'd be able to quit when the perfect murder had been accomplished. The same way he believed that he'd quit smoking cigarettes when he turned fifty years of age. The same way that he believed that he loved Tawny, or any of the others whom he'd loved then killed throughout the years.

"Today they will hunt me down and kill me. Today they will lock me away forever."

Bracken spoke the words aloud then stubbed out the cigarette, ran a hand over his shaved head, felt the stubble there, then got up from the bed and stretched his body and reached for the ceiling.

"The *fuck* they will," he said with conviction, and walked into the adjoining bathroom to take his morning shower and prepare for the day.

DRESSED, SHAVED, IN today's hunting outfit, smelling clean and feeling relatively good, Bracken walked down the stairs to his kitchen, saw Tawny standing in front of the stove. From behind Tawny looked almost like a teenager, long brown hair falling to the middle of Tawny's back, an apple ass tucked into faded jeans. Tawny was wearing heeled cowboy boots, which made Tawny appear taller than Tawny was. Muscular calves pushed out at the fabric, strong bare arms were moving before the stove.

Tawny was thirty-six years old, and Bracken knew all about Tawny's life. Knew almost every minute of that life before he'd ever slept with Tawny, and used that knowledge to check Tawny out, to try and catch his little Tawny telling him a lie.

Which he never had, and that was surely a surprise; people like Tawny generally lived lives of total and complete deception. For months, though, he'd checked Tawny, asked Tawny veiled questions and listened carefully to Tawny's responses, Bracken's face showing only concern and understanding; compassion and sensitivity being traits he could imitate at will. At last he began to trust Tawny, and after a year together, Tawny was the newest trusted member of his circle. What he liked to think of as his familiar, the one who walked out front and took all the simple risks without ever knowing the truth about what Bracken really did.

There'd been seven of them before in his life, and only one that he'd loved. The first one, Terri, dead these fifteen years. Terri's death had taught him that romantic love was for the weak. The others, he'd killed himself, as he had murdered Terri, when he thought that they were weakening, felt that they might be having second thoughts about what they did for him, guilt closing in on them when they found out it was all for real, when they realized that a life on the outside was not at all sentimental.

Children with their fantasies, for a time they could be so adorable.

He walked up to the stove and hugged Tawny around the waist, nuzzled Tawny's neck as Tawny gave a little jump of surprise.

"I didn't hear you come down the stairs."

"A little too low, it's basso, too deep."

"I didn't hear you come down the stairs."

"That's much better, Tawny," Bracken said.

"I heard you in the shower, I'm making you some eggs."

"Over easy, Tawny."

"I *know*, James."

Bracken poured a cup of coffee and sat down at the table, looking around at the black marble floor; at the wide window that protected his home from the eyes of the pedestrians outside on the sidewalk; he could see out, onto the street, but passersby could see only their reflections. Every window in the house had been done this way, the glass two inches thick, embedded well into the walls, their frames made of reinforced steel, set into concrete. The windows in Bracken's house would stop anything short of a full frontal assault by a heavily armed invading force that knew what it was doing.

Your average SWAT team would have trouble trying to break into this house. The glazier's bill had been enormous, but the price was worth it to him, Bracken hated curtains and blinds. Hated being restricted, hidden away where he couldn't see. He wanted to be able to see everything around him, with those people around him seeing nothing, wanted to be able to come and go freely and do as he pleased, without anyone being able to get at him for his actions, ever.

92

No one could ever get to know him, no one he did business with would ever be able to recognize him when he was in his natural element, when he was being himself. It was one of the reasons that they called him the Chameleon.

Security was of the utmost importance to Bracken. In addition to the windows, he had other safeguards that made him feel secure.

The front door was a good one, but behind it was yet another door that was more likely to be found on a cellblock than in a house, with squared iron rails instead of bars, the edges of which had been patiently and sharply honed. A master thief who had managed to get through the first door would slice his best tools— his hands—to ribbons, testing the strength of these steel bars. There was a six-digit number that had to be punched into the pad beside the door to open it, to click it open, and it had to be carefully closed from its farthest edge.

Upstairs, the windows were all separately bugged, each single alarm independent of the other, none of them needing ComEd power, and the alarm batteries were charged each month; that was one of Tawny's duties. There was a single balcony outside the front second-floor window, and the indoor-outdoor carpet had been wired. Anyone who stepped on that carpet weighing more than ten pounds would alert Bracken to the presence of an intruder on that balcony, and he'd respond accordingly.

Naturally, none of the alarms were tied in to a police agency, not the city police department and not to a private security company. Bracken's alarms, when disturbed, were wired to a console in his bedroom and when they were disturbed, a single light would flash and a soft beep would be emitted, telling him which window had been tampered with, telling him where to go to protect the security of his household.

None of the windows had been stickered, it was impossible for anyone but the best of thieves to look at the place and see what he had come up against, to be able to recognize the challenge. He'd had to check out breaches of security only three times in the eleven years that he'd been there, and he believed that the streets of New York were safer for his efforts; three thieves had been surgically removed from the ever-growing pool of criminals.

Feeling absolutely secure, knowing he was safe, Bracken added cream and sugar to his coffee, lit a cigarette while he waited for his eggs, Bracken looking with pride upon his home, at the place he'd worked so hard to build.

From his seat, he could see the hall that connected the kitchen to the living room. He could see the old comfortable leather chairs in the living room, the matching hassocks out in front. Could see the locked steel door of his private office, where the scrambler phone sat upon the bare desk.

That entire room had been plated with steel, drywall and wallpaper covered the metal. That room could withstand an attack by any army, it would take the best professional lockpickers hours with blowtorches to get into that room, and that would give Bracken time to figure out his options.

In a closet in that room was his personal arsenal, what he would have to use if the time ever came. Either to fight if the odds seemed reasonable, or to kill himself if he were overwhelmed. They and the .38 in the desk were the only guns he owned, and they never left the closet except for once a year when he took them out for cleaning. He would only use them if his dark prophecy came true, would only open that closet in anger if they were coming to kill him. Or to try and lock him away.

There were three other downstairs rooms that he couldn't see from where he sat, large and airy rooms that Bracken had redone when he'd bought the house. Every room was painted in brownish colors, all the furniture was heavy and dark; all the wood solid and heavy, none of it pressed, none of it condensed. There were no antiques in the house; anyone visiting would immediately know that it belonged to a real man.

"I'll take that," Tawny said, and waited, holding the plate of eggs, until Bracken nodded his head. Tawny took the cigarette from between his fingers, placed it between sensuous lips, and Bracken looked away. He hated when Tawny did that, it made Tawny look so damn butch. Tawny put the eggs down in front of him, the bacon on the side. Two pieces of buttered toast were in a corner of the plate.

He loved this house, took great pride in the place, in what he'd done with it in the years that he'd lived here. This, and his car, were all that were keeping him here, were really all the roots that a man like Bracken could ever have. But as much as he loved it, it wasn't the only place he had. In case they ever were waiting inside for him, there were other places that he could go.

Disguises, cash, identification and passports were set up in two different places, one on the East Side, one on the West Side, in case Bracken ever had to leave the country in a hurry. The most highly trained investigators in the world, armed with recent photographs, could not recognize Bracken when he'd turned chameleon, not even if Bracken walked up to the man and asked him directions, or for a light for his cigarette. He was confident that in the event of an emergency, he could escape, slip away from them, with a minimum of effort.

But that day, he knew, would most likely never come. He was too good at what he did, too prepared for every hunt. The only way they could ever get on to him would be through an informer, and that was an unlikely scenario, as nobody knew his business. Not even Tawny, not anyone.

Tawny said, "You want some juice?" and Bracken was jerked out of his reverie.

"It was all I was planning on having, that, and maybe some grapes."

"I stayed home today, it's the day I check your mail."

"Monday already." Bracken shook his head, as if he'd forgotten, and he heard Tawny softly laugh.

"As if you didn't know."

"I might have given it a thought."

Tawny put the juice down in front of him, sat back and looked at him, sizing him up.

"My God, you're good at that. Even *I* wouldn't recognize you on the street."

"It's what I do, Tawny."

There was an expensive brown wig covering his shaved head, glued on to perfection, every strand in place. Plain-glass aviator glasses were perched on top of his nose. His thin eyebrows had been thickened and combed out, so that now they were bushy, like Donald Trump's. There were cheek implants inside his mouth, which he now removed to eat. They'd made his cheeks appear far fatter, his face fuller, in contrast to his slender body. He was wearing a suit that he'd burn in the fireplace tonight, fifteen hundred dollars on Fifth Avenue, a tie that had cost more than Bracken's first car. Comfortable leather shoes that had special steel toes built in.

Tawny covered the cheek implants with a napkin, sat down and sipped at a cup of coffee.

Tawny said, "Sometimes I'm in awe of you, the way you change what you look like. It's frightening."

"You'll be in greater awe in a couple of days," Bracken said, and shut his mouth. There was no use in telling Tawny anything that Tawny didn't have to know, not until the time was right. Tomorrow, when he was packing, would be the time to break the news. Paris, for a month or so, where he liked to go after every successful job. A man like Bracken could fit in in France, they didn't judge you so harshly over there, as they did in this country.

"Come on, *tell* me!"

"Tawny . . ." Bracken said, and that was all he had to say. Bracken was wiping the egg yolk from his plate with the last of his toast when Tawny put the fresh cup of coffee down in front of him.

"I hardly recognize you," Tawny said, then, casually, "You look sharp today." Tawny prying again.

"I've got a date later this afternoon," Bracken said, more than he should have, he could tell by the look on Tawny's face. "It's my business, Tawny, don't ask me about it."

"I thought you trusted me." Listen to this, sulking.

"With your end of the business," Bracken said.

"I thought we had no secrets."

"*You* have no secrets. That's the deal. Me, nobody knows my business but me, not even the people who hire me."

"But a *date*." Tawny now pouting. It was very unbecoming.

Bracken put his coffee down and stared at Tawny, brought his forefinger to his temple. His thumb was in his cheek, knuckles close to his nose, his elbow resting on the table. Bracken deciding something, casually, bushy false eyebrows raised, lips pursed. Tawny looked away.

"I didn't mean it."

"My business is none of yours."

"I know that, I know the rules."

"If you forget this rule, how do I know you won't forget the others?" He was questioning softly, speaking as much to himself as he was to Tawny.

"I didn't forget, I just made a mistake."

"In my business, Tawny, you can't afford to make even one mistake."

Still casual, Bracken hadn't changed his position nor raised his voice. Tawny still wouldn't look at him, was rising and reaching over to pick up his empty plate when Braken grabbed Tawny's wrist.

"I have no time for games, I have no time for jealousy." His voice was soft and he wasn't squeezing hard, just enough pressure to let Tawny know he was serious.

"I have certain responsibilities that are none of your concern. It's not that I don't trust you, Tawny, rather that the people who hire me have no reason to trust you. I can't do that to them, do you understand me?"

"James, I am so sorry, I don't know what happened to me. We had such a nice weekend, I just started seeing us as a regular couple."

"We're not that, and we'll never be that." He let go of the light grasp, sat back in his chair. "We're so far above that shit, Tawny, I'm surprised you'd ever want it."

"I don't James, all I want is you."

He let Tawny walk away, Bracken sitting there, thinking. When they started asking questions, when they started getting possessive . . .

Tawny came up behind him, was licking the back of his neck, fingernails running down the front of his shirt, teasing at his nipples. "Got time to play?"

"You haven't bathed, I can smell you."

Tawny's voice came into his ear soft, hurt.

"How can you tell?" Then playfully, "How do you know I didn't bathe down here this morning?"

Bracken gently pushed Tawny's fingers away and shook his head, smiling faintly. He lit a cigarette and took a deep drag, tossed the napkin away from the cheek implants. He inserted them back into his mouth, popped the caps over his back teeth and moved them around with his tongue until they were properly in place. He bit down on his teeth several times, to make sure that the implants had been inserted properly and wouldn't be in the way of his tongue, would not interfere with his speech.

Tawny came around and sat down next to him, took one of his hands and squeezed it, tightly. In the bright spring light coming through the kitchen window, he could see the lines on Tawny's face. Without make up the thirty-six years were apparent. The hair was parted down the middle, falling gently down either side of Tawny's head. In the brightness, Tawny no longer looked like a teenager; Bracken could see the signs of some miles driven over a rough road. The thin nose that had had work performed upon it. Lips that had had injections. The brow was a little too thick, the Adam's apple defined. Thin, slender person, his Tawny surely was.

Still, up close like this, without makeup and with foreknowledge, was the only way to really tell that Tawny was a man.

"I forgive you, and you'd better clean up and shave," Bracken said. "Now, Tawny, if there's nothing else you want to talk about, I have to go to work. You have the mail here when I get back, would you? That's a good girl."

THE GUY WHO really ran the fourth-floor gym was a black man by the name of Delmar Lewis. Del was an ex-fighter who hadn't been very good, who'd quit the ring and had then gone into management, and had been in the corner of a number of Chicago's greatest fighters, and he never let anyone forget it. Like right now. Old Del was holding four pre-teenage newcomers captive with his stories, as Mark walked into the entrance of the youth center.

They would have been sent here by their schools, would be troublemakers who had been sent here as a last ditch effort to help them straighten out. Mark knew that there had probably been seven or eight of them who'd actually been sent, the decision to send them made by the school juvenile justice committee that was headed by a grade school principal, the group meeting after classes every Friday afternoon.

Four had shown up this morning, released from the school after classes had begun. Half was about average. The school would check up later, if anyone remembered to call, and Del would give the school the names of these four. The others would be truants, as if that would matter to them. Kids like these ate truant officers for breakfast.

But they weren't eating anything now, that was for sure. Del's ancient voice was loud, carried throughout the gym, over the sound of a heavy bag being hit, the rat-a-tat-tat of a couple of speed bags being tattooed by guys who knew what they were doing. The tiny little man was captivating his audience, holding their attention without half-trying.

The large loft-type gym was nearly empty, but there were five adult male youth center graduates working out before heading off to their jobs. They ignored Del, having heard it all before. Mark and Del, to them, were part of the furnishings; they wouldn't pay much attention to them unless either of them had a problem or some trouble. Then they'd pay attention. Strict, and if need be, brutal attention. A couple of them felt that they owed their lives or at least their freedom to one or the other of those two men.

There were half a dozen heavy punching bags hanging from chains around the gym, strung up at spaced and staggered intervals. Six pro speed bag stations were set against a far wall. Mats were laid out on the hardwood floor, and that was where the clients boxed, because there wasn't a boxing ring; they cost far too much to have one installed. There were situp benches, though, and dip bars to improve your strength.

The only concession to modern robotic boxing training were lightweight hydraulic devices that attached to your wrist, they looked funny, but they did the job; you squeezed them to build strength in your hands. A dozen well used jump ropes hung from pegs on the wall, over an equal number of worn leather medicine balls. There were cloudy mirrors bolted to the walls so the kids could watch themselves shadow box.

There were no weights in Del's gym, no running machines, no stationary bikes or StairMasters had ever been in this place. You ran on the street and you came in winded and sweating or Del's wrath would descend upon you, and nobody wanted that. Del ran a tight, old-fashioned ship, and there was no doubt in anyone's mind that he himself was the captain. Evander Holyfield would not even know what he was seeing here; but Mike Tyson would recognize the place, as would Marciano.

Another thing you rarely saw in Del's gym were white people. Del didn't like them. Del didn't trust them. Mark was, supposedly, Del's boss, but neither man ever mentioned the fact. Mark listened to Del's tirades against the white man and had long ago learned not to argue with the man. He was pleasant enough to Mark and the other white people who worked upstairs. If he wanted to discriminate against white kids in his gym, then Mark and the others would find them other places to go. It was unpleasant and sometimes led to arguments, but it was the way it was; the old man was set in his ways.

"You kids want to be fighters?" Del was saying, "Let me tell you about being a fighter." He set his narrow, bony shoulders and put his hands on his hips, Del about to impart the wisdom of the ages to them, and he had those kids—gangbangers all—eating out of the palm of his hand. Del was a living legend around here, even Mark could be sometimes intimidated by him.

"I was with a guy who fought LaMotta and beat him, who fought Zale four times, and beat him *twice*. My man's name was Nate Bolden, boys, and that name might not mean much to you. But I'm here to tell you he fought Blackjack Billy Fox, Archie Moore, Lem Franklin, Lee Savold, and Gus Dorazio. You wouldn't know those names, but Muhammad Ali could tell you who they was. Before any of your mamas was born I was in his corner at the old White City in Chicago, at his first fight in thirty-seven when he fought a guy called the Ace of Spades and he beat that man in a decision with a bunch of hand speed was quicker than lightning, with a jab that could have rocked Joe Louis in his prime. We fought in White City, at the Marigold, the Coliseum and the Rainbow, and years later, when they built it, at the Chicago Stadium. You want to see the Coliseum, what's left of it? Go down eight, nine blocks, right down Wabash here, you'll see the stone remains. Walk inside there at night and you'll feel the ghosts of some of the all-time greats."

The kids were enthralled, as they always were at first. They wouldn't have heard of any of the fighters, but some of the places might be familiar to them. Del spoke with passion, with knowledge and sincerity. His accent was pure South Side ghetto, his tone filled with bitterness at the stolen opportunities, the breaks that should have come the way of his fighters but hadn't, due only to the color of their skin.

"You youngbloods all talk about discrimination, but you don't know nothin' about it." Del's voice dripped with his disappointment. As he spoke, he turned his glare onto each child in turn until he was sure that they wouldn't challenge him. Even at their age, with their badass street attitudes, the kids' faces showed pain at the intensity of Del's stare. They understood what he was talking about, took it for granted as a part of their daily lives.

"Sure, the white devil motherfucker give you his shit, it the way he is, but *we* went through things that you boys would not believe. Back in those days we couldn't even use the *bath*rooms of the places we was fighting out of, nor the showers. We couldn't stay in their damned hotel rooms nor eat our meals out of their restaurants. Imagine yourself, you're Joe Louis, you're fighting for the heavyweight champeen-ship of the entire god-damned *world*, and having to go all the way to the other side of town, down to what they all called niggertown, to get a shower and a meal after winning a fight. Joe Louis having to lay his head on soiled pillows. Del grunted and nodded, confirming to them that it had actually happened.

"You wear your baseball hats cocked to one side to show your love of some street gang, and you resent it when we make you take them off when you're in this place, but back then, somebody would'a *shot* them caps offa your fool heads, taken a bunch of your brains along with the hats, too!" Del looked at them, waiting for one of them to defend their gang. None did. A rarity in here.

Del continued, "You boys wanna hang in here, you got to live by the rules. No fighting amongst opposite gangs allowed, no weapons, no caps allowed, no colors represented *a*tall, not once.

"You break the rules once, we all vote on what to do with you. You break 'em twice, you ass be out there on the streets again, we ain't got no room in here for no troublemakers.

"And remember, we's only the gym, down here. We ain't but a wee small part of the entire youth center, all of them offices is upstairs, manned by *white* peoples. And you still got to go through us to get to the center, to get your mandated counseling. You gotta pass through us to go upstairs a'*tall*. How that make you feel, bein' a loser been dumped out of here, passin' by us twice a week to go see your white counselors, huh?" Del's gaze softened, as did his tone of voice.

"But if you play by the rules and want to learn about fightin', if you cares about doing that right, I can help you with that. Me and the boys been around here awhile can teach you to be as good as you can be, if you got the discipline and know how to listen.

"And remember this and don't you never forget it: Life ain't nothin' but sufferin' for us, and it ain't but one damned fight after the other. And if you don't learn how to do it right, if you don't learn to dance and weave and wait your time to make your move, then you ain't never gonna be nothin' but a convict or a junkie. Enough of the boys come in here wind up as one or t'other." Del paused, letting them savor the wisdom of his last words.

Del said, "Now ya'll go on to school and think about which *ya'll* want to be, then get your asses back here this evenin', after you done all your homework assignments. We'll start working at five-thirty, not one minute past."

Mark watched the kids run past him, none of them acting like wiseasses now, none of them making any jokes as they passed him by. One or two of them might be back tonight. He kept his face stony as they passed by him. He'd had his heart broken too many times to look at them seeking hope.

Over by one of the heavy bags a guy the gangs had christened to be Thunder stopped punching, looked over at Mark, and nodded his head, half-smiling. Thunder had been sixteen when Mark had first met him. He was twenty-three or four now, and far more impressively built than he had ever been back in his gang-banging days.

Mark nodded back, and winked at the guy who was now referred to as Mr. Thornton at the grade school where he taught Black Studies. Mark didn't know what they called him at night, when he went to college, working toward his doctorate.

Sometimes, his heart didn't get broken, but was filled. There was an ugly scar on Thunder's left bicep, large and round. The gang had cut their name off the tattoo that had been there when Thunder had turned his back on them and begun his life as a free man.

"Mark, how the hell you doin'?" Del had spotted him, was walking over to meet him on legs that were bent and twisted. They'd been broken at the kneecap years ago by some mobsters who'd wanted one of his fighters to throw a fight. Del never had played that shit. Mark shook his hand, warmly, forced a smile for Del. They had an understanding, and Mark was treated mostly with respect, although he often felt like an outsider down here, even when he was teaching a young kid how to fight.

Del was a little guy, had never been more than a bantamweight. Del was bald now, and what hair he had left on the sides above his ears was snow white and cut short, down to the skull. His head looked like a bowling ball with talcum powder slapped on the sides. There was no fat on him, Del was spare and tiny. Nothing but a sunken-chested, crippled, shriveled up old man. Until he opened his mouth. Then you could get a glimpse of the man he used to be. He ran the gym with an iron hand, and God forgive the punk who judged him by his looks and decided to play tough guy. There were plenty of real tough guys who hung out here, men who loved old Del with more passion than they had ever loved a father.

Mark said, "Del," and let his hand go.

Del seemed troubled, and Mark thought that he needed something. Del hated to ask him for anything. Mark didn't know if that was due to the man's independence, or to his blatant distrust of the white race, of which Mark was a member.

Del said, "Had a problem in here last night." Del shrugged. "Boy forgot what we got goin' here, decided he was just high enough to come in here and call us all names, decided to come on in and kick him some ass."

"I didn't get a call."

The old man's voice softened, and he looked around, made sure nobody could hear him. He had a way of doing that that showed the people he was cutting out that he was doing it for their own good, making a pact with the devil that they didn't need to know about. If Mark had done it, pickets would be set up.

"Didn't need you. Nor the police, neither. Thunder was here, with his new wife, showing her around the place, introducing her to those that couldn't make the wedding. Sweet woman, Mark, should'a done better for herself." Del chuckled at his gag, and Mark smiled, tolerantly.

"Was some other boys here, too, helped me calm things down. Then it got a little ugly. Turned out the boy had him a gun." Del shrugged.

"Boy got dropped off in a alley a few blocks down, an anonymous call went to nine-one-one. You hear about anything, any complaints, let me know. I take care of them."

"You think we'll get sued?" Mark smiled to show he was joking. The old man shook his head, slowly, not playing. He didn't see anything funny about the situation.

"Don't figure that's likely to happen. Some lawyer might come around, though."

"I'll send him on down to see you."

"You do that. And Elmer ain't here yet," Del said as Mark walked over to the iron railing that would take him to the second floor offices. A small thing but Del felt it was important enough to mention to Mark.

"He's not?" Mark was surprised. Elmer was usually here before everyone but Del, who lived here, slept on a cot in a first-floor closet. Mark had a quick, vague sense of unease, a premonition that he quickly forced out of his mind. He'd been having too many of them lately to take any of them seriously anymore.

"He comes in, let me know, send him up right away to see me, would you?"

"His granny called, though. I took one call down here, and then told her to call your number upstairs, to leave a message for you."

Mark looked at the face that was a roadmap of a long, rough life. It was giving nothing away. He nodded and hurried to his office, unlocked it and went inside.

It was a small office, like all of them in the center. The top two floors had once been lofts that had been cheaply partitioned off by unskilled but free laborers. Almost everything that was done around here was done for next to nothing, the work performed by the kids and the staff, or donated by one of the few corporations that were involved in what they were trying to do here. One of the *very* few corporations.

The walls in his office had never been painted, he could still see the studs through the flat drywall. The floor was hardwood, bent in places, rotting in others. A potential corporate sponsor had been saying for a couple of years that it would donate enough to fix the place up right, but the money hadn't come in yet, and Mark wasn't holding his breath.

The South Loop Youth Center didn't have a high profile name like the Michael Jordan Foundation—from which they'd received donations in the past—or Ronald McDonald house. Corporations weren't lined up around the block to donate money or expertise to help solve the sort of problems that they dealt with from in these rooms. Such as gangbanging, black-on-black crime, street violence and drug abuse.

The heads of corporations generally turned their faces away from such problems, saw them as police problems, instead of the problems of society in general. Mark didn't care that they closed their minds, his problem was that they closed their wallets, too. And the ones who *did* want to give big bucks wanted a place on some board of directors, along with direct input into how the place was administered. That, to Mark and his staff, was unacceptable. There wasn't enough money to ever give anyone power over them. They'd given enough up to the government and the state, had to kiss enough ass for the yearly quarter million that the state and federal governments threw their way. One of his assistants, Zack, was an expert at applying for grants, it was his job to milk every one of them that he could find, and he brought in enough to pay the permanent staff and to keep the lights turned on and the rent paid each month.

So what got them by was that, the infrequent donations from private citizens and industry, and the United Way, God bless them. It brings out the best in all of us . . .

The money that didn't go to the necessities went to the programs, which found for the kids who needed it, professional psychological counseling and often drug and alcohol counseling, the center paying for it when Zack couldn't find a government agency that would give the help for free. There were now a total of seven full-time staffers in the center who worked far more than the forty hours a week for which they were paid, counseling the troubled youths, teaching them to read and write, about birth control, handing out rubbers . . .

With enough money, though, with enough programs like this for these kids, crime could be cut in half, he knew. He believed it in his heart, as he saw the success stories every day of his life.

Saw the failures, too, and it looked like Elmer might become one.

His grandmother's message had told Mark that Elmer would have to go back into the custody of the state. She'd called him for advice, for help. She thought that was what he was there for. He could hear the desperation in her voice, the old woman reaching out to him as someone she could trust. She didn't know, as Mark did, how much it would hurt Elmer to have to be committed to an institution once again. The kid had seemed to be doing so well.

But Mark didn't live with him, she did. And she knew Elmer better than Mark ever would.

Reluctantly, Mark listened to the message again, jotted down the number she gave him for a call back, then reached for the telephone and dialed the woman's number.

BRACKEN LIVED IN what was called the Mews, in Greenwich Village, owned a small 3-million-dollar house that was surrounded on all sides by invading junkie scum. Street fags and dope dealers,

NYU free thinkers mingled with advantaged tourists loving April in New York, all of them thinking they were safe in the Village. None of them had any idea of how wrong they were. Maybe someday he'd show them, give them a small glimpse of hell.

The house would be worth a fifth of that amount in any of the surrounding affluent New York City suburbs. It was worth so much only because it was in Manhattan, was exclusive, with private, personal curb-side parking spaces reserved for the wealthy homeowners, whose vehicles reflected their overinflated incomes.

Bracken's house was in an enclosed area, with tall iron fences on either side of the semi-private street. The huge cast iron drive-through fences were locked around the clock, but the man-doors on either side were only locked from eleven at night until seven each morning, after that you had to use your access card to get in. Bracken wished that the walk-through gates were locked 24 hours a day. That would keep all the people from cutting through, looking at the quaint little houses.

His house was one of five that were connected by adjoining walls. Rowhouses, they'd been called, way back when they'd been built. The street outside still had the original cobblestone from 150 years before. You parked your car in front of your house and set the alarm and your car would never be stolen, because only the owners had the security cards that would open the mechanical iron gates.

The front doors of the houses were oak, heavy, with good locks that Bracken had improved with a variety of his own; his house, he knew, was as much a fortress as it was a home. There were private second-floor balconies with assorted chairs and Weber kettles and Hibachis scattered around the high porches, safe from walk-by thieves, although every now and again Bracken would go out and notice that one of his neighbor's grills or chairs would be missing.

The houses had a single flat roof. Bracken knew that his section was the only one that had been alarmed to detect even the smallest human intruder. There were no pigeon coops on top of the roofs. Bracken's portion of the roof was separated from his neighbors on either side by a two-foot privacy fence that couldn't be seen from the street.

His neighbors went in for pastel trim, painting the wood that surrounded all that good red brick in disgusting pink or green, but that was not for Bracken. His trim had been lacquered, was deep brown, rich and shiny.

The best part of living there, as far as Bracken was concerned—beside the sterling investment—was the complete and total privacy. Eleven years he'd owned the home, and in that time the house's value had quadrupled, and he'd never done more than formally nod at his neighbors, at the rich older people who lived on either side of his house.

And it was quiet. Sometimes he'd hear classical music late at night coming from one of the neighbors' homes, but the buildings had been erected before the turn of the century, when houses had still been castles, private and secure. With his air-conditioning on, or the heat in the winter, he could believe that he was alone, living in Paris, in exile with a lover. It was a fantasy he enjoyed, albeit one that was dangerous.

Late Monday morning Bracken stepped out of his house carrying an empty suitcase in one white-gloved hand. He pulled the door shut behind him, his head down, the collar of his topcoat pulled up around his cheeks. Anyone seeing him would think that he was a visitor, his appearance was so radically transformed that not even an ex-lover would know him if he passed them by on the street. If he'd had any ex-lovers who were still alive.

His car was at the curb, the black Jag sedan that he loved so dearly. Summer was coming up, and he'd have it stripped bare and painted yet again. Although there was no vehicle traffic on the private street, you couldn't stop the tourists and the natives from passing through the courtyard, and every year, without fail, at least one time someone would run their key across the side of his car, scratching through the finish, through the paint, sometimes right down to the steel. Jealous scum with nothing, hating those who possessed.

Bracken walked a few blocks, hurrying, wanting to get out of the area. He caught a cab and gave the driver an address several blocks away from where he planned to go. Bracken sat in the back, smelling stale sweat and ancient smoke, while the skinhead kamikaze Arab with a beard sang along off-key with the song that was playing on the radio.

"Aye nevah weel forgeht, the way you looook toniiiight!" My God, he sounded terrible, the man's voice shrill and whining, but Bracken let it pass. He was working now, going to his job, and like most men who loved his work, he was happy this Monday morning. And who deserved his attention more, this guy who was trying to fit into a foreign country, or a woman who spoke like the heroine in a dimestore romance novel? Besides, with Leehanna, there was a hefty profit involved.

They passed a group of young black kids walking down Broadway. One of the boys was carrying an oversized radio that blasted out rap music with lyrics that some could consider offensive, and the cabby stopped singing his song, looked at them in undisguised disgust as the boys passed a woman and shouted things at her as she hurried past, obviously frightened, trying to ignore them.

"So, they been here three hundred years, eh?" The cabby looked in his rearview mirror, seeking Bracken's approval. Bracken sniffed deeply, as if telling the man that he stunk. The cabby's eyes went back to the road, and the rest of the trip passed in total silence.

He got out at Park and walked a few blocks north, crossed over and walked east to 5th, walking easily in the early lunchtime traffic, fitting in, not allowing himself to get upset at the jostling and the jockeying for position.

There was an attractive long-haired woman standing behind a card table set up at the curb, shouting for people to sign the petition she had set up on one side of the makeshift desk. Atop the table stood a poster-sized color picture of another woman, not unattractive, the woman in the photograph tied up, lying on a grimy, stained bed, with a man with a belt in his hand standing over her, grinning. It was obvious that he was about to bring the belt down on the woman's buttocks. The woman's backside was already heavily marked, one-inch welts criss-crossing one another. Her face was tear-streaked, set in an expression of terror.

"Stop violence against women—stop *Spank* magazine! Sign the petition and stamp out *Spank!*" Her voice was passionate, filled with her outrage. She sang her theme song loudly, her voice filled with her fury.

Bracken had to hand it to her, she knew how to draw a crowd. Around her, women who were strangers to each other were speaking as if they were old friends, leaning over to sign the petition, their sex drawing them together for once. Bracken spotted a pickpocket crew working the crowd, three of them, well-trained. Spotted, too, mixed in with the well-dressed business people, two men in suits, staring in druglike euphoria at the picture on the poster. One of them had his hand deep inside the pocket of his cashmere coat. Bracken excused himself, worked his way through the crowd, avoiding the pickpockets, and moved on, although if he hadn't been working he'd have had to take some action against them, would have tried to move behind the woman at the card table, shown her what he thought of her and her movement, of her goddamned preaching on a city sidewalk, so righteously, at lunchtime.

There were times when he wasn't working when he would scratch some idiot simply for standing in the middle of the sidewalk and gabbing with somebody else, the two of them showing who they were, how important, the idiots proving that they had the power to make masses of humanity walk around them rather than simply stepping out of their way. Bracken would flick out a credit card, held down low, cut through the pants or pantyhose and if he was lucky, he'd slit an artery. He'd have the card back in his pocket before the victims realized that they were bleeding.

But not today. Today was not for sport. The woman would get a pass because today was purely business.

Bracken politely held the suitcase out in front of him, excusing himself when it touched someone's coat. Trying not to draw attention, as he practiced at blending in; he'd done this sort of thing many times before in his career.

Bracken entered the Plaza Hotel from the Central Park side, strolled up to the reception desk and registered with a false credit card. He kept his head down as he signed the credit card slip, accepted the key and refused the bellhop's help. Walked quickly to the elevator behind the desk and slightly to the right, across from the concierge's desk, Bracken looking at the carpet.

He could hear violin music coming from the Palm Court, he knew that tea was being served, finger sandwiches and cheesecakes, coffee and liqueurs. The elevator doors opened and he stepped through them, and hit the button for his floor, then stepped back to let a bellman with a luggage rack inside, nodding at the man's courteous thank you.

Bracken got off on the 13th floor and had to walk a ways to his room, he'd purposely taken the wrong set of elevators, had not wanted to walk past the crowded Palm Court and the main entrance of the hotel. He would have passed too many people if he'd gone to the proper elevators.

When he found it he was happy, as it was a good room, on the corner, the windows facing front. Across from him was the front street, the hotel's drive, the fountain, and then open space; to the left, Central Park. To the right were office buildings, but he had to lean far over to see them.

Bracken closed and locked the windows and pulled the shades, leaving the suitcase on the bed, turned and checked out the room, liking what he saw.

The door was brown, heavily painted and steel, it closed quietly and had a good lock, with a deadbolt that turned once to double-secure the room. There was a short hallway with a bathroom on the right, leading to a king-sized bed in the middle of the room. The bed had a maroon-trimmed, multi-patterned bedspread, a pattern that was duplicated on the headboard, the curtains, the cloth that covered the sides of the nightstands, and the tablecloth on the small dining table. There was a marble-topped desk against one wall. The nightstands were miniatures of the desk, set on either side of the bed. White shades pulled down tightly; no one would see them, see what he was doing.

The walls were cream-colored, as was the rug. There was a large chest of drawers set against one wall, with a TV in the top section, with six drawers underneath on the left, and a miniature bar on the right. There was a fake fireplace next to the desk, with small, maroon-colored pieces of glass sitting inside a black iron log holder. Bracken flicked a switch and the glass began to glow. He left it on, nodded his head. She would see such tackiness as being somewhat romantic.

The bathroom had a long sink, scrubbed down and sparkling clean. Like the room itself, the high ceiling gave it the appearance of being larger than it actually was. The bathtub though, was very large; there'd be more than enough room for the two of them in there . . .

Bracken left the room and hung the "Do Not Disturb" sign on the knob and closed the door behind him, walked all the way down the hall to the same set of elevators he'd used to come upstairs. He checked his watch. It was just eleven-thirty. There was plenty of time to walk. He was meeting Leehanna Staples less than a mile from the Plaza.

THE COURTROOM WAS old and had bench-style wooden seats, all of which were filled with mostly black women and children. Their men would be in lockup, in the detention center, waiting for their names to be called so they could come out and tell the judges that they were innocent, had been framed. They had been arrested and bond had been set, and some of them would have already had preliminary hearings to ensure that the arrest had been righteous. This was their arraignment, where they would plead before the judge.

The suspects' handcuffs would be removed before they were allowed into the courtroom, unless they were violent or abusive, then the cuffs would stay on, behind the back, or, if the accused was particularly violent or seen as an escape risk, he'd be shackled around the waist and the ankles before he was allowed to come in and make his plea.

Mark watched it all from a seat at the back, with Mrs. Griffin, Elmer's grandmother, sitting close behind him. She held on to his arm as if for dear life, he could feel her fingernails through his jacket, pinching.

This is what it is supposed to be like; outside was what it really was.

In here, there was decorum, courtesy, majesty, even, and, mostly, a total respect for the way the law worked. People looked up at the judge sitting at her bench and they felt it, that grab in the balls, deep down, primeval fear; you were accused of doing something offensive to society and this was where you wound up, afraid and alone, facing your country's highest authority. This wasn't mommy and daddy; this wasn't the principal's office. Nor was this a juvenile center, a social worker's office or the youth officer's department. This was for real, and scary, that judge sitting up there was a woman who had the power to take away large chunks of your life, or even the entire thing; if she felt like it and your crime demanded it, she could lock you down in the pen forever, and see how you liked that.

Not that anyone who ever appeared in front of her would ever see themselves as deserving of such punishment. Mark had dealt with admitted killers, had looked them in the eye and asked them why they'd done what they had, and there was always an excuse, some rationale for what they'd done. "Motherfucker got into my face," he'd heard, and lately, the hot word was "dis'd." "He dis'd me" said in explanation, as if the words said it all, as if no more explanation was needed.

What would this judge do if someone told her that as a reason for committing a crime? The judge had probably heard it, at one time or another.

But more often than that she'd have heard heartfelt pleadings by people well trained in oratory, the lawyers crying out for justice against an unjust, racist system, speaking in articulate sentences that their client could not understand. They'd get the feeling, though, the gist of what was being said. Hang their heads and look sad, repentant. Life on the streets made me kill, Your Honor. The system made me do it. Black robes, white justice, Judge, it's the white man keeping me down. He dis'd me.

He wondered if sometimes the judges forgot that the world didn't work under the same restrictions as the courtroom. How many times had he seen it, stupidity rewarded, in the name of the law.

A kid he knew, a stone thief with more arrests for muggings and purse snatchings than his mother had had children, had taken a seat at an outdoor cafe, drinking coffee and staring intently out at every woman who passed by. A waiter had watched him closely, saw him tense up as certain women walked by, then relaxing for some reason, sitting back in his chair. The waiter asked the guy to leave, politely, and the guy had done so, although not without an argument. He'd sued the cafe and the waiter and the judge ruled in his favor, said that his record had no bearing on what had happened that day, as the waiter could not have been aware of it. And now the cafe was in real trouble, because the complainant was a black kid and the waiter had been white, but the civil jury that would hear the case would not be allowed to know about his record.

He'd never felt comfortable in these places, in a so-called court of law. The hypocrisy involved made him sick to his stomach, the way justice was done in the hallways when the right amount of money changed hands.

Even in Mark's worst days, he'd been, plain and simple, a thief. He'd tell you as much if you asked and he liked you. He didn't try to sugarcoat it and hide behind a respectable front. If he didn't like you he'd tell you to go fuck yourself, but that, too, was if nothing else, honest. Not like the shit they pulled in these supposed halls of justice.

Rights were a joke, the privilege of the rich, or so they thought, but really, when you looked at it closely, no one had them, not anymore. Stop & frisks were common in every poor neighborhood in the city these days, and very few poor young black people would ever dare ask the offending cops about such sophistry as illegal search and seizure. They preferred that their bones remained unbroken.

As for the rich, what right did they have to simply walk the street? Mark would hear it, from even the smartest people, after a crime was committed upon a person of means: What were they doing in *that* neighborhood? What were they doing in the park after dark? The cops would put the word out, you were looking for drugs or whores, you could be walking innocently down the street and that's what they'd say you were doing. Limited imaginations and past performances of others gave them the right to deliver their quotes, and they'd say them, to the newspapers and the television cameras and you'd see you face at six and ten, while the cops destroyed your reputation as you lay, beaten, in some hospital, blameless.

And the people who had been mandated to protect your rights, the lawyers, they'd do it all right, jump in front of the cameras if they were sure that they had a case they could win, if they were sure that the person, place or thing they were suing had the wherewithal to make it worth their while. They would go before the Supreme Court if they had to, in righteous anger, shaking their fists and protecting your ass for thirty-three and a third of whatever the jury might award you.

Lawyers, man, did Mark feel hatred toward them. There were no slander laws to protect you from what they said about you when they were trying to protect their client, or slam you down like an animal. They could call you anything they felt like, accuse you of anything, and if they couldn't prove it, well, your name and reputation were still shot to hell. The things they had said about him when he'd been trying to do right for once in his life, the names they had called him, the way they had looked at him . . .

Lawyers were the single class of people that Mark had never learned to accept. Cops, even judges, he'd come to terms with them over the years. But lawyers, they were no good, he would never see them as being human.

The courts, too, God, how Mark hated them. Hated what they'd become, the way the game was played. Rights didn't matter, obscure points of law and kicking ass were all that either side really cared about. It didn't matter if you were guilty or innocent, all that mattered was the language, not saying a single word that could overturn a case somewhere down the line.

The rules had been laid out to him by an assistant U.S. attorney, back in the days when he'd still been testifying against the mob: "They're all wrong, they're all guilty. We know that, and so do they. The side that can get the jury to believe the most of their bullshit wins."

It was the way the law worked, and he'd seen it from personal experience, Mark testifying in sixteen cases when he'd agreed to testify in seven. Mark being coached, told to lie on the witness stand, sending three men whom he'd never even met to the federal penitentiary. Mark being pushed around, treated like dirt by men who set themselves up as society's supposed protectors, Mark's child's future threatened by such men when he even dared balk at their ugly, brutal directions.

They cared only about convictions, nothing about justice. Had Mark by the balls and knew that his mind would follow. And he had, for a time, gone along with their cruel deceptions. Until it got too much for him and he'd shared his suffering with Andrea Bella.

Thank God for Andrea, and for her husband, Dan, too. Although he never wanted to see them again, Mark felt that he owed them a debt. Felt safer thinking about them, too, than about where he now was or why he was there, although he could put it off no longer, the paper in his hand seemed to be burning Mark's palm.

Mark had known the presiding judge for a while, and he knew her to be fair, although he wasn't sure how she'd look at the paper he'd brought with him today, whether or not she'd sign it. She was a tough one, though, the judge, with a sense of humor to boot.

She'd once sentenced a thieving street-rapper to probation while singing to him, in language he understood. "If I ever see your backside in my courtroom again, I'll send it away, for three years in the pen." She'd rapped it out with a straight face, not M.C. Hammer, but not too bad for off the top of her head.

Another time she'd been kind to a thief, sentenced him to six months in the County Jail when the maximum she could have laid on him was five years penitentiary time. The tough guy had looked up at her and sneered, told the judge that he could do six months while standing on his head. The judge had gone icy-eyed, had stared at the young man and spoken the words that were quoted as a program ending anecdote on all three local news stations that night. "In that case, sir, I sentence you to six *more* months, so your circulation can get back to normal."

She seemed to be in a good mood today, though, and Mark wondered now, what she'd think of Elmer's case.

It was for Elmer's benefit to be put away, he could no longer fend for himself. The boy building labyrinth scenarios in his head all the time, committing acts and then denying that he'd done them, even to himself, Elmer having the capacity to convince himself that he'd done nothing wrong, even when confronted with evidence, even when you'd seen him do it.

Mark had witnessed the behavior, Grandma hadn't had to do much convincing. He would look out his window and see Elmer in the alley between Wabash and Michigan, with a dead rat in his hands, swinging it around his head in an arc and then letting it go at the windshield of the first car that came up 13th Street. Mark would ask him about it later, ask him why he'd done it, and the boy would look at him innocently, "Done *what?*" Elmer would say, having forgotten the entire incident.

Elmer saw Mark as his counselor, referred to him as such, but Mark wasn't, not really. He just let the kid hang around and run some errands.

Elmer was reliable, most of the time, when he took his medication and didn't wander off in the middle of a chore. He had some mental problems, but Mark thought they were, for the most part, under control. The medication seemed to be working this time, in the last eighteen months since Elmer had been released from state care.

Still, it broke Mark's heart to do this, to help put the boy away. But it was something that he had to do, there was no putting it off. What if the boy stopped taking his medication and really hurt someone this time? Mrs. Griffin said that he'd been attacking girls around his own age, grabbing at their private parts, slobbering as he did so. What was he now, eighteen? If one of those girls decided to press charges, Elmer would be in front of this judge, and facing serious time. Judge Kitner was hell on sex crimes.

A young black youth was in front of her now, looking up at a woman who could have been his mother. Judge Kitner's black face was impassive, professional, showing neither solace nor rebuke. She heard the charges against him and questioned him carefully, asked him if he could afford counsel, if his rights had been fully explained to him. The boy seemed to be around seventeen years old. He leaned against the judge's bench, a look of disdain stamped on his face. He answered with "yeahs," without respect for her position of power over his life, or for her status as a sitting judge. Judge Kitner ignored his impertinence, simply made notations on something Mark couldn't see. Maybe the kid's file, maybe a notepad. Or maybe she was just doodling, her mind in half-gear. She only looked up when the youth pleaded not guilty.

She gave the kid a continuation, time to consult with his court-appointed attorney. At the next hearing, she knew, the lawyer would speak for him, would accept some form of plea bargaining, and then she would sentence him to what the prosecutor and public defender had agreed to, anything from time already served in the County lockup to a stiffer sentence that would have to be served out in the pen. The boy was pulled away, and Judge Kitner called for a recess before the revolving door began spinning again.

THEY STOOD IN her chambers, Mark respectful and polite. Mrs. Griffin was ashamed, he could tell that by the way she was standing with her head hanging, silently sobbing. He tried to distance himself from her, to be a professional here, doing only what was in Elmer's best interest.

Judge Kitner finished reading the document and looked up over the rims of the half-glasses she'd put on.

"Who's the doctor who signed the order?"

"Elmer's mental health physician, assigned by the state. He's been working on the case since Elmer was a child."

"And Mrs. Griffin? Ma'am?" Elmer's grandmother looked up, fearfully.

"You sincerely believe that your grandson is a menace to himself and the community? There are other options here, you know. Involuntary commitment is only one of them, no matter what the doctor signed."

"He won't take his medication, he throws it away . . ."

Judge Kitner sighed. She saw enough suffering every day in her courtroom, and now it was once again dragged in here, into her inner sanctum. She scrawled her name on the pretyped involuntary commitment order Mark had prepared and handed it over the desk to him. She avoided looking at the old woman standing at Mark's side, now holding onto him for support, as if she'd fall without his help.

"There you go. Keep me informed of his progress, and I want to know when he gets released."

"Thank you, Your Honor," Mark said, and they left.

OUTSIDE, IN THE car driving her home, Mark told Mrs. Griffin what she'd now have to do.

"All you have to do is call a private ambulance, and they'll take him away. Once he's committed to an institution, you call me, Mrs. Griffin. I'll go up there with enough people to convince him that he'll have to learn to take his medicine if he ever wants to get out of there for good."

"I don't want to do this!" Elmer's grandmother was suddenly stricken with guilt. "That boy goes crazy when he sees anyone in a white uniform!"

"It's too late now, Mrs. Griffin, you have the orders signed by a physician and a judge. If Elmer doesn't go for help, *you'll* be held in contempt, and he'll still go away."

He drove in silence, staring straight ahead, trying to ignore the stinging sobs of the woman seated beside him.

TOMCZAK SAT IN the deep leather chair in the waiting room of the ad agency, with two of his scripts in his lap, nervous and unaware that he was breathing through his mouth. He could see, through the window that separated him from the secretary, that even her office was large. Hell, the reception room he was sitting in was big, and it had class. There were good Steve Campbell prints on the wall, dark and grieving, frightening. Tomczak liked them, but he now tried not to look at them; Campbell had always made him tense unless he was looking at the work all alone, Campbell's pictures in a book, Tomczak in the safety of his own house at night.

He was on an upper floor of the Sears Tower Building, and he could feel the building swaying beneath him, it threw him off, made him dizzy. He had to fight with himself to stay where he was, to not leap to his feet and run out of the place.

He'd worn the sort of clothing that he thought big time ad execs would admire: a light brown corduroy sport coat over jeans, with a red and white lumberjack shirt and a black knit tie. He had the knot of the tie pushed all the way up. He'd finished the outfit off with dark brown, highly polished cowboy boots.

He'd combed what was left of his hair straight back, so they wouldn't think that he was ashamed of his baldness. He'd scrubbed under his fingernails and he'd shaved carefully. Now he sat straight up in the chair, in case the big shots asked the receptionist what she'd thought of him, how he'd waited, if he'd appeared intimidated or apprehensive. Creative people took input from everyone, even from the help.

Tomczak looked up and saw that the receptionist was looking at him, there behind the glass, and she smiled at him, bit her lower lip while she held a slim telephone receiver to her ear. Big-titted woman with dyed blond hair. She'd have gotten the job by blowing one of the partners. Well, she'd be blowing *him* soon, because he knew that he'd score the job. He smiled back, though, wanting a confederate inside the place, even if it was only this woman who answered the phones, smiling at him and rolling her eyes now, showing him that she was talking to someone she didn't much care for.

The inner door opened fast and he couldn't help himself, it scared him and he jumped, then he covered it up by getting quickly to his feet, pulling hard down on the hem of his jacket. A tall, thin, well-dressed man with a full, rich head of gray hair was coming toward him, striding fast, his hand held out for a shake.

"Lloyd Tomczak? I'm Peter Gerald." Jesus. Peter Gerald, of Burnhamm and Gerald himself, come to greet him. They must be taking his job appointment seriously. Tomczak gave him a two-handed shake, his scripts under his arm, hoping that his palms weren't too wet. He felt the sweat seeping out from under his armpits, was glad that he'd worn the thick sport coat because the sweat couldn't stain through his shirt and embarrass him.

"Thank you for seeing me, sir," Tomczak said.

"Number one, call me Pete, we don't stand on formality around here." Gerald began to walk quickly and Tomczak followed him, back through the door he'd come from, Gerald still talking.

"Number two, it would have been hard *not* to give you an appointment, as persistent as you are. And besides, Mr. Burn-hamm insisted that we speak with you, together. We pride our-selves on always being on the lookout for new talent, as I said, we don't stand much on formality around here."

They didn't? You could have fooled Tomczak, as he walked behind Gerald, down a carpeted hallway that had brightly painted walls. Almost every time they'd pass a doorway, the people work-ing inside would jump at the sight of their boss, some would smile, while others would quickly pull their feet off the desks. One of the women tried hard to look seductive, the rest of them were too busy, they smiled professionally, and that made Tom-czak happy. Maybe he'd find a replacement for Aiko somewhere in this building, a hard-working woman who didn't eat meat and loved all living things.

It was obvious to Tomczak that the people who worked here feared their boss; maybe they feared him informally, didn't stand on formality, just hated him a little bit, casually.

The offices were all well appointed, though, these weren't real estate office cubicles here. Tomczak got glimpses of deep, dark carpets, saw framed pictures on the wall, easels set up in corners, for showing their ideas. Each office had its own personal desktop computer, and several workers did not even look up at them as they passed, the industrious workers who were intently pounding on their keyboards, lost in their artistic expression. Tomczak en-vied them.

Every door on both sides of the hall was open, and that didn't make sense to Tomczak. What sort of company had a policy that demanded you keep your door open? Did Gerald or his partners like to spy on them, or were they afraid that their employees would fuck off if they weren't being watched all the time?

The artwork here was far different than that in the waiting room. On these walls were silver-framed posters of advertisers' products, large, glossy pictures, in glass that wasn't streaked. Soap and hot dogs were in these pictures, insurance companies and automobiles.

Gerald looked into every office, walking slowly now, not miss-ing a trick. He'd be a good boss, a good administrator. Tomczak would bet that he knew how to kick ass. Well, he'd never have to kick *his* ass, not if Tomczak got the job.

The last doorway they passed was half-closed, and Tomczak noticed that the little black plastic nameplate holder in the center of the door was empty. Gerald stopped abruptly, and Tomczak almost walked right into him. He caught himself and stopped, waited as Gerald looked into the room. He could see over the man's shoulder. There were a couple of workmen in there, painting, their dropcloths over a desk, covering the carpeted floor.

"You about wrapped up in here?"

One of the men said, "Yes, sir," snappily, while the other one kept painting. Gerald sniffed.

"I can hardly smell the bastard anymore. Good work, fellas," Gerald said, and closed the door.

Tomczak didn't know if he was supposed to laugh at Gerald's comment, so he didn't, he just stood there, and waited for the man to lead him away.

There was a huge double doorway at the end of the hall, and these were the only doors Tomczak had seen that were closed. The doors were made of very dark wood, with inset paneling and brass knockers and handles, or maybe they were gold. This would be Gerald's office. Gerald led him toward those doors, asking insane, small talk questions. Now that they'd passed the workers' offices, now that there was nobody to check on, Gerald's step had sped up again. Tomczak tried to answer the questions in a witty, self-deprecating manner. Gerald pushed the doors open and walked through and held them open for him, and Tomczak stepped in, and Gerald let the door go, and they closed with a whoosh of compressed air. In spite of himself, Tomczak had to stop and gawk.

He'd thought that the outer offices were plush, but he'd been wrong. This in here, now, *this* was plush, and he hadn't even seen past the outer secretary's office.

There was white shag carpeting on the floor, wall to wall, with a large, circular emblem in the middle of it, the emblem multi-colored, the insignia of Burnhamm and Gerald Advertising, Inc. There was a knockout model type manning the phones, with long, glistening black hair, perfect teeth, wearing a high-cut white silk blouse. Tomczak could see her bra right through the fabric. She smiled brightly at the boss, and as soon as he'd passed, she sized Tomczak up, and he could tell from the way her smile dropped that she didn't much like what she saw.

He looked away quickly, embarrassed, lowered his head and kept following Gerald.

There were three more sets of large, shining double doors against the walls of the outer office, and Gerald strode to the center set, opened them, stepped back and held them open so Tomczak could walk through first.

A very old man was sitting at a large conference table, glaring at Tomczak, as if he knew that he was wasting his time by even allowing someone like Tomczak into his presence. This would be Mr. Walter Burnhamm himself, the moneyman behind the business. It was the way that Peter Gerald described him in the interviews Tomczak had seen on TV. "He's the moneyman," Gerald would say, "I'm the ideaman, the front man."

Burnhamm was the man who drummed up the business, who was old friends with the people who owned Lever Brothers and automobile companies. Burnhamm never did interviews, never spoke to the press. He never attended parties, was never seen at public functions.

Tomczak was sweating from the fast walk down the hall, breathing heavily, his mouth still open. He could feel a warm river of sweat flowing down his ribs and chest, the sweat that would about now be staining the waistband of his pants.

"Come in, Lloyd," Peter Gerald said, and Tomczak walked further into the room, stood before one of the dozen chairs at the far end of the table and waited until Gerald sat down and nodded at him before he dared to sit down himself.

"You write for the *Leader*," the old man said, accusation in his tone. It was not news he was happy to be discussing.

"I do, sir, yes, only until my novel sells." He could not imagine ever calling this man Wally. He doubted if Burnhamm's wife even did. Burnhamm was looking at him strangely, as if he didn't believe him, the old man's liver lips twisted down in disgust.

"You've written a novel?" This came from Gerald. His eyebrows were raised, as if in surprise.

"A novel, and a number of screenplays, yes. The *Leader*'s only freelance, I sell them stories and pictures."

"A renaissance man," Gerald said, and smiled.

The Burnhamm-Gerald emblem had been sculpted into the center of the table, had been painted in its traditional colors,

bright and carefree, yet businesslike. There were professional por-
traits on the walls, in heavy, expensive metal frames, pictures of
the people who owned the products that these men had made
millions advertising.

"I understand you have an idea for saving LNA for our company." Burnhamm's mouth was still turned down, his eyes giving
off all the warmth of a serpent's.

Gerald said, "Nasty business, that hitting the papers, the man
who leaked it wound up out on his ass."

"I read about it in the papers, yes, sir, I read that you were
about to lose the account. But I really don't believe it will be a
loss for you, or, for that matter, for me, either. I think it's my
ticket in, sirs," Tomczak nodded his head, first toward the old
man, then toward Gerald, including them both in his address,
then looked directly into Burnhamm's eyes.

"I've brought scripts with me, that I can produce and direct
myself, I have the equipment, I can have a demo videotape ready
for you in a month, bring any of the three in for under fifty
thousand, total." Burnhamm's eyes squinted even more, Tomczak could not see his eyeballs from where he sat, just wrinkly,
old, yellow flesh. He hurriedly continued.

"As you said, I work for the *Leader*. Before I get into LNA, let
me run this by you." Tomczak ran his hand through what was
left of his hair, looking down at the first script as he licked his lips,
then he looked up, sure that he knew how to present his idea.

"The *Leader*'s an alternative, right? It's, as it were, Chicago's
Village Voice. I'm locked in there, started freelance, and now, even
though I'm still freelance, I have a weekly column, they like me
so much. They'll put this idea in, too, if I tell them, for the right
price." He smiled to take the sting out of his statement, to show
that he wasn't pretentious or arrogant.

"You got a beer company to do the ads for?" When neither
man answered, Tomczak got nervous. He fought it and said, "All
right, let's just say you do. You know how they do those TV
commercials, with all the sharp young chicks in bikinis running
around on beaches? OK, here's the deal, we hire one of those
chicks. We do a closeup, of her face, get her to lick her lips
suggestively. Under it, we put the caption, 'Buy our beer, and
she'll suck you dick.' " Tomczak paused, looking at them, seeing
if either of them got it. They didn't seem to, they were just staring
at him.

He said, "Here's what we're looking for, exposure, right? It's the *Leader,* covered by the first amendment, we run personal ads, people looking for discipline, want to have sex with nuns, shit like that, all the time. This is protected speech, see? Covered by the first amendment. It's a brilliant ad, if I say so myself, because it shows the commercials for what they are, which is bullshit, while at the same time, it makes a statement. It says the same things the commercials don't have the balls to say, follow me? And no matter what, you *know* it'll get a ton of free publicity and controversy."

The two big shots were looking at him strangely, as if they hadn't understood a word that he'd said. All right, he'd run that one by them later, after he gave them the knockout punch.

"I have another idea, too, for any major religious organization that might wish to advertise, the way the Church of the Latter Days Saints does."

Gerald cleared his throat. "Let's stick with the LNA Insurance Company, Lloyd?"

"Certainly."

The old man harrumphed, and Tomczak wanted to spit at him. Who did he think he was, why had he agreed to meet with him if he was only going to be rude?

He fought his anger, stared at the man and looked down at the third script, cleared his throat, then laid out his brainchild, his advertising masterpiece.

"Picture this, sir: You have cartoon characters, a man, a wife, couple kids, a dog, they're drawn wholesome, in their nice little house, full color, virtuous. Leave it to Beaver time, right? Well, they step outside, and then the house is on fire, they're all in terror, but, suddenly, a pair of large caucasian hands comes down from the sky, and the hands are together and they lift the entire family up into the palms—"

"Lloyd, Lloyd, come *on,* that's Allstate, for Christ's sake—"

"Will you please let me finish, Pete!" Lloyd regretted the anger in his voice, but this bastard, he'd wrecked the delivery. A delivery that Tomczak had stayed up with most of the night, practicing it in the mirror. Gerald sat back in his chair, appearing half-amused, and Tomczak thought that he might admire aggression. Burnhamm certainly did, he was grinning openly for the first time since they'd entered the room.

"Go on, finish," Burnhamm said.

"Thank you, sir," Tomczak said. "So, picture it in your mind once again, sirs," he nodded toward Gerald, there was no sense in alienating the idea man. "Picture these hands, with this loving all-American family inside, the hands are lifting them up over the flames that are devouring their house, and the family's starting to dry their tears and smile, the dog's wagging its fucking tail, when all of a sudden—" Tomczak jumped to his feet and slammed his right hand down on top of the scripts in his left.

"*WHAM*, the hands slap together hard, and even though the family's entirely covered by the back of the hand, it's family entertainment, I know, but the viewers *they* know as they watch that the hands have crushed them all to death, right? So now comes the voiceover, *our* man, but he sounds like theirs, he says, real sad-like, 'And you always thought that you were in good hands with Allstate . . .' then we go on to describe what LNA can do for them that Allstate can't . . ."

Tomczak's voice trailed off. The men were staring at him, aghast. Burnhamm broke the silence first, chuckling deep in his throat, a rich man's chuckle. It was the chuckle that Tomczak imagined J. D. Rockefeller had chuckled, as he'd watched the poor children fighting in the street over the shiny new dimes that he'd thrown from the back of his limousine. Gerald didn't join him, though, just sat there staring at Tomczak, appalled.

Burnhamm stopped chuckling, said, "Very good job, young man. I'm sure they love you over at that commie rag you work for. But it doesn't work with me, I've never been that naive. I'll tell you what I'm here to say, then I'll bid you a good morning."

Burnhamm rose, and Gerald joined them, the two of them staring down at Tomczak, ganging up on him.

Burnhamm said, "I have lawyers I pay to do nothing more than what I tell them, men, and now women, too, who work for me, on a full-time basis. If you and your rag think you can write an expose, think for a second that you can use our losing LNA as some silly cover story to show that we're going under, I will sue you, and spend millions if I have to, to close that paper down once and for all."

"I—they don't even know I'm here . . ." Tomczak was confused, what was this man saying to him?

"If we see you, or any of your people, hanging around our

offices, if any of our people come to us, and they *will* come to us if you try and pry information from them, I'll have the security guards throw you from the goddamn windows. I did not spend a lifetime getting where I am in order to let some wet-behind-the-ears punk like you write garbage about me, or about my company."

"Sir, Mr. Burnhamm, it's not what you think."

"Come now. Why do you think we brought you in here? If we thought you were really looking for a job, we'd have let Personnel handle it." Burnhamm wagged a finger toward him.

"I by God wanted to look you in the eye and let you know where you stand, sonny-boy, wanted you to stare right at me, rather than sitting home in your little bungalow, thinking you're some tough guy and are going to kick our asses for us. Now get out of here, before I have security throw you out."

"But my presentation . . ." Tomczak was crushed. It was hard for him to keep from crying. Three weeks he'd worked on this!

Gerald said, "I have a newborn granddaughter, Lloyd, who could reach into her diaper and smear her ka-ka on the wall, and what she'd smear would be more creative than that piece of shit you just presented. Now, will you see yourself out, or shall I send for security?"

Tomczak gathered his scripts to his chest, kept his head down so that they couldn't see how they'd hurt him. He turned and spun, walked to the door. He stopped before he opened them, and turned, fighting his tears.

"That script is copyrighted, if you use it, I'll own this fucking company, you bastards!" Then he walked out of the door and tried to slam it behind him, but the hidden hydraulics caught it, forced it to close slowly.

All the time that he was pulling on it, Tomczak felt the eyes of the model on his back, watching him. He glared at her as he passed her desk, heard the door to the conference room open behind him. He would have cursed her, would have told her what he thought of her and how she'd gotten her job, but he knew that Gerald was watching them, and Tomczak lost his nerve.

He waited until he was out of the waiting room, in the hall-way and waiting for the elevator, before he let himself break down and cry.

*   *   *

BRACKEN WALKED UP the church steps, past the glassed-in let-terboard that today carried the message: "Come pray for peace with Our Lady of Fifth Avenue." Even as excited as he was, closing in on the kill, Bracken had to smile inside. He could picture her, such a woman, wearing a mink coat with rouged cheeks, bright red lipstick over sharp, nicotine-stained teeth, speaking in a high nasal whine: "So, you want peace? Peace where? Middle East peace is a thousand Hail Marys. World peace is gonna cost you extra, Bubelah."

A bum was lying on the concrete directly in front of the church doors. There was maybe a foot between him and the large double wooden doors that opened onto the church. Bracken, early, stood and watched the action, saw that half the people who entered or left the church banged the door into the wino while the other half stopped and squeezed through, stepping over the man. He appeared to be sleeping. Maybe he was dead.

Sculpted wooden saints looked down at Bracken from pedestals set in alcoves; he could see the scrub marks where custodians had scoured off graffiti. The statues were set back, out of the elements but still outside, all looking alike, basically, even though some had hair and others were bald, some had beards and others were clean-shaven. It was as if they'd been produced on an assembly line; one face and body structure, thinly disguised after construction to give them some sense of verisimilitude.

Bracken was much better at making himself look different.

He wanted a cigarette, badly, but Leehanna didn't smoke and he knew she would smell it on him if he had one now. He'd scrubbed his teeth and gargled twice with Listerine before he'd left his house, and, staying in character, he didn't have any cigarettes on him. She claimed an allergy to cigarette smoke, it was her diplomatic way of excusing herself from the presence of those who still indulged. Still, it would taste good, a nice English Oval right about now. Maybe two or three, and a glass of Scotch, a single malt.

Later. In an hour. Maybe longer, maybe less. And there'd be other things he'd want, tasks for Tawny to perform. Tonight they would celebrate, but first, the matter at hand.

SAFE HARBOR

*   *   *

SHE FOUND HIM sitting in a pew four rows from the back, and she genuflected and slid in next to him, got down on the kneeler and pretended to pray. Bracken knelt down next to her, amused, his face not showing it. He had to fight the urge to reach out and pinch her on the ass.

Around them, maybe twenty people were spending their lunch hour in some sort of worship. Bracken was surprised at how young most of them were; he considered religion to be the superstitious bastion of the guilt-filled old. Some were on their knees, heads bowed in humble prayer, others sat staring at the statue of the dying Jesus on the cross, the life-sized figure hanging above the altar, Christ's face a mask of agony. It was a much better sculpture than the cheapo statues outside, and this one didn't have pigeon shit splattered all over its body.

One young woman was grinning up at the figure, a rapturous, stupid look on her face. Had her prayers been answered? Bracken wondered. Had she gotten her promotion, a nice, fat raise? He had to hide his contempt for them, for these superstitious yuppies. Leehanna might grow skeptical if it showed in his voice or manner.

She was wearing a silk scarf over her hair, large sunglasses, and a lightweight spring suit. There was very little makeup on her face, although he could see plenty of lipstick. She'd carried a jacket in with her, a black thin leather car coat. Leehanna had dressed way down for him today, even better than Bracken had imagined. Then again, she knew better than anyone how much this deception might cost her if it ever was exposed.

"May we go now, please?" Leehanna pleaded in a whisper. Her face was pained, she seemed next to tears. "I feel like such a hypocrite, in here, on my knees."

Bracken rubbed her back. Gently patted her neck. "Let's go," he said, and rose to his feet.

They were in the elevator by twelve-fifteen, Leehanna strangely quiet, maybe ashamed. Subdued and submissive, not like her at all. Bracken played it straight, not wanting to blow the play before they'd gotten into the room, keeping his mouth shut and following her lead; once they were inside, he'd own her.

But he felt the need to be chivalrous, as her fantasy lover might be.

He stopped outside the door and she lagged behind him, as if frightened to enter, Leehanna now trembling, eyes lowered, silent.

"You don't want to do this."

Leehanna shook her head.

Bracken folded her into his arms, rubbed her back, feeling through the thin leather jacket. He felt the back of her bra, patted her gently right under it. Kissed her neck and pulled his head back, and when he spoke, his voice was filled with sympathetic understanding.

"Don't you know you don't have to? I'd wait for you forever. Until you're ready, darling."

"I've never cheated on him before, not in all my years of marriage. I feel—dirty." She still hadn't raised her head; he imagined that she was biting her lower lip.

"Then we wait. I can wait for you."

"No, I don't want to wait."

"Tell me, Leehanna, shall we stay or leave? The choice is yours and yours alone."

"Oh, William, I do love you so . . ." She was kissing him, smashing her teeth into his, leaping up and laying one on him, all of it part of her game. He imagined that she was soaking wet down below, running this scam to disavow herself of any responsibility for what would happen inside. She pulled away from him, tears running down her cheeks, her eyes shining brightly. Leehanna speaking in a husky whisper, Ava Gardner to Clark Gable.

"Open the door, darling, open the door to a new life for both of us."

He could tell that she didn't think much of the room, thought that she and her husband probably had an upstairs balconied suite let by the year, in case they wanted to have parties and not get the marble floors at any of their mansions smudged. Still, she put on a good show, walking around, looking at everything, at the glass glowing in the fireplace, her shyness a thing of the past.

She turned to him, fire in her eyes. Crooked a finger his way. "Come here," Leehanna ordered.

Bracken went to her, slowly, now acting shyly himself. He took her in his arms and lightly touched his lips to hers, just brushed them, licked at them once, then kissed her again, passionately.

"I want you to take me, I want you to take me now!" Leehanna said, and Bracken almost smiled, was tempted to tell her where she was about to be truly taken. Instead, he licked her neck, brought his hands up and wiped at the lick mark, put his gloved hand to her lips. She licked at it and he gently traced her lips with a finger, smudging her lipstick, wiping any of his saliva that might have stuck there off her mouth, her neck.

She reached behind her and undid her zipper, stepped out of the dress and then stepped back, showing him her acrobicized cross-trained body, standing in high heels and nylons held up by a garter belt, wearing only that and a wide bra that had the nipple-coverings cut out of the front. Not too bad, really. What did she have, two teenage kids?

"Come to me, James, come to me *now*."

Bracken slowly began to undress, letting his clothes drop to the floor, enjoying the look in her eyes when he removed his shirt, Leehanna seeing the deceptively strong muscles in his chest and arms for the first time. He tightened them a little, playing with her, as he reached down to take off his shoes, stripped his socks, letting his pants and underwear fall together . . .

She suddenly appeared stricken, then caught it quickly, looked up at his face.

"You're not—ready."

He averted his eyes and acted ashamed. "I'm afraid."

"Oh, darling, don't be. I'll overcome your fears."

She came to him, kissed him, fondled him lightly then harder, feeling lower, to his scrotum, her anxiety growing as he stayed soft down below. She squeezed him too hard and he took in his breath, stepped back.

"Did I hurt you?"

"I'm all right." He paused and smiled weakly. "Would you join me in the shower?"

"The shower?" She was disappointed, then raised her eyebrows and smiled. "Why not?" Leehanna said, then walked past him, reaching for the bra clasp. "But I get to soap you down. We'll see how long it takes me to get you ready, William."

TEN MINUTES LATER, Bracken straightened his tie in the bathroom mirror. His jacket was around his shoulders, draped Continental style. The water was running hot in the shower, and the mirror was beginning to steam. He'd closed the door, so the escaping hot fog would not set off the smoke alarm. He smoothed back his hair, made sure the wig was tightly secured, then nodded to himself, pleased.

Now, he was hard. Erect and eager to find release.

Still, there was work to be done.

Bracken searched the room, in case a credit card had fallen, a button or even a toenail, anything that could tie him to the room. He found nothing. He searched his pockets carefully, until he was sure he had everything with him that he'd left his house with earlier. He was breathing shallowly, excited, wanting release.

But still, he had to see her again, wanted to say goodbye.

Leehanna lay in the tub, hot water pounding down into the open unfocused eyes. The water had washed away the blood that had spurted from her forehead. In the middle of her forehead was an indentation the exact size and shape of the shower pull that was set in the center of the silver water faucet. Bracken had gotten behind her and had thrown her down hard, had smashed her skull into the nozzle, had stepped back and then out of the shower. He'd taken a dry towel, had turned off the water and had wiped her down from head to foot; fingerprints could be extracted from skin, Bracken knew. He then wiped the tub thoroughly, lifting her easily with one powerful, gloved hand. Turned the water back on and left it running in case a single pubic hair had been washed from his body, a single strand of nylon from the expensive wig on his head.

He'd used the hotel-provided blow dryer to dry that wig, the same towel he'd used on Leehanna to wipe the water off his body. Had then used the towel to wipe down the floor. The towel was now in the suitcase, which was closed and ready to go.

Bracken went into the bathroom again and looked down at her, feeling slightly dismal. He'd grabbed her from behind, and she'd never had a chance to look at his hands once he'd removed the gloves. He'd wanted her to see them, he wanted to know what her face looked like when she realized that it had all been a lie. Wanted to know if she was smart enough to figure out that it had been her husband's doing all along, Bracken simply doing his bidding.

And now he'd never know.

There was always something on every job, something that

was lacking. This hadn't been the perfect job, and he'd have to do it again. And again and again, over and over, until he got it perfect, worked it exactly as he'd planned.

Then, he knew, he'd be able to walk away from it all.

Bracken backed out of the bathroom, opened the suitcase and got out the towel. He crawled into the bathroom and wiped the floor again, just in case the soles of his shoes had left an impression in the water that had settled there from the steam. He felt a few drops of it drip onto his back as he worked, falling from where it had gathered, water droplets slowly fattening, on the high ceiling of the bathroom.

Bracken backed out of the bathroom, put the towel back into the suitcase, carefully checked the hallway before stepping out into the hall, and left the Plaza Hotel without anyone ever noticing that he'd even been there in the first place.

TAWNY WALKED THROUGH the main hall of Grand Central Station, in a hurry, not paying any attention to the high stupid ceiling or any of the other things the tourists flocked to this useless homeless shelter to see.

She knew that she had angered her lover and was frightened that she'd lose him. He was the best thing that had ever happened to her, without a doubt, in her life, and now her neurosis, her incredible stupidity, seemed to be putting that relationship into serious jeopardy.

If he asked her to leave, she'd have no choice but to kill herself.

She'd been nothing before finding him, a confused, terrified little animal looking only for someone to love her and making terrible life choices in that search, and what does she do when she finally finds true love? She breaks the rules, rules that she'd been told about up front, and was driving James away from her with her incredible insecurities.

She wouldn't blame him if he kicked her out. Who could love someone like herself? What man like him—with money, a beautiful home, good looks and that incredible urbane manner of his—would want someone like her for long? What could she possibly have to offer? He'd given her the world, and all he'd asked her for was privacy, to accept the few things that he wanted to share with her without question, and to never pry into his business. So what does she do? She begins to pry. As if she didn't already know more than she wanted to know in the first place.

There were other things James wanted, too, but those things were more of a pleasure for Tawny to perform than a task. He was the first man she'd ever met who'd truly treated her as a woman, and even when he was mad at her, he never made fun of her or ridiculed what she was.

And what was *he*, really? An international assassin? With the CIA? Tawny did not know. And it was really none of her business. He treated her well, she wanted for nothing. And she believed, in her heart, that he loved her. Or that he had, at least, until she'd started to become a pest.

It wasn't easy, being Tawny.

She walked out of the station at Lexington, stopped at the corner and looked behind her. She'd taken a cab here, had it drop her off three blocks away, the same as she always did. Then walked through the station, to throw off any tail. They were James's orders and she followed them, no matter how silly she thought them to be.

Now, sure that she hadn't been followed, Tawny turned and walked to the middle of the block, stepped into the post office branch where James kept his lockbox.

James seemed to always understand, had always been there for her, or had been, at least, until Tawny had felt comfortable enough in the relationship to begin feeling jealous, to want to know about things that he didn't want to share. At first though, and for many long months, it had been her belief that he would tell her everything once she proved her loyalty, once he was certain that she wasn't just another whore.

But it had been more than a year now, one of total honesty on Tawny's part, and nothing had much changed. Except for her new belief that James didn't want her anymore, was no longer attracted to her body as he once had been. The new and painful feeling that he didn't love her anymore.

Things had changed just recently, and Tawny was unhappy about those changes, about having to sleep in a downstairs bedroom these past few weeks, about being more of a cook and housekeeper than a lover or a friend. She was no longer sure where she stood with him. Which wasn't really that strange a feeling for Tawny to have; she'd felt that way for as long as she could remember.

But how the hell else was she supposed to have acted when he told her that he had an afternoon date? Wasn't she supposed to be upset? Or maybe it was just his way of keeping her on her toes, making her feel insecure, or, rather, more insecure than she normally felt.

Who could be secure when nature had spent the entirety of your life playing a cruel, mean trick on you? Locking a woman inside the body of a man? She'd always been frail and small, even when she'd been a little boy, always wanted to wear dresses rather than the cowboy clothing that her father had forced her to wear. She'd always hated that slender round flesh that hung from between her thighs, she'd always wanted it gone. It was so ugly, so unnecessary . . .

James understood that, knew how Tawny felt. Had paid for the lip injections and the estrogen implants, paid for everything, really, from the electrolysis that had removed the hairs the estrogen hadn't, and he'd paid for the bleached teeth that gave her such a lovely smile, for the psychological counseling that was supposed to prepare Tawny for the big operation, for the expensive racy underwear he liked for her to wear around the house at night, and he'd paid for the silk, see-through negligees that he insisted she wear to bed. Soon, eleven months from now, he'd see more through those nightgowns than that repulsive penis that now hung there. Tawny stifled a giggle; actually, he'd see less.

Part of the deal was, she had to live as a woman for two solid years. James seemed to understand that and he took it in his stride, but it had enraged Tawny when the doctors had told her about that. She'd been a woman for her entire life, had known she was one since she'd been of the age of reason, so what difference did it make at this stage if she dressed like one for two years? Why couldn't they just do their damned operation and get it over with once and for all?

Too many problems, too many troubles. Too many damn things for her to think about, to worry about. Such as, would he still love her when she was a total woman? Physically as well as mentally? When there was a vagina for him to stick it into instead of Tawny's anus? Oh God, for him, she'd even cancel the operation.

But did he love her anymore? Was James still committed to the relationship?

He'd certainly paid more than lip service to it; they'd even had their own special ceremony, had married themselves in his home. "Till death do us part," he'd told her, thirteen months ago, and she'd taken the same vow, had consecrated it with their blood. He wanted all his needs met, and in return she wanted for nothing. Quite a deal for a woman who was virtually unemployable.

Tawny walked into the large room that held the hundreds of P.O. boxes, dressed as she'd been when James had left the house, the only additions being a rabbit fur jacket and a purse on a long slender strap. She held the purse in front of her, right hand gripping it firmly. Now she reached into the purse and removed James's lockbox key, stopped before his box and began to insert the key into the slot.

Then stopped, cautiously, and looked around. He'd insisted on that, on her checking the vicinity for cops, back when he'd first entrusted her with his weekly mail checks. She thought that it was silly, a little overly dramatic, but he was the boss, and his punishments could be as cruel as Mother Nature's; just his angry silences could hurt Tawny worse than any physical beating.

She'd seen him watching her, three times in the past year, dressed in one of his strange outfits, mingling into the crowd. She believed that she could always pick her man out, even with a mask over his face, but who knew for sure? Maybe he'd watched her five times, ten, and she hadn't seen him, hadn't been able to recognize him, as good as he was at disguising his appearance, God, sometimes, he was frightening. The last thing she wanted to do was alienate him further. This morning, ugh, the way he'd looked at her, the tone of voice he'd used! As if throwing her into the street would be no more difficult for him than having the oil changed in his car. Just the thought of that ever happening made Tawny shiver in fear.

Tawny looked around, at the hustlers checking their mail drops for money orders or cash contributions that had been solicited in magazines and tabloids and alternative newspapers for everything from beauty creams to child pornography, at the people so steeped in urban paranoia that they lived in terror of someone learning their home addresses; at housewives who'd taken P.O. boxes in order to correspond with their secret lovers . . .

Looked and saw two heavyset dark men approaching her, not bothering to hide their amusement. Cops? They were coming directly at her, she'd better decide right away.

Tawny put the key in her mouth and was ready to swallow it, was prepared to choke to death before giving up the anonymity of the man she loved more than life. She wiggled it with her tongue to the back of her throat, was working up saliva when the men stopped, a few feet from her.

"We don't want the key, love-buns, don't scrape up the inside of your neck." The one who spoke was heavier than the other one, although they were both fat, incredibly out of shape. Younger than James, but he'd take them both in seconds. Tawny could see bulges at the sides of the men's belts, covered by their sport coats. Pistols, barely concealed.

The second man said, "Swallowing a key's gonna hurt this gump? You got any idea how many things a lot bigger than that key been inside that long, slender throat? I'd take a shot at him myself, we was in the pen. Gaze into them eyes and think I was with Raquel Welch."

They talked like cops, were sarcastic, caustic, thinking they were witty and superior and not knowing that everyone but themselves and their type would see them as nothing but fools. Tawny glared at them but kept her mouth shut; she knew what might happen if she overreacted.

They'd either lock her up in a men's holding cell where she'd be raped and possibly infected, or they'd run her in and make fun of her, question her for hours and not let her make any phone calls, just to be mean, just to show her who was boss and how little power she had over her own freedom, over her life. Both scenarios had happened to her before, and it was one thing to take such abuse when you were twenty years old and part of a street culture which expected such disrespect from the law, but quite another altogether when you thought of yourself as an urban housewife. She'd keep her mouth shut and see what these men wanted, and odds were that one of them would be back alone, some other Monday, looking for her, wanting her. Cops were so predictable.

"Listen, stuffed crotch," the first one said, "a good friend of ours wants to talk to your boyfriend." Tawny became immediately alert. These weren't cops; dear God, they were mobsters.

"And he don't write no letter or make no phone calls, if you know what I mean, honey." The son of a bitch, he winked at her.

Tawny nodded her head, a thrill of fear, excitement, running through her spine, down into her groin. She could feel that hated excess flesh beginning to stiffen up.

"This afternoon, five o'clock. Mr. P. wants to see him. He'll know where, and if he don't show up, we'll decide to blame you. And then we'll be back." The second one reached out and pushed the front of her jacket aside, just boldly reached into her coat and squeezed her left breast, hard.

"I'll be goddamned. It sure feels real."

Shaking their heads, chuckling, the two men walked away from her. Tawny used shaking fingers to take the key out of her mouth, bowed her head to avoid the giggles and stares and comments of the insensitive boors who were now making fun of her, stealing away what was left of her dignity, robbing her of her self-respect.

Even in her humiliation, she was aware enough to know that it would be the wrong move to check the mailbox now; too many people were looking, too many people were laughing at her. Tawny put the key back in her purse, threw her head back and, holding her head high, walked past them without giving them the satisfaction of even acknowledging their existence.

BUT JAMES SURE wanted to acknowledge hers, that was for sure.

He'd been waiting for her, and he grabbed her just as soon as she walked through the door, James standing there in a silk robe, out of uniform now, himself once again, that cute stubble on his shaved head glistening, slick with sweat. He was so worked up he almost hadn't waited for her to close the silly door that was more of a large razor blade than anything else, grabbed her as she walked in, not noticing her upset or maybe not caring about it, slammed her up against the wall as soon as the door was fully closed, then he was on her, pawing her, ripping her jacket, tearing the button on her jeans . . .

Tawny dropped the purse and held his head to her neck as he sucked on it, closed her eyes and let the pleasure course through her, breathing through her mouth, grateful to be loved.

It took away the fear of the monsters, the men who had tormented her, grabbed at her breast and squeezed it . . .

She felt safe, completely protected, accepted at that moment. James's attention made her forget her humiliation, the shame she'd suffered at the hands of the mobsters at the post office.

Now, later, sharing an English Oval in his bed, Tawny spoke her first complete sentence since she'd walked through the door of the house.

"My God, James, that was in*cred*ible."

"Don't say *was*, Tawny, we're not through yet."

She laughed, a little apprehensively. "I'm so sore, it's been so long."

"Has it?" He cut her with the remark, to the bone.

"Of course it has. You know I'm faithful."

"Maybe."

"James, you have to trust me by now, you must. You must know how I love you."

Suddenly he turned to her, his face showing his rage.

"Don't talk like that." His voice was cold but his eyes were afire, blazing, and Tawny looked at him, trying to figure him out.

"Like *what?* What'd I *do?*"

He was relaxing, slowly, took a deep breath and let it out through his mouth, a weary sigh that only he could know the meaning of. James reached out a hand and patted her absently, took a deep drag off the unfiltered cigarette, leaned over and smashed it out on the ashtray on the nightstand.

"Like a fifties screen siren. I had a little trouble with one not too long ago."

"You had a problem with a fifties screen siren?"

"A bitch who acted like one. Dialogue straight out of a Joan Crawford movie." He shrugged, seeming embarrassed. "It bothered me, that's all. For a second, you sounded just like her."

"I'm sorry."

"Don't be."

"You know I just want to please you."

"You do that, Tawny." The man she loved nodded. "You do that better than anyone has in years and years and years."

"Not better than anyone, ever?" She'd gone too far, playing the coquette. His face darkened, but he didn't get mad, just looked terribly unhappy for a minute, then turned his head away from her.

"No," his voice was firm, strong; he wasn't mad at her.

"There was someone else, once, a long time ago. Someone I loved more than anything."

He was sharing with her. She'd have to be careful, here. Push too hard and he'd clam up and get mad, but still, she wanted to know, needed to know more about this.

"What happened to her?"

"Him. His name was Terri. He's dead now, Tawny. You don't have to worry. Terri's been dead for over fifteen years."

Although she felt elation at hearing that, she kept it out of her tone of voice when she said, "I'm sorry."

"No, you're not." James was half-smiling. "But it was nice of you to pretend you were."

He reached for her, erect again. Where did it come from, this impulsive wanting after weeks of nothing at all? Tawny had no idea, but was not about to question it.

She took him in her arms, but he did not want to be held. She let her head be pushed down onto his chest, Tawny darting out her tongue, quickly, licking at his nipple. She allowed her head to be guided down his body even further, thoughts of Mr. P. and the two insensitive oafs he'd sent now the furthest thing from her mind.

She'd tell him about them later, after he was through with her.

ELMER LEE GRIFFIN was even more confused than usual, and that was saying something to anyone who knew the boy. A child of the streets who'd been abandoned by his mother then taken in by his grandmother after the grandfather who hated him had died when the boy was eight, Elmer had seen his share of grief and suffered more than his share of pain.

They'd put him in a "home" when his mother had abandoned him, back when he'd been just a toddler, and after Grandma had taken him away from that, the boy had never been right in his head, or so everyone in the neighborhood, including his grandmother, said.

Later, when they'd proved him to be violent and incompetent, they'd sent him to different places, institutions, they called them, but Elmer knew that they were really the nuthouse and he hated them worse than almost anything. He'd spent nine of the last twelve years in those places, and his mind these days was made up: he would never go back.

Now he stood in the basement of Grandma's high-rise CHA apartment on Chicago's West Side, a gray, ugly, multi-unit building that looked like every other building for as far as Elmer could see, Elmer holding the pistol-grip shotgun in one large hand, shaking and shivering, crying bitter tears. Grandma had gone back upstairs to her first-floor apartment, screaming, some time back, it seemed like hours to Elmer, and he could see now even through the block glass basement windows that it was getting late in the day, that it would soon be dark. Elmer hated the nighttime, too; there were a great many things that Elmer hated. He especially hated upsetting Grandma though, she was such a sweet and kindly old woman, and Elmer really and truly loved her.

Had the sweet and kindly old woman he loved gone upstairs and called the po-lices? Elmer wondered. He hoped that she hadn't, 'cause then there'd be trouble. And if she didn't call them, then those ambulance people would, trying to take Elmer away, who did they think they were? They'd backed off pretty quick when Elmer had pointed the shotgun at them. They'd definitely call the po-lices, even if Grandma didn't want them to.

He hated them those po-lices, for the way they did him, for the hurtful names that they always called him.

They'd pull their cars to the curb outside and order Elmer and every other black male on the street to line up against the wall, would slam them hard in the head if they didn't. They called it gang sweeps, but Elmer called it bullshit. The special CHA security po-lices were even worse. They walked the area, hands on their pistols, black people not trusting other black people, shouting orders and telling Elmer to do things he didn't understand. Like disperse. What the hell did disperse mean? And how could Elmer do it if he didn't understand it? He'd try to explain and they'd laugh at him, call him names, the same way that the gangbangers did. As far as Elmer was concerned, the only difference between the two groups was that the gangsters were better armed.

But Grandma or the ambulance guys would have called them, and they'd come when they got the time, and Elmer would fight them and maybe hurt one or two before they kicked the shit out of him and locked him up in the nuthouse for the rest of his natural life. They were probably too busy to come and mess with him just yet, out collecting bribe money from the Ma-fi-a or the drug lords. Or maybe they were sending for reinforcements, knowing from experience that Elmer was no slouch.

He considered it an insult if they sent less than three officers to expedite his occasional but violent apprehensions. Because all that one of them would have to do was touch him, and the gentle giant turned into a raving madman, and all the hate came right to the surface. When Elmer got going good, no one man could stop him.

Elmer stood six feet, three inches tall, and weighed 295 pounds. He didn't believe himself to have a mean bone in his entire body, he thought that he had inherited his grandma's innate sweetness. The po-lices, he knew, thought differently, but Elmer knew the truth. The thing of it was, what drove him nuts, was when someone put their hands on him. Yell at him, curse him, talk about his mamma all you wanted, none of that kind of kid-ass shit would ever get a violent response out of Elmer. It would hurt him but he wouldn't show it, would ignore it most of the time. But touch him once, even in friendship, and Elmer would go off on you; it was only the way he was.

Lying on him, too, he struck out blindly when some motherfucker lied on him, said he did something that he knew he didn't do. It wasn't too bad when he was taking his medication but he sometimes forgot to swallow the pills on time, and every time he forgot about them, something bad always happened, someone always lied on him.

Like now, look at him, getting snot all over his favorite T-shirt, with a color picture of the Teenage Mutant Ninja Turtles on the front, and waiting for the po-lices to come and kick his ass for him, haul him away to a nuthouse. But what else could he do? He hadn't taken his pills in a while, and he hadn't taken a shower in a while, and now Grandma said that he had to go away again, said that he'd been out there bothering girls again. Elmer hadn't bothered anyone. He wasn't a raper mans, like they all tried to say. The frustration of being lied on like that made Elmer very angry today. Why did people always pick on him, why did they call him stupid? He simply couldn't stop crying. If he didn't kill himself the po-lices would come and arrest him and everyone would know that he was just a big baby, blubbering and whining, the whole neighborhood would know, and would believe them when they said that he was a rotten raper mans.

Well, to hell with them, with the stupid people and the gang-bangers on the block. They had started the trouble every single time, those big dumb blabbermouths who needed guns to be tough. Maybe when the time came to say goodbye, he'd blow out the block glass window and take a few of those punks with him before he turned the shotgun on himself.

And kill himself he would. He had heard Grandma talking to the ambulance men, going on about his latest involuntary commitment, telling him it was for his own good, and he'd plugged his ears with his fingers and had hummed real loud to make her disappear. He knew what those words meant: involuntary commitment. It meant he'd go into an *institution* again, they could call it a "home" all they wanted; no matter what they called it, an institution, a nuthouse was what it really was. And he'd never forgotten what had happened to him the first time the state had put his ass in a nuthouse.

Sometimes he'd wake up crying and screaming, Elmer in terror at the memory of that place. He'd never told anyone about what had happened, although he'd come close, with his best friend in the whole world, the white man, Mr. Torrence.

Mr. Torrence would not let them put Elmer away; if only he had a way to reach him, Mr. Torrence would make things right, because they couldn't go much more wrong. Involuntary commitment, Elmer's black ass. He'd rather be dead, which is why he'd run out of the apartment and had stolen the shotgun from Mr. Pryor's apartment, from that nice Mr. Pryor, who lived next door to Grandma. Stolen the gun and come down here to the basement to hide from them, but that hadn't worked, they'd found him.

It was a nice little thing, looked something like a toy. Half the size of a regular shotgun and he could hold it against his broad forehead with one large hand. The way he'd shown Grandma and those crazy people ambulance drivers just a little while ago.

"I kill myself before I go to a nuthouse." Elmer had spoken the words while holding the gun up alongside his head, and Grandma had flown up the stairs like a teenager, thinking that Elmer was going to kill her, too.

How could that woman think that, as much as Elmer loved

her? She'd never liked him, though, he believed that to be true. Took him in out of a sense of responsibility, and was putting him away again because she didn't love him, didn't even like him. Grandma had taken him in only because she was maybe just feeling guilty over the junkie ho her only daughter had become as a little girl. Grandpa had set Elmer straight right quick as to what those words meant before the old man had died; they were the words he had used to describe his daughter, the way he had always referred to Elmer's mother.

Elmer thought of Grandpa now as he stormed and raged throughout the basement, kicking the walls, striking out at things with the shotgun barrel, Elmer waiting for the po-lices to come, waiting for the battle to commence. Elmer in a filthy stinking basement that had gang graffiti everywhere. He had to be careful where he walked, there was human poo-poo everywhere, in piles.

Skinny old man, his grandpa was, always calling everything *shit*. "Go get me my shit," he'd tell Elmer when the boy was visiting, and Elmer never knew just what to fetch the man, and when he asked in terror the old man would call him stupid. He, too, liked to accuse Elmer of doing things that the boy hadn't done.

"You been out clutchin' them puthies agin?" Grandpa would demand, when one of the liar girls on the block had accused young Elmer of molesting her. He never clutched any pussies. Elmer hated to touch human beings almost as much as he hated them touching him. Those people were always lying on him, and everyone always believed them.

He made himself stop thinking about the old man, things were bad enough. He had to think about other things, about a way to get out of this mess he was in. But it hurt him to think, it always made his head ache. Still, there was no way out before the po-lices came and killed his ass.

There was a wall phone that the gangbangers had mounted on one of the three wooden posts that held up the stairs that led to the first floor, to the hallway of the building, and Elmer stood before it, wishing he had Mr. Torrence's number. Mr. Torrence would know what to do, would find a way out of this for Elmer so he wouldn't have to go to the nuthouse. As things stood, Elmer was only waiting for the sounds of sirens to smash the night's silence.

When he heard that sound, he was planning to blow his head off.

Elmer walked over to the wooden stairway and looked up at the door at the top of the stairs. A ring of light glowed around the door's edges, and it frightened Elmer to be down here in the dark. But the light switch was up there, right next to the door, and there was no way Elmer was going up there, not with the chance that there were po-lices hiding right behind the door, waiting to pounce on his big black ass, the same way they always did when they came to haul him away.

Elmer put his back against the wall and slid down slowly to the cold gray concrete floor, holding the shotgun between his legs. He was in anguish, shock, and he couldn't stop shaking, cowering there on the floor in Grandma's basement, wondering how everything could have gone so bad in his short and miserable life.

He was slow in his head, he was aware of that, and wasn't too ashamed of it, he thought that it was normal. He was a man now, though, at least in the eyes of the law. He was eighteen now, and even though he couldn't read or write, he was old enough to go to the penitentiary, at least.

Or another one of those adult "homes" that were really institutions, where they shot you up with Thorazine and you wandered the halls all day or watched soap operas in the day room with the other drugged-out zombies.

Slow and fat, everyone used to think, not understanding back then that Elmer had a lot of muscle under all the blubber. They looked at him as the big fat dummy who needed medication to stay sane. Well, he knew that he wasn't insane, it was just that they didn't understand what had happened to him. And after *that*, after what they'd done in the first juvenile mental "home" they'd sent him to, and later, after what had happened in the institutions, he'd come back to the neighborhood and everyone had been making fun of him ever since, even when he kicked their asses for them and made them eat dirt.

Elmer lifted up his shirt and looked at the three star-shaped scars on his rubber, bouncing belly. Bullet wounds; Elmer had been shot and still hadn't quit, hadn't stopped fighting until he'd passed out from lack of blood. You'd think that would have earned him some respect, you surely would but it hadn't. They would still taunt him, drive by in their fancy pimp type cars and call him names out their windows then drive away real fast, their laughter ringing in Elmer's ears, Elmer trying to ignore it. Passersby would yell things at him on the street if they were far enough away where they knew he couldn't catch them. Even the little girls, doing double-dutch rope jumping, would laugh at him behind his back, snicker at him as he passed their concrete playgrounds.

Elmer's fat was the sort that fists bounce off of without doing any damage, and his physical strength was tremendous. He never cursed anybody and he never started a fight, so why did they always make fun of him, why did they have to hate him? And why oh why did all the women say all the time that Elmer had clutched at their pussies?

His usual mental state was one of confusion and hurt, even on good days, and he spent a lot of his time wondering why he never fit in. He never meant to hurt anyone, never meant any harm. On bad days, man, forget about it. It was all he could do to keep from killing someone on bad days, and nobody ever appreciated the restraint that Elmer showed at such a time.

"Elmer, you okay down there, buddy?"

The soft male voice of a white man made Elmer jump in fear, and he leaned back further against the cold gray wall, trying to force himself through it, wanting, trying to become invisible. The light switch was flipped and the bulb above Elmer's head flicked on, and without thinking about it he grabbed the shotgun and placed the butt against the floor and his forehead against the barrel. Hunched down over it, Elmer put his thumb on the trigger. When he spoke his voice was cracking with terror, but still, it carried conviction.

"OK, that's it. Party's over. You come down here and I kills myself," Elmer said, meaning it. His shaking thumb was banging back and forth between the trigger and the guard and Elmer eased it off a little bit, held it against the guard and tried to control the shaking.

"I'm not coming down, Elmer, relax, buddy, just try to take it easy."

Elmer slowly, carefully turned his head so that the barrel was now at his temple, Elmer sniffing at the tears that were running down his cheeks, straining his eyes to try and see who was at the top of the steps, Elmer seeing a tall white man in a suit with a badge hanging off of the front of his belt. Good-looking guy, for a white man, with short blond hair. The man didn't look mad or even mean, and he wasn't pointing his gun at Elmer, although Elmer could see his holster, hanging off his belt on the left side of his waist.

"You the po-lice."

"Yeah, my name is Eddie, and you're right, Elmer, I'm a cop, but I'm on your side, Elmer, I really am. Why don't you call me Eddie, OK? And I'll call you Elmer." The blond po-lice, Mr. Eddie, held his hands out at his sides, palms toward Elmer so he could see he wasn't holding a weapon. Slowly, he opened his coat, held it away from his side, like batwings. He wasn't packing; the brown leather holster hanging off his pants was empty.

"I want to talk to you, Elmer. I want to be your friend." The man took a step down, and Elmer saw his game and decided to stop him in his tracks.

"You take another step, we gonna get pretty friendly. I gonna blow my brains all onto your fancy suit, Mr. Eddie, I swears it."

He watched as Mr. Eddie took a backward step up, and stood at the top of the stairs.

"Don't do that, Elmer. Don't do that, and don't shoot me. I've got a wife and two kids at home who'd really, really miss me."

"Ain't nobody gonna die this evenin' but me, Mr. Eddie, I swears. I is the only dumb motherfucker gonna die in this basement this evenin'."

"You're not dumb, Elmer. You're pretty smart, aren't you? You've got forty or fifty cops standing outside, waiting to see what you want to do, I wouldn't call that dumb. You've got an entire gang outside on the sidewalk, afraid to come down and deal with you. Name me one other man can scare a gang like that? And what makes you think that you have to die? You don't have to die, Elmer. I can fix things for you, if you'll work with me on it." Mr. Eddie smiled at him, like the two of them were insiders.

"Nobody wants you to die, Elmer, in fact, we all want you to live. We want to work this thing out with you." Mr. Eddie smiled again.

"Listen, today's my day off, buddy. I got called in because I'm trained for this work and it's my area, I work nearby, my office is in the headquarters building, over at Eleventh and State. They called me in on my day off just to come and talk to you. What does that tell you? Doesn't that tell you that nobody wants you hurt? Nobody wants you to die, Elmer. The police department's paying me overtime just to come here today and talk to you."

Mr. Eddie stopped talking, and it looked like he wanted Elmer to say something, but Elmer couldn't think of anything to say to him, his mind was racing too fast as it was, his head was beginning to ache.

Mr. Eddie said, "The other cops out there, when I decided to come down here? Man, they went *berserk.* I'm not supposed to be doing this, Elmer; I'm never supposed to come into contact with a man with a gun if I can help it."

"So you is in trouble, too?"

"Maybe big trouble, I could even get kicked off the negotiating team."

"I kills myself, what happens to you?"

"Oh, man, don't even say it. You do that and I'm off the team for good. My boss, he's a good guy, but he's one of those bosses who goes strictly by the book, you know what I mean? Everything has to be according to the rules, or he goes cra—gets mad at me."

"I think I in some trouble, too, Mr. Eddie."

Hearing about Mr. Eddie's problems with his boss had calmed Elmer down a little. At least he wasn't crying like a big baby anymore.

He said, "Cecille call me a raper mans, everyone always say I a raper mans and I isn't." Bitter, angry tears now began to flow again, streaming heavily down Elmer's cheeks, and he turned his forehead back to the barrel so that Mr. Eddie wouldn't see him whining like a baby.

"I won't let them put you in jail, Elmer, if that's what you're worried about. Not even if you did something wrong. Jail's for bad guys, and you're not a bad guy. All you need is a little help. I want to get you that help, Elmer, I *promise* to get you that help. We all know how people sometimes lie just to get somebody else in trouble. That's what it looks like here, as far as I can see. Let me look into it. I'll need your help. You and I'll sit down and get to the bottom of this, and we can take all the time we want. All you have to do is give me the weapon and I promise you you'll be safe."

Elmer wanted to believe him. It was hard *not* to believe him, the way the man talking, so slow and casual, so calm and relaxed.

But still, Elmer knew what would happen to him if he gave Mr. Eddie the gun.

"I can't do that, Mr. Eddie, uh-uh. I can't go back to no nuthouse."

"That's fine, that's all right. You won't have to go anywhere, Elmer. You and I, we can talk, and we've got time. Just don't shoot anybody."

Elmer said softly, "I ain't *gonna* shoot nobodies, I only gonna kills *me*." Elmer again moved his head back and stared down into the barrel of the shotgun, his eyes crossed, squinting, trying to see the shell.

"Can you get me Mr. Torrence's number, so I can call him up on the phone? He the only mans I ever met can make me feel good when I get de-pressed. Can you get me his number? I ain't got it with me."

Mr. Eddie said, "Mr. Torrence?" and Elmer heard another voice speak from behind his friend Mr. Eddie, a gruffer, tough-guy voice. The regular po-lices, the ones who would kick his ass and take him away as soon as Mr. Nice Man Eddie came down and got the gun out of Elmer's hands. He couldn't hear what the other man was saying, but he could tell from the tone of voice that it wasn't something nice.

Mr. Eddie said, "Get back, goddamnit," hissed it at the other man like he was real mad, then said to Elmer: "Mr. Torrence is a friend of yours?"

"He my *coun*selor." Dumb white man, don't even know who Mr. Torrence is. "He talk to me over to the youth center on Wabash every day. Sometimes I even work for him, Mr. Torrence gives me jobs to do."

"Youth center?" Mr. Eddie smiled. "*I'm* a youth officer, too, Elmer, that's my regular job. And I want to be your friend. Tell you what I'll do, Elmer. You promise not to kill yourself while I'm gone, and I'll go and get his number for you, and you can give him a call. What do you say, Elmer?"

Elmer turned his head again and watched Mr. Eddie back into the door, watched him push it with his backside and saw it open wide. As Mr. Eddie backed through the door, still half-smiling at Elmer, Elmer saw a whole bunch of other po-lices in blue uniforms behind him, these men all wearing heavy blue vests and helmets that had masks attached to them, the men all looking down into the basement, holding all sorts of weapons. Before he closed the door, Mr. Eddie smiled down at Elmer and spoke to him as if they were good buddies.

"You promise me, now, Elmer, right?"

Elmer said, "Where you a youth officer at, Mr. Eddie? Not over to Area One; I be knowing them over there up until I turned sixteen."

"I'm at One, but only since January."

"You young to be a youth officer. I know that shit. Usually it a payoff for being in tight with some politician, ain't that right."

"Not all the time, Elmer. Sometimes, ability counts for something, even in the police department. Now, you have to promise me you won't hurt yourself if I go and get you Mr. Torrence's number, all right? Do you promise me, Elmer, do you give me your word?"

"I promises you. And could you leave the light on, please, Mr. Eddie? I hate the dark, I really do."

"MR. P."

He was lying on his back, with his hands behind his head, an empty champagne glass standing on his chest, James drawling the words, almost with bemusement. There was a cigarette hanging from the corner of his mouth, and he was playing with the ash, letting it burn long and then blowing it off the tip, trying to get it into the glass. His chest and the bed sheets were covered with ash stains. She'd have to change the sheets as soon as they got out of bed.

It seemed to Tawny that she couldn't do anything to upset him this afternoon, all of a sudden things between them were once again the way they used to be, and she was elated, in her glory over that fact. She'd told him about the visit at the post office, what had happened that afternoon, and the only thing he'd really been upset about was the way the men had treated her; he wanted to know her feelings, how much pain their ignorance and insensitivity had caused her. Her sweetie looking at her with loving eyes, concerned about her emotional state.

Now, though, he wasn't so solicitous. He'd said the name a half a dozen times, James appearing pensive.

"Mr. fuckin' P." Spoken thoughtfully, this time, with respect. "Day late and a dollar short."

"From what?"

"You don't want to know."

"Are you going to go? It's almost four, now."

"I can't not go. He'd see it as an insult, and he's not the type of man you want to insult unless there's no other way around it. But he's in for a disappointment."

"Don't do or say anything to those two men of his, please. They'll hold it against me, they'll come and get me when you're not around."

"They will never, ever bother you again."

"How can you be so sure?"

"By tomorrow at this time, you'll be the last person alive they'll ever want to see again. They'll be told how it is this afternoon, reasoned with. They'll have to understand that it's an eye for an eye."

"James, please, just let it go. You don't have to do that for me."

James laughed lightly, as if bemused by her misunderstanding of his words.

"I'm not doing it for you, Tawny, I'm doing it for me. If guys like that think that they can ever get away with disrespecting you, even once, then it only goes downhill from there. Until the time comes—and it *will* come—when they start laughing at you when you walk in the door, making fun of you to your face. And if you kill one of them, it gets to be more trouble than it's worth. Even though none of them could ever find me, where I live, I'd have a lot of trouble working in New York again if I ever murdered one of those greaseball slobs. So I have to straighten it out right now, before it gets to that point."

"*Kill* one of them, what are you talking about!"

He looked at her, as if just now noticing that she was there. He'd said too much, she could see it in his face, he was upset because, thinking aloud, he'd given away too much of himself. Still, he didn't do anything, just put the glass on the nightstand and rolled out of bed, told her to get cleaned up and get dressed while he was gone, they were going out this evening for a big night on the town.

TUESDAY MORNING, AFTER Leehanna's death was splashed all over the airwaves and the newspapers, a money transfer would take place, and Bracken's Bahamian account would have added to it a half million dollars, cash. He kept all his money where he could get at it; in the event of his death, it would all rot without anyone ever having spent it.

There were those he knew—and the mobsters were the best at this—who put their money in the hands of friends, who trusted them to watch over it and give it to them when they needed it. Then they'd go to prison, and things would suddenly change. The people who had been entrusted began to look for someone to kill them in a jailhouse riot, so that they could keep all the money for themselves. Bracken would never be that stupid. Bracken didn't trust anyone. Sometimes he didn't even trust himself, his instincts.

Leehanna was the first job he'd done in a year, although he'd checked out more than a few. Dropped them for one reason or another, sometimes simply because he disliked the person who had wanted the work performed. This was the first job he'd done since he'd had Tawny with him, and he didn't understand how the dagos had found out about him. And, more important, why were they at his P.O. box in the first place?

Pete Papa was a heavyweight, the most powerful man in New York. He was not a man to disrespect, you had no choice but to show up when he called you. Bracken would go, and would tell the man that he couldn't do his job for him, would find a way to straighten it out without a problem, and then he'd have a talk with the two who'd bothered Tawny.

What Tawny didn't understand was that they'd been disrespecting Bracken, not him. He wasn't even a part of it; if it hadn't been Tawny, they'd have found another way to do it. The two of them more than likely were only angry because the boss had called Bracken in instead of letting them take care of whatever the problem was all by themselves. Some of these guys would take issue with that; they wanted to enhance their rep, or sometimes it was just the extra money that they craved. Seeing all that cash go into a stranger's pocket would be difficult for them to tolerate.

Bracken didn't come cheap. And it didn't matter one whit to him that a couple of fatass guineas had made fun of his boyfriend. What they thought of him didn't matter. The only thing that mattered was the illusion they had thrown out into the world, their misguided belief that he was someone they could play around with. Which was why he'd go without any of his sharp-edged weapons, he had to do this one on one, or one on two, if they preferred.

He took a quick shower and spent a minute looking at his wardrobe, picked out just the right outfit. For this meeting, he'd need some makeup, would want to change his appearance even more radically than usual. Bracken didn't want to just blend in with the crowd this time, he wanted to be a part of the furniture. Even at this time of day he was no more than ten minutes away by cab from where the meeting was to be held, it would take another five minutes for him to make his way to the candy shop after having the cab drop him off several blocks away. It gave him time to prepare.

EDDIE DOLAN WAS arguing viciously with the ERT guys. With their sergeant in particular, a fat son of a bitch named Lawlor. Around them, in the hallway, the rest of the Emergency Response Team unit stood ready for action, impatient, wanting to prove their effectiveness. Raring for action, these men were, looking forward to charging the basement.

Dolan's group leader, Sergeant Wilson, was standing in a corner of the hallway near the front door, calmly talking to Elmer's grandma, trying to elicit information they could use in their discussion with Elmer. Poor little old woman with her gray hair pulled back tightly, in a bun that was held in place in back by a blue rubber band. She was worrying some prayer beads, twisting them around in her hands.

The door to her apartment was to their left, and pushed wide open. There were spray paint markings on the door, declaring the property and the people inside to be under the protection of some voodoo religious sect. A feather was thumbtacked to the door, directly in the center, above the religious symbol.

Eddie could hear black male voices coming out of the woman's apartment every so often, affirming information that the woman was giving the sergeant.

There was supposed to be another barricade and hostage unit member here to relay whatever information the sergeant got from Wilson to Dolan, but she hadn't shown up, maybe she had her beeper off. Wilson was pissed at Dolan, Dolan could tell. He'd broken a major rule of barricade negotiation; he'd gone unarmed into the lion's den.

The hallway was small, filthy, in contrast to Mrs. Griffin's apartment, which was tiny but compulsively clean, with plastic slipcovers over living room furniture that was faded now, but had at one time been white. Dolan could see a glimmer of light from her apartment from where he stood in the middle of the hall, arguing with the lardass sergeant. Arguing in a low, intense voice so that Elmer wouldn't hear them and do something he wouldn't live long enough to regret.

Outside, there was, for the moment at least, controlled chaos. Children were dancing in front of the tripod-mounted TV cameras, throwing down their gang signs at the reporters. A holiday atmosphere had filled the night, people without hope suddenly getting their share of attention. There were dozens of uniformed police officers out there, manning the wooden barricades. Keeping the gangbangers out of the building. It was the police presence that had drawn the reporters, as the reporters had drawn the fun-seeking crowds from the other ghetto buildings. The same reporters who would be angry because they hadn't been told anything, who were now speculating live, on the air, as to what was going on inside the roped-off building.

Outside the building, snipers and other ERT units, up to fifty armed officers, would be lined up against the basement walls and in other strategic, secured spots around the immediate area, checking out the windows, their weapons aimed at them, at any of the building's doors, in case Elmer somehow got by the unit in the hallway and tried to effect an escape. The SWAT guys didn't leave a whole lot to chance. They would be into position with their rifles, ready to act if needed. But in here, it was down to just Dolan and Lawlor. Dolan the chief negotiator this time around, Lawlor the ERT chief.

Dolan said, "We have two more negotiators coming to the scene, and I've already established a strong rapport with Elmer. Shit, Sarge, you and I aren't even supposed to be talking! The liaison man will be here soon, and he'll coordinate things between us, all right? But until then, there's no sense in our getting into each other's asses. So let's just calm down and take a rational look at the situation."

He could tell that his logic wasn't getting through to the sergeant. The man was standing there squinting at Eddie as if he were an annoyance, an insect about to be slapped away. Eddie jumped into the silence, forcing himself to speak slowly and clearly so this bastard wouldn't know that he was scared out of his wits.

"Elmer believes what I say and he trusts me. We can sit here all night and talk to him, for a day, even two days if we have to, until he falls asleep or hunger drives him out. He doesn't have any hostages, and he's no threat to the neighborhood. The basement windows are made of glass block, and the shotgun pellets would more than likely just bounce off them if he shot at it. Besides, we've got the neighbors out of the first-floor apartments, just in case. The stairwells and elevators are ours. The situation is under control, and directives state that as long as that's the case, we use as much caution as the negotiator sees fit before we take any direct action. Our primary job is to save lives, in this case, Elmer's. He needs help."

"Oh, Christ," Lawlor said. "And it's racism made him do this, and it's poverty, and it's social injustice." Lawlor wasn't holding his voice down, and Dolan's face was pained. He wanted to shush him before the grandmother heard what he was saying, but it would look bad, would get as big a laugh out of the other ERT cops as Lawlor had just gotten with his take on Elmer's social situation.

"You had no business going on down there, Blondie. You want to talk about the regulations, you've busted a shitload already on this deal."

"The man's mentally ill, he's got a history, Sergeant. I needed to see if he was stable, or if we maybe should try and take him."

"You make those decisions here, do you?"

What was with this guy? Eddie had worked with many ERT units in the past, and he'd never come across a cowboy like this before. The man was sneering at him now, smiling openly as he spoke.

"His being crazy is all the more reason for you to step aside, Blondie. A nutcase like that might mistake a good-looking sucker like you for some white girlfriend rejected him sometime in his sordid past, shoot you on sight when you open that door again."

Chuckle chuckle chuckle. The rest of the ERT guys were eating this up. Standing around looking like Robocops, with their weapons at the ready and their helmet shields down in case

Elmer made a banzai suicide charge up the stairs. Dolan wished that the liaison sergeant and the rest of the hostage negotiating team was there for moral support, wished that his sergeant wasn't working so diligently trying to get the old lady out of the stairwell and back into her apartment; she was now arguing with Wilson loudly, telling him she wouldn't be taken away from her own grandson while the ERT guys ignored her and let Wilson handle her by himself. She wasn't their job. Their job, as far as Dolan could see, was killing Elmer.

Lawlor said, "Look, Blondie, we let you go down there against our better judgment, because you said you were going to and there wasn't much we could do to stop you. We ain't here to shoot other cops, but you know as well as I do that there was no call for it, and it's against the regulations and everyone here knows that, too. You want to play hero, pal, do it over at the Youth Division. This is our call now, and I say we're going down."

Dolan smiled at him, at the big fat asshole with the oversized Navy bulletproof vest that made him look like a baseball umpire, his shield pushed up on his helmet so that he could talk to Dolan. The guy was cute, throwing out lines he could repeat later in some bar when he had an audience. Forgetting that he was dealing with a man who knew some psychology and who knew how to channel his anger.

For instance, if he had something to say to the man that would make him feel challenged, it couldn't be said in front of his command, or else Lawlor would feel the need to respond negatively, if only to prove to his men that he was the reincarnation of Randolph Scott.

"Sarge?" Dolan said, and slowly backed away toward the entrance door, where the grandmother and the sergeant were deep in lively conversation. "Would you step over here a minute, please?" Dolan was smiling widely and using his best ass-kissing tone.

He backed completely to the doorway, out of the range of hearing of the ERT members, past Wilson, who saw what he was doing and stopped talking to the old woman—thank Christ—and looked at Dolan, curiously. Lawlor was swaggering toward them, as if he knew what Dolan was trying to pull and was man enough to handle it without any help from his crew. The grandmother had moved closer to the sergeant and had now fallen silent, wanting in on it, wanting to know what the secret plan was that they were devising for her grandson. Good. Dolan had planned on having a pair of biased ears right there, to hear his comments for the record so he could win without getting into a fistfight with this idiot.

When they were right at the front door Dolan dropped his ingratiating smile and stepped up close to Lawlor, nonthreatening but in a way that showed that he was Lawlor's equal in size. And in far better physical condition. Inside the apartment, two other family members, older black men, were watching them timidly, but intently. Outstanding.

Dolan said, "Lawlor, the kid's got a shotgun, and he's all alone down there. I've been down there without forty pounds of weapons hanging off me, and I judge him to be unstable but harmless to anyone but himself. He's made statements to the fact that no one else will get hurt tonight." Grandma's eyes were large and she wasn't missing a word.

Dolan said, "Now, we both know that we're supposed to coordinate on this and work together, but what it comes down to is: I'm in charge. Until the liaison officer responds to his fucking beep. Me and Sergeant Wilson. And I'm saying you don't go down there blasting unless or until we tell you to." Dolan was in darkness, standing in a tiny foyer, his back to the closed front door. The Mars lights from idling squads flashed through the small window of the door, casting blue and red shadows over Sergeant Lawlor's face. Even in the dark, Dolan could see that Lawlor's face was flushing.

Dolan said, "This isn't some fucking TV show, and you ain't John Wayne. And if you charge down there and that boy shoots himself, I swear to God, fellow cop or not, I'll testify as to what I've said to you in front of a jury in a court of law. And see to it that you can't even get a job supervising janitors for the Chicago School District."

"They wanna kill ma boy?" Elmer's grandmother said. There were low angry murmurs from the men standing at the door, just inside the old woman's apartment.

Dolan stared into Lawlor's eyes and smiled, letting him know that he'd talked him into a trap. He turned to Mrs. Griffin and dropped the smile, looked at her with all the compassion he could muster.

"Nobody's gonna kill anyone, ma'am," Dolan said to the

woman. "We're just getting the ground rules straight, aren't we, Sergeant Lawlor?"

Lawlor was staring hatred at Dolan, and decided not to answer.

"I need to use your phone, ma'am, if you don't mind?" Dolan took his eyes off Lawlor for the first time since they left the basement doorway, left him standing there with Sergeant Wilson, who would try to calm him down.

He was walking into the apartment, heading toward the telephone, before he stopped and turned and called Lawlor's name and Lawlor stared at him, one hand gently masturbating his M-16. It chilled Dolan, but he didn't let it show.

"My name's Dolan, Sergeant Lawlor. Detective Edward Dolan. Not Blondie. And when you're over on that end of the hallway with your goods, and that basement door is open, you keep your goddamned mouth shut. I won't take my eyes off that boy and risk getting shot because you want to know what's happening down there." He turned away without another word and smiled at the two older black men.

"OK to use the phone?" Grandma's voice answered him, right behind him and loud.

"You can just wait a minute before you use any damn phone. I want to call my lawyer and get him over here with a Camcorder, in case that motherfucker over there go down and shoot ma boy." The woman spoke and Dolan smiled, but did not turn to Lawlor. He would have heard the woman, and besides, Dolan had made his point well enough, there was no sense in rubbing it in any more than he already had.

BRACKEN DIDN'T SEE the feds, but he knew that they were there. Papa had beaten a couple of big federal cases in the past couple of years, and they didn't much care for that sort of impertinence, looked down on it, in fact, and were capable of seeking revenge.

He tried to spot them, walking toward the candy store, letting his eyes roam the street casually, Bracken hunched over, walking with a cane, another old man on a street filled with older people. He wore a dirty old fedora pulled down low over his face, a baggy suit that had been padded, the suit adding an easy thirty pounds to his appearance. He shuffled along slowly, eyes darting up, trying to catch them at their game.

Bracken looking for customized vans, ComEd trucks, Bell workers, even construction workers tearing up the street. He looked up at what used to be tenements, apartments that were now being renovated and turned into condominiums, what had once been slums would soon be turned into prime real estate. It amused him, the thought of it getting trendy down here, on the west side of Broadway.

Up there, in one of those places, that's where they'd be, he decided. They'd have talked some Republican junior crime-busting contractor into letting them use one of the apartments under construction, would have told him that he was performing a valuable service to his country. He wouldn't give them anything, all they'd get on their stupid film was what he wanted them to see.

Murder, RICO, conspiracy, extortion, how many charges had Papa beaten in his life before a jury of his peers? There'd been two or three more big ones in the last five years, cases that had been highly publicized. Bracken had known Papa since he'd been a little kid, and in all that time Papa had only gone away to the pen one time, had served three years of a nine-year rap, Papa down in the pen on the word of a stoolpigeon, copping a plea just as the jury was about to decide his fate in a windowless room. The evidence against Papa had been overwhelming, and the stoolie's testimony had been crucial, damning.

Bracken couldn't think about that too long, or he'd go mad. The man that had put Papa away had been responsible for the death of the only man that Bracken had ever really loved, and he'd already been dwelling on Terri's death too much already today. Terri, with his perfect yellow hair, his straight white teeth. The all-American boy who'd loved James Bracken more than he'd loved his own life.

He'd been Torelli's rap partner on a big uptown score, and when it became apparent that Torelli had started singing, Bracken had been forced to kill his lover.

Terri, dying, had looked up at him and had asked him why.

How many reasons could he have given the boy? If they'd had time, he would have enumerated some. Because Torelli's testimony would put his lover in prison. Because Terri was too cute, too young, too fragile to ever do time. He would have had to turn punk or turn informer, and either resolution was unacceptable to Bracken.

He shuffled into the entrance of the candy store and stopped, his back to the street, Bracken's head down, his cane held in front of him, in both hands, patiently waiting to be asked inside. The door had been open this calm April afternoon, and Bracken didn't have to bother to even clear his throat, his shadow had alerted the old men inside. They ushered him in, and Bracken waited at the card table, calmly, still with his back to the door, being carefully watched by one of the old men while the other went to summon his master.

Bracken made sure that he kept his back turned. They'd have video on him now, the feds would, he knew they were out there and he knew they were pros, would have filmed him coming down the sidewalk, heading into the store. They would want to know who this old guy was, how he fit into the conspiracy, how they could use him to their own greatest good. Bracken knew that they could take raw videotape and do funny things with it, run it through a computer and strip Bracken of his mask. These guys weren't worth it, he wouldn't allow himself to be placed under surveillance for simply speaking to a wiseguy and telling him that he wouldn't work for him.

The old man came through the door from the back and nodded, and Bracken walked past him, the old man staring at him blankly until Bracken passed through the doorway. Into the smoky back room, past booths filled with men drinking wine, eyeing him. Past filled card tables, no one in the room speaking, all of them with their eyes on him, trying to make him, trying to remember him from other times that he'd been there. The kids that worked there were making themselves busy elsewhere, not wanting to see him, not wanting to have Bracken look their way, showing more intelligence than the testosterone loaded fools at the tables, staring at him.

It filled Bracken's heart with joy, the fact that they all feared him.

Pete Papa came out of his private office and made a move to hug him before he remembered who Bracken was. When he did, he just held Bracken by the shoulders, then let his hands run down to the middle of Bracken's arms, the old man nodding gravely as he studied him.

"Who the hell is this, it looks like my father come in here to see me!" On cue, the men in the room laughed, but not too loudly.

There was something wrong here, Bracken could smell it in the air. The old man was putting on some kind of a front, but through his biceps, where the old man held him, Bracken could feel that the man was shaking. Papa was scared. Something had him terrified. And the men in this room were no dummies, they'd smell his fear the way a dog would. Papa slapped him on both arms, pointed with a thumb to his private office.

"Come inna back, I got something to talk to you about." He turned without waiting for a response, hollered over his shoulder, "Ey, Alfie, bring us some coffee back here." He went into his office and Bracken followed him.

Bracken waited silently, patiently, until the coffee was served, and then he didn't accept any, sat back and watched Papa stir his. The fat man blowing on it while Bracken relaxed his body, his face.

Papa did not look good, the years had not been kind. There were deep lines on his face these days, etchings of a brutal past marking him, making him ugly. His thin hair was now all gray, and combed straight back, held down with some kind of gunk. He breathed in great gasps, wheezing with each breath, his large belly jiggling as he coughed, and he coughed often.

Death was close, but the old man was sly. He would have a few tricks left. Papa's only fear would be dying behind the walls of a federal penitentiary.

Pete Papa was playing the game, going through the motions now for Bracken's sake, but he was terribly upset, his fingers trembling, eyes darting.

Bracken sat straighter in the chair, stretched out his legs, took off the hat, placed it across his knee, Bracken looking around, at a room that hadn't changed one bit in thirty years.

There was the leather-topped desk, Papa's pride and joy. There was no phone on that desk, not one shred of paper. Pete Papa would leave no paper trails that could be used against him later. Could he even read and write? Bracken had no evidence either way. The room was the size of the outside candy shop itself, the walls thick. Instead of insulation, there were bricks between this drywall and that of the outer room. Bracken suspected that there was a sheet of steel there now, too, so that even state-of-the-art long-range listening devices couldn't hear what was being discussed inside.

There was only one chair facing Pete Papa's desk. He never spoke business to more than one man at a time, there would be no corroborating evidence ever used against him in a court of law. The chair was comfortable, deep, old, polished and shining leather.

Pete Papa was watching him, the old man's eyes widening, watching the chameleon shed his skin. "Christ, that's scary," Pete Papa said.

"Pete." Bracken spoke for the first time. The don raised his eyebrows.

"Two of your men disrespected me today." Papa's eyes narrowed, it was the only sign of his displeasure. "That's inappropriate, Pete, they never should have done that."

Pete Papa sighed. "They don't know no better, these kids I got now. They don't know you from the old days. All they know is stories, shit they talk among themselves, blow things all out of proportion, and they want to test themselves, like little kids."

Papa said, "They come in here, with their mouths, talking worse than the niggers, bragging all the time. 'I kicked this one's ass, I killed that motherfucker, I tortured this son of a bitch on a meat hook for fourteen hours.' I look at 'em, it's like they was raised in the jungle. I try to tell them, 'the people who need to know, they know what you did. The people who *don't* need to know, you don't *want* them knowing anything. Shut your mouth,' I tell them, but they don't understand how it is, Jimmy. How it has to be to get ahead in this business, how hard it is to get there."

Pete Papa became solicitous, looked at Bracken with grave concern.

"You still calling yourself Jimmy, right? I ain't talking out of turn here calling you by a name you ain't using no more, am I?"

Bracken shook his head and made a gesture with his hand. It was a mark of respect that Papa had even asked. He would not point out to him that nobody ever called him Jimmy.

"You know what the boys call you, some of them out there?"

"What's that, Pete?"

"The Sandman, on account of when you come calling, people go to sleep."

Bracken didn't answer, just nodded his head; he kind of liked the nickname.

Papa said, "They see movies, some tough guy actor is making billions of dollars two days after getting off a banana boat from somewhere, they watch the fucking movies and they want to be like him. They don't remember the end of the movie, where the faggot actor gets shot for about an hour with Uzis and AKs and M-16s. They don't think that shit can ever happen to them. The difference is, the actor gets up and walks away after the scene is filmed." He pronounced it, "fill-um," Papa having trouble understanding anything more complicated than radio mysteries.

Pete Papa shrugged.

"I guess all the good ones, all the smart ones these days, all the guys like the ones I used to want with me, guys like *you*, they're going to college now instead of coming to me. There's opportunities out there for them they didn't have forty years ago."

"There are no guys like me, Pete."

"Don't I know it. But these others, what I got here today, they know you only by rep, and they don't like that I go outside the family for something. Don't worry about it, I'll take care of it. They got to learn not to disrespect a man of your standing."

"*I* got to take care of it, Pete, or it won't mean anything to them, you know that." Papa put his hands out, palms up, giving in without an argument.

"Fuck 'em. Somebody gotta teach 'em manners. You want them in here, or outside?"

"On the way out. I want the others to see what happens."

"They'll be pissed at you, at me, too, for not stopping you."

"I'll get my respect my way . . ." Bracken shrugged, letting the sentence trail off, implying that Papa would have to get his own respect his own way. This, too, uncharacteristically, the old man let pass as if he hadn't caught it. Bracken thought that he must want his help very badly today.

"It ain't like it used to be, that's for sure," Papa said, and Bracken leaned back, got ready to listen to the lecture. "Times have changed. Once," Papa said, "I could walk out of this room and look around me, and bet my life that I could trust every man in that room out there. Today, Jimmy, take my word for it, that ain't no longer the case." He leaned forward now, regretting what time had taken from him, expressing that regret to Bracken, one of the few men Papa thought might understand the loss that he had suffered over the years.

"There's *dope*, Jimmy, and these guys are into it, they got that shit coming out of their ears. There's too much money in it to keep them away from it for good, and what am I gonna do, kill everyone I find playing with that shit? I'd'a had no one left, there'd'a been no one left in my family. So I give it the okay, take my piece and I'm happy, pretend I don't know what the fuck is going on. Somebody wants to use that shit, fine, they deserve what they get. At least if they get it from us, they know it ain't laced with strychnine.

"Jimmy, I ain't talked onna phone in eleven years. I ain't accepted a piece of mail or mailed one in that same amount of time. I ain't said ten words of importance out there in my own candy shop, for Christ's sake, because I gotta worry about who might be droppin' dimes, who might have a friend looking out for him in the F.B.-fuckin'-I., get him out of some little shit he gets himself into in return for some information on the old man himself. Me, I can't worry about it too much. I got a half a dozen layers of insulation these days. I'm seventy-two years old and I can't play with my grandkids out inna backyard, I gotta worry about some son of a bitch with a long distance mike and a video camera watching us.

"I tell you, it ain't like the old days." Papa sipped his coffee once, dropped the spoon and took a sip, then let the cup rest on his lips as he swallowed the first taste. He nodded, then drank the rest of the cup down, fast, put it down on the desk in front of him.

Bracken said, "For me, things are only getting better."

"And I'm gonna make them even better yet, Jimmy. Tonight, I'm gonna make you a millionaire."

"I'm already a millionaire, Pete."

"Richer than you ever dreamed, and that don't mean just in money."

Bracken waited, letting the old man play his game. He'd never known any of these guys to come right out and say something, and Pete was the best at it, the best that Bracken knew; he talked more about past glories than about what was going on now.

He was also the only one in the entire crowd, however, who presumed to be Bracken's friend. Thought this was so because he'd known Bracken all his life. What the old man forgot, was, he was the one who'd sent dear Terri out with Torelli that night. He thought that he'd been doing the wildest, youngest hit man in New York a favor, letting his boyfriend get his feet wet, allowing him to make some money with a man that Papa trusted like a son. As far as that trust went, it was a one-way street.

Bracken didn't trust him, he didn't trust any of them, but he especially did not trust Pete Papa.

"I got feds climbing out of my ass, Jimmy, night and day, they're watching me. I get this place swept every fucking day, costs me an arm and a leg. How'd you like to live like that? It ain't no way to live. I look out the window in the morning, there's the feds. I open the window in the john, there's a fed, with his nose open. I go home at night, what's the last thing I see when I pull down the blinds in my bedroom? Feds.

"They don't forget, Jimmy. I beat them three times the last few years, and they're pissed off about that. Want to take an old man and lock him away for the rest of his life, just to get even. They want me to die in the joint, want me buried in some pauper's grave behind the penitentiary. And these bastards, these federal guys, you can't pay these fuckers off, the way I did all my life with these local cops."

"Revenge, Pete, you should know about that."

"Revenge, that's one thing. These guys, they think they're fighting *crime*. I tell 'em sometimes, when they get too far under my skin, 'Whyn't you guys go bother the niggers, leave me alone?'" Papa pounded his fist on the table to emphasize his point.

"The jigs," Papa said, *"they're* the ones fuckin' up the city, makin' it unsafe for the rest of us. Shit, for fifty years, this was the safest neighborhood in the world. Now, look at it. I gotta hear rap music pounding through the windows all night."

"So how can I help you, what can I do to make your life better?"

"Ain't my life gettin' better, it's *yours* gonna get better, Jimmy." Pete Papa rose and stretched, his huge belly jutting out, quite a sight. He was proud of his belly. He sat back down and patted his gut, rubbed it a few times, then let his hand drop to the desk. He flipped his fingers back and forth.

"Guys been after me, since I walked out of the joint twelve years ago. I spit in their face three times since then, walk out of the Federal Building a free man, and now they're pissed, trying to come at me from twenty different directions." Papa paused, uncomfortable.

"You know Tulio?"

Bracken pursed his lips and nodded slowly. "Sure I know Tulio."

"Tulio's turning." Oh, Goddamn. No wonder the man was so afraid, no wonder he'd gone on and on about the old days, about times when everyone he knew, he could trust.

Bracken could not believe it. "Get out of here," he said.

"He is."

"Never happen."

Pete Papa nodded his head, grievously.

"He's been with me since before you was born; Tulio and me, we built this thing up from the ground, from nothing, just the two of us, together." The hurt was right up front on Papa's face. For a second, Bracken thought that he might break into tears. His voice was low, his tone exposing his bitterness at his betrayal.

"His grandkid is engaged to my brother-in-law's niece, you didn't know that, did you?" Bracken shook his head.

"The girl, she's one of us, an Italian, college kid, but with heart. Don't ignore her family because she's smarter than them. She comes to all the weddings, the christenings, cries at all the funerals. A real throwback, this girl. It would'a made a good marriage. So all of a sudden her boyfriend, Tulio's grandkid, her fiance, he's antsy, tells her he can't finish the school year out."

"When's this?"

"Just yesterday. Takes off, leaves her right there on the campus alone, no explanation, nothing. She's crying, upset, but she's got our blood and she's mad at the kid, see, so she follows him to his dormitory, looking for the reasoning behind all this, and what does she see?" Papa nods his head, confirming the disloyalty.

"She sees a bunch of son of a bitches in sunglasses and cheap suits loading a car with his shit. Naturally, she calls her dad, tells him what's going on. Him, he comes here to see me, alone, so nobody knows about this except me, the girl, her old man, and now you."

"And anybody that might have been listening in to the phone conversation between the girl and her father."

"Don't even say that, I got enough fuckin' problems."

"I can't believe this," Bracken said.

"How you think *I* feel? I send a guy out to talk to a guy, who talks to another guy, who then talks to someone else, who turns out to be a solid citizen just happens to owe somebody I know some money, and this last guy, he don't know shit except that he's gonna get some of the debt wiped out for doing a guy a favor, he winds up taking a ride past Tulio's house in a car that even J. Edgar Hoover himself couldn't trace back to me. He don't see no strange cars in the driveway or on the street, but as he turns off, a car follows him, and he looks in his rearview mirror, sees someone talking into a radio, probably reading off this guy owed somebody money's license plate number."

"When you think he'll run?"

"This guy, he went out to the house just this morning. Now, they're either in the talking stages, or Tulio's thinking things over, cause he was here just yesterday, in that very chair your ass is in right now. That bastard, that traitor fucking Benedict Arnold, he kissed me when he came in, kissed me again when he left. I see him again, I'm gonna give him something to kiss."

Papa said, "I have somebody call his house, tell him to come over here, but what do they say on a tapped line? The feds would *want* him to come here, then disappear. They'd have enough just from that tape to put me away, the way the juries are acting today. You see what a problem this is for me? How do I tell any of those boys out there that my right hand is flipping over? That I was so wrong. They'll see me as weak, as if I ain't already got enough problems trying to hold onto what I got." Papa shook his head in disgust. He looked as if he was about to spit across the desk.

"That little bastard, that college kid, I'm his Godfather, for Christ's sake. Helped raise him, I was always here for that little son of a bitch."

"Tulio could do it to you, Pete."

"Me, and all the guys I know. Everyone except you, Jimmy. Even *I* couldn't put you away. I could kill you, but I couldn't put you in prison."

"You might not be able to kill me, either, Pete. First, you have to find me. And nobody can find me. And after I'm found, the guys who found me would wish they'd stayed at home that night." Pete Papa shrugged this off, did not see it as worthy of response.

He said, "Fifty years I know Tulio. He knows everything,

Jimmy. Earned good, too. I made his family successful. What can they offer him that I ain't given him?"

"Forgiveness." Bracken said it immediately. It was a concept he understood, but one that would never cross Pete Papa's mind.

"What?"

"He's getting old."

"So? *So?* He spends more time in the fucking church than he spent with me, the last ten years. You think your time's close, you go to the priest, you say you're sorry, Jesus Christ, if the priest got any sense, if he knows what's good for him, he forgives you."

"He's making it right. Check with his doctor. What do you want to bet old Tulio's dying, Pete?"

"Guess who's gonna *wish* he was dying, if Tulio turns the trick? I'll give you a hint: Me. Where'm I gonna go? Some federal pen, I'll be in Lewisburg or Atlanta, they won't send *me* to some country club, you can bet your ass on that. Not the way they feel about me. I'll be in some shithole of a federal pen, right next to forty other guys Tulio sent away. You think they'll blame him?"

"You want Tulio dead."

"And his wife, his kids, anyone in the fucking house."

"Including federal agents."

"Them, they're up to you. All I want is the clan dead, as a sign of my discontent."

Listen to this guy. He still couldn't drop the mustache Pete language.

Bracken said, "How do we follow them, find out where they wind up, with a helicopter? It's not possible, Pete, these feds don't play around. They'll take him away in a ten-car convoy, split the cars up one by one, and they'll have a crash car for each one, some guy driving who'd see it as an honor to die for the Marshals Service. An army couldn't follow them, couldn't find out which car has Tulio."

"See, it ain't gonna be that hard, Jimmy. Cause you go in tonight. I give you everything you need, but you go in tonight and you whack that cocksucker out."

"Forget about it, that's crazy. I don't even know what the house looks like, how many feds might be there with him. The floor plans, how many servants he's got, I know nothing. To-night's out of the question, it can't be done in less than a month."

"For two million dollars, cash."

"I'd never live to spend it. I wouldn't do it for ten million. With all respect, Pete, I understand your problem, and I'm sorry for you. I wish I could help, but it just can't be done."

"Two million dollars . . ." Pete let it dangle, some of his old strength back now, eyeing Bracken, about to offer him something more valuable than money.

When he spoke now, his voice was low, seductive. ". . . and proof of where Torelli's hiding."

Bracken's face fell. He lived a great part of his life being somebody else, acting, with his guard always up, showing people nothing. But now he couldn't help himself. Torelli. Tommy Torelli. The stoolpigeon who was the reason Terri was dead. He took his time, was afraid to seem too anxious, did not want to beg, either. When he finally spoke his voice was a malevolent whisper, toxic, deadly, a man who'd better be hearing the truth.

"You know where Torelli is?"

"I got proof, I got a picture. I know the city, I know everything. I got connections into every major police department and almost every major newspaper in the country, Jimmy, and I never stopped looking. Everybody knows how important this is to me, this was the only guy ever sang on me, and he couldn't be allowed to get away with it forever." Papa's voice dripped poison, it would be an effort for him to not kill Torelli himself.

"Now, I could send a crew out there tomorrow, there's enough guys around still remember what he did. They'd do him for free, just as a favor."

"No! Don't send anybody. Torelli's mine."

And suddenly Pete Papa was his old self again. His hands weren't shaking, his voice was strong and powerful. He had someone squirming, in his control. He was doing what he did best. Manipulating someone.

"Can you imagine the look on that bastard's face, when my people show up to kill him? The confusion, the terror? There he is, living in what he thought was a safe town, out of sight, out of mind, feeling safe after all these years. Then my people show up and start to carve the skin off him, inch by inch, maybe boil him in water. If I wasn't so old, if the feds weren't constantly on my ass, Jimmy, I'd do it myself, just to see his face. Either way, I'll have them take pictures. Polaroids so I can look at them and get a hardon." Papa smiled to show that he was only kidding, then he went hard, quick, his facial expression changing at the speed that a window shade flies up when its string is abruptly pulled.

"I offered you a place with me now almost thirty years running. Gave you offers other men would kill their children to get, and you turn me down, you hide from me, the guy who gave you your start. I want you and I got to go through forty moves, like you're the boss and I'm some hit man, looking for an audience.

"But I held my tongue, Jimmy, I ordered no reprisals against you. But you turned me down, and if you hadn't, you'd'a been the first to know about Torelli, I know what he cost you. The deal between us has always been, cash up front for services rendered. Only this time, *I* got something *you* want, and believe me, Jimmy, I don't tell you nothing unless you tell me that you do this thing for me."

Bracken didn't hesitate, he wasn't about to negotiate. He said, "I need to know the layout of the house, everything you know, Pete. How many rooms, how many bathrooms, where the old man sleeps, where the bedrooms are, everything."

He said, "I've got the hardware, I'll use my own weapons, I don't trust your sources or your people. I go in the house, Tulio dies, you tell me where Torelli is, that's the deal, right?"

"And the two million, don't you forget about that."

Fuck the two million. He'd pay two million and kill Tulio, Pete Papa, and the mayor of New York himself for the information that this old man was able to give him. But he didn't tell Pete Papa that, just nodded his head in acceptance.

"What if he's not there? What if the feds have him in a safe house already or on some army camp?"

"Then you lose two million, and I'm dead."

"I get the information?"

"It dies with me."

Bracken looked at him hard, saw how much this man was enjoying the bargain he was driving. Was he that stupid? Did he take Bracken that lightly? Bracken hoped that he did, it would work to his advantage.

And now it made sense, the way the two punks of Papa's had treated Tawny. The disrespect had been communicable, they'd caught it from their boss. From a man who feared what Bracken was capable of, but who saw him as just another faggot, just someone else to bring in here and reminisce with. Someone who could be trusted as a killer, as a man who would keep his mouth shut, but someone to be taken lightly as a man.

That was, as far as Bracken was concerned, beautiful. Wonderful. It actually couldn't be better.

Bracken didn't want this man to ever know what he was truly made of. Not until it was too late.

So he said, sincerely, "Talk to me, Pete, and don't leave out a single thing. Talk to me, now, tell me everything you know."

IT HAD BEEN a pretty busy day, and Mark was grateful for that. He hadn't been forced to think about Caroline, about what he'd say to her when he finally saw her, when he went home from work tonight. If he ever got there; it looked like it was going to be another long night.

He was walking along the lake with a kid who'd wanted to talk to him, with darkness falling now, a good spring chill in the air. People passing them would look at them strangely, and he could see it in their eyes, their interpretation of what was going on.

Mark was dressed in an old suit jacket over a white shirt that had a frayed collar. He hadn't shaved today. He'd pulled the collar of his jacket up around his neck to ward off the early evening chill. He had combed his hair carefully that morning, but hadn't thought about it since, he knew that it would look unkempt, it was too long and a little wild, he could use a haircut.

The kid whose street name was HardWay was wearing an oversized leather jacket with an emblem of a huge 8 Ball trapped in a large yellow circle on the back. He had a Chicago White Sox cap on his head, turned to the left, the price tag still attached. He had on starched khaki pants and had expensive shoes on his feet. The belt on the pants was hanging open, unbuckled, and HardWay's zipper had been pulled down all the way. It was the new thing with teenagers, saying they were always ready for anything, fucking or fighting, it didn't matter to them. The only thing they admitted to enjoying even more than those two things was making money when they could, from whatever source was available.

There was a line from a rap song that Mark could never forget, street poet imagery that haunted him, how they felt: "Life ain't nothin' but bitches and money," sung with sincerity, in a tone that implied its undeniable truth. Could it have really come to that? Mark truly hoped, wanted to believe that it hadn't.

The look that the passersby gave them told Mark what they thought; what they, in their superior wisdom, had immediately figured out. They thought that Mark was hustling the kid, or the kid was hustling him, one or the other.

People like this couldn't see past that, wouldn't be able to understand that someone could do something for somebody else without having something tangible in it for them. The people who passed them had combed their hair many times a day, rubbed mousse into it, and plastered it down with hair spray. They would have designer deodorant rolled onto their under-arms. They'd make fifty grand a year and believe that making that kind of money would somehow keep them safe from the dangers of the street. They'd probably showered before putting on their jogging clothes, to bring them down after a hard day at the office, playing with somebody else's money. They had their evening meal catered to them, on disposable plates, knife and forks delivered, scented candles, too, if they wanted them. They looked at HardWay as the enemy, as the inferior troublemaker that made their city look bad. Mark didn't know what they thought of him. He had learned long ago that he didn't much care.

These people would go home to their matchbox, noisy apart-ments with nasty views, and enjoy the fruits of their profligate spending, these people who saw banks as only institutions for which they should work, savings as something that only the el-derly needed to do.

Yet many of them would be going back to work tonight, the men trying to climb that ladder, the women looking to burst through the glass ceiling. Mark tried to ignore them, and Hard-Way succeeded in doing so; to him, they were barely even there, just another piece of ugly business that had to be put up with in his life.

A great many people passed them, too, as the two of them strolled slowly along the lake, walking on the concrete away from the jogging path—most of them young, almost all of them in shape. Joggers and bike riders and people on rollerblades, whiz-zing by without warning, close to Mark and HardWay, two men who knew a great deal about violence ignoring people who only thought they did.

It was easy to ignore fools on a night as beautiful as this one. The dying sun was reflecting off the side of the John Hancock building, onto the water, staining the dark blue to orange, blue and white. The waves diffused the light, made it ripple and dance on the whitecaps. The city of Chicago as seen through the eyes of Dali, surreal, gorgeous, stunning in its ephemeral beauty. Waving goodbye, disappearing, then materializing once again as the new wave rolled in.

HardWay was discussing things that Mark had heard before, and he went out of his way to let the kid think that he hadn't, that what he was saying was singularly unique, Mark mostly just nodding his head and mumbling encouragement whenever the young man paused. There was anger there at first, as there always was, HardWay for a time trying to justify his past behavior.

"I'm standing on Twelfth Street just last night, after working out at Del's, me and James Tokin. We ain't doing shit, but two squads pull up, on either side of us, the pigs get out of they cars with they shit *pulled*." HardWay's voice told Mark of his resentment, of the anger he felt about the way police had approached him.

"It was *cold* last night, man, and we had our hands in our pockets, and they yelling at us, cursing us, before their doors are even open: 'Get those fuckin' hands out where I can see them!' They throw us up against the car, yelling and screaming for us not to take our hands off the hood, call me a nigger motherfucker maybe ten times while they pat me down. Take me off the car and throw me against the wall, tell me to get the fuck off *they* street, like it ain't mine, too."

Mark jumped in, feeling on safe enough ground to contribute. "If you're not home watching Street Babe reruns, they figure you're up to no good."

"Why they do that, Mr. Torrence, why do they always fuck with us?" HardWay asked, and Mark had to admit that he simply didn't know.

"The thing is, this is a big city, HardWay, that's part of it. They know that for the most part, they can get away with it. In small suburban departments, where they go to training every year and learn how to deal with people, they're more polite, because they know better. And out there, in the suburbs, they're not dealing with death and destruction every day, drug overdoses and insane people shooting at them. Sometimes, in the North suburbs, *years* go by without a killing, HardWay." Mark spoke in surprise at that idea, and HardWay grunted, he could not believe the concept, either.

Comfortable with the way the conversation was going, really wanting to give this kid a good answer, Mark said, "Those suburban cops, they know, too, that there are thirty or forty of them on the force, tops, in towns with twenty or thirty thousand people. Here, man, there're four and a half million people, and twelve thousand people with badges and guns, they've got a lot more anonymity, they know they can get away with a lot more. With some of them, it goes to their heads."

"So they get to break the law, because they got a badge."

"All they have to do is say that you acted in a suspicious manner, and they've got a right to detain you."

"Don't seem right, especially when they lie to the judge like that. I wasn't doin' *nothin'* wrong, Mr. Torrence, I was just standing there."

An honest exchange of candor, and the boy began to open up.

HardWay told Mark what he'd really wanted to say all along, that he didn't want to be a gangbanger anymore, had figured that out now at the age of fifteen, three years after being recruited into his set. He thought that it was too late for him, that his life had been fixed on a course that could never again be altered.

Mark walked on, looking out at the lake. Not saying anything now, the time for that would come later, after HardWay figured out what it was that he was truly saying. Then all it would take would be a gentle nudge, and he'd be on his way out. It would be a tough decision, but it would be all HardWay's.

If he was serious about it, escape would surely cost him. He'd be violated and beaten, what was called "eighty-sixin." HardWay would have to stand inside a circle of his homies and take their beatings, his hands down at his sides, under orders not to use them except to help himself off the ground if a punch should knock him off his feet. If he lifted his hands to his face to protect himself, he would get out of the gang forever; somebody would shoot him in the head for his cowardice. After the beating, while HardWay was unconscious, any tattoos that he had on his body showing any signs of his gang affiliation would be scraped from his physique with a straight razor, the work done brutally, and it would take a long time for the razor scars to heal.

How many times did Mark do this every year? Forty? Fifty? The number had to be well up into that range. Mark somewhere where the kid would feel safe, listening to intelligent kids who'd maybe been busted for something heavy and saw for the first time where it was they were truly heading, the kids with enough imagination to see the penitentiary in a light that the less imaginative among them could never grasp.

HardWay was feeling that now, the pressure on his young shoulders, seeing where the gang was leading him, seeing too that it was no longer fun, that certain acts were expected of him that he had no wish to perform.

They'd put a gun in his hand soon, if they hadn't already done so. Drive by someone and tell HardWay to pull the trigger. Thousands of people were shot and survived it every year in the city of Chicago, the murder rate would be through the roof if most of the shooters weren't frightened kids who closed their eyes when they jerked that trigger.

HardWay had a sensitivity about him, a quietness that a lot of boys like him seemed to have. More like prisoners than outright gangsters, they'd joined the gang out of necessity and soon saw that it wasn't for them.

Mark walked on silently, and let the boy express his feelings.

The lights had come on in the downtown buildings, and Mark walked over to an empty bench and sat down and HardWay joined him, barely stopping in his narrative, the boy talking haltingly, but talking all the same.

How long had it been since HardWay'd had to articulate something of importance to him? A fifteen-year-old dropout with no future that he could see. HardWay could see it now, what was ahead of him if he didn't change. Death or prison, the cemetery or a cage. Some choice to make when you by rights should be worried about being promoted into your second year of high school. Mark and the boy looked out at the lights, at five miles of them, lining Lake Shore Drive.

There was a building to their right that appeared to have some fire damage near the roof, you had to look closely to see that it wasn't smoke on the top of the building, but rather, clinging vines. All the way down the Drive you could see what looked like a million street lights in perfect symmetry, curving out, gracefully, seeming to finally be swallowed up by the buildings of Michigan Avenue.

Ahead of him, the Drake Hotel's pink neon sign was flickering to life, the "R" barely lit at all, the sign from here read D AKE. From where they sat Mark could only see the antennas of the Sears Tower, overlooking the lakefront, lights at the top flashing white in syncopation. Headlights of commuters, heading home, moved along the Drive. Over the lake, the sky was orange and pink and dark blue, rapidly fading to black. Far off in the distance, the huge dinner yacht, The Star of Chicago, was pulling off for a night on the town.

There were couples everywhere, jogging together, walking together hand in hand. Some were May-December, without discrimination toward sex. Some were interracial, and not the least bit embarrassed about it.

At times like these, he could almost believe that he was safe.

Except there he was, with HardWay discussing his life in the gang.

"Right here, not two years ago, I was thirteen and still in the sixth grade." It was easy to understand the kid, he was relaxed and speaking calmly, seeming far older than he was, Mark's peer rather than his charge.

"We come across this tourist, 'bout three in the morning, the man walking around drunk with his hands in his pockets, shit, acting like he was home in his cracker backyard surrounded by his friends. Man had his sleeves on his suit pushed up, like they do on 'Miami Vice' reruns? Seen a watch, man, gleaming gold." HardWay's voice trailed off, and Mark took his eyes off the false beauty of the city and looked at its true reality.

HardWay's face was rigid, set in a look of self-loathing and pain. Mark didn't have to imagine his inner torment, he could remember it from his own childhood, how he felt after an act of particularly harsh violence.

"We walked up near him and when he seen us," HardWay said, "and the man, his face went all lit up. Here's this bunch of twelve- and thirteen-year-old black choirboys, walking up to him, grinning. He was a big guy, musta thought he had nothing to fear from a bunch of little kids."

"In Minnesota, he'd run a candy store."

"You know about it?" HardWay was staring up at Mark, confused. Mark nodded, his lips turned down, his arms across the back of the bench. He looked back out at the lake, and when he spoke, his voice was casual.

"Read about it in the papers."

"Man, I ain't said shit." HardWay was now frightened, his eyes large, cautious.

"Whatever you tell me, it stays with me. If I had a big mouth, I'd'a been found in the trunk of my car a long time ago, believe me, HardWay. Back when I was your age they'd'a found my ass, dead."

"Man, I'm *hurtin'*."

"Yeah, I know."

"You ever do it, Mr. Torrence? You ever carry that around inside you? Two year now, all I can do is think about that white man, unless I'm high, then it's a righteous thing. I sober up, though, man, and I got to live with it, seein' his face. He had a wife and a bunch of kids, he wasn't doin' nothin' wrong. I think about him and I wonder if I'm goin' to hell for what I did. It's like a cancer, man, eating at my soul."

"You believe in God, you got to believe in forgiveness."

"But how He forgive something like that? How could He do that?"

"God's job is not to punish you, I bet. If he's there, I figure his job is to set you straight. Maybe by making your conscience bothering you, maybe that's His way of telling you that you got to get right with him. And if you don't, *then* you go to hell." Looking out at the lake tonight, Mark could almost believe it.

"You get right, Mr. Torrence?"

"I'm doing all I can."

"So you think if I leave the gang and I get a job, that He'll forgive me?"

"I think if you do that, God forgiving you won't be your problem."

"The gang, they'll be my problem."

"For a time, but not for long."

"Then what?"

"Then," Mark said and paused, and looked back at the boy and stared at him with all the sincerity he possessed, "then, Hard-Way, you have to learn to forgive yourself."

"Yeah."

Mark looked back at the lake, eyes roaming, seeing everyone coming toward them long before HardWay noticed them.

He would think that he was the toughest thing out here, that no one would dare mess with him. Mark knew better, knew just how tough the two of them together truly were. One skinny little crazy man with a gun, and it would be all over.

There were things he could do for this boy, if he was serious. Jobs he could get him, Mark's Rolodex was worth more than the gold those kids had taken off the corpse of the Minnesota conventioneer. He could even relocate him, if that's what Hard-Way thought he wanted, move him to another part of the city or out to a rehab center or a halfway house out in one of the suburbs. The choice would be up to HardWay, and if he made it, Mark would help him.

HardWay said, "They talk about you, sometimes, about how they might take you out someday."

"I've heard the rumors, and I'm still here."

"A lot of them don't like you, but the ancients think you're solid."

The ancients. HardWay's voice revealing his awe, the kid discussing men who were in their late twenties and early thirties, considered ancient simply because they'd lived to such ripe old ages. Men of respect, of HardWay's set, who had gone before him and had lived to tell the tale.

Mark said, "The ancients have a secret. They know something, HardWay, took them fifteen, twenty years to learn. Something you already know, that you learned before you were sixteen."

"What's that?"

"That the gang life is just no way for you to live. That the gangs won't help you or save you, that if you let them they'll only destroy you."

"Man, I want to live."

"I'll help you if you'll let me."

There it was, out in the open, and what would the kid do with the offer now that he had it? Mark looked over, watched him casually, saw the boy's face brighten.

"I was meanin' to ask you, I mean, I wanted to know if you would . . ."

"If I'd what?"

"Help me, man, help me to get out."

All right.

Mark said, "Let's go back, HardWay, and let's talk to Del.

There'll be a whole crew of guys there by now, who already did the same thing that you want to do. We can go into my office, the bunch of us, and they'll talk to you, and you can tell me which way you want to go, which path is right for you. Then we'll take it, starting right now, tonight. Whatever it takes, I'm willing to do. I'll go to the wall for you, if you're serious about this."

"I'm serious, man," HardWay said, and stood. "Let's go back and talk to them homeboys."

"*Ex*-homeboys."

"Right, *ex*-homeboys."

"There's a place in Crete where you can spend the night, if you want to leave tonight, HardWay. A boy's home where I know the director."

"Where's Crete?"

"South suburbs, thirty-five, forty miles away from here."

"Suburbs? Man, I heard about them suburbs. They got snakes out there, shit, raccoons come up and eat your garbage. I'm better off out here, with asphalt under my feet. Besides, the D's, my set, they moving out there, to the south. In Country Club Hills, Matteson, they go out there behind the Gang Crimes guys all the time busting they asses."

Snakes? Mark didn't want to hurt his feelings by laughing.

He said, "We'll talk about it when we get back to the center."

But they didn't get a chance, not right then, because as soon as they got back to the center the cops grabbed Mark, told him he had to come with them, there was an emergency and Elmer Griffin needed him.

DOLAN HAD A cellular phone to his ear, was talking to Elmer who was listening to him on the bootlegged phone line the gangbangers had set up down in the basement.

"We played hell getting a hookup to that line, Elmer, the guys who use it didn't want to tell us what the number was. They tapped into the Safer Foundation's line. Only use it at night, when nobody's at the office."

Keep it light, kid around, that was the way to play it. Keep the kid's mind off his problems, off the shotgun. Try to make jokes with Elmer while Lawlor and his men stood glaring at him, some of them with their face shields down, ready for immediate action.

There was a lot of brass milling around outside, too, talking to the reporters and the camera crews. They wouldn't come in here if you stuck a poker up their ass; they knew about negotiations, who was in charge, and they wouldn't be taking any orders from some lowly youth officer. They'd wait until the situation was resolved, one way or the other, then they'd storm in and want to take over.

"Now I can't come down there again until you lay down the shotgun, Elmer. That's the rule, and I have to abide by it. The good news is, we got all night, buddy. More than that, if you want it. We'll take all the time we want, all the time you need to figure things out, pal. Just don't do anything silly, don't do anything that would make your grandma and Mr. Torrence mad at you."

Don't mention suicide again, don't even repeat the word. This call was being recorded, would be evaluated later. And Eddie had no doubt that when the ERT guys were debriefed, he'd catch enough hell without being caught making procedural errors in the general conversation.

"Did you call Mr. Torrence, Eddie? You call Mr. Torrence up?"

"We sent a squad to get him. He should be here anytime."

He didn't tell Elmer that he hadn't bothered to call Torrence on the phone. When you were on the phone in the safety of your own house or in your place of business, it was easy to say no. With a couple of uniforms standing in front of you it was an entirely different thing.

"When he gets here we'll let you talk to him, you can talk to your friend, no problem. Put the gun down and you can take a walk together, just the two of you, alone. It's a beautiful night out tonight, Elmer, maybe sixty, still. Light wind and a full moon, you wouldn't believe how pretty it is. The Sox're winning. Cubs are off. Bulls heading back into the playoffs again."

"Mr. Torrence walking around *this* neighborhood? His white ass with me? It wouldn't be a pretty night for long. It get awful hot real fast, Officer Eddie. They hate white mens as much as they hate raper mens."

Eddie laughed, hollowly, trying to think of something to say. Behind him, Lawlor cleared his throat, and when Dolan ignored him, Lawlor tapped him on his shoulder, and Eddie put his hand over the mouthpiece, looked behind him and nodded. He removed his hand and said, "Somebody just pulled up, Elmer, let me go see if it's Mr. Torrence." Eddie hit hold, cutting Elmer off in mid-sentence.

"What!"

"This is bullshit, Dolan, the kid's down there alone. There's a thousand monkeys hanging around outside, waiting for the fireworks. We got to take him now, before they charge the building and take *us*."

"You want to call those people monkeys when the phone's live, when it's taping? How about I step out there and call one of the captains in; one of the *black* captains?"

"Look, motherfucker—"

Dolan turned his back on him. "Talk to Sergeant Wilson." Where in the hell was the liaison man? Try to find an officer on a Sunday night. At least one that you'd want around. He turned the phone back on and softly said Elmer's name.

No answer.

"Elmer!" Said loudly. They'd have heard a shotgun blast through the door. Where the hell was Elmer?

"*Elmer!*" Dolan shouted the name, stepping to the door before Lawlor's hand pulled him back roughly.

"Don't get that close to it, pal. He fires through that door, you're dead." The son of a bitch, he was speaking for the recording machine.

Calmly, Dolan said, "Elmer?" into the phone.

"I here, Officer Eddie," Elmer said, and Dolan sighed in relief. He could feel the sweat trickling down his spine, on his temples. Running onto his cheeks. He ran his forearm over his face, took a deep breath and relaxed.

"Where'd you go?"

"I had to take a leak. They's a washtub full of pee-pee over next to that ratty couch."

"Think the bad guys use it for a bathroom?"

"How else it get full, fool?"

Dolan laughed, the joke on him.

"Was that Mr. Torrence?"

"No, Elmer, not yet."

"Damn."

"You getting hungry?"

"Sure am. What you got?"

"I'll get you a pizza, trade you a piece for a shotgun shell."

"I ain't that hungry."

"Give you half the thing, one half-pizza, one shell. The whole thing, two shells. You want something to drink, I'll send down a quart of Pepsi, for another shell, Elmer."

"That pizza sound like a good deal. Fucks the Pepsi, though. How I take the shells out?"

"Let me order the pizza, and I'll tell you how to take the shells out while we're waiting for it to be delivered."

This was a good sign, Elmer enjoying the task of negotiations. Getting off on being important for the first time in his life. He was telling the cops what to do, ordering them around.

Eddie had seen it go the other way, too, where the barricaded suspect with a gun had enjoyed the power too much, had fired shots through the door just to scare away the cops. When that happened, the ERT moved in, and the guy all of a sudden stopped being so important. Elmer though, he was doing all right.

There was a commotion over by the front hallway, murmuring as the ERT men turned to see who was daring to come through the door.

It was a muscular white man, wearing a beat up suit, a white shirt without a tie. Tall guy, not too bad looking, with good shoes on his feet. Swarthy, looked Italian. Suspicious of the ERT guys, shooting them a quick disapproving glare. Not shy, though. The man walked straight past the ERT, not even giving them a second glance, held his hand out for the phone and said, "I'm Torrence, let me talk to the kid."

"Not without proving who you are, asshole," Lawlor said, worked up, mad because the guy wasn't acting intimidated or impressed. Torrence turned and looked at him, as if seeing him and his crew for the first time.

"See you," he said, and began to walk through them.

Eddie said, "Mr. Torrence? For Elmer's sake, come back."

"The second these SWAT guys are cleared out of here, send for me. I'll be outside, talking to the TV reporters. I got a few things to say to them." He was speaking over his shoulder, as if giving instructions to his children, not angry or coming on though, just strolling and talking, cool as could be.

Eddie smiled. He raised his eyebrows and cocked his head at Lawlor. "What's it gonna be?"

Lawlor said, "Mr. Torrence, come back here a second. Please."

Torrence ignored him, was at the door now. Opened it without looking back and was about to step through when Lawlor threw both his hands up, most likely thinking about what this guy would say about him and his crew to the TV stations. "Goddamnit, let's go, outside, everybody."

Torrence stepped back and let the door close, stood inside the hallway with his hands clasped in front of him, looking straight ahead as the ERT left the building. Dolan watched him, saw him notice the sergeant and the three black people who were now all just inside the grandmother's apartment door. Torrence nodded to them formally, and the old woman stepped through the doorway. That was strange, the two of them gave each other a really funny look, each of them looking guilty at the other. The old woman reached out and touched the man's arm lightly.

"You gonna let them kill ma boy?"

"Nobody's gonna kill anyone, Mrs. Griffin," Mark Torrence said, then patted her arm gently, and began to walk back toward Dolan.

"Can I have the phone now?" Torrence said, and Dolan handed it to him, gratefully.

"Push hold. I didn't want him to hear your exchange with the ERT. Once it's off hold, the call's being recorded, Torrence, you should know about that. For your own good, watch what you say."

Torrence pushed hold and said, "Elmer? You there? It's Mr. Torrence, Elmer. So what the hell'd these idiots get you into now?"

LAWLOR IGNORED THE shouting reporters and the hollering coming from the hundreds of black ghetto-rats that were standing behind the barricades, and pulled his crew to the corner of the building, away from the other cops. He didn't even want the other ERT units to hear what he was going to say.

"There's uniforms watching the windows, you replace whoever's at the window furthest from the subject, and do it now. Get into the sniper's range. Fuck them, even the other units; it's our call, not theirs."

"But Sarge—"

181

"Shut the fuck up and do what you're told. Find their weakness and a way to break them, quick. I don't care if you have to wire them up with plastic, just get it done fast. When we strike, I want two seconds wasted on those windows, no more. The windows go out and the stun grenades go in. Two seconds after that, you're in there, and if he doesn't drop his weapon, *you* drop *him.*"

"Check." A group of voices sounding off as one; it was music to Lawlor's ears. As the men dispersed, a captain walked up to him, swaggered, really. Lawlor could smell the whiskey on the man's breath when he spoke.

"What the hell's going on in there?"

"Some asshole civilian wouldn't talk to the suspect without us leaving the area. Now that he's on the line, let's see what he does when he sees me." Lawlor stepped past the captain—he had no time to waste on drunks—and headed back toward the building, walking quickly, determined.

MARK SAID, "ELMER, forget about the pizza." The kid had been fast-talking, something Mark was familiar with. Elmer had done it before often enough, whenever frustration got the better of his emotions. Elmer would begin to rattle on, going off on tangents, talking a mile a minute and saying absolutely nothing. It was the last thing he always did before he broke down and cried. When he was like this, he needed a firm hand, he needed guidance.

"Elmer, what you do is, talk to me. Tell me what this is about."

"You ain't spoked to the po-lices?"

"What for? I'm here to talk to you."

It was strange, hearing Elmer's voice, coming at him in stereo. His voice coming at him through the door, and in the earpiece of the cellular phone. Elmer must be on the stairs. Was he pointing the gun at the door? Mark stepped back, leaned against the large-tile wall.

"They-said-I-done-clutched-Clarisse's-pussy-but-I-didn't-clutch-no-pussy," the kid was hyperventilating, making wheezing sounds as he spoke.

"Elmer, calm down!"

"Then - Grandma - got - one - of - them - involuatory - order - things -
to - send - me - to - the—"

"*Elmer!*" Mark said it harshly, wanting the kid's attention.
It worked.

"Shut up, now, relax." He spoke softly now, with feeling.
"Calm down, Elmer, I'm right here with you."

"No you *ain't.*" Elmer was crying now, sobbing into the
phone. Mark could picture him, snot running down his nose,
Elmer swiping at it with his arm, getting it all over his forearm,
his shirt.

"You out there, with the po-lices, you on they side."

"No I'm not."

"I gotta talk to you, Mr. Torrence, and not over some fucking telephone."

"Elmer, hold on."

Mark put him on hold, turned to the cop, who was already
shaking his head.

"Out of the question, forget about it. We never give up a
hostage, Mr. Torrence, not for anybody, no matter what they
think they can do. Hell, we never even give up a hostage for a
hostage, or send a cop in exchange for an innocent woman or
child. That's only on the TV, Mr. Torrence, I can't let you do it."

Behind the cop, Mark could see the big mouth SWAT guy
coming back into the building, his face showing his fury. He was
alone, but he was a big guy, could prove to be a handful. Mark's
back was to the door, the cop was a couple of feet in front of
him, looking stern, his mind made up. The big slob in full riot
gear was getting closer.

It was now or never.

He tossed the cellular phone at the cop and as the cop reached
for it he turned around and was through the door before anyone
could stop him.

And found himself looking down the bore of a single-barrel
shotgun, the hole looking big, about the size of a cannon barrel.
The weapon wavering in the shaking hands of Elmer, the kid
scared to death.

"How you doing, Elmer?" Mark said, and Elmer lowered the
gun. Mark lowered his head, shook it once to clear out the terror
and to try to regain his composure.

"Elmer? Step back, son, I'm coming down the stairs now."

Outside the door, he could hear the big cop shouting at the

blond cop, the blond cop shouting back, then many voices, all yelling at one another at the same time. Mark smiled slyly at Elmer.

"We got them going out there, don't we?"

"What they gonna do, Mr. Torrence? I'm so scared."

"It's all right, I'm here with you, they're not gonna hurt you."

Elmer's face was tear-streaked, twisted with his fright. His eyes were big and round, and he was breathing through his mouth, his large chest heaving with every breath he took. Mark walked down the steps carefully, Elmer not moving back, just standing there shaking, looking up at him.

The kid was flop-sweating, smelling bad. His eyes never came off Mark's.

"Don't worry, Elmer, there's TV out there, everywhere you look. They can't play hero, come down here and hurt someone, not with the cameras rolling. They'd lose their jobs, they'd go to jail."

"But I just a nigger to them, I know that." The belief in Elmer's voice made Mark's heart ache. Elmer stepped back and slid down the wall. He was crying terribly now, his lips curled up, his teeth chattering.

"They tell me all the time, that shit, that I ain't nothing but a nigger to them!"

The basement was a nightmare, filthy and rat-infested. Spiders were everywhere already, even this early in the year. In the middle of the floor was a puddle of filthy water, over the drain, where it had backed up. Mark breathed through his mouth, fighting his own fear. Elmer was his friend, Elmer would not hurt him. Elmer did not know that it was Mark's fault that Elmer was in this position.

He stood next to Elmer and put his back against the wall and slowly slid down, sat down on the cold wet concrete, his shoulder touching Elmer's. The gun was between Elmer's legs, the stock on the floor, the barrel pointing at the ceiling. The tip of the weapon came about to the middle of Elmer's chest. Upstairs, the voices had stopped screaming. Mark couldn't hear anyone up there anymore.

"This is for real, ain't it, Mr. Torrence. I ain't never been in this kind of trouble before."

"Elmer, give me the gun."

In a flash, Elmer's head was down on the shotgun barrel.

How could he stay in one piece, the way he was shaking? Mark had never seen anyone tremble this violently before. He began to fear that Elmer would accidentally pull the trigger.

"You touch the gun, I pull the trigger."

"Elmer, relax. I know you didn't hurt any girls. I know you don't do that."

"But they don't know it, out there, *they* think I did, they *all* think I did, Mr. Torrence, even my own Grandma!"

"You don't think that I can talk to them, tell them you didn't hurt anyone? You don't think they'll believe me?"

"They still put me away. Grandma still got them commitial papers."

The boy could see no way out. With a chill, Mark realized that Elmer was just trying to work himself up into enough of a frenzy to pull the trigger. When he spoke, it was as quickly as Elmer himself had spoken before, the words coming out of Mark in a rush.

"Elmer, come stay with me, come live with me and my family."

Elmer's face brightened. He smiled through his tears.

"You let me do that? Would the cops let me do that?"

"I'll become your guardian, I'll take care of you. We'll let you stay with us for a while, then you can move into the gym over at the youth center with Del, as soon as the doctors say you're ready. We'll give you a job, you can work there, too, every day, with me and Del."

Elmer was calming down, seeing a solution. He lifted his forehead off the barrel, turned his head so their eyes met. His temple was still just inches from the barrel of the weapon. Elmer smiled through his tears.

"You do that for me? *You* do that for *me?*"

"You've got my word. You ever heard of me breaking my word, Elmer?"

Elmer's smile broadened, adoring eyes shining. The tears he shed now were tears of joy. They ran into Elmer's mouth, no different from the other kind.

"Okay, okay, Mr. Torrence, I can do that, if you give me your word."

"I already said I did, didn't I Elmer? Come on, don't dis me now, not if you're gonna be my son."

"Ain't never had me no daddy before." Elmer leaned back

against the wall, out of range of the shotgun, and Mark sighed, relaxed. Elmer was still smiling.

"Ain't got to go to no nuthouse, Mr. Torrence, not even for a night, right?"

"They'll want to look you over—"

"No!" Elmer was terrified again. "I can't go back there, Mr. Torrence." Elmer leaned into him, whispered in Mark's ear.

"They fucks you in there at night, Mr. Torrence. They dope you up, then they come in and fucks you, the orderlies do, did it to me when I was a little boy." Elmer leaned back, his face set. He shook his head.

"Ain't going back to no nuthouse, not ever."

Mark closed his eyes and shook his head, back and forth, twice. Was this boy never to have relief? Was every human being he come in contact with going to somehow hurt him?

Mark said, "You're a man now, Elmer, and I'll be with you every day. Soon as they let you out, bam, you come and live with me."

"I can't go back there."

"I won't lie to you, Elmer, I'm not the cops. They'll take you in for observation, but I'll be right there with you. Get you a good lawyer, too, to make sure nobody hurts you even a little."

"You be there with me?"

"Every damn day. You got my word on that, too. All I ask of you, in fact, I demand it, is that you take your medication, every day, like you're supposed to."

Mark could see him thinking, Elmer's face all scrunched up in concentration. Finally, it relaxed.

"All right. I go. But you gotta take me in."

"Give me the shotgun now, Elmer."

"All right, Mr. Torrence."

Elmer looked at him, trusting him, was lifting the shotgun up slowly as Mark reached over, even more slowly.

"That's it, Elmer, give it to me . . ."

Mark had his hand on the barrel when the far window blew out with a blast that shook the building, thick glass was flying at them, cutting them, and Elmer was screaming in terror, looking at the window, breathing like a thirsty dog as the stun grenades went off, blinding them in flashes of pure white light.

Mark heard Elmer scream one last time, felt the shotgun barrel pulled toward Elmer's forehead, felt it there, the boy's head one with the shotgun, right on top of it again, and he had time to scream *"NO!"* before Elmer shouted in agony and pulled the trigger, and then all Mark could feel was wetness splattering all over his face.

THERE WAS BLOOD in his eyes. Mark could see the film of redness and feel the burn behind his eyelids. The bright white was fading, and he knew that he wasn't blind. Thank God. His ears were ringing from the sound of the grenades and the blast of the shotgun, Mark in pain, wondering if his eardrums were broken, suddenly freezing cold.

Voices were shouting in front of him, boots pounding down the stairs on his left. Excited men, scared men, he'd heard such voices before.

Hands were on him, pulling him up. "On your feet, asshole." A gruff voice, disgusted. Then another voice said, "Jesus Christ," softly. He heard the voices through the ringing in his ears, as if from far away.

"Put him down Sarge, he's hit." There. Another voice, different, with a little compassion in it.

"He ain't hit, that's splatter, Lonnie." The same guy that had dragged him to his feet and called him an asshole.

What was he talking about, splatter? Mark stood there, disoriented, rubbing at his eyes. A hand touched his shoulder and he shook it off, nearly fell.

"Leave me alone. What the hell happened?" What *had* happened? What were all these voices, all this shouting . . .

Elmer.

Blinking rapidly, Mark waited, wondering what the hell had happened to Elmer. He and the boy had been sitting there, sitting there shoulder to shoulder.

Good Christ, they'd stormed the basement.

Mark ignored the pain in his eyes and forced them open, wide. His face was bleeding, he could feel it everywhere, as if every pore of his skull was individually oozing. It was in his eyes, on his nose, his cheeks, on his neck. How badly was he hurt?

He didn't feel any pain, but he knew that was normal when you were in a state of shock. Did Elmer shoot at them, had they shot back and killed him?

Mark looked down, waited until his eyes could focus.

The blast had thrown Elmer back, stabilized him against the wall. It looked as if he was wearing a red bandanna, a red hand-kerchief across the upper portion of his head.

"Oh, no," Mark said, a moan, realizing what had happened. Elmer had killed himself. The top of his head had been sheared clean off. From the eyes down, he could be sleeping, but up above, nothing.

On the wall behind him was what was left of Elmer's brain, splattered along the concrete, a single slice of it hanging from the ceiling, like a slim filet stalactite, dripping bright red blood. The shotgun had bounced off the floor and wound up on Elmer's lap, across his legs, pointing at Mark.

Jesus Christ in heaven, it was all his fault.

He had a sudden urge to pick it up and use it on this son of a bitch in the armor suit in front of him.

"Get the civilian out of here," the sergeant said. Mark felt a hand on his shoulder again, gentle.

"Come on, Mr. Torrence, let's go."

Mark looked at him. It was the blond guy from upstairs, the hostage negotiator. He looked a little white around the gills, him-self, swallowing a lot.

Around them, pandemonium reigned. Cops in white shirts were everywhere now, barking orders, stepping all over evidence. Somebody kicked the shotgun out of Elmer's lap, as if it were still somehow a threat to any of them.

Mark didn't trust himself to speak. He was shaking, he knew that he was probably in shock, although he was certain now that he hadn't been hit. The pain would have set in by now, and the cops wouldn't have dared to manhandle him if he was shot. They'd have a big enough lawsuit from the grandmother as it was.

Mark bowed his head, so he wouldn't have to look at any of them. The blond cop had his hand on Mark's shoulder again.

"Take your hand off me." Mark said it softly, but firmly. He was pleased to hear that his voice wasn't cracking. He felt the pressure go off his shoulder and he began to mount the steps, still looking down. Mark got to the doorway, marched past a bunch of uniformed cops, ignoring them, not paying any atten-tion to their comments. They were confused, not knowing where he fit in or what he was doing there. He didn't feel the need to share it with them. He had something else to do, no matter what it cost him personally. Elmer had something coming to him.

"Hey, Mr. Torrence, where you going?" The blond again, gonna take command. Mark kept moving, slowly, toward the doorway. The cop hurried in front of him, stood blocking the door.

In the apartment, Mark could hear the old woman screaming. There'd be cops in there with her, stopping her from going outside and talking to the reporters. Containment, they called it. Until they could haul ass. Maybe have a doctor sedate her, so she couldn't go out there and raise holy hell until after they were all gone.

Mark knew from personal experience how coppers could lie to you.

He had to hurry, get out there before this kid in front of him decided to contain him.

"I need some fresh air."

"Not that way, God, you serious? There's a thousand reporters out there. You need to be alone, Mr. Torrence, you need to get cleaned up."

"Shit," Mark said. "I can't let *them* see me."

The cop gripped Mark's arm by the elbow, was looking down the hall, at the stairway, the elevator.

"Come on, we'll hit the roof, you and me, you need a chance to talk."

"Fine. Do me a favor, take your hand off me, would you?"

The cop looked at him a second, then let go of Mark's elbow.

"Let's go," the cop said, and began to walk down the hallway.

Mark turned and ran through the steel entrance door, and a thousand flash bulbs went off in his face, a half a dozen minicams turned spotlights on him as he ran toward them. He heard a communal gasp, some frightened cries. He stopped, cupped his hands around his mouth and shouted, loudly, so they wouldn't miss it.

"They killed him!"

Mark heard the roar that met his shout; angry, shocked, outraged.

"They killed him, shot him down in cold blood! He was giving up the shotgun, handing it to me when they shot him down like a dog."

The blond cop was at his side now, trying to push him back

inside the building, and Mark shoved him hard, a good one, caught him off guard and knocked him on his ass.

"They don't want you to know!"

A bunch of uniforms were walking toward him now, reporters were shouting questions over the militant shouts of the crowd. They pushed against the barricades. A few of the braver ones broke through and started to follow the police officers, shouting at them.

"They want to cover it up!" Mark shouted. "They killed Elmer and they don't want you to know about it, they'll say it was a suicide!"

The blond cop was in front of him again, disheveled, breathing heavily.

"You're under arrest."

Mark glared at him.

"For inciting to riot and assaulting an officer." The cop grabbed his left arm, roughly, and Mark looked over at the people, could hear the shouts of "Let him go, motherfucker!" the crowd worked up and ready for some action.

"I told you twice to take your hands off me."

"It's not a matter of choice now, mister."

The cops that had been walking toward them were now back at the barricades, had pushed the stragglers who'd followed them back, were looking scared, their sticks out, holding them across their chests and pushing at the crowd that was threatening to overwhelm them.

"Fuck you," Mark Torrence said, and punched the cop, hard, once across the cheek.

It didn't knock him down but it did move him back a little, the cop staggering, the lights on him, flash bulbs exploding all around them as Mark advanced on the man, hands up.

The angry crowd broke through the barricades, screaming, shouting their rage, as the cop reached for his hip, felt his empty holster. Mark backed away from him and tried to melt into the crowd, but a different pair of arms grabbed him, hard, around the chest from behind. He felt cold steel clamped hard on his right wrist, then his left; could hear a lot of movement back there, there was more than one cop attending to him. The crowd behind the barricades began to curse what was happening, he could hear them shouting for the cops to let go.

"Don't you move, you son of a bitch, or I'll squeeze the life out of you right here." Mark recognized the voice behind him as that of the sergeant, the big bastard from SWAT.

"Go ahead and pinch me, motherfucker," Mark said. "I already did what I came here to do."

BRACKEN LET HIMSELF into his house carefully, deep in thought, trying to figure everything out. It had taken too long, the discussion with Pete Papa, it was after eight now, and he would have to get moving. He didn't begrudge himself the time he'd spent, it had to be done, the old man had to believe that he'd told Bracken everything a dozen times. Near the end, Papa had been quizzing him, asking him questions and trying to catch Bracken in a mistake. Fat chance.

He brushed by Tawny with just enough of a look at him to see the hurt appear on his face as Bracken walked by, Tawny now in a silk outfit, pants and top, with a pastel silk shirt open enough to show the top of the tits that Bracken had paid for.

He didn't have time for Tawny's neurosis right now. In fact, it would soon be time to replace him. There was something deeply erotic about screwing a transsexual, but the novelty was wearing off for him, Tawny's constant need for attention was beginning to get on his nerves. And, within a year, if all went well, Tawny would be a full-fledged female. Bracken could not imagine making love to a woman, even a pretend one such as Tawny would be. Silly little self-hating fool, all the time referring to himself as a woman.

But he had other things to think about now, such as his continued survival. And the death of the man who'd caused Terri to be killed. The death of Tommy Torelli.

Bracken walked to his private office and unlocked the door, entered, closed the door behind him and locked it again from the inside. Now, totally safe, he could think without any distractions.

What could he do, what were his options? He had a pretty good idea of what he would do tonight, but impulsive activity could be the death of him; Bracken had to break things down, analyze them and look at every possibility, before he made any moves that could make his worst nightmare become a brutal reality.

So, what could he do? The first move, and maybe the smartest, would be to do nothing. Sit back and let Tulio turn, watch Papa's family be destroyed from the inside out. What would it lose Bracken? Nothing, really, at all. He didn't make the bulk of his income from Pete Papa's family. He'd worked for the man on and off for over twenty years, but he'd never felt any filial loyalty toward him, he didn't feel that he owed Papa anything. If he let things progress along to their logical conclusions, Papa would be in prison for the rest of his life, and Tulio would be so securely hidden that a legion of hit men wouldn't be able to find him.

But if he took that stance, let things happen, he'd lose his chance of finding where Torelli was hiding out.

What had Papa said? He had a picture, along with proof, evidence of where Torelli was hiding.

Bracken had been on a total of nine fruitless hunting expeditions over the years, trying to find Torelli. In every case, the search had cost him money. Money paid to informants, travel expenses, the little things that added up once he got to the place Torelli was supposed to be. The things he had to do to approach the man with caution—finding out about someone's life wasn't as easy as some might think. It took time, and money, to go all the way back to the day of somebody's birth.

All the time that it took for him to do these things, Bracken would be fighting the urge to rush the job, go in, find out if the man was Torelli, kill him and his entire family if he had one, then get out. It wasn't like a job, a paid performance. Killing Torelli was personal. Bracken had a great stake in finding the man and bringing him to justice.

But he couldn't bring himself to just rush in, no matter how much he wanted to. He was too much of a professional, and he had to believe that Torelli had safeguards, wherever he was, that he knew that Bracken and the mob would never stop searching for him, no matter how long he was underground. There might even be federal marshals still with him, if not living with him, then at least nearby.

Every thread, every hint as to where Torelli might be, had to be carefully checked out, approached as if the tip were completely legitimate and Torelli had indeed been found. They all had to be carefully checked out, no mater how impatient he was to see him face to face.

And every time, it hadn't been Torelli.

There'd been men who'd looked like him, men who might

look like him after his appearance had been surgically altered, men who resembled Torelli with an extra fifty pounds on their frames, and still others who would have been a dead ringer for him if Torelli had been anorexic. Not one of the nine had been a true spotting of the man, and not one of the nine had been a joke, a waste of Bracken's time. They all *might* have been Torelli, and that was all Bracken needed to go out on the hunt.

Major cities, mob cities, weren't even a consideration. The FBI would not send a witness into an area where there was verified organized crime influence. It would be too risky, too likely that he'd be spotted. They could not afford to lose a man—if they did, they'd get no new recruits. No, the perfect record had to be maintained, every protected witness had to stay alive, or the program would be destroyed.

Bracken's problem with that, was: Who would know if a protected witness had been killed? The FBI wouldn't call a press conference, would not allow the murder to become public knowledge. For all the public knew, dozens had been killed already. Rumors of such murders cropped up regularly in the underworld.

But if Torelli had been hit, Bracken would surely have learned of it. Whoever it was that had performed the task would have made sure he'd known, in order to win Bracken's all important favor. He was the best, and they all knew it, which was why his services were so much in demand among men who had brutal and casual killers around them every day. No, he'd have learned about it. Torelli, he was sure, was, somewhere in this country, still alive.

Somewhere in Utah or Nebraska, or maybe Beloit, Wisconsin.

Someplace where organized mobsters would not waste a lot of their time. Maybe in the Midwest, maybe even on an island. But he wouldn't be hiding in New York or Los Angeles, Las Vegas or New Jersey, he'd never be in a major city. He'd caused too much damage to Pete Papa to stay in any large city; there'd always be someone, somewhere, keeping a casual eye out for him, and for the same reason that the mob would have informed Bracken in the event that Torelli had been hit: they'd want Pete Papa's gratitude, he was the most powerful single gangster in the entire United States.

So, what Papa had, what Papa must have, is a picture, of Torelli, sent to him by someone else in one of the other mobs. With something else in the picture that gave away the man's physical environment. A statue or a monument that would prove where Torelli lived. Some concrete evidence that Papa had chosen to bargain with.

It would have to be proof, beyond a shadow of a doubt. Pete Papa would know that to lie to Bracken about such a thing would be a cordial invitation to his long overdue funeral. There were lies that you could tell, if you were powerful enough to get away with them once the lie was disclosed; if you had the juice to look at the person you'd lied to and tell them to kiss your ass.

This wouldn't be one of those lies. This would be beyond redemption, if it turned out that Papa was lying. Because Bracken would risk his life to get the sort of information that Pete Papa was promising. And would be more than willing to take a life— even if it was Pete Papa's—if that information was even slightly less than true.

No, Papa was not a stupid man, no matter how desperate he might be at the moment. He had some sort of proof, visual, undisputable proof that he was willing to hand over to Bracken, along with two million dollars, for the death of Don Tulio, Papa's best friend and lifelong crime partner.

So, option number two was to risk everything tonight, Bracken's life, his future, his freedom, everything, for what Pete Papa had tucked away somewhere, the proof of Torelli's refuge.

Blackmail, was what it was. How long had Papa been holding it? How long had he had knowledge of Torelli's whereabouts, and hadn't done anything? Was he that smart? Bracken believed that he was. The man liked to ramble on with people he thought he could trust, but he hadn't lasted fifty years by being anyone's fool.

Even though Torelli had cost him three years of his life, and the services of many men who'd been valuable to him for much longer than that, it was just like Papa to wait on punishing him, not risking any of his own people, not taking the chance of a murder conspiracy rap putting him away in some prison for the rest of his life.

Protected witnesses were the government's first line of attack against the mob, they had to be protected and kept alive under any circumstances. If Torelli were to be hit, the FBI would use every ounce of power it had to put his killers behind bars for the rest of their lives, if they could. Papa would not want anyone knowingly associated with him to do such a job, not when a stranger such as Bracken could be used.

There was one other problem with this line of reasoning, one that deserved Bracken's attention for a moment.

If Papa had been sitting on the information for a time, Torelli might have moved, the government might have changed his identity again. That would have happened many times, in the last fifteen years.

All Torelli would have to do was get himself arrested, or in some other situation where police attention would be drawn to him. Or the feds could come into information that they thought might do him harm. Any reason, no matter how flimsy, would be cause to take Torelli away, change his identity again and let him start over in some other town where nobody would have ever heard his name.

Papa would know this, would be aware of such things. And he wouldn't dare blackmail Bracken and then not come through with the goods. So the picture had to be current, had to be something he'd come into just recently.

And all Bracken had to do to get his hands on this picture was to breach the security of a house that was quite probably guarded by an army of federal agents, kill everyone inside that house, and get away again, scot free.

Was there any other way for Bracken to get the information, the picture that was in Pete Papa's possession? No, if there were, he would have had it by now. Someone would have made sure that Bracken had gotten the evidence, there were enough people out there who knew how dearly Bracken would pay for that one little picture.

Enough people who knew, too, what Bracken would be willing to do to get his hands on the thing, the work he would perform for free for proof of Torelli's whereabouts.

It was a good gamble for Pete Papa to take. If Bracken got caught, Papa would believe with all his heart that he'd never give Papa up to the law. He was a professional killer, his discretion and lifelong silence came as fringe benefits of the large price tag you paid for Bracken's services. If Bracken *didn't* get caught, all Papa had to do was hand over a picture and a ton of his stolen money, and everyone would be happy, life would go on as before.

The deal wasn't as sweet for Bracken, he had more to lose than Papa. He was nearly thirty years younger, and he hadn't even come close to doing everything that he wanted to do with his life. His compulsions, his needs, what they forced him to do, had held him back since he was a child, kept him shackled to people like Papa, who paid him great amounts of money for doing what he did so incredibly well.

But that wouldn't last forever. He'd do a perfect hit, someday. And when he did he knew that it would be over. When the flawless murder was committed, when Bracken felt in his heart that he'd committed that act, he could take what he had and retire, spend the rest of his life in Paris . . .

But that time hadn't come yet, and it might not ever come. And tonight he had work to do; there was a picture he needed more desperately than he needed oxygen to breathe.

There was another picture, in the bottom of his desk, that meant the world to him. Bracken unlocked his drawer and took it out, looked at it, put it atop his desk and stared at it longingly.

The picture was in a gold frame, sitting on his desk, the only sign there was in this world that Bracken suffered from the human failing of love, locked here in his office, and then inside his desk, locked away where it could never betray him.

The boy in the picture was young, early twenties, and movie star gorgeous, blond and smiling and carefree and in love. He had his arm around a much younger Bracken, who was smiling woodenly into the camera.

Terri. Terri. God, he'd loved that child. Besides his sister, he couldn't think of anyone else he had ever loved. Just she and Terri, and now they were both dead.

Bracken picked the picture up and hugged it to his chest, rocked back and forth with Terri in his arms. He began to sob, silently, as he did a lot these days, thinking of Terri and how it had been, how vastly different things would be today if the boy had only lived. When he was done, he put the picture back in his drawer, locked it again, then wiped at his eyes.

Bracken went to his closet, unlocked it, disarmed the separate alarm, then opened the door and studied the weapons inside. He shook his head, then closed the door slowly. There was no reason to not play with what got you into the game in the first place. There were men who were better with guns than he could ever hope to be. He'd be coming across such men in a little while, later tonight. But he was the best that lived with his hands, his feet, and with sharp-edged weapons, that he'd lovingly honed himself.

If such weapons weren't good enough for the task at hand, then tonight, his nightmare would come true. Tonight, they would just have to hunt him down and kill him.

HIS BEEPER WAS turned off and in his coat pocket. Mark looked at the dashboard clock and marveled that it was only closing in on eleven. He drove with the feeling there was no sunlight left in the world anywhere anymore, feeling it, sensing it, that the sun would never rise again.

He'd killed Elmer as surely as if he'd stuck the gun into his forehead and pulled the trigger himself.

Sure enough, he was right. He jumped as reality set in, the remembrance of the night overwhelming him, depressing him. Frightening him, too. Elmer, good Lord, poor, stupid, sweet young Elmer.

Talk about stupid; look what he himself had done. Fifteen and a half years of hiding out in peace, and he blows it all in one hour, jumps his dumb ass in front of a half-dozen TV cameras, God knew how many 35-millimeters and personal recorders, minicams, and Polaroids.

If he had to come out of the closet, though, what better cause could he choose for a springboard?

Mark drove slowly, not wanting to get home before Caroline was in bed. Had she seen what had happened on the TV? Surely, someone she knew would have called. Christ, he was depressed, could not remember the last time he had felt so low. Then again when was the last time he'd sat in a cramped jail cell for five hours? He used to get out of them a lot quicker when he was back with the wiseguys, when the cops knew who he was and feared the people he worked for.

There he was, thinking about it again, about what he used to be.

Mark steered the car along Lake Shore Drive, taking the scenic route home, in no hurry. How long had he slept in the cell? It had to be two, three hours after they'd made him take a shower and printed him and taken his picture; they'd impounded his clothing for evidence, and now he was wearing sweat clothes with tight laceless sneakers on his feet. They'd locked him up and twenty years had gone by, he'd gone over to the wooden bench cot that was bolted to the wall and he'd laid back on it, his wet head atop one of his arms, and he'd immediately fallen asleep, he'd been drained. He'd only got up twice: when the blond cop had come and talked to him, and when the turnkey had told him that a lawyer was there with his bond money.

He'd been in the jail shower for some time, too, scraping at his skin, scrubbing Elmer's blood and brains and skull off himself long after he was clean. He hadn't slept well in the cell, didn't feel rested, thoughts had raced through his mind, and his sleep had been disturbed by nightmares.

Why did it have to be like this? Why was there always so much confusion? There would be people at the youth center who'd think that Mark was part of a conspiracy, that Elmer had died because of Mark's hatred of his race. Nothing he said would be able to convince them differently; they could look at a video-tape of the entire event and still believe Mark guilty of the boy's murder.

He worked in a place where most of the people in the building did not like him, it was as simple as that, Mark knew that and had thought that he'd accepted it. And for no other reason than because he was caucasian. There were those who knew better, who would die for Mark, but a lot of the time they'd turn their back on him, after they were out of the gangs for a while and had been politicized by Del. It hurt him, people he cared deeply about, people he'd gone to the wall for, snubbing him. Sometimes he just wanted to give it all up, sometimes he wanted to walk away from it all and pretend that life was safe and good, pretend that all that mattered was his family.

Elmer had never looked down on him, had never even mentioned the difference in their race. Elmer had liked him, loved him, had trusted him. And now Elmer was dead, and the second-guessing would begin.

Mark pulled over at an all-night South Side diner, walked inside and ordered a cup of coffee, feeling a few aches and bruises. It hadn't been a pleasant ride to the station last night. There was some common-knowledge street wisdom that had come true in his life last night; don't ever hit a cop and then pretend that you have rights.

The diner was almost empty, a couple of older black cops in

uniform were sitting at a booth, the only other customers. They'd looked up at him when he'd entered, then gone back to their discussion, talking together in low voices, as if not wanting to destroy the quiet peacefulness of the place, or perhaps they had so little peace in their night that they'd grab what they could on their coffee break. Their radio never shut up, though, crackled with action that Mark couldn't understand. He turned back to see the young black waitress standing in front of him, smiling.

"You want some pie or cake with that coffee, mister? How about some fresh fruit?"

Mark stirred the coffee and ordered a nectarine, chewed at it, wanting something in his stomach other than caffeine, stared at the coffeepot behind the counter as it brewed a new pot, Mark deep in thought, wondering where it all would lead.

What would Caroline do, what would she say? She'd have to have seen the broadcast, it was right there live on the six o'clock news. He tried to say a prayer, to pray that she wouldn't leave him. He didn't know what he'd do without her. Maybe wind up in a basement somewhere, with a pistolgrip shotgun clutched in his hands.

Someone from the government would come out now, Mark knew. The cop, Dolan, who'd arrested him, had taken his picture and his prints, and the feds, those bastards, still had a hold on them, there was no information available without calling a certain number and explaining what information was wanted and having to reveal why. He'd walked away from their program over thirteen years ago, and they were still a part of his life, still there to haunt him.

He resented it now, their arrogant goddamned belief that sometime, somewhere, he'd screw up again and wind up in some jail. Resented their patience in waiting so many years, updating software to include his name and fingerprints, believing Mark was an habitual criminal and would remain one for the rest of his life.

"Why's the FBI hiding your identity?" the cop wanted to know when he'd come and awakened Mark in the cell.

"You that stupid?" Mark had asked, wanting the guy to come into the cell with him, just for a minute.

He'd been the supposed negotiator. He was the one who was supposed to have ascertained that Elmer posed a danger to no one, he was the one who was supposed to sit on the basement door until Elmer fell asleep. And he was the one who had to take responsibility for what had happened, no matter who it was who had actually come charging through the window.

"You look that stupid," Mark said. It was getting to the cop, Mark could tell. Good.

"Tell you what, Mr. Hostage Negotiator, why don't you come on in here with me, and I'll tell you all about it. Go back and get your gun if it'll make you feel safer. Matter of fact, it'll look better for me later, if you come in with the gun. I'll give you every chance that your buddies gave to Elmer."

When the cop spoke, it was as a professional, but Mark could tell, he was copping a plea. You didn't have to be jumping up and down and shouting to try and rationalize your way out of your own stupidity.

The cop said, "I didn't order that assault. I never gave them the green light. There was never an impasse. Everything got screwed up, nothing went properly over there, right from the start." The cop had been talking in his courtroom testimony voice, without emotion, but if what had happened hadn't bothered him, then why had he spent so much time trying to explain things to Mark?

The cop had said, "There were people who were supposed to be there who weren't there, and plenty of people who *weren't* supposed to be there who were there before even *I* was. Some of the wrong people, this time."

"Bet they'd 'a showed up if some white guy on the North side had gone ballistic, I bet you wouldn't have had any trouble finding enough of the right people then."

The cop had walked away then. When Mark had been bailed out, the cop had been nowhere in sight.

Chris, the lawyer, had told him that several units would want to be talking to him, and soon. The Office of Professional Standards, the Internal Affairs people. Mark would probably be called to testify before a grand jury. And the press, whatever you do, Chris told him, stay away from the press. They'd crucify you in court if you turned this into a celebrity case. Only the prosecutors were allowed to do that in this city.

Mark hadn't bothered to tell him that he'd do no such thing. Wouldn't appear before any grand jury, wouldn't speak to any cops from any inter-departmental headhunting unit. His face, with Elmer's head all over it, had been shown on TV, he'd be all over the morning papers. By Friday at the outside he would be yesterday's news, but the mob, they never forget you. And Chicago was a mob town. And those guys, they could hate each other, but they'd still be looking to take off a stoolie, Chicago for New York, and the other way around, because when one guy went to jail due to the testimony of an informer, it meant that anyone could go to jail for the very same reason. These guys, they didn't even like to *think* about the pen. Maybe even now, there were people being mobilized.

He had to get out, had to beat feet quick, before they came hunting, sniffing around his family.

Goddamn.

Mark lifted his hand for another cup of coffee, wanting to make the night last, not wanting to go home. He nodded when she poured it, shook his head when she asked if he wanted anything else. Mark turned on the stool, unconsciously looking out the diner window. All he could see was his car, the four-year-old Ford Crown Vic that he'd bought new and had been so proud of back then. Mark looked at it now and thought that it might wind up being his casket. Mark didn't have a driveway, nor did he have a garage. The Torrences kept their cars out in the street, where anyone could tamper with them, anyone could plant a bomb . . .

It surprised the hell out of him, how easily he slipped back into it. The mindset of the wiseguy, always thinking, always preparing. Nothing was too outrageous, no act too treacherous. Where Mark's mind was now, there were no friends, nobody to be trusted. There were people to be used, and people trying to use you. And people to protect; he had three of them, who through no fault of their own were now at risk.

All right then, run with it, sit here at the diner alone and drink your cup of coffee, think it over the way you would have when you were twenty-one years old, when your name had been Torelli.

He had kids, if he was going to think about it the right way, he had to understand right up front that he'd put them in serious jeopardy. Caroline, too, her life would be in danger. There was a stab of guilt over that, and he quickly, easily suppressed it. He had to not think about putting three children and an innocent woman at risk because of what he'd done to avenge the death of a black man to whom he was not related in any real way.

What he'd done had been the act of a rational, caring man. The man Mark was today, and he had to now think as the man he had once been. Now, he had to think like an animal.

Would they come after his wife and kids to try and make him suffer, or would they kill him on the street, just to put past business to rest?

He had to figure that they'd go for the family first. For two reasons, what they'd see as good ones. First, to make his family suffer for the way their own families had suffered while they were away, doing time for crimes that Mark's testimony had convicted them of. And second, to send a message to anyone else out there thinking of rolling over to the G. See how we treat those who disrespect us? We kill their families then make them die slow. It was the way that men like this thought.

It didn't matter that it was all fifteen years ago; it wouldn't make any difference to them that there were now thousands of tough guys on the program. All that would matter to them was that one of them got what they saw him to deserve.

And if Pete Papa was still alive, he might come out himself, to join in the fun.

The coffee was gone, Mark was staring down into the dregs in the bottom of his cup. He nodded at the waitress when she got off her stool down at the end of the counter and came by with the pot, pointed at his cup. She did not ask him this time if he wanted anything with his coffee.

How big would the story be, really? When you thought about it rationally, maybe not that big at all. A few lines in the paper, the dramatic footage for the TV news, but all in all, it wasn't that important. All they had was a dead ghetto kid and wild accusations made by the boy's social worker. In a city of three and a half million people, it wasn't really important. Maybe it would blow over. Maybe it was no big thing. No reporter would come to the house; they wouldn't know how to find him. The house was in Caroline's name, given to her by her father, and she hadn't taken his when they'd married. Maybe the wiseguys wouldn't find him, either. Maybe he'd get away scot free.

And maybe there was a Santa Claus. He had to stop thinking like a square john, like a working stiff. Still, it had to be considered. Maybe they wouldn't find out about him. His face had been covered with gore when the flashbulbs had gone off. His nose had been worked on many years ago.

Was that a risk he wanted to take? At the very least, he owed his wife the truth. He'd tell her about himself, lay it all out, then let her take it from there.

She'd wanted to know since January, had been throwing subtle shots since then. Growing bolder as he evaded her, until now she was demanding what she saw to be her right; tell me about your past, Caroline would say; let me know what formed you. As if he were a plastic life-sized toy that had been put through some kind of mold.

He hadn't told her out of fear of losing her, and now he had no choice but to let her go. For her sake, for the sake of the kids, if he was going to be cold, totally pragmatic, he had no choice but to leave. And if he was any kind of man, he'd have to tell her what he was.

What he'd *been*.

It was impossible for him now to separate the two, the past from his present, what he was from what he'd been. The man sitting at the restaurant counter wouldn't dream of helping someone like Elmer Griffin, not unless there was a profit in it for him.

Somewhere in the back of his mind, on some level, he had to admit that he always suspected that someday, they would find him. Why else did he have all those weights in the basements? Why else did he work two or three hours a day on his body? Why else would he have stayed in such condition, watched his diet as he had? Because he knew.

He'd even dream about it. See those bastards come kicking in his door, automatic rifles blazing. See, in his dreams, his children's heads filled with lead, cut in two, or the top gone, like Elmer's had been this night.

And what would he do with that body of his, now that his secret might well be out? Could he use his physical strength to kill a man today? He'd never murdered, even back then. Could he cold-bloodedly put his morals on the side and take a man's life, kill without emotion?

It was something to think about. Something he had to consider.

It was different if you came home and found somebody raping your wife. Or if someone molested one of your kids. Then, in the heat of anger, in the passion of the moment, most men—or women—could kill, and could probably do it easily. Later, they would feel remorse. Later, they would cry. Take a look at what they'd done and maybe sink into the pit of despair. But at such moments, in times of fury, Mark believed, anyone was capable of murder.

He spent most of his working days with the type of kids who'd sometimes brag to him about drive-bys and setups, hits, revenge killings. Dis murders that occurred for no reason other than somebody had gotten into somebody else's face. They'd boast of their exploits, knowing their secrets were safe with Mark, and he'd talk to them, calmly, point out to them the error of their ways. Sometimes they'd break down in grief, other times, they'd laugh. Depended on the kid, on how callused he'd become. If the stories were true, or even exaggerated, a large number of these kids had already wasted their lives.

He knew that there were kids out there who looked at killing as a part of life. That there were kids he saw each day who had performed murders for candy bars, starting before their teen years. Kids came into the center, teenagers who'd been shot more than once before they celebrated their thirteenth birthday. Kids with one lung or missing an eye, kids with a limp, ten-year-old cripples.

He'd heard stories of legendary South or West Side killers who giggled as they murdered, or sang punch lines from rap songs. Heard about kids who'd bend over their kills if they had time, would study the corpse with interest, looking for what was missing, trying to see if a soul escaped. Kids, not yet twenty, with dozens of kills to their names. They had no sense of responsibility beyond their own immediate wants or needs, could justify anything they did in a minute, blame it on society, the white man, or their enemy.

How many times had he heard it, going back to when he was a child? They had it coming to them. They made me do it. Rationales for everything from a street fight to a murder, blame it on somebody else, accept no personal responsibility.

When black ghetto kids became organized criminals, they were called mutants, gangbanging sociopaths or animals. When white men did it, movies were made about them, portraying them as men of respect. Only the white men's rationales were different; they were only protecting their families.

Mark knew better, from personal experience. He'd met a lot of men who talked about their kids, bragged about their sons as if their wives had given birth to the second coming of Christ, and then he'd found out later how badly the kids had been abused, how often the daughters had "seduced" their mobster fathers, how terribly the kids were beaten, simply for acting like kids. He'd have to ask Caroline about that someday, if things ever got back to normal. Were all criminals degenerates? Was it something twisted in their minds, something they picked up in jails?

There wasn't much difference in the two sets of people, only the cultures were different, the rationalizations more acceptable for one type than the other. And the color of their skin, that was different, too.

Mark had lived with and been a part of both types, and now, being cold, he had to admit that both types scared him out of his wits.

And he knew why. It came to him with a sudden clarity as he sat at the restaurant counter, the sound of the cops' radio tinnily blaring out the unspeakable things that people could do to one another.

He had told himself and the law fifteen years ago that he'd done what he'd done to be doing right for a change, but he knew that to be a lie. Had known it to be a dishonest statement even as he was saying it. He could pinpoint it back to the exact moment when it first struck him, staring through a thick window at a lower West Side hospital back home: When he'd first lain eyes on his son, he'd had something to lose.

What did he care about before then? What could have mattered to him? He'd loved his mother, sure, but he hadn't gone home for her funeral. Still in the program back then, living in Omaha, Nebraska, jetting back in under heavy security to testify at various trials, it had just been too dangerous for even a private viewing, they had told him, in private, and in his heart he'd had to agree.

It was when he'd seen his son, his flesh and blood in that room, that Mark realized that things had changed forever, that nothing would be the same again.

Because he had something to lose he also had, for the first time, the fear of it being taken away from him.

He would have left Pete Papa and the rest of them alone, would have spent his life in prison and never said a word if they'd taken care of Mario, seen to his financial needs. But they hadn't, they'd threatened the child, were going to kill him if they thought Mark was talking, and that was too much for Mark to bear. Something he couldn't live with.

And if his love of Mario alone had been enough for him to change his life forever, to turn his back and rat out people he'd known and admired his entire life, then what was he willing to do to preserve what he had today? How far would he go to protect the family that he loved so deeply?

Mark decided, there at the counter in a diner he'd never been in before, with two cops sitting not fifteen feet away, that he could indeed kill without emotion. Because the things on earth that he was most afraid of losing—his family—also brought him strength.

Mark got up off the stool and laid two dollars on the counter, he walked out of the diner with his head down, his keys dangling from his finger. His mind was made up, he would go home and take a shower and get dressed. He'd shave and brush his teeth and then go downstairs and see if he could manage a bit to eat, get himself into the right frame of mind. Then he'd go upstairs and wake Caroline, and hope that he'd somehow have the courage he needed to finally tell her everything.

"TELL ME EVERYTHING! You want to tell me everything?" Caroline wasn't calm anymore, the professional veneer was gone. She hadn't been upstairs sleeping, had been down here waiting for him the entire time.

They were in the living room, the two younger children upstairs—herded up there by a mother who'd heard her husband's key in the lock and ran them up the stairs with hardly a hello to their father—blissfully unaware of what was so suddenly wrong in their lives. They were probably happy to have been allowed to stay up so late on a school night. Mark had no idea where Mario was.

He'd begun the conversation standing in front of her, looking down at Caroline sitting on the couch, but had started to move, to pace, as soon as she'd begun the tirade. He thought she'd have been at least a little more compassionate.

"It's a little late for that, Mark—or do you want me to call you Tommy?"

"What?" Mark spun on her, astounded. "What did you just say?"

"You heard me. Goddamn you. You owed it to me to tell me the truth. I deserved it, I had at least that much coming to me before you married me." He looked at her, at the anger so apparent on her face. She wasn't about to break into tears, if anything, she was liable to hit him. He'd known her for eleven years and been married to her for ten, but he'd never seen her show this kind of anger, not even during their worst newly-wed arguments.

"What the hell are you talking about?"

"Don't play stupid with me, I know about you. The full implications of what could happen didn't hit me until today, but I've known, Mark, I've known for a while, and you haven't been man enough to ever tell me the truth." Caroline rose now, unfolded off the couch like a gymnast from a mat, her fists at her sides, eyes blazing.

"Mister sensitive. Mister caring. In college when you meet the dumb medical student you're going to spend the rest of your life bullshitting. You told me you wanted to make a difference, told me that you wanted to change society. All the time you were just hiding, doing the work you thought would draw the least attention to yourself from *them*. You *used* me, you set me up. *And* our children."

"That's not—that's not how it was." Could she really believe the words she was saying? Could anyone know him as well as she did and still think him capable of such cold, brutal manipulation?

"Convince me of that now, go ahead, eleven years after you first had your chance to tell me everything. I had a right to know, Mark, I should have been given the option. If not then, then later, after you knew that you could trust me."

He still couldn't bring himself to tell her the truth. That he'd thought he'd lose her if she'd known.

"How long have you known?" Mark's voice was flat, without emotion.

Everything he'd ever wanted he'd had, up until just now. Now it was all going up in smoke, now it was as if he'd never had it to begin with. He had to stay under control, keep everything in check, even though it felt as if his life was ending right here, this early morning.

"It doesn't matter how long I've known." She must have seen the flinch of anger across his face, because she challenged him, came stomping across the room to confront him, Caroline right in his face, unafraid.

"What? What are you going to do? Beat me if I don't tell you what you want to know? Is that what's really inside of you? You think I'm going to jump at your command?"

"I've got rights here too, Caroline." It wasn't easy, staying calm, not when she was testing him like this, mad and shouting at him.

"Go ahead, Mark, talk to me about *your* rights." She was sarcastic now, Caroline going for the knockout punch. "What rights are you referring to, the right to beat your woman if she doesn't do what you say, doesn't answer your questions to your liking?"

That was it. Did she think he was one of her clients?

"Shut up, Caroline, just calm down."

"Is that an order?" Caroline crossed her arms, she glared at him, venomously. "Are you giving me orders now, Mr. Mafioso?"

"That's bullshit, I don't know where you got that!"

"Are you denying your name is really Tommy Torelli, is that what you're doing? Are you going to stand there and lie to my face, try and tell me that you weren't a protected government fucking witness? You tell me about your rights, but what about mine? What about the kids' rights? Didn't I have a right to know, before I decided to marry you? Didn't I have a right to the truth before your face gets splashed all over the newspapers, all over the fucking six and ten o'clock news?"

"You still don't know the truth."

"The hell I don't. I've known it for months."

"Who told you, your father? You started prying into my past right after Christmas. What did he do, feed you some speculation along with some 'facts' he picked up out there playing rent-a-cop, playing big shot fucking copper in Phoenix?"

He was shouting too, now, advancing on her. Caroline didn't give an inch.

"He never said a *word* about you, not a word, until tonight!"

That stopped him. Tonight? What about tonight? The old man was in Phoenix, Arizona. How did he find out about any of this?

"When did you speak to him today?"

"Call him and find out."

Mark had had enough of her self-righteous anger. This was a matter of life and death, and, like it or not, she was now a part of the equation. He grabbed her arms and shook her, once.

"Goddamnit, just for a second, forget you wouldn't have married me if you'd known. Try and forget your whitebread scorn long enough to understand we're in trouble."

He let her go and she stood there, as if she were seeing him for the first time. Looking at him in the manner in which she might look at a strange new client who had come into her office and assaulted her. As if the last eleven years didn't matter, had never passed.

Softly, hurt, Mark said, "It's important, Caroline. Important that I know."

"I called him." She was rubbing her arms where he'd grabbed her. Mark could see red marks there, she might bruise up, later. "After I saw you on the news," Caroline said.

She said, "You can look down your nose at the law all you want, you've been doing it for as long as I've known you, and now I understand why. But your arrogant brand of criminal ignorance only makes it easier for them to catch people like you. He was never stupid, and neither are his friends in the force. He's gotten calls all night from them, wanting to know if he could talk to you, straighten you out about what you'd done, the lies you told the public, before things got too far out of hand. For God's sake, Mark, do you realize what you did? There was a *riot* there after you were arrested. Stores are still burning. Spring's not even half over yet and the newsradio stations are predicting race wars all summer over what happened tonight. Elmer Griffin has become a ghetto saint."

"You called him or he called you, either way, what did he know?" She hesitated, as if she wasn't going to answer. She dropped her hands from her arms, shook her head. As if finally fully realizing her own stupidity in marrying him.

"Word's out throughout the department about you, that the government has a hold on your prints, a notice to call if you're ever arrested for anything. That only means one thing, Mark, and they know what that is. And they're not as stupid as you think. Before you were even printed, they knew who your father-in-law was. And he wasn't even going to call me about it, to give me a hard time. He said when I called that I knew where he was if I needed him. He never even told his friends on the department anything about you tonight. He loved you like a son."

Loved. Caroline had used the past tense.

Mark said, "He couldn't have learned my old name, couldn't have found out about that from his friends out there. If they'd found out who I was already, they'd have released the name and the details of my past, Caroline, trying to discredit me, to save face. Your father didn't tell you about me. Not tonight, not at Christmas."

"It's not your business who told me."

Mark grunted. He thought he had her number.

"I see. No more of my business now than my past was your business, is that the game we're playing?" She didn't answer him, shook her head, repulsed by him.

"You ignorant, hateful man. How could I have ever been so blind, so goddamned stupid?"

"Be morally offended later, Caroline, right now, it's important, for your sake as well as the kids'. Who told you about me?"

"*I* did," Mario said, from where he was standing in the doorway.

SEEING THE KID calmed them both down. For a minute, Mark could only stare at him, feeling many emotions, the strongest of which was betrayal, as if the two of them had ganged up on him, worked against him, to try and hurt him.

That feeling couldn't last for long, though, seeing the kid, standing there, so afraid. Mario's lower lip was trembling, as Elmer's had been hours ago, yet he stood there defiantly, staring back at his father.

"You gonna hit me, now?" Mario said, and the terror in his voice broke Mark's scornful silence.

"When have I ever hit you?" Mark's voice was just above a whisper, he spoke incredulously. "In your life, Mario, tell me, when have I ever hit you?"

"You were about to hit Mom, I saw you grab her."

"Been there a while, watching? All right, tell me this: When have I ever hit your mom?"

"I knew he was there," Caroline said.

"You should have told me."

"Why? You'd act differently in front of him? Modify your behavior depending on who's in the room with you? I wanted him to see you as you are, not just see what you wanted to show him. He's seen enough of that in his lifetime."

"I don't know what you mean by that, Caroline . . ."

"No, you don't. This boy has suffered deep emotional trauma since the day he was born. First he had a thief for a father, then a prisoner, then a protected witness, then a college student, then a social worker. You spent more of the past ten years with gang members than you did with any of your own children, but Mario was the one who needed you most, he was the one you dragged through the dirt with you. He didn't know the real you, never saw what you really are. It's not that he's that dumb; it's that you're that good. You pulled the wool over all of our eyes, didn't you, Mark?"

Mario was on the couch now, looking down, ashamed. In spite of his anger, Mark's heart went out to him, was breaking at the sight of his boy, sitting there, blaming himself for this fight. Didn't he know that it had nothing to do with him? Didn't he know that everything Mark had done back then, he'd done to protect Mario? Mark had never told him that back then, he didn't want to make the kid feel guilty over Mark's actions. Mario hadn't chosen to start his life as the son of a thief and a half-a-hooker.

Now Mark fought to say the right thing, had to settle for two words he hoped would convey his feelings.

"I'm sorry . . ."

"For what, Mark?" Caroline said. She was angry and he couldn't blame her, he had no right to blame her. "Sorry that he told me, or sorry that you got found out? Sorry that you ever were a mobster in the first place? Sorry that you turned government witness against your friends? What the hell are you really sorry about, Mark? That's the thing you have to figure out."

Her voice was calm, that unveiled disgust still there in her tone, but at least she wasn't yelling anymore. Mark didn't know what to say, did not know how to respond. He ignored Caroline. The fight was all out of him. He looked at his son, who was looking at him with eyes that spoke of sorrow so deep that no sixteen-year-old should ever be aware of it; sorrow Mark had seen before, many times, in the eyes of children much younger than his son. Like HardWay. He had eyes like this.

"I'm sorry," Mark said again, and Mario nodded his head. The boy was crying.

"Me, too," he said.

"I'm taking the children away from here."

That got a rise out of him, a small one, but from the heart.

"They're my kids, too. You can't just take them from me."

"I won't put them at risk. The teachers will question Elaine and Kenny all day tomorrow, at this point, their father's a hero. When the truth comes out, this house, their schools, will be over-run with reporters, with people wanting to see the big mobster's kids. I won't subject them to that. And how long will it be before someone *else* comes looking for you?" She pointed her head at Mario, as if she were keeping the truth from him. "You know who I mean."

His resolve from the restaurant faded out of him. Back then, trying to be cold, he'd wanted to leave, to set them free of him. Now the thought of living without them terrified him, the thought chilling Mark right to his soul.

"I'll handle that. We'll go away together, all of us. I won't let you destroy everything I've spent fifteen years building, Caroline." He was doing exactly what she'd accused him of earlier. Regulating his behavior because Mario was in the room. There was an emptiness inside him, coupled with an insane longing to destroy. He was abruptly very happy that Mario was sitting there on the couch.

"All you've built were lies, Mark, these past fifteen years." Her voice gave away her exasperation, her regret that he couldn't see the truth as she did. "Home, family, marriage, job, it was all a lie, and you let it become real to you. It was all founded on a lie, it was all fed on a lie. It turned into a lie, finally, because none of us knew the truth except Mario and you, and you, Mark, weren't talking. You can't think for a minute that we'd all go away together. Go away where? On the run the rest of our lives? No, you made this bed of lies, now you have to live with the truth. You won't drag these kids down with you. It's going to be hard enough as it is, breaking the truth to Elaine and Kenny."

"Take them to your dad's, then, Elaine and Kenny. Where you'll be safe. After you've calmed down, Caroline, we'll talk, I need to talk to you."

"I'm going with Mom," Mario said.

"You can't mean that. You can't," Mark said.

"He's going with me. And there's nothing for us to discuss. Your 'need to talk' to me should have been expressed eleven years ago, Mark. Or even yesterday, before this happened. Things might be different, if you had."

He was standing beside her, but he'd never felt so alone. Mario was on the couch, looking up at him now, his face filled with so many different emotions that Mark could only nod, try to assure the boy with that simple act that he understood his decision.

"Take care of your mother, Mario," Mark said, and there was no emotion in his voice. It was flat, cold, a computer voice without inflection.

"Come on, Mario, we've got to pack. The kids are already packed and waiting upstairs, they think they're taking a vacation to see Grandpa."

Mario was anguished. "What about school, Mom? What about Diane?"

"I'll call the school, tomorrow," Mark said. "They'll give me the records, I'll send them wherever you need them to go." Nothing had changed in his voice. It sounded as empty as he felt.

"What about Diane, Mom?" Mario's voice was a plaintive wail. "I love her, I've got to tell her where I'm going."

"Mario, no one can know where we're going. Your father's ensured that we can't trust anyone but your grandfather right now, until this thing is resolved." She left the rest unsaid: Until your father's dead.

"You can stay." One last shot, if he could get the kid to stay for one reason, maybe Mark could convince him to stick around for other ones.

"Mario," Caroline said, "go pack."

Without another word, Mario, hanging his head, crying, walked slowly to the stairs, mounted them silently. They both watched him go, Mark thinking of the way he used to have to tell him not to run, not to bounce up that same stairway. From here, his son looked like an old, old man. He felt Caroline looking at him, felt her eyes burning into the side of his head. He did not want to look at her, forced himself to do so. When she spoke she made him feel like the worst of criminals, Caroline using a tone of voice he'd heard before, but not from her.

It was the voice a defense attorney would use years ago, telling the jury what he thought of the stoolpigeon, Torelli.

"See what you've done with your lies, your deceptions? See what you've done to your family? Does it make you proud, Mark, to see your son like that?"

He had no answer, could not respond. He said, "I'll drive you to the airport, make sure you get off okay."

"You've destroyed our family. You've destroyed our lives. You've destroyed our home. You've destroyed my practice. I think you've already done enough for one lifetime, Mark. You stay home. *I* can take care of them, better than you'd ever know." She paused, eyeing him, without any compassion or understanding.

"There are late night flights to Las Vegas. We can catch a connection from there, or rent a car if we have to. When we leave, it would be better for the children if you're not there."

Mark looked after her, watching her as he'd watched his son, as she mounted the stairs, her shoulders bent from the burden that he'd laid across them, the burden she was willing and more than strong enough to bear.

He waited, silently, until he was sure she was in their bedroom, so that nobody could see him weak, nobody could see him falling apart. It wouldn't be good for the kids, wouldn't be good for the kids . . .

Mark's face crumpled, slowly, as he lost the battle to keep it together, as the full realization of what was about to happen hit him with full force. This house, which had always been his refuge, the place where he felt most safe, was now a mockery of that safety; the home was now his tomb, a casket about to close on what was left of him.

Upstairs, the only people he had ever loved were packing, preparing to leave him forever. The only woman he thought could ever truly understand him now only looked at him with hatred in her eyes. His first born son, the baby he'd worshiped, was now nearly a man, making his own decisions to walk away from his father. The younger children, Elaine and Kenny, would forget him easily enough. In six months, they would not even remember what his face looked like, how his body was shaped.

It was so delicate, reality, it could change on you in a second with no advance warning. Yesterday at this time his greatest worry was some slob who lived next door to him, and his worry that his wife might be going through midlife change prematurely. Today, there was nothing left. He was totally alone. Again.

His lips curled up and his eyes squeezed shut. Mark felt the strength going out of his legs, and he fell to his knees. He lowered his head to the couch, fighting the urge, the need to cry. He breathed in huge gasps, sobbing as he let the breath out, buried his head in the cushion, and screamed into it, once, blindly punching the cushions with curled fists, symbolically beating the property, the house that had been so cruelly a part of this great self-deception, until the tears began to flow, and then he covered his head with his hands and let his anguish overwhelm him.

BRACKEN WAITED UNTIL midnight, until he saw that most of the house was dark. From his vantage point in the trees far above the property he could look down upon the target house, see how difficult it would be to get into. What he was seeing did not give him hope.

He'd spotted four men guarding the grounds, with weapons, staggered, each walking alone. No dogs, which was a relief. Bracken hated animals. He had no idea how many other guards there were inside the house.

He was high up on a hill, on top of the western peak of a small valley in Connecticut, looking down at a house that most likely had sold for twice what his own house was worth, a house that was easily ten times larger than his own. The house he was looking at had to be on ten acres, most of it frontal land, surrounded by a stone fence on three sides. On plenty of private property, some of it wooded, the house with many rooms, lots of fireplaces. Behind the house was a wood, and behind that, these small mountains. It was like having fifty acres. The man knew his business. An hour and a half out of New York City and here they were, in spacious countryside.

Bracken was wearing skintight black stretch pants and a matching turtleneck shirt. Black gym shoes with rubber soles. He would have to always be vigilant of the fact that he wore no gloves, he must not touch anything inside, would have to always be aware of that and not touch anything that would leave a print. He might need his sharpened fingernails; he suspected that he'd certainly need the callused sides of his palms. Gloves would blunt the blows, and the fingernails would be useless inside them.

There was a black military web belt snapped around his waist which carried the tools of his trade, the knives in leather sheaths, hanging on tiny hooks.

He was frightened, in fact, terrified. He had not killed like this since he was a very young man, going in cold, without preparation or planning, back when he'd just have to kill someone, either kill or go insane.

This was not his way. It was for cowboys, for punks. There was too much risk involved here for him, he had to fight the urge to run away, had to force himself to stay where he was, not to go back to the car and blow the whole thing off, head home and find another way to get the picture of Torelli.

But he had to do it. It was the only way to get his hands on that picture.

The night was chilly around him. He'd been sitting so long that the crickets had accepted him as part of the landscape, were chirping again. Every now and again he'd hear something thrashing through the woods, some small wild nocturnal beast, searching for its evening sustenance.

He saw his opening, saw human error in action. Slowly, so as to continue blending in with the background, he began to make his move, sliding down the hill by inches.

Bracken waited, knowing the way the guards were walking, how long it took them to get around the house, having timed them during his watch. There wasn't supposed to be a moment when any single side of the mansion was totally out of someone's sight, some guard was supposed to turn the corner at the same time that the other one was turning the far corner. The guy inside this house was planning on trouble, on a full frontal attack from some quarter, and he was prepared.

More prepared than his guards were, at least for right now.

Bracken could hear two of them talking, could smell their cigarette smoke. The mistake they'd made, that would cost them their lives. Wanting to be social, to have someone to talk to, to break the boredom of their vigil. Bracken smelled the smoke and craved it, had not dared to light up on the hill, could not risk the flash of a lighter or the smoke being spotted, floating against the moonlight.

The two talkative guards were on the left corner of the house, and Bracken went there, lay flat against the stone wall, listening. Floodlights lit the interior of the fence, and the long shadow covered Bracken well. Someone could be standing atop the fence and not see him, flattened there, breathing silently through his mouth.

He could hear them, now moving, talking in low, kidding tones. A third voice, louder, joined the conversation, warned them to keep moving, to split up and get back in position. Bracken heard a muttered, sarcastic, "Fuck you . . ." while the other guard asked the third one who'd died and made him boss.

It was what he'd been waiting for.

Bracken kneeled, then slowly straightened until he was standing on his toes, looking over the top of the wall. He saw two men's backs turn the right corner, saw another man, a muscular man, holding his weapon casually, the gun hanging from a strap around his neck, the man's left hand on top of the barrel, his right stuck deep in his pocket. The man was looking at the ground, and he did not look happy. He was in the middle of the grounds, halfway to the corner. Thinking hard, trying to figure out what *fuck you* meant.

There were maybe fifty feet separating the wall from the house. From the hill Bracken had seen a long, paved drive, twisting through trees, curving out a long way to the street. The front of the house was as well-lit as the back. The sides were dark, without floodlights. The master of the house must keep the bedrooms on the sides.

Bracken boosted himself to the top of the wall and began to run silently along it, until he was ten feet from the end of the house. He jumped lightly to the ground—the point of no return— just as the man was about to turn the right corner of the house.

Bracken made it to him without being heard, and slit his throat from behind, holding one hand across the man's mouth, not looking at his work, but rather at the retreating backs of the two men ahead of them; they were just turning the corner as Bracken dropped his load. The man died silently, there in the side yard, his blood staining the maintained lawn, the man never knowing what had happened to him.

As the next single guard turned the corner Bracken slashed him quickly, across the middle of his throat, with the sharp edge of a long blade. The man's face didn't even register surprise until he was already a bloody mess, a fountain of blood spraying out of him, onto the man who'd killed him. Bracken grabbed the man and pulled him toward him, carelessly tossed the body behind him to die. He pulled a second, similar knife from his belt and stood waiting, crouched, a knife in both hands, hearing their voices before the sound of their footsteps, the last two guards still together, socializing. If he misjudged their distance from one another, this might be tricky; this might even get him killed.

As they turned the corner he leaped, stabbing upward with both fists, hitting the first guard high in the neck, cutting him bad, although the slash was not deadly, the blade brushing the throat then being deflected off of the bone of the jaw. He'd hit the mark on the other man, though, the knife had gone in under the chin, straight up into the brain, and Bracken knew he was gone the second he struck, turned his full attention to the man who'd survived the first strike.

He hadn't survived by much. He was staggering backward, trying to draw in breath, the underside of his jaw cut open to the bone, the bone itself cut nearly in two, the skin was dangling from the side of his face, blood pouring over him, onto his chest. Air escaped from the hole in his neck; his trachea was cut, it was only a matter of minutes.

The man was still staggering backward, the weapon dangling at his side, forgotten, both hands wrapped around his throat, survival now the only thing on his mind, the man still thinking that if he stopped the bleeding, he'd be able to breathe again. Bracken moved to him and pulled him to the dark side of the house, looking into the eyes, knowing the precise moment when the man became aware that he was going to die, seeing the panic there, Bracken studying it clinically.

He held the man up until he died, then, gently, Bracken lowered him to the ground. He was no longer afraid. This would be easier than he thought. These were well-trained professional guards? They were bones for a dog to chew on, now, fertilizer, nothing more.

HE FOUND THREE more guards in the house, two of them sleeping off duty, one in the kitchen, having a midnight snack. Not one of them heard him coming, none of the three was a problem.

Nor was the old woman in the downstairs bedroom, or the

young man, in his twenties, who was in the bedroom upstairs. Bracken silently, thoroughly, and quickly searched the house. There was only one room left, an upstairs bedroom, and he could hear a television blaring from inside. He'd saved it for last, knowing his man was in there.

He opened the door and pushed it wide, holding a slim, double-edged six-inch blade in his right hand.

A filleting knife.

The old man on the bed looked up with the resentment of the powerful at being disturbed. Then he saw who it was, saw the blood-drenched madman, and his resentment turned to horror.

There was a plate on his chest, the old man was having a bite to eat. Bread crumbs were on the front of his robe, on the plate, on the blanket at his side. He was dressed in a maroon silk robe, the robe tight where it was tied around his belly. His bare feet had gnarled toes, corns and calluses everywhere. This man lived in a multimillion dollar house, and didn't want to spend the money to go to a foot doctor. Bracken smiled. He'd cut those corns off, toe by toe.

"Hi, Pete," Bracken said, before Pete Papa screamed for help.

"Go ahead, Pete, yell it a little louder. See if you can raise the dead."

"There's guys, there's guys . . ."

Bracken shook his head.

"No more guys Pete; there's just you and me."

"Tulio! I paid you to hit Tulio!"

"You didn't pay me shit. You'd'a paid me, those'd be federal agents lying out there, rather than your bodyguards and half of your family. You were blackmailing me, Pete, and that's not the way I operate."

"You can't do this, they'll hunt you down like a fuckin' dog, my family'll massacre you, everyone you love!"

"They'd have to find me first, Pete. Name me one of them who knows what I look like. Where I live. Even my real name. All anyone in this business knows is the P.O. Box number that I trusted you with, and they know what Tawny looks like. The box'll be out of commission tomorrow, and Tawny, too, for that matter." He smiled.

"Besides, who's gonna kill me, Pete? You said yourself, there's no one like me anymore." He shrugged. "Judging from the talent you had here guarding you from the feds, I don't think I have anything to worry about. You don't have any real chips to lay on the table anymore, old man."

Bracken had moved closer to the bed as he spoke, until he was standing right at the side, near the nightstand.

"Got a gun in there, Pete? In case the feds come calling? Tell you what, I'll make you a deal. You give me the pictures I want, right now, and I'll use the gun on you and make it quick. If you don't give them to me, right away, then by the time I'm done with you, you'll *want* to use it on yourself."

It was dawning on Papa now, what Bracken had had to do in order to get in here.

"My son? My *wife?*"

"All gone."

He had to hand it to him, the old man still had balls. He made a move at Bracken, careless, sloppy and slow, and Bracken backhanded him with his free hand, watched him flop back down on the bed, then moved in quickly and slashed at his right eye, cut it open, down the middle. It burst open like a squashed bug, fluid oozing onto his cheeks before Papa could even close his eye in pain.

Pete Papa screamed.

"Go ahead, Pete. This house is older than your grandmother, and the closest neighbor is far enough away, gunshots couldn't wake him. Nobody can hear you, you go right ahead and scream if it'll make you feel better."

"No!" Papa had both hands up, in front of his face. His eyes were closed shut. Blood was seeping from under the right eyelid. "No, please, don't take the other eye, please!"

"Give me what I want and I'll make it nice and quick."

"What do you want? What do you want?"

"Come on, you forgetting already? The picture, Pete. I want the picture you held over my head, the picture you tried to use to blackmail me."

"The picture, the *picture?*" Papa was acting as if he'd just now figured things out. "You killed my wife, my son, you blinded me over a *picture?*"

"That's right. Gonna cut the skin off your fat ass for it, inch by inch, too, Pete. Now, where's this picture? Where do you have it?"

"For Christ's sake it's in the closet! Right there in the fucking closet! You didn't have to do this, I would'a given them to you!"

Papa's eyes were still tightly shut. Tears were squeezing out of the left eyelid, diluted blood out of the right, mingled with tears. Papa rolled onto his side, as if hiding from Bracken. When he'd spoken, Bracken could tell from his voice that the old man was crying.

"The picture's in your *closet?*" Bracken almost laughed. "You were going to have me kill federal agents and then hand me a picture I could have just broken in here tomorrow and gotten?" Bracken shook his head.

And he'd almost taken up Papa's challenge, had almost gone out to kill Tulio.

For a picture that was so easy to get.

"Goodbye, Pete," Bracken said, and cut off Papa's scream before it fully formed in his throat.

THE PICTURES, NICE and neat. There was little doubt about it, it was Torelli or close to his exact double. A little heavier, a little more muscular, older, naturally, and there'd been good work done on his nose, some scar tissue around his eyes that Bracken didn't remember, but this looked very much like Tommy Torelli. At least it was the best lead he'd had in fifteen years.

Bracken, wearing a long winter coat he'd taken from Papa's closet to hide his bloodstained clothing, walked slowly through the silent house of death, down the stairs, deep in thought, thumbing through a stack of pictures that had been sitting atop a shelf in an envelope in the closet, ignoring the carnage around him; the bodies weren't even there to him anymore.

So Torelli was in Chicago? What kind of place was that to hide from the mob?

If these pictures were of Torelli, it could only mean one thing. He'd dropped out of the Witness Protection Program. Once you did that, once you signed the papers, Bracken knew, you were free to go out on your own, and if you got killed, well, the feds weren't at fault. They'd tried to keep you safe and you'd walked away from their protection. It was the sort of thing they would publicize. See how we take care of those who come to us? See what happens when they leave our protection?

On the back of the pictures was a rubber stamped name and address, the legend above the name saying: PROPERTY OF.

Bracken memorized the name on the back, filed it and the address away in his personal file: Lloyd Tomczak, and a Chicago street address. The guy could take a good picture, that was for sure.

Some of them were closeups taken surreptitiously, with a telephoto lens. Candid shots, the guy who looked like Torelli walking around, getting into and out of a car, mowing a lawn with a jacket on. In that picture, Bracken could see a tall wooden privacy fence behind Torelli.

In other pictures the subject didn't look quite so domestic. He was scowling at the camera, cursing at whoever was taking the picture. Giving him the finger. At this Lloyd Tomczak guy. Bracken would be needing to speak to him soon.

At last, he'd finally felt that he'd found the bastard, all wrapped up, with a house of his own. Unless he did landscaping work, but Bracken couldn't picture that. No, this Lloyd Tomczak would know where Torelli lived, and if the man truly was Torelli. All Bracken would have to do was ask him. Nicely. Check him out real well before he paid a call on the man in the photos.

And he'd done a solid favor for the rest of the mob tonight, too. Gotten rid of this fat old man with his old-fashioned ideas, put him in the ground where he belonged, now a new regime could take over.

What a stupid man, having the pictures right there where Bracken could get them. He'd been sure that all he'd get out of Papa was a place where they were supposed to be, he'd never dreamed that he'd have them that close, so easy to get to that it could have been done without any of the violence.

But no, if he'd only stolen them, Papa would have known who had taken them. And, too, it wasn't too dumb a move, keeping them in the house, not from Pete Papa's point of view. He'd thought that the house would be invulnerable, that he'd be safe from anything or any one. Had he ever been wrong.

Bracken walked out of the front door, saw headlights on high beams, flashing lights ripping through the trees, bearing down on the house, fast. The lead car turned the corner, and there were several more behind it, and Bracken turned, first right, then left, caught like a frightened deer in the glare of many spotlights as the first car squealed to a halt, barely feet in front of him.

Men in suits were out of the car in seconds, high-powered rifles, shotguns and pistols were pointed at his chest. Bracken raised his hands high, followed the orders of the man who was shouting at him from behind his car door.

"Hands up high, higher, motherfucker!"

Words ran through his mind, in his own voice.

Today they hunt me down and kill me.

They were here, ready to do just that.

"Slowly, down on your knees, *don't move your fucking hands!*"

Bracken obeyed, seeing many men and women with small arms drawn, racing toward him, guns pointed at him. "Don't move those *hands!*"

Bracken didn't

Some ran into the house, others waited until he was spread-eagled on the ground, Bracken noticed this in the jumble of confusion as he felt the muzzle of a weapon slam against his ear, as hands pulled at his arms, as handcuffs were snapped on tight.

He heard one of them run out of the house and retch, throwing up on the lawn.

"Jesus Christ," said in total disgust. "It's a slaughterhouse in there."

"I escaped, some maniac was in there, killing everyone," Bracken said. "I escaped, you've got no evidence on me."

He was dragged to his feet roughly. He could see several faces staring at him, some of them quite emotionally. That would be those who had been inside the house, had seen his work first hand.

The leader was standing in front of him, an older man, wearing what he probably thought was a well cut suit. The man was watching as Bracken's web belt was ripped from his waist, eyeing the bloodstains on the front of Bracken's clothing, on his hands . . .

"How about those knives at your waist? Those aren't evidence?"

"That's it. Charge me with something. I'm not saying another word."

"You don't have to, asshole," one of the feds said. "We've got you on tape, saying more than enough. To Pete Papa in his bedroom. We've had the house wired for more than a month now, you stupid prick."

Bracken looked at the lead cop in the cheap suit, saw the man staring at him with a look of utter contempt.

"You killed how many altogether? Nine, ten? In one *night?*"

"All these assholes are the same, Milt," a woman's voice was saying, as disgusted as her boss's. "They have to talk sometime during the kill, have to show how smart they are." She shook her head, glaring at Bracken. "You just had to carry on a conversation, didn't you?"

Bracken thought, *Today they will lock me away forever.*

Good God, it had come true.

TWO A.M. IN the city of Chicago, on the far Southeast Side.

Mark looked at the moon, sitting on an aluminum chair in his fenced backyard, defeated, empty, totally alone. When was the last time he'd been so alone?

In a jail cell, fifteen years ago, that's when.

Even when he'd been in the Witness Protection Program, even on his worst day back then, testifying eye-to-eye against Pete Papa before the operation on his nose had partially altered his appearance and forced him to testify from behind a curtain, he hadn't been this alone. Mario had been back in a hotel room or a safehouse, Mario had been somewhere, waiting for him. Just the thought of that had given Mark strength. Now, there was no one. Now, pushing forty, he was completely, totally, maddeningly alone.

Mark did not trust himself to be inside the house when he was feeling this way. Suicide would never be an option with him, but there had been a time when his first instinct in troubled times was to destroy things, and even though he believed that he was now Mark Torrence, he was feeling a lot like he used to when he was still Tommy Torelli. And he didn't like it, it was eating him alive. He'd look at the Uno box or the Parcheesi game that they kept on top of the refrigerator, and he'd get the urge to push the thing over, stomp it until it was just a hunk of twisted, broken metal.

The fact was, it wasn't even his house, even thinking that it was had just been more of his wishful thinking. The house was in his wife's name, it belonged to her. She'd want him out of it sooner or later so she could sell it, and he would have to move on.

There were no more tears, although he wished that they would come, could even feel them in the back of his eyes, hiding there, pressing hard, only lifelong habits and beliefs preventing them from escaping. In the house, though, earlier, crying had made him feel better, at least for a short time. Good enough at least to get out of the house while his family took their midnight trip to the airport, Mark not wanting to see that, unable to watch them leave. Mark using that time to drive down to the 7-Eleven and pick up the first pack of cigarettes he'd bought in over thirteen years. The same brand he used to smoke, non-filtered and strong.

It had tasted good, that first cigarette, made him light-headed and slightly nauseated. It somehow made him feel young again, too, as if smoking the damn thing would wipe out the last thirteen years of his life and give him the opportunity to start over again with a clean slate. As he'd lit the second one he'd realized that he was, once again, a smoker. Like love, or trust, you couldn't turn it on and off whenever you felt the urge, not without suffering. He'd learned that lesson the hard way, hadn't he, just this afternoon. Too late for it to do him any good now, though.

It was better to look at the cigarette, at the glowing tip, at the controlled fire, smoldering, or up at the moon, at the cloudless, dark sky, that was safe. It was far easier to look at anything else than it was to look down, within himself. He didn't know what he'd seen there, or how he'd feel about what he'd find.

He hadn't quit smoking for reasons of health, lung cancer didn't much frighten him, and death by a heart attack had been back then, to a man in his line of work, considered to be death by natural causes, no matter how young he might be when it occurred. There were too many tons of toxins sent into the air by the government that had protected him for him to think that smoking cigarettes was going to kill him on its own. He'd only quit for the little edge that he believed quitting had given him, back when he'd known for sure that he was going to drop out of the program.

The mob would be looking for a relatively skinny man with jet black hair, a mostly flattened nose; a man who smoked and enjoyed drinking beer, who drank whiskey to excess after the successful completion of a score that had fattened his bank account. They'd be looking for a man who liked to gamble, who liked going to the track and to Vegas for weekend jaunts when he was doing pretty good, a player was what they'd be looking for, and he had stopped being one, just to get an edge.

He couldn't remember the last time he'd had a drink, not even a cold beer in the summertime or a glass of wine with a meal. It had been a long time, maybe even since the day of his wedding to Caroline. He'd needed a few drinks that day, man, with a room full of cops, the family and family friends of his brand new wife, a lot of them wanting to know where *his* own family was. Taking pictures, too, it was the last time anyone had snapped one of him until that son of a bitch Tomczak had moved in next door.

He'd given the cigarettes up back when he was still living in a safehouse, his mind made up, Mark knowing that he'd have to take full control of his future, a future that did not include any federal agents, not even Bella. Knowing too that every move he made, everything he did, not only impacted upon him, but upon an innocent child, young Mario. So he'd changed himself, the way he looked and acted, the habits he had that could be spotted by someone who'd know what to look for.

The feds had paid for the nose job, and the two years in captivity had added some weight. Maturity and working out did the rest, filled his body out for him. He didn't look anything at all like his old mug shots. In those pictures, he'd been young. Now Mark was middle-aged.

And, after a year or so back then, he'd no longer had the nervous energy or any of the other compulsions that had driven him for so long. At first he had learned to control them, then finally he'd discovered how to simply live without them. Mark no longer had the insatiable sex drive, no longer had the two or three sleepless nights each week that he'd once spent gambling, playing cards until dawn. Even back then, two years into the program, he had already lost most of the primitive urges that had once ruled his life. He'd rested well and kept regular hours, with the marshals—most of whom he'd never learned to fully trust—guarding himself and his son. He'd exercised behind drawn white curtains so that no one in the courtroom could see the way he'd changed.

And there were other things he'd done, subtle things that he knew contributed to the killing of the personality that had been Tommy Torelli.

He'd spent countless hours looking into the mirror at night, had learned to change his facial expressions. He taught himself to smile differently, got rid of all the personal facial expressions of his past. He would stand over against the far wall and walk toward a full-length mirror, modifying his gait, changing the walk over from the arrogant swagger of a street punk to an anonymous, average step, Mark practicing for long hours until the walk, the facial expressions, became second nature to him, became the habits of the man that he had turned himself into. And after several unsuccessful attempts, he'd quit smoking, too. Given the smokes up, and the reliance on booze to help him sleep at night.

They were slight edges, but sometimes that was all you needed to win.

What difference did it make now? They were on to him, or if they weren't, they certainly would be soon. He could smoke all the cigarettes he wanted to now, and get drunk if he felt like it, go out to the track, walk with a swagger again and stamp his face with the hatred and resentment that had once been so much a part of his emotional makeup. Those negative emotions had not been strong elements of his life for a very long time, but they were now back with a vengeance, and, just like the addiction to nicotine, they were back as if they'd never been gone.

Everything he'd worked for was gone. The people he'd loved had left him.

Mario's actions and feelings probably hurt Mark the worst. There'd been a time, right after Kenny had been born, when Caroline, mainly out of surprise, had bragged to her family and to her friends about what a wonderful father her husband was, how proficient he was at changing diapers, warming bottles, getting the baby to eat. She seemed almost shocked that he'd been so good at tending to a child.

She didn't know that he'd done all those things for Mario, all by himself. Had taught himself to be a good father, made himself one, and it was an easier thing for him to do than learning to change his looks, the way he walked, far easier than giving up the cigarettes had been.

He'd held baby Mario in his arms and he'd rocked him to sleep, singing to him softly, a song he'd invented just for the child, with a lot of la-la-las sung in a soothing, lullaby, hushed-voice style.

He'd applauded that baby when he'd first successfully learned to use his potty seat, had been kneeling before him when he took his first tentative, shaky steps. Even the few guards on the detail who hated him, who saw him as a dishonorable snitch, had to admit that he was a good father, and they helped Mario make the adjustment to life on the run, the feds always somewhere nearby, clapping for Mario along with Mark when the kid did something new for the first time.

Mark smiled bitterly, sitting in his backyard in the dark, looking at the moon.

Mario's face would break into an angelic grin whenever he was praised, and that kid was often praised.

Mark never left any of the male marshals alone with the baby for any extended period of time, he didn't trust any of them to look after his child properly. His lifelong hatred of the law had prevented him from leaving his beloved son alone with them for any more than an hour or two at a time. But he had, out of necessity, been forced to make a compromise. There was a woman he'd met, Andrea, the wife of one of the marshals, who'd had her own children at home, and Mark had demanded that she stay with them if they wanted him not to have a convenient lapse of memory on the witness stand. She'd taken the mother's place in Mario's life for a little while.

And did she ever love that child. She'd play with Mario while Daddy was gone testifying, the two of them in an anonymous hotel room somewhere, the woman teaching Mario his ABCs, teaching him how to read. Mark would come into the room and the child's face would light up with joy. Mario would hear the hotel room door open and he'd call for his dad, come toddling in and laugh while Mark whisked him into the air and kissed him, hugged him hello. And whenever Mark had to leave, oh, how that baby would cry. He wondered if that had left any scars on the child's emotions.

The last time he'd seen that kid, Mario had been once more crying, the kid blaming himself for the ugly breakup of his father's once happy marriage. Mario hating himself because he felt more loyalty toward his adopted mother than he did toward the father who'd raised him for six years, alone.

How could Mark blame him for that, how could he hold it against the kid? Caroline was a better parent all the way around, and a better person, too.

He sat there, thinking about this, about the type of father

he'd been. He'd been nowhere near a good enough father, he realized that now.

If only he could have them back again, if only those kids were still here! He'd never be too busy for them, never ask them to leave the room when he was talking on the phone to some idiot who didn't matter a damn in any of their lives. He'd work regular hours and let the kids at the center fend for themselves, he'd be home before the younger kids went to bed, every night, if only he had another chance, if only they'd come back.

A time machine was what he needed, to take him back, just one lousy day. He could forget his ego, put it on a shelf. If he had another chance he would smash the heavy silences that descended upon them whenever Caroline and himself were in a room together, alone. He'd tell her about his past, gladly, he'd tell her anything that she wanted to know, throw himself at her mercy and see which way she played it. He'd only be telling her what she obviously already knew, but it would be good to see how she'd take it when she heard it from his lips.

Which was all she'd really wanted in the first place. The trust that he hadn't been able to give her. A trust she'd certainly earned, after all those years together, years without questions, years without doubts.

If he'd trusted her, if he'd told her the truth, she wouldn't have left, he was sure.

Selfishly, worried about losing her, Mark had frozen her out, slowly destroyed the love she'd had for him until there wasn't enough left of it to make her stay, when he'd finally gone too far.

She'd known, and she'd stayed. For months, she'd stayed, until last night's publicity had forced her to take the kids and leave. Why hadn't he trusted her? It would have meant the world to her, he knew, if only he'd have told her, if only he'd have trusted her.

If only he had that time machine. If only, but he hadn't.

He understood that even having them all in the house together—even with Mark and Caroline mad at each other all the time as they'd been lately—was better than not having them around at all. She could be at her worst, and he could be thinking of divorce, but they were still in the house, still together, and there was always the chance that things could be worked out.

That chance was gone now, he'd thrown it away by his lack of confidence in her love, in his lack of confidence in her ability to forgive and understand. By his lack of confidence in her, by his belief that she'd take the kids and leave him if she ever learned the truth.

He hadn't been wrong about that, though, had he?

The thought flashed through his mind unexpectedly, in a moment of fleeting self-pity. That wasn't fair, to think that way, Mark knew better, had direct evidence of the fact. She'd found out through Mario months ago, and Caroline had given Mark every opportunity since then to tell her about his past. Shit, she'd nearly begged him, Caroline only going into herself, suffering alone, when he'd rebuffed her too many times for her to think that he'd ever be upfront and honest with her.

He wished now that he'd never met her, that he'd never fallen in love with her. That he'd left the emotional walls up as high as they'd been for most of his life, that he had found hookers to satisfy him sexually, he would have pretended to love them for the time that they were together. It would have been better than looking for a woman to share his life with. Better than the gross impertinence of believing that he had a right to live like everyone else, to seek the happiness that others had. Better than destroying the lives of four people who'd trusted him, four people who until today had needed him to be a part of their lives.

They sure didn't need him now. They'd suffer for a time without him, but they'd forget him, they'd get on with their lives. Even the younger kids would be okay, after enough time passed. They had a good foundation, and they had a wonderful mother. A mother who would someday—maybe soon—find another man to love her, a man who'd understand what she had to offer, and who would never be fool enough to do anything that might cause him to lose her.

No, they didn't need him. They'd be all right without him.

So, that left him. What about him, what about the man who'd destroyed the reality his family had once enjoyed?

Who cared? Did he? He wasn't sure right now, couldn't think in matters of long-term realities. Right now, he knew, he'd never deserved a family like them in the first place.

What he'd done to them had been unthinkable, marrying a woman who'd had no idea what she'd been letting herself in for, fathering two children and raising a third who could someday potentially face a death sentence simply because of who their father was, what he used to be. Poor Mario, what Mark had done would be just another terrible blow to a child who'd had more than his share of them already. To a kid who'd been literally bought from his mother, then grabbed out of his grandmother's arms, forced to live a life of hiding, a life of lies for his first six years on earth.

He should have left Mario with his grandmother, should have gone into the program alone. Pete Papa would not have killed that baby, if word got around about his doing that, he would have lost the respect of all of his men, the respect of the entire neighborhood. Someone would have taken him out, killed him in a takeover bid and not gotten a lot of grief from the other New York families.

What would Mario be today, if raised by Mark's mother? God knew, the boy had only been three when the woman had died. And if his biological mother had raised him? What would have happened then? He'd be a thief today, a hustler if she had. No, Mario had been taken on the best route for the boy. The trouble being that the best route might not have been good enough to save him. Only time would tell, and Mark would not be there to see the final result, what Mario became.

None of his children had come into the world by choice, but Mario had been the one who had been used the most, hurt the most. If he could somehow kid himself into believing in some god, Mark would gladly turn to Him now, ask Him to give him a long, lingering, fatal cancer in return for emotional health for Mario. Weighing heavily on his mind right now was the fact that he'd had other children at all. Convinced Caroline to have them, in fact, when she hadn't been sure that she'd wanted them. As if he had some inalienable right to that, the right to create lives and then to destroy them.

He couldn't think about that, not right now. There were too many people who owed him favors and who had cold guns lying around that he could borrow.

He would have to make a goal, and right now that goal would be to survive. He had to stop thinking about anything that would make him want to die, anything that would give him cause to put a loaded gun inside his mouth. He had to stay within himself now, could not think of the kids anymore.

So what would he do now? What would Mark do, now that his secret was out? Now that the entire city, everyone he knew, everyone he'd met in the past thirteen years, knew or would soon know of what he was and what he'd been.

He wasn't running, not anymore. That was out of the question. What could he do, go to the feds, ask them to take him back and find another place for him to hide? He'd rather die first. He'd left the Witness Protection Program under less than friendly terms; his leaving had, in fact, derailed the career of Dan Bella, an up-and-coming computer wizard who'd given him the Torrence identity. Even if they would take him back, he couldn't bring himself to ask. Not after what it had cost Bella, the husband of the woman who had taken such good care of Mario. The last time he'd seen Bella the man had told him what the price tag had been, what it had cost to secure Mark's safety. And he'd made sure that Mark knew that he'd done it only for Mario. That Andrea had made him do it, had told him he owed it to the beautiful little child . . .

If Caroline was still here, if the kids were still in danger, he'd do it, in a second, swallow his pride to protect his loved ones, to keep any kind of harm from befalling them. But they weren't here, they would be halfway to Vegas now. Safe in a house that by morning would be as well-protected as Fort Knox. Mark could picture it, see Caroline's dad calling in the troops. There would be fifteen or twenty employees of the guy's security firm hanging around the house soon, legally armed, listening as the old man told his daughter what an asshole she'd married. A couple of them would have no choice but to be attracted to her, would feel sorry for her, and Caroline would be vulnerable, suffering, maybe needing a shoulder to cry on . . .

Jesus Christ, knock it off.

The family was gone and it was only him, and he knew with crystal clarity that he didn't matter anymore.

What was the worst they could do to him? Kill him? It'd be a blessing, dying, the way he felt right now. It would release him from his suffering. Release Caroline, too, from any sense of responsibility or guilt that she might be carrying. All she'd have to do when she was feeling bad about leaving him was think that she'd be dead, too, her and possibly the kids, if she'd have stayed. Caroline may love him, but she was also pragmatic. Had a logical mind. She could live without him far better than he could live without her.

So maybe he'd get lucky and they'd come and kill him in his sleep.

It would be nice if they'd come tonight, he'd welcome their profane company. There would be no warning, he knew, no threatening phone calls, the mob would not try to scare him. They would not know if the feds were still protecting him yet, although they might suspect that they weren't. Still, they'd be cautious about giving him any advance notice. They'd charge through the door with weapons drawn, shooting anything that they found inside that was breathing. They'd kill him over and over again, shoot him until even the Cook County coroner wouldn't be able to identify him after he'd assembled the parts. He was a rat. A stoolpigeon. Nothing but a fucking snitch.

He had a college degree, a good job, insurance policies, a house that wasn't in his name, but still, it was fully paid off. His identity had been changed twice: once when he'd gotten through testifying, and once again by the compassionate fed Bella who'd felt for Mark when Mark was thinking of dropping out of the program. Bella and his wife were two of the very few people he'd known who'd truly liked Mark for the man he was, instead of just pretending to like him until he'd used up his usefulness; Mario always believed they were actually his aunt and uncle. As far as Mark knew, they were the only two people in the world who knew what Mark's name was today, because Bella had gotten that name for him. Along with a Social Security card, a credit history, an entirely new life. What he'd done for Mark had cost the man his ranking position in the marshal's office, but he'd given Mark and Mario a new chance, a shot at happiness, a third life for them to live.

He had all these things tonight, and a driver's license and credit cards in his pocket that announced to the world who he was. He thought of himself as Mark Torrence, it was who he believed himself to be.

But in his heart he knew that he was still Tommy Torelli, and that he was nothing but a fucking snitch. Was that and nothing more.

He heard barking from close by, then the sound of someone pulling hard on the gate of his privacy fence. Mark turned his attention to the gate, surprised that he was unafraid. He would not seek safety, would not even go inside and look for a weapon to use to defend himself. What he did was all that he knew he could do, and in a corner of his mind he hoped that when he did it, that it would be them, come to kill him.

He got up and walked over to the fence and unlatched the gate and pulled it open wide.

IT WAS A slow night in the Hammond, Indiana, federal marshal's office. Dead quiet, as it always was, when he pulled this kind of duty. Bella had long ago given up the hope of ever getting a call to action when he worked at night. Even if something *did* come up, which would have been highly unusual, they wouldn't give it to him. He had enough political pull—thanks to Andi's uncle— to still have a job, but the service never forgives, not even after nearly fifteen years.

But still, the post had to be manned, and even the type of fuckup that his superiors saw him to be could be expected to handle this kind of duty; a federal prisoner was being transported here for trial, by car. He would arrive sometime between midnight and eight a.m. The marshal's service had learned, through trial and error and their innate paranoia, not to tell even their own destination offices their full itinerary, where they were coming from, what their route was, who it was that they were transporting, or when they would arrive. It was for their own safety, they were told, and that was just another of the many directives that made less than a hell of a lot of sense to Bella.

What would happen if Bella told his wife about the trip, by her bedside before going to work? "Honey, that kill-crazy maniac from California's coming in tonight to begin his trial in the morning. I have to be there at ten, that's when he's coming in." For all the government knew, Andi might get on the phone, call her aunt, tell her about it. And God only knew who Andi's aunt might know. Or, for all the marshal's service knew, Andi's aunt, old May, he called her Maybelline the Talking Machine, might herself be in cahoots with the killcrazy maniac, or might get all sexually excited at the sight of the guy, at the mere mention of his name. May might wind up outside the Hammond Federal Building with a machine pistol under her coat, her eyes blazing with lust, her husband the Senator's power behind her, letting her literally get away with murder.

Now that he thought about it, when he put it that way, the directive made sense. There was no way of telling what his aunt-in-law might pull.

Bella got up from his desk and looked out the window, at the street below, empty now, the lights shining on pavement, throwing few shadows tonight on the barren pavement. He yawned. He felt better than he had in a while, Andi was making a faster comeback than usual. She'd sat up in bed by herself today, and he hadn't heard her vomit, not once, all day. He'd spoon-fed her soup and he'd held the glass of water under her chin, saw her drink of it, robustly, Andi rolling her eyes at him. Her spiritualist friends had called all day, but none of them had come over, at least while he'd been home. He hadn't thought of killing her and himself all day long.

Bella shook himself, that fantasy would make him crazy. When he was at work like this, out in the civilized world, he became frightened when he remembered the sort of dark thoughts he had at Andi's bedside.

She'd talk of her recovery, what they'd do when she got better, and he'd laugh with her, kid around with her about heading out to Las Vegas, about going out there and winning one of those superjackpots. Her religious beliefs forbade gambling, but she didn't argue with him, did not give him a hard time about his harmless fantasies. They both knew that he was only making conversation, and going to Las Vegas was no more far-fetched an idea than Andi's recovery in the first place; they were both pipe dreams.

But in the light of the office, with his suitcoat on and his tie up at his neck, with his weapon strapped on his hip, the thought of murder-suicide was far from Bella's mind. He could slip back into his armor, be a professional and pretend he did not have problems. Do the job he'd been doing for over half his life, sit at the computer and play with it, find out what was going on . . .

The phone rang.

"Federal Marshal's Office, this is Bella, may I help you?" Another directive told him how to talk, what he had to say when he answered the phone. The exciting life of a federal marshal. Matt Dillon was probably spinning in his grave.

"Dan, sorry to call so late, it's Clive."

"Clive?" Bella recognized the voice. The East Coast wiseguy tone. What was Clive doing calling here this late at night? Had he been transferred out of the New York office, or worse?

"Listen, right up front, we never had this conversation, all right? How're the phones on your end."

"Come on," Bella said. "The government cut way down on listening in on the convicts at the penitentiaries, Clive. You got guys making drug deals from pay phones in the pen, ordering murders, doing business with leaders of Arab nations, and we're not listening in even half the time anymore. You think they're gonna waste money listening in on you and me?"

"Unless you're under suspicion again."

"Clive, I'm a stone around their neck, is all I am. A couple more years and they can put me out to pasture. Andrea can't wait. I should have done it at twenty, she says. They don't care about me. They just can't find a good enough reason to can me, one that'd satisfy her uncle. Thank God he's stayed in office all these years."

"Andrea said you'd be there until morning. She sounded tired. I just got off work, I'm calling you from home."

Please God, don't let him ask why Andi seemed so tired.

Quickly, he said, "How's Val?"

"Gone. Two years now."

"It's been a long time."

"Would'a been longer, but for some reason I still got a conscience, even after working for the government nineteen years."

"So what's eating at it? You owe me money I forgot about?"

"I owe you more than I ever earned on this job, what you did for me in eighty-three."

Good to hear, but it would have been better to have the man's loyalty through a sense of friendship than through a sense of obligation over a ten-year-old debt. Still, it showed that Clive had some sense of honor after all. It showed, too, that Bella still had things to learn. If asked, he would have said that he'd believed Clive not to have any sense of honor.

He said, "Forget about it, Clive, I already have."

"No, you'll want to know this. They brought a guy in tonight, under extreme security, a guy who killed a shitload of people, like a dozen of them, somewhere in Connecticut."

"Christ."

"Christ had nothing to do with it, more like the devil, you

ask me. The guy's a stone killer, Dan, supposed to be the best hit man anyone's ever heard of. I guess the FBI's known about him for years, but never had more than a profile made up, never knew his name, where he lived, how his clients got ahold of him, nothing."

"So what's that make him, Spiderman? Without informants or a piece of direct evidence for them to dissect, how *could* they have anything?"

"You're not listening to me. This guy's supposed to be some sort of superman, a hit man's hit man."

"All right. So what?" Just like Clive, making mountains out of molehills. Who gave a damn about some killer who'd done his thing in Connecticut? Clive was the type to give criminals romantic notions that they, by their nature, could not ever really have. Even years ago when Bella had thought that they were close, Clive had watched too much television. He tended to be impressed by things like a criminal being able to evade the FBI.

"So this, Dan. The bureau got him, caught him with the weapons, after he hit Pete Papa."

"No shit." Pete Papa dead. Brought back memories better left undisturbed. "How old was he, seventy-five, eighty? Who'd put a hit out on Pete Papa?"

"It wasn't a hit. It was just a fucking fishing expedition. Get this, Dan, this guy, this killer, he wiped out about a dozen people just to get his hands on a picture. This bureau guy, a rook, he spent half the night sitting in the coffee room in the federal building, bragging about it to anyone who'd listen. All those dead people, one of them a mob boss, just to get at a picture, what you think of that? This new bureau guy, he was in on it, it was his first major pinch and he couldn't stop talking about it."

"And his last, the bosses find out he was fraternizing with the enemies over at the marshal's service."

"Are you listening to me? This guy killed the most powerful mob boss in the world, Dan, just to get a fucking *picture*." Now Clive was delving into the melodramatic. Dan knew he'd have to bite, or the guy would play it off for another hour.

"Who was the picture of? It was the right question to ask. It had to be an important picture, or nobody, even a psychotic hit man, would ever take the kind of risk that came along with killing a mob boss. Clive let the tension build up, leaving the wire silent. At last he spoke, in a whisper.

"Torelli, Dan, he was looking for a picture of your boy Torelli."

"Oh, my God."

And all of a sudden Mark Torrence had come out of the blue to haunt him. How long had it been since he'd seen Mark's face, since he'd heard his voice? How many years had it been since he'd spoken to the man face to face? Now tonight, there Torrence was, the target of a killer, who was willing to kill ten or eleven people and a mob boss, just to get his hands on Mark Torrence's picture. Didn't he have enough problems? Weren't things tough enough?

He should have put it together when he'd heard Pete Papa's name. He was slipping, first about Andi, now about this. But he knew how to make it up.

"Listen, Clive," Bella said, casually, "this guy, this hit man, what was his name?"

"Nobody knows that, they're not giving it out to *any*body. The guy I talked to, this rookie, he couldn't even tell me why this guy wanted a picture of Torelli, what he was going to do with it. All I know is, they had the house wired, caught the guy talking to Papa, cutting on him to get what he wanted. Word is, he cut one of Papa's *eyes* out. The bureau guys are in the shit, Dan, they had the house wired, and this guy still got in under their noses, wiped everyone out before the bureau could even get there."

"Did he get the picture?"

"Whole bunch of them, they're in black and white, I know that much."

"Wait, Clive, what you're saying is, this killer, he went over and tortured a mob boss, wiped out a bunch of people, just to get some pictures of Tommy Torelli?"

"What do you think I was trying to tell you? What do you think I called you for?"

"That doesn't make sense."

Clive said, "There're millions of crazy people floating around this city, but this one's different, this one kills a mob boss just to get a batch of pictures."

Bella understood it, knew how it could have happened, but he didn't say anything to Clive. Would let him figure it out for himself.

"So they've got the guy, anyway, right? Torelli's safe, at least from him. He's going down for a bunch of life sentences, ten, eleven times."

"No, he's not."

"Don't tell me this, Clive, don't even tell me."

"They took him to Jersey. You know what that means."

"They're bringing him into the *program?* I can't believe it, how fucking dumb can they get?"

"He'll never see daylight. He'll give them half the New York mob, then they'll bury him on an army post somewhere, with his family if he's got one, protected for life, but he'll never be free. They can't do that, not for a stone killer like this. But he won't spend his life in Atlanta, either. He'll have it pretty good compared to his options."

Bella had to bite his tongue. He saw things here that Clive wasn't seeing. And probably shouldn't see, the kind of mouth he had on him.

"Thanks, Clive, I appreciate your calling."

"Listen, we're even now, right? And I figured you should know, after the kind of trouble you got yourself into over that guy. Ruined your career, you had this much coming." Clive paused, as if wondering if he should go on. Or maybe he'd realized that he'd already said too much.

Clive said, "And we both know how it works, right? I mean, the kinds of people this guy can put away, the bodies he's gotta know about, Dan, they might even throw him Torelli, just to keep him happy."

So Clive was smarter than he acted. How about that?

"Thanks, Clive," Dan Bella said, and dropped the phone back in its cradle.

The FBI had a hit man in custody who wanted to kill Torrence bad enough to kill Pete Papa, the most powerful wiseguy in America, just to get a picture of the man. Dear sweet Jesus Christ.

What he had to figure out now was, how much did he care about Mark Torrence?

He owed the man nothing, if anything, Torrence owed him, and in fact, he owed Bella quite a lot. Clive, in his ignorance, had to go and make a big deal out of it, but the fact was, Bella *had* destroyed his career, any opportunity he'd ever had of advancing, by protecting Torrence, by giving him that name.

He'd never told the government why he'd done it, nor had he told them what name he'd given the man. And they'd never forgiven him for it, for creating a life for Mark Torrence that they didn't know about. Just for giving him and his kid a shot at a decent life. But what had his options been? Back then, Torrence had been falling apart by inches.

They'd had him testifying as an expert in trials, telling lies on the stand about guys he'd never met, and knew nothing about. And when Bella had changed his name, had made him Mark Torrence, there'd been a clear understanding of what he'd do if they fired him. He would tell the papers why, go to the press with the story.

The kid, Mario, would be what, sixteen, seventeen now? Bella wondered what he'd look like now, if he'd take after his old man. Bella hoped not. The teenage years were tough enough.

He knew that he'd have to go talk to the man, run him down in the morning and go see him after his duty was over. He'd have to do it, even if he didn't want to. All Andi would have to do was hear about this—and she would, Bella told her everything—and she'd want them to take the family in, want him to find Torrence and his entire clan and bring them home to live with them.

For the kid, more than for the father.

Andi would to this day see her greatest personal achievement as a two-fold attainment: raising her daughters properly, and taking care of the children of protected witnesses and never getting one complaint.

Which was saying something. Some of these Mafia wives, they got put into protective custody and started to think that they were suddenly Liz Taylor, always demanding things, ordering people around. You had to play them by ear, judge the value of the husband's testimony in weighing your response to their demands, how long it took for you to let them know their new place in life. But even the worst of the bunch loved Andi, wanted her to watch their kids.

And did she fall in love with them? My God, more than once, Bella had been jealous.

The first one had been that Mario kid, Andi traveling the country with the father, babysitting Mario at the government's expense. After that, it was the job of choice for her, making an extra income for them, Andi's heart going out to the poor kids who had no decision in the process as to who had fathered them.

But Mario had been the only one of them all who'd not had

a mother, whose father was raising him alone. Her first, and her favorite.

It had turned into a career for her, Andi in demand, getting a full salary with overtime, free first class air fare when she had to leave the state.

Bella had wanted to know, back then, what was going on. His wife was traveling everywhere with this protected program wiseguy whom her own husband had introduced her to, and suddenly she'd been giving up weekends, any days off, all her free time that she used to spend with Dan and the girls, and Dan had wondered, had wanted to know if she'd gotten a taste of the other side.

"He trying to get in your pants?" he'd ask, and she'd glare at him, but it stayed in his mind, until he got to spend time alone with them all together, Andi and both the witness and the kid, no other agents, no work to be done, and when he'd seen that, he had finally understood.

That kid was the most precious, adorable baby either of them had ever seen, excluding their own, naturally. In spite of the circumstances he had to live under, Mario was always bubbly and happy, big-eyed and full-lipped, loving and wanting to hug and be hugged. How did some mob scumbag father a child so sweet? The answer was easy, once you saw the two of them together and you knew where to look. Bella could remember how the father's face would light up at the sight of his baby, no matter how beaten down he'd been when he'd come through the door. All the weight of a day of crucial, damaging testimony against men who wanted him dead would fly off his shoulders when he saw little Mario, as soon as he saw his son.

It wouldn't matter how many times he'd been called a rat or a liar or a stoolpigeon that day by defense attorneys. It didn't matter how many fingers had slid across throats from the spectator section when the punks thought that the judge wasn't looking, none of that mattered, because when he saw that kid, the man would positively radiate.

And Andi knew why he'd decided to rat out his friends, and she shared the information with him once he'd stopped bugging her about whether she was maybe banging the guy. He'd done it for his kid. What a love story for the eighties. The man whose name was once Torelli had taken his very life into his hands, just because he loved his kid. How could you not help out a guy like that, no matter what he'd done with his life before you'd met him?

The last time they had talked, Bella had been even more uncomfortable than Torrence, the two of them trying to be casual, but really having nothing to say to each other. He was married by then, Mark was, with a kid on the way. The wife hadn't known anything about Mark's previous life. Bella did not think that Mark's keeping his past from her was a very smart move. But, as Torrence had pointed out to him, that was none of Bella's business.

He said he just wanted to be normal. He said his wife did not bother him about his past. He said it wasn't even an issue between them, she loved him for what he was today, and that was what he'd been searching for.

Maybe he'd found it, but he wouldn't have it for long. Not if the government gave him up to this hit man.

Bella's first instinct was to leave it alone, mind his own business and let what happened play itself out. But Andi would never forgive Dan if he let anything happen to any of the Torrences, and Dan could not imagine doing anything that would hurt her.

Bella sat back in his chair, with his hands behind his head. Forty-six years old, with just a couple years to go until he got a pension for life. His plan then was to get another job, maybe with the post office, collect two government pensions when he turned sixty-five. Could he live without one of them? Andi and he would make do. If she survived. Because there was no doubt that the service would dump him, get rid of him for sure this time, if he did anything more for Mark Torrence, no matter *how* cute his son had been fifteen years ago.

But what did he have to lose? What could they possibly do to him? His wife might well be dying and he was already broke. What would they take from him, his pension? He already had his twenty years in, the pension was already locked in, unless he broke the law. He wouldn't perform any criminal activities for the man, would only go and see him, see if there was anything he could do that could help. It would take him out of himself. He might, if he was lucky, even feel like a cop again. The worst that the government could do to him was force him to retire. Could he afford that? Maybe he should leave it alone.

Still, they'd been almost friends at one time. Maybe it would be worth looking into, if only to finally ask the guy what single protected witnesses did for sex.

Bella made up his mind. He'd wait for this prisoner to come in tonight, then he'd get on the horn in the morning, see if he could shake up anything else from any of the people he was still tight with in the service. Which wouldn't take long; there were damn few of them these days.

MARK OPENED THE gate and stood there while the stupid dog from next door jumped up at him happily, missing Mark's groin by inches, its paws catching on the fabric of Mark's pants, scratching at him. The dog made him jump back, and that gave the asshole, Tomczak, the opportunity to step past him and into the yard. Tomczak smiled at his dog indulgently.

"Come on, Meeky, be nice, don't jump on the man." He closed the gate behind him, Tomczak somehow getting it in his head that he'd been invited in. Mark was eager to let him know that wasn't the case.

"Tomczak," Mark said, softly. "Turn around, take your fucking dog, and get off my property. I mean it. Right now. You don't know what you're getting yourself into, here."

Tomczak took a quick step back, forgetting that he'd shut the gate. His back hit it and he swallowed, looked at Mark, fearfully. He found his voice, and spoke with anger laced with fear.

"There's no reason to act like that. You're not being very neighborly. I'm here, actually, in my official capacity as a journalist." The man was talking fast, trying to make his point before he got tossed off the property. Mark glared at him, trying to center himself.

"I saw you in the yard from my upstairs window and came over to talk to you, man to man."

"Man to man? Man to *man*? There's only half what's needed here for a man to man talk." Mark watched as the idiot stood there thinking about what he'd just heard, trying to figure out if he'd been insulted.

"Listen," Tomczak said, "you're in enough trouble already. You want to go to jail again? No judge is gonna give you an I-bond for assaulting two people in twenty-four hours. How'll your family make out then?" This little baldheaded bastard, he was playing him, thinking Mark gave a shit one way or the other about going to jail.

And maybe he did. Maybe he had to. It would be easier for them to get to him on the inside. Mark would die hard in there, stabbed over and over with homemade shanks, or maybe doused with a flammable liquid, with a match then being tossed through the doors of his cell.

Tomczak said, "I saw it all last night, what happened, I was there." Tomczak suddenly looked away from Mark, and squinted.

"Meeky! Stop that!" Mark didn't bother to turn to see what the dog was doing. It didn't matter now; the dog, Tomczak, nothing was important.

Tomczak said, "The paper sent me out. They wanted me to cover it, what the pigs did to the man."

"Go away, Tomczak, I'm telling you, go away . . ." Tomczak stepped forward warily, pulled the gate open and took half a step through, and spoke with one foot in the backyard, the other planted outside, ready to run in the event he had to make a fast getaway.

"You'll want to hear this, you might want to talk to me."

"What for?"

"I got it all, what the cops told me, and we've got pictures. They said the boy committed suicide." Tomczak smiled, to show that they both knew better. "You can bet that their autopsy will back them up. You talk to me, tell me what *really* happened, and I put your story on the front page of the *Leader*, guaranteed." He smiled again. Mark had the urge to punch that grin right off his face.

"I've certainly got enough of a story to be able to give you my word about that. Elmer Lee Griffin's a folk hero in the ghetto, and you're not very far behind him, buddy."

"I'm not your buddy, and I'm not interested."

Tomczak's face showed his disappointment. He could not understand that anyone would turn down a chance at the front page of the *Leader*.

He said, "It's your chance to tell the real story, all the words you want. We're not like the other papers, we don't have restrictions on a good story, we can write all the words we need to tell our stories."

"Go away, Tomczak, I won't say it again."

Tomczak stepped all the way through the gate, making kissing noises at his dog. Mark stepped forward, never taking his eyes from his neighbor's face. When the dog brushed past him, Mark closed the fence. Not seeing Mark's face gave Tomczak renewed courage. He spoke in a loud, vicious whisper, as if frightened about waking the other neighbors.

"You can't threaten the press! You can't scare me off! Didn't you ever hear of the First Amendment? The story'll run, Torrence, this Friday, you'll see, and you won't like what you read, not after this!" All Mark could do was lock the gate; he couldn't even feel anger anymore tonight. All that was inside him right now was a freezing emptiness, and even a guy like Tomczak couldn't work up any of his passions.

He went back to his chair, reached into his pocket, and took out his packet of cigarettes, was slightly surprised to see that there was only one more left. He lit it, took in a deep drag, the chain-smoker having a nightcap, and wondered if he should go out for another pack, or wait until morning.

Too big a decision to make right now. He'd smoke the thing down, see how he felt after it was gone.

Mark turned the chair so that Tomczak could not see his face from his second-story window, and looked up at the moon again, taking a deep drag on the cigarette, and let the loneliness overwhelm him.

DESPERATION AND TERROR took turns washing over Bracken in powerful waves, but nobody else in the room would ever be able to know that. He kept his face blank, uninterested, aloof and above the people he was being forced to keep company with. His emotions could run wild and rage inside him, but he was a man who viewed those emotions only as human failings that had to be endured. There was nothing he could do about them but make sure that he kept them a secret.

He was polite, courteous, slumping forward with his muscles loose. He knew how skinny he would look in the baggy clothing they'd provided, how harmless. Without his knives, they would think that he was nothing. Which was exactly what he wanted them to think.

"Would you care for a cigarette?" the fed wanted to know, and Bracken wanted to jump at the offer. But he kept himself cool, raised his eyebrows at the man speaking to him. Senior Special Agent G-man Bittner, trying to be his friend. The man had no idea who or what Bracken was. For all this man knew, Bracken was just some psychotic who'd gone on a late night rampage for a thrill. He had yet to disabuse them of such notions, would not give his best ammunition to anything less than the boss himself.

So this guy was playing him, being cute and maybe even worried about his job because he was waking up the boss, the head man himself, to come over and speak with Bracken, and he might well think that Bracken was nothing more than some wild killer. If that were the case, this Bittner would be out of a job.

But he couldn't afford to take that chance, they would have to check out Bracken's statement, the single claim he'd made to them. They'd told him that they'd known about him, were well aware of who he was, that they'd been on his trail for years, but that was probably just FBI bullshit, garbage they'd told him to make themselves feel important.

Yet they'd know that if Bracken could deliver even half of what he'd promised, this guy would not have to worry about his job, he'd be in line for one hell of a promotion.

So they'd be courteous to each other, the man would be solicitous to him. But he had to be careful. Even restrained as he was, Bracken lived on a greater plain than Bittner. He could not allow too much of his natural superiority to shine through just yet.

It was obvious that the G-man was nervous. He was twirling a ring of keys around on his finger, stopping them with his palm after every ten or fifteen circuits. He'd shake them, unconsciously, then begin the process again. Bracken never looked at the keys, he didn't want the man to even know that he was aware of what he was doing. You could never tell when information could be used as ammunition, to be used against your enemies. Sometimes, he knew from vast experience, that information could cost them their lives.

So he said, "No, thank you. They're not my brand."

"What'a'ya smoke, I'll send someone out for a pack."

They were waiting for the U.S. attorney himself to come and listen to Bracken's story, the feds now going out of their way to please him, to not show their revulsion at the crimes he had committed.

"I had a pack in the car . . ."

"We've got the car, it's in our lot downtown. Everything in it's been inventoried and bagged, the cigarettes, the lighter, everything." The fed smirked. "The guy you stole it from is gonna have a classic, a collector's item. You have any idea what that car will go for at auction after he gets it back? The car that was driven to the Connecticut Massacre. If John Gacy and Richard Speck can sell their paintings, then every idiot in the world with a little dough will want to own that car. If I made more money, I'd even bid on it myself."

Bracken nodded his head in acknowledgment. He was aware of the greatness of his actions, their impact, and wanted Bittner to know it. Wanted him to believe that he was well enough off to pay for the car out of pocket change that would never be missed. A specialist who'd caught an unlucky break and was now looking for nothing more than a way out of the trap.

The fed was smoking, sitting on the couch next to Bracken's leather chair. Bracken was in a jumpsuit that they'd given him after his shower, and he was shackled. These boys were taking no chances.

Chains were wrapped through beltloops on the jumpsuit, and attached to Bracken's wrists. Another chain at his wrists ran down his body and was attached to both his ankles. A single ratcheted cuff trapped one of Bracken's ankles, the other cuff was attached to the claw foot of the large, heavy chair that Bracken was sitting on. A canvas strap ran around his torso, he could feel the buckle pressing into his spine whenever he leaned back. The confinement was making him crazy, and they were watching him closely, seeking a reaction.

So he forced himself to appear relaxed, in control, above their petty games. His face gave away only his bemusement, his sad, detached, professional disapproval of their paranoid little security preparations. He wanted them to believe that he was a virtuoso, one who was totally aware that it was all over for him. That if he was given what he wanted, he would sing for them forever. He wouldn't show fear or anxiety, would not bargain from a position of weakness. They'd give him what he wanted or he'd go to prison in silence.

"I smoke English Ovals, unfiltered," Bracken said.

"We can get you maybe a pack of Lucky Strikes, a Pall Mall." The fed turned to the room. "Anybody got a Camel, an unfiltered cigarette?" There were murmurs, discouraging murmurs, some even sounded disgusted. These weren't the sort of people who would smoke. This fed Bittner was older, he was their boss. No one had yet complained about his smoking, at least not to Bittner's face.

"I'll get you a pack," Bittner said, and got up off the couch.

"Let me try one of those, would you?" Bracken said.

The man handed him a single cigarette out of his pack, and Bracken took it in both hands, holding it as he would a tiny flute, then lifted his hands as he leaned down as far as the strap would allow. He could barely make it. Bracken bit off the filter. He spat it onto the floor in front of him. He turned the cigarette around and stuck it between his lips, leaned back and accepted the flame of the federal agent's lighter, then nodded his head in thanks.

"I'll send someone out for a pack of non-filtered. You'll be talking to the man for a while, I'd assume, you'll need your own. Can't promise any English Ovals, that's a pretty exotic brand, but I'll get you something else, all right? Something you won't have to chew apart before you smoke it." Bracken nodded, and the man rose and placed an ashtray in Bracken's lap, then walked away.

Bracken did not look around, did not show any interest in where the man was going, or to whom he spoke. He needed to give the impression that *he* was using *them,* instead of the other way around. And he could not appear too anxious to please, too awed at their position of power. They had to believe that he had no interest in them other than as a means to an end. He wanted them to think that once they'd served their usefulness, he would not even deign to speak to them again.

It had been a tough choice, how to play them after they'd caught him. His first instinct had been to act the role of beggar, humbly pleading for them to give him a chance to talk. That would have put them off their guard, but they wouldn't have respected him. It would have been better for his eventual purpose, but might not have gotten him through the door of any of their superiors. They would have used his apparent weakness to further their own gains, to get him to talk so they could rise above their lowly status and maybe get assigned to a permanent position, teaching at the academy.

As it was, they'd tried grilling him for hours in the Federal

Building on Broadway in downtown Manhattan. Wanted to know what he could tell them, and he'd told them only one sentence. "I can give you the heads of all five borough families," and they'd known what he'd meant, known that he'd been referring to the Mafia. He'd said it coldly, without any emotion, a bargaining chip to get to speak to someone of weight. The chief interrogator, Bittner, who'd been out there when Bracken had gotten caught, had stopped cold, looking at Bracken, who'd stared back without blinking. He'd still been sitting in his work clothes, covered with blood, and he'd smiled. The man had turned away and had gone to converse with his superiors.

He'd come back with a couple of them and Bracken had repeated his phrase, and told them one thing further: He would tell his story only to the United States attorney himself, and to no one else. He'd speak only to the man who could absolutely guarantee his safety, write his contract for him even as they spoke.

Oh, how they hemmed and hawed. Told him it couldn't be done. Bracken had offered them only a frozen smile. "Then charge me and send me to the MCC." He'd turned his eyes away from them. That had taught them that he wasn't some sniveling coward of a small time mobster whom they'd be able to push around.

Now, he turned his thoughts to his immediate problem: escape. The sooner he made his move, the better his chance of getting away with it. Once he was ensconced on some army base somewhere, being debriefed, once he was in their element totally and completely out of his own, he would never have a chance of getting out of their clutches. If that ever happened, Bracken knew, he'd be watched 24 hours a day by people who were well trained to do only that. There'd be an order to everything, organization and structure. Tonight would be the last time that even the slightest confusion would reign around him. Right now, they were all in a place they'd probably never been in before, doing things they might not have done before, with a man they really knew nothing about except that he was a killer. Tonight would be the last chance Bracken might ever have. Because he was serious about his offer, it hadn't just been a ploy to buy him time.

He would not go to prison, would not rot in a penitentiary. He'd die inside, no matter what precautions were taken to protect him. He'd murdered the most powerful mobster in the world this night, and every second that he lived after that murder would be on borrowed time. The feds would know that, and would use it to their advantage. It would be the chip that could make the stakes too high for Bracken, as far as they were concerned. They knew what would happen to him in prison, and would use that fact against him.

Yet what he'd done would have been worth the risk, if he'd gotten away free. Knowledge of Torelli's whereabouts had been worth anything, even his life.

But nothing was worth going to prison for. Not when the world at large would know who he was.

They'd printed him and taken his picture, but that was unimportant. He was The Chameleon, the master of disguise. A picture of him sucking in his cheeks, with his head shaved, his eyes opened wide, would be worthless.

As would the fingerprints they'd taken be of little use to them. Bracken had never been printed before, had never even been arrested, nor had he been in the service. All he'd have to do was escape and not get arrested again. He'd managed to evade arrest for 44 years, and for over half of those years he'd been involved in various criminal activities. They would never have gotten onto him if they hadn't gotten a lucky break, if Tulio hadn't ratted and given them probable cause to wiretap Papa's home.

And they would never catch him again, he would never in his life be as impulsive as he'd been this night. With what he had saved right now, money that the feds could never find out about, he could retire from crime. Go to Paris and live out the rest of his years. Try not to think about what he'd been forced to give up. His house. My God, his freedom and his work.

But first, he had to escape. And he didn't have anywhere near the sort of information that he'd need in order to make that escape good, there was far too much that he needed to know and didn't. And some things that he wanted to figure out, things about this house that baffled him.

There were plenty of federal agents in the building, Bracken knew that much. And something was very strange about this house, there were a number of things happening that made absolutely no sense.

Three carloads of feds had driven him here, wherever the hell they were. They'd driven Bracken here masked, in the gutted interior of the middle vehicle, a new van, and they'd driven for some time. He'd been in a wheelchair, strapped to it, the wheels locked into braces that had been bolted to the center of the vehicle floor. His hands and feet had been shackled, his forehead strapped to a headrest on the chair. There'd been straps around his legs, chest and waist. They'd been taking no chances; he hadn't had even a ghost of an opportunity to escape from their custody then.

The van had slowed, turned off concrete onto bumpy gravel, as if in an alley. It had driven down on a steep angle, then up again, slowly, making a sharp turn, as if turning into a garage. When they'd pushed Bracken out of the van, he kept all his senses alert, trying to discover hints as to where they were, what the hell was going on.

He could hear their voices booming, as if they were in a large open space with walls, a warehouse of some sort, perhaps an underground loft. They'd unstrapped him and a powerful hand had gripped each of Bracken's biceps and propelled him blindly forward, and he could tell when they'd gone through a doorway from the way the agents had positioned him. One of them had been forced to let go his bicep, while the other one had hung on, but had stepped behind Bracken, one hand on Bracken's back, pushing him forward.

He'd sensed that they were no longer in a large, open area. Could feel the men right next to him, as if cramped walls had forced them to move in closer to him. To test this, he said, "Is the mask still necessary?" They didn't answer him, but he'd learned what he'd wanted to. He'd heard his voice bounce back at him, could now hear it in their footsteps. They were in a very close, narrow space, but it was long, they'd been walking for some time.

They'd come to a flight of stairs, and he'd been led up, told that there were nineteen steps, so he wouldn't fall down as he reached the top.

Nineteen steps. When they'd shackled him to the chair and taken off the mask, Bracken had been amazed to see that they were in a house, a two-story, that didn't seem very large, and certainly not all that wide. From where he sat, chained to the chair, Bracken could see the stairway leading to the second floor.

There were only eleven steps.

What the hell was going on? None of this made sense.

There was a door that led to a basement, and Bracken, concentrating, could hear the agents coming up and going down those steps, regularly. He'd close his eyes and concentrate mightily, count their steps as they walked up or down the stairway. Seven stairs, no more than eight. Where had the nineteen steps come from? And why did the agents keep going up and down that stairway?

Sometimes they'd go up and down the stairway that led to the second floor, different faces going up than those coming down. What was the secret? How did that happen? He knew how many agents were there at any given time, counted them, put their faces with a number so he wouldn't lose track.

The number of agents stayed fairly regular, but the faces changed. How odd.

Something was going on here, there was more happening than he knew. Bracken hated mysteries, not knowing what was going on around him. He'd watch, carefully, and learn the secret, he was certain. Maybe it was even something that would work to his benefit before this ordeal ended.

Bracken could now see bright light breaking around the blinds of the window to his right. So it was daytime. He could hear the sounds of human yawning every so often, hear someone standing up and stretching behind him, jaws and knees and elbows popping as they drew in extra breath. They were tired. That was good. It would make them drop their guard.

He looked around casually, saw six men and one woman in the room instead of the eleven people who had been in there with him earlier. The ones who noticed him looking evaded his gaze, dropped their eyes, which did not offend him, in fact he saw it as wonderful, it was a sign of their submission. They were afraid of him. Good. He wanted them in fear. If he could get loose, he could use that fear to his advantage, make it work for him and against them. They'd be seeing themselves as they'd seen the bodies in Papa's house, slashed, cut, bleeding to death . . . They would not be as courageous as they would be with someone they saw as just another criminal.

But first, before he could use their fear against him, he had to get loose from his bonds. And to get his hands on one of their weapons.

*   *   *

SAFE HARBOR

AS SOON AS he awoke, Mark felt the pain. In the back of his throat and running right down from there into his lungs, the strange soreness unfamiliar, a burning sensation. Mark tried to take a deep breath, coughed before he could pull in much air. The cough turned into a spasm of phlegmy, wet coughing, making the burn go deeper.

Damned cigarettes. Look what they did to you. It was scary, how they could hurt you. The scariest part was, he wanted to smoke another one, right now. Mark could already feel the withdrawal pains, the wanting, the longing for nicotine.

He looked through sleep-slit eyes at the other side of the bed. Caroline was not there. A wave of longing passed over him, but he quickly shook it off. He could not live this way, constantly thinking of her. He had to be pragmatic, be the man he used to be. Get all the romantic bullshit notions of love out of his head right now. All that thinking of her and the kids could do right now was cause him more pain, and he had enough of that already, enough to last him forever.

He rolled out of bed and checked the clock, saw that it was only five-fifteen. He'd made it through the night, they hadn't come to kill him. Yet.

Maybe they'd wait awhile. He went into his bathroom thinking about this, wondering about it as he cleaned up, took his shower and shaved. Thought about it as he dressed, too, about the psychological game they might be playing.

Would they give him time, make him feel as if he'd made it home free before they came? Not Pete Papa. Papa would want him dead, and fast.

Unless he himself was dead. That was something to think about. Papa would be an old man now, and in his line of work, there were very few really old men. At least in terms of years. That was a good thought, that Pete Papa was dead. Unrealistic, but comforting.

Mark wondered about it, about who'd come after him if Papa was indeed dead. Some of the guys from New York? Some Chicago wiseguys? They were all of them on the run, Mark knew that much just from reading the papers. A lot of the old guys were either doing time or were dead, and U.S. attorneys across the country were burying more and more of them in one of those two places at a near daily rate. If Papa was dead, he might even pull it off, walk away scot-free, after all, who would know about him? Who in Chicago would recognize him? It had been over thirteen years since he'd testified against any of them, and not a single trial had been in Chicago. Even though there was a strong mob influence out here, if Papa was dead, the others, especially in Chicago, might no longer care.

But he would have heard about it if Papa had died. Would have read it in the papers or seen it on the news. He was hot copy, Papa was. An important man. A folk hero back home, in Little Italy.

Mark shook his head, not thinking clearly, needing a cigarette to calm his jangled nerves. Maybe, after he'd quit his job, he'd even go out for a drink. Booze was a relaxer, and what did he have to come home to? He was thinking about that when he left the house, thinking about how booze used to numb him, make him forget his problems on the rare occasions that he got really drunk. Thinking about it as he walked to his car, thinking about it when the car pulled to the curb and honked at him and scared him half to death.

Mark turned quickly, crouched, teeth bared. Terror gripped him, twisted at his stomach, flew up into his chest. In spite of last night's thoughts, he found he was not yet ready to die.

He looked at the car behind him, saw something vaguely familiar about it. Recognized what it was as he stood up, trying to relax, to appear normal.

It was a government car, and the guy getting out of it was his old protector, Marshal Dan Bella.

He looked terrible. Bella had lost weight, seemed bent now, and old. What could he be, in his mid-forties, five, six years older than Mark was himself. He looked twenty years older now, his hair was thinner, going gray.

Mark hadn't seen him in a number of years, he couldn't remember if both of his kids had been born the last time the two of them had talked. He seemed bigger then, stronger. Now he looked like a beat up, broken down old man.

Dan said, "Mark, how you been doing, guy? What have you been doing with yourself?" and the only thing Mark could think of to say was, "Trying to keep a low profile, that's what."

Bella didn't extend his hand, nor did he acknowledge the dig. He walked up to Mark and never broke his stride, sunglasses on against the early morning glare. He put his hand on Mark's shoulder and spun him around, kept it there as he forced Mark to walk alongside him slowly.

"You got problems."

"Don't I know it."

They passed Tomczak's house, and Mark looked up, out of habit. What was that in the picture window, something throwing off a tiny red glow?

"I think I can help you."

Mark stopped, angrily, shook Bella's hand off his shoulder.

"Help me? You want to *help* me?" He forced himself to lower his voice, he hadn't realized that he was shouting. "Keep walking," he said, "I think that son of a bitch in there is videotaping us."

Bella was good. He didn't look up, didn't even look curious. He simply put his head down and started to walk alongside Mark.

"You want to help me," Mark continued, "so you pull up in front of my house in a car with government plates. That's a smart move."

"If you're being watched, it *is* a smart move. They'll think we're guarding you, that there's more of us in the house."

"The only guy watching me is that asshole next door. He thinks he's Mike Royko."

"Watching you?" Bella said, more than normally interested.

"Forget about it."

Bella didn't, Mark could tell. But he let it go for the moment, said, "We took a guy in last night, a guy who might solve some of your problems."

"Yeah? Who's that, St. Peter?"

"Better than that. Guy named Bracken, a friend of yours, remember?"

"No. I never heard of him."

Bella seemed taken aback, it was obvious that he thought that Mark would have heard of the name.

"Worked for Pete Papa years ago, we think that's where he got his start. He's a killer, Mark, does that ring a bell?"

"Can't remember anyone named Bracken."

"He's heard of you."

"Lots of people heard of me, and most of them work for Papa."

"He doesn't work for Papa anymore."

They had passed the corner and crossed 112th St., the two of them heading into the forest preserve property, their heads down, speaking in low voices. The cars that passed them on the boulevard would see two men out for a stroll, neither of them appearing to be in much of a good mood.

"Come on, Dan, what's going on."

"Papa's dead, Mark. Bracken killed him."

"Jesus Christ, thank God."

"Yeah."

"You said you took him in. You mean you arrested him, right?"

"He's under arrest, yeah." Bella seemed uncomfortable. Mark was not in the proper frame of mind for this sort of bullshit.

Bella said, "There's something you need to know, Mark, and I've been elected to tell you." He stopped, put his hands in his pockets and looked at Mark intensely. "This guy Bracken, he killed Papa's wife and son, wiped out a bunch of his bodyguards, just to get some pictures of you. Papa had them, wanted him to kill a guy for him before he'd give them up."

"Of *me?* What the hell would he want pictures of *me* for?"

"We were hoping you could tell us that. Bracken isn't saying."

Mark saw it then, what was really going on. In a soft incredulous voice, he said, "He's protected, isn't he? You've got this guy in the program as a witness."

"The bosses are trying to keep it hush hush, but they know I came out to see you. They approve. I was going to come out anyway, no matter how they felt."

He started walking again, his hands still in his pockets. Slouched over, the weight of the world on his shoulders. What was with this guy? He didn't get like this out of his concern for Mark. Mark followed him, and stuffed his own hands deep into his jacket pockets. He didn't want Bella to see that they were shaking.

"I heard about it from someone else, someone who owed me a favor," Bella said. "That was before you got your face splashed all over the front of the papers, before the CPD started making phone calls to anyone they could think of in the government, trying to find out why we had a hold on your prints."

"So they called you."

"The big shots did, yeah. Later this morning, after I made a lot of inquiries. They came back to me and told me that it would be a good thing if we talked. It was logical enough. I get the impression at first that they just wanted me to pump you for information about this guy. I've been on their shitlist for thirteen years, they think I'd jump at the chance of getting back on their good side."

"And you did."

"I shit on their good side." The bitterness in Bella's voice made Mark look up at him, curiously. Was he that resentful toward his bosses, even all these years later? Then he should quit the job, get out of it while he still had a chance to do something else with his life. Mark had his own problems, such as figuring out what in the hell the government wanted from him now, all these years later. Why some guy named Bracken would kill Pete Papa just to get some pictures of him . . .

Bella would think that Mark owed him, Mark knew, and in his heart he believed that he indeed did owe him. In the early morning silence of the woods he looked at Bella, wondering what he really wanted, how the guy would call in his markers. Whatever they were, Mark would have to guard against his emotions, as he knew that he would immediately feel the urge to pay them in full. Thirteen years of complete freedom was better than no time at all.

Bella shocked him by reading his mind. He said, "You don't owe me anything, Mark. Get that clear up front. Or the government. You made your deal and you did what you said you'd do, and if they want to hold it against you for not wanting to lie for them, or for not wanting to live in Dinosaur, Utah, for the rest of your life, then what are you gonna do?"

"And what about what they held against you?"

"I did something for you, for your kid. But mostly, Mark, I did it for my wife."

"How is she?" Mark remembered Andrea now, her happiness, her joy, and in spite of his troubles, he had to smile. Andrea had treated them well.

"Fine." A curt response, without feeling. "What's important is how *you* are. And what you're going to do."

Mark said, "What *can* I do? I've got the smell of a young kid's blood still in my nose, Dan, parts of his brains on one of my suits, sitting in a cage at police headquarters. My suit's evidence, in protective custody. I got my picture on the news, in the papers. I got some killer out East killing mob bosses to get pictures of me. I got Pete Papa dead. You tell me, Dan, what the hell *can* I do?"

Dan looked off into the woods, thinking. To Mark it looked as if he was debating whether he should even bother to tell him what he'd come out here to say. Dan took in a deep, weary breath, spoke as he let it out.

"This guy, he's been talking all morning to the U.S. attorney himself. He'll put away all the top New York mob guys if what he says pans out. They'll know by now that the FBI has Bracken, after what happened to Papa, not even they could put a lid on it. And they'll panic and start running. Between Bracken and a guy they already were bringing in, one of Papa's own people named Tulo or something—"

"That's Tulio, he's Papa's right hand. Tulio's turning?"

"He's croaking. Wants to get right with God."

"They told *you* this?"

"If they wanted me to talk to you, they had to tell me what I needed to know. Anyway, New York's gonna be reeling. The way things have been going the last twenty-five years, everyone knows that Bracken and Tulio are only going to be the tip of the iceberg. With two witnesses corroborating each other, hell, Mark, it's a dream come true, a first. They'll have these so-called wise-guys falling all over themselves to jump into custody with their families. A protected life at Eglund Air Force Base with the wife beats the hell out of life in the penitentiary, alone, with a husband named Bubba."

"So what's this got to do with me, why did they send you out here, Dan?"

"Like I told you, I was going to run you down anyway, Mark, to warn you about this Bracken character. At first I was thinking that the FBI isn't above killing you to get Bracken to do what they want."

"Jesus."

"Look, they'd discredit you first, if they really wanted to hurt you. Tell the locals who and what you were, and let the papers do the rest. But if that failed, if they needed Bracken that badly and he wouldn't talk unless you were dead, well, it wouldn't be the first time somebody had an accident to keep the wheels of government running smoothly. I told them that, told them I was planning on warning you off, to put you on the run. Told them that I'd get you another entire set of ID if you wanted it."

"I won't do that."

"How about for your family?"

"They're gone, Dan. Caroline took the kids and left me last night."

"She took Mario?"

"He went with her." Mark tried to keep the sadness from his voice, knew that he had failed.

"I sat at the kitchen table this morning drinking coffee with the ringers on all the phones turned off, and still, all I could hear was the whirring of the phone machine, people calling, wanting to talk to me about what went down. She was right to leave. The house is in her name, but it won't be long before some idiot reporter, or somebody a lot worse, with connections to the phone company gets the address to the house."

"The question you have to ask yourself is, are you worth it to them? The New York wiseguys'll have enough on their plate, they won't care about you. The Chicago outfit never got along very well with the New York mob to begin with; this crew out here has always been outsiders. Papa's dead, and whoever this Bracken guy is, he's in custody."

"What if he was working for someone else, was sent to get the pictures?"

"Why, Mark? The guys your testimony put away were all from Papa's crew."

"So you think I'm safe? You think they won't come after me?" The sudden hope lifted his spirits, he could see it happening.

"I think you should be aware of all of your options. The AIC I spoke to got highly irate when I questioned the integrity of the bureau. But he still asked me to come see you. They want to coordinate with the U.S. attorney out here, get you covered, make a double strike, out there and out here, if someone comes after you."

"They want me to play along?"

"They'd appreciate it if you did."

"Why the hell should I?"

"You're not planning on going anywhere, anyway, are you? Your family's gone, you said. They make a move on you, we grab them. In the meantime, you're guarded, around the clock, you're safe. And when it's all over, if they come after you, you get a new life, just like before."

"And the college degree I busted my ass for? Does that come along with me? My life, the life I've built, what about that, I just throw that away?"

"You knew you were at high risk from the day you came to us."

"Goddamnit. God*damn*it! That was fifteen years ago, Bella. I've built something, I've worked like an animal since that time. In the last thirteen years, I've changed, I'm not that man anymore."

"And you're not Mark Torrence, either. You never really were."

"I should have let that whole thing alone last night. I should have stayed out of it, let the cops handle Elmer any way they wanted."

"That," Bella said, "wouldn't have mattered one bit. The pictures Papa had of you didn't come from any newspaper. He had them before you got in trouble, before you got your face in the papers. Hell, Mark, none of the cops or reporters out here know who you are, even now. The government still hasn't told them anything."

"They're waiting to hear from you, is that it? If I do what they want, then they don't destroy me in the papers."

"I didn't tell them anything, what your name is, where you lived after I found you."

"What did Papa have, Dan? Where did he get those pictures?"

"They came out of Chicago, from the offices of a regional newspaper. Something called the *Leader*, you ever heard of it?"

"Son of a bitch."

"Yeah. We've got the photographer's name, and the FBI is running a check on him right now. What they need to know is if he got the pictures of Papa himself, or if someone else at the paper saw them and knew what they might be worth. The nose job obviously wasn't the disguise we thought it would be."

"Or it could have been someone at the photo lab where the pictures were developed, my God, there's a thousand ways they could have gotten those pictures, ways Papa could have wound up with them."

"It's being checked into, and right now the chief suspect is the guy they belong to. These weren't copies, Mark, they were originals, and the man who took them was so proud of them he had his name and address and phone number stamped on the back of the paper."

"Tomczak, right?"

"Your next door neighbor."

"FBI knows more than it's telling you, Dan."

"They usually do."

"There's more to this than they're telling you, they don't care about me. Wouldn't ask for my approval for their surveillance. And it doesn't matter that you wouldn't give me up, because if they know where Tomczak lives, how long will it take before they make the connection to me? Shit, all they'd have to do is ask the little bastard, he'd turn me over just to get a story."

They began to walk back now, out of the woods and back toward civilization. The vehicle traffic on 112th St. was building up as people who worked in Hammond and Whiting, Ind., headed off to their jobs. Mark thought about what he'd learned, resentment raging inside him.

"Last Friday, when I spoke to this idiot, he told me he had connections, that I didn't know who I was fucking with."

"That's good to know, those words might hang him."

"But I don't believe he's connected, at least not to the mob. The guy's an animal rights activist, Dan, for Christ's sake."

"Or he's pretending to be. We'll find out, though, won't we? Soon, too, if I know the FBI."

"Tell them I won't do it." Mark stopped on the corner, not wanting Tomczak to record this confrontation. He stood breathing heavily, a foot away from Bella.

"Tell them if I see one of their cars on my block, I go to the press, say it's federal harassment for what I did the other night. I'll say it's political and demand an investigation. I'll tell them every word we said today, tell them everything you've told me."

Mark paused and stared hard at Bella, so he would understand that he meant every word that he spoke.

"I had dealings with them before, they seem to forget that. The marshal service protected me, but it was the FBI that brought me in, federal prosecutors who made me lie in courtrooms. I know about their arrogance, how they feel about guys like me. All they want is some testimony to back up some half-ass investigation so they can get their mugs in the papers, and get convictions against the mob. So they can retire and go into politics, I know how they act. I haven't forgotten, Dan. They'll prep me like they did before, have me lie to get their convictions. That's why they sent you, because I got so many convictions for them before. They want more, on the back of what I'd done before.

"Tell them to go fuck themselves, Bella," Mark said.

"You act like that, I tell them what you said, and the government'll go hard. They'll let the word out about who you were, why they had you on a print hold. What do they have to lose? You're not with them anymore, they have no vested interest in protecting you."

"Yeah, and they never lost a witness who was protected, right? Let me ask you this: How would anyone know if they *had*? It's just more of their bullshit, their PR routine. Forget about it, Dan, I won't *let* them protect me anymore. The people who I didn't want to know already know. I don't care what anyone else thinks they know. I'm Mark Torrence, Dan. I may not have my family, I may not be protected anymore, but I'm still me, and I won't be anyone else, not ever again. I'm through running, I'm through hiding."

Dan shrugged, as if it did not matter to him either way.

"I'll tell them."

"Make sure that you do," Mark said, and walked ahead of Dan all the way to his car, then turned back to see Dan watching him, standing by his car and coolly looking at Mark, the way a visitor at the zoo might look at some new, exotic arrival.

When he spoke he didn't much care one way or the other if Tomczak recorded his words. He half hoped that little bastard would come outside right now. If he did, Mark knew, he would put him in the hospital.

"You tell them what I said, and you tell them this, too: If they want to get hard, if they want to send someone to settle this Bracken's score for him, you tell them not to send the second team, you hear me?" Mark said, and did not wait for an answer. He got into his car and started it, then took off without looking behind him even once.

"LISTEN, DO YOU want to take a break yet, are you ready to get some sleep? We can rest for four, six hours, then continue this, refreshed."

Bracken sat at the old wooden table and listened to the man, to Mr. United States Attorney Fred Tallman himself, and knew that the man was speaking for his own benefit more than he was for Bracken's.

There were dark circles under Tallman's eyes, and he was yawning a lot, rubbing his hands over the stubble of his beard, washing his face with them, trying to keep awake. Solicitous bastard, now that he had a confession, going out of his way to show Bracken what a regular guy he was. He'd keep doing so until he got everything that he wanted from him.

Every word that Bracken spoke was being recorded three times, twice on tape—one cassette and one large reel to reel, expensive machine—and once on paper, his words tapped out by a male stenographer who never looked up from his machine, the stenographer one of Tallman's hand-picked crew. The machines were set up on the table in front of Bracken, and papers were scattered around it, a suitcase was standing open on one mahogany end.

The first move they made was to get him to make a full confession. It was there on the table in front of them, signed and witnessed, Bracken's name scrawled along the bottom, each page initialed: J.B. The stenographer had typed it out on a portable Underwood. His deal was there, too, what the government was going to do for him in return for his full and unrestricted cooperation.

Bracken would be protected, given a new name, a new identity, access to the funds that he'd told the government about, in return for his testimony. Fat lot of good it would do him. He could use the money to spruce up the room they'd give him on some federal reservation, in either an unused Army barracks or, at least, on their land. He'd be free, in a sense. Freer than he'd be in the Lewisburg federal pen.

He'd have to be protected, though, away from society, forever. There was no way that Bracken could ever be set free again in his lifetime because he'd have to tell them the truth, that was part of the deal, too. If he lied to them, if his confession proved false, they had the right to rescind their deal, to lock him away in one of their cages.

They'd already caught him on Papa's property with a number of kills to his name. Even if he'd denied committing those murders, the government had enough evidence to convict him anyway, they had the tapes, eyewitness accounts from the agents on the scene, and they would use that evidence to destroy him. So he'd told them the truth, about Papa's murder and many others, every dealing he'd ever had with the man was now being set down on the record, three times.

In return, he got amnesty. The government would not prosecute him for any of his crimes, he had total immunity from prosecution, as long as he told them the truth.

Over the past couple of hours, some of it had even been fun. He'd seen it, had known when he'd told them something that Tulio hadn't bothered to, the old man protecting people he cared about, conveniently forgetting about things that should have been part of his testimony. Tallman and one of his stooges would look at each other quickly when this occurred, and the stooge would write things down on a legal pad, then leave for a minute, sending one of the FBI agents out on an errand to jog Tulio's memory. Maybe they'd even revoke his deal, let Tulio fend for himself in a world that he'd soon be leaving.

They had plenty of conferences, too. The FBI, AIC, Bittner, would knock on the door, and one of them would answer it, then Tallman would go over to the door and have a hurried, whispered conference with the man before coming back to the table. He was being kept informed, updated, he would call it.

Politicians and their political appointees, how stupid they could be.

After the first confession and Bracken's deal was prepared, they'd removed the chains from his hands so that Bracken could read them and smoke, unencumbered. His legs were still chained, he could only move them about eighteen inches apart, but his hands were free and neither of his ankles was chained to any of the furniture.

He used his hands again now, wanting them to get used to his moving them around freely, Bracken tapping a Pall Mall on his knuckles, sticking it in his mouth, stretching and yawning before he lit it.

"Maybe we should get through the Tulio material first," Bracken said. "I'll tell you what I know about what he's said, then we'll call a break. A couple more hours is all it should take. We should do it, sir, before old Tulio realizes I'm in custody. If you don't know by now, he has an ego. When he finds out that you're here, talking to me personally, he might clam up on you just because his feelings are hurt."

264

Tallman grunted. "He'll never know, and if he does find out, he'll *still* do what he's told."

Tallman was a large man, with a lot of fat on him, his hair blow dried and graying, with the haughtiness of one who was always in control of his environment. He had the knot of his tie pulled down now, the first button on his shirt undone, his jacket off and his sleeves rolled up to the elbow. A working man, or rather, Tallman was pretending to be one. What did he think, that Bracken had a voting card? The act might play on the nightly news, might make this toad look like a man of the people, but it had no effect on Bracken. He saw Tallman as nothing more than a brownnoser, a lawyer with connections, whose daddy had bought him legitimacy, Tallman appointed by a president for whom appearances was all.

No matter what image he tried to convey, Bracken knew better, could see through it. He could smell the man's fear, could see his true softness through the tough front of authority that the man worked so hard to convey.

Tallman had turned on a ceiling fan, so that Bracken's cigarette smoke wouldn't choke him. He said, "Believe me, he'll do what he's told, even if he does find out. You guys are getting a ride, here. Neither of you is a movie star."

Tallman said, "But you're right, let's get the Tulio thing over with this morning. That way we can present grand jury evidence about Papa's entire family before you even wake up from your nap." Tallman smiled.

"By the time we get around to a different mob family, the men you've told us about from Papa's crew will already be rounded up and sitting in the MCC."

"The other four families, we can work on them later tonight."

"It will be a pleasure to work on them, I assure you, Jim," Tallman said. The three armed flunkies that were in the room laughed at Tallman's ironic tone. The stenographer didn't, but he didn't type the last exchange up, either. He knew when to stop, had obviously been through this drill before. The little man sat there without ever breaking a smile, more of a robot than a man, never getting flustered or asking anyone to slow down. When the time came, Bracken would enjoy killing him the least.

The FBI agents were somewhere outside the room, steaming. They'd wanted in on this, there had even been a heated discussion about it that Bracken had overheard, the Agent-in-Charge arguing that Bracken was too dangerous to be in the room with Tallman without FBI protection. Tallman, in his arrogance, had ordered the man to shut up. Told Bittner that he had his own men, who'd been trained for just this sort of service. Subtly saying that the FBI wasn't as good as Bittner might think it to be.

Bracken had smiled inside, but had kept his face impassive.

He knew their game. They would pump him for all that they could right here, while they could, give him rest a little at a time so his memory would be fresh, and then jump right back on it again, until they'd pumped his well dry, and then they'd lock him away somewhere, in a place that would be heavily guarded, and they'd forget about him until it was time to prepare him for the trials.

Until he'd worn out his usefulness, they would treat him like a king. Bring him cigarettes and coffee, whatever kind of food he liked. Tallman was going out of his way to be gracious, was treating him like an equal, as someone to be respected. The man was far too wrapped up in himself to be effective at it though, at least with Bracken. Such manly camaraderie might have impressed Tulio, but Bracken saw it for what it was, patronizing nonsense, calculated and foolish.

It made Tallman vulnerable, though, his wanting Bracken to believe that he was one of the boys. Right from the start the fool had given Bracken valuable information as he tried to calm Bracken's nerves.

"It's not like it used to be, not like it was back with Vincent Teresa or Jimmy Fratianno, or even Henry Hill. We've come a long way since then, the last fifteen, twenty years. They got treated well, even Fratianno, who admitted to murder, he's free today. But of course he only killed his own, not like what you've done, Christ, the guy's wife and kid." Tallman laughed nervously.

"Half his mob family. If we should cut you loose into society, do you have any idea what we'd catch from the press? If only we could have kept a lid on it, Jim, you got to believe me, I tried."

Tallman had been soothing him, but showing how honest he was, even before the confession, and Bracken let him, listening to his friend, to the man who'd "tried" for him. To the hypocrite.

"We've come a million miles since Valachi. You look right outside that window, Jim, and you'll see trees, sidewalks without cracks, gutters without papers or dirt. We're in a real *neighborhood* here, Jim, not in some loft district in downtown Manhattan."

Tallman had smiled. Had told Bracken that they owned four houses on the surrounding block, that every house they owned was manned with armed and well-trained agents, that he might well be the safest man in America at this very moment. The house directly behind the one they were in was one of theirs, and the trees that had once been on the property had been cut down so that the back could be watched at all times. The entire square block area was being watched by people who knew how to do it, who knew, too, how to keep a low profile.

"The guy down the street mowing his lawn in sweatclothes, he's one of us. The woman driving this week for the grade school car pool, with the curlers in her hair, she's with us, too. Those are *her* kids she's driving, and that lawn, that's our man's. These people *live* here, Jim, it's their neighborhood, and they fit in. They go on red alert only when we get someone like you in this house here. In seven years that we've had this place, we've used it a total of three times."

Bracken loved this guy, the way he was giving information away. Keep it up, fat man. Keep thinking that you're God. This fatass didn't have any idea how weak his beliefs really made him, how vulnerable.

Bracken would point out his defects to him soon.

"We even have plans for you in the event of a nuclear attack," Tallman had said, and then smiled at Bracken, smugly.

Bracken had given in then, had begun his confession, acting as if it were impossible to argue with Tallman's special brand of logic. He'd gone out of his way to make sure that Bracken knew that he was not only safe, but that it was virtually impossible to escape. What he didn't seem to understand was how very much he'd given away.

The rest of it, Bracken figured out for himself, his mind working as he spoke, occasionally testing them, seeing what they had.

They were at their highest level of alertness when he stood or went to the bathroom. It got their attention, and they stood tall, ready, their hands on their weapons until he came out and sat back down.

He soon learned that the bathroom would be useless to him. The glass in the small, old-fashioned iron lift-up window had been replaced with thick bulletproof glass that had wire crisscrossing the panels; its frame had been welded into place from the inside. Even if he could somehow find a way to get it open, it still wouldn't be big enough for anyone larger than a small child to fit through. When they'd remodeled this place, the feds had been taking no chances.

The house was very old, Bracken could tell that from the architecture alone. Even the converted bedroom they were now in had arched doorways. The walls had been paneled in dark, rich wood, the molding was side. All the wood was freshly, highly polished. The windows in here had been covered with very thick, dark drapes. Bracken wondered if they were made of bulletproof material, if the glass behind the draperies was the same as that in the bathroom.

No one could get in, and no one could get out. Anyone who walked out of the room was immediately spotted by the FBI honcho, Bittner, standing right outside the door. Bracken could tell that it was him without having to turn around; when the door opened, Bracken could hear the keys spinning into the palm of the man's hand. When it was closed, he could hear nothing. The door was thick and old and real wood, it closed out any sound. It would keep sound in, too.

He lit another cigarette and blew smoke out, toward the ceiling.

"I want to give you something, Mr. Tallman," Bracken said. "A gesture of good faith."

Tallman spread his hands wide. "That's not how it works, Jim, I have to be honest with you. I don't give a shit about good faith." He smiled painfully, letting Bracken know that what he'd said hadn't been personal.

"Then let's make a trade, how's that? I need freedom for Tawny, a full pardon. He's never been involved in any crimes, Mr. Tallman, he knows nothing. The worst he's ever done is check my mail for me once a week, now is that a crime? I never told him anything about my business."

It was difficult, for Bracken, being respectful of this man. Bracken sensed his cowardice, knew what an egotistical pig he truly was. It was going to be a pleasure to kill him, when the opportunity arose.

"He's being debriefed now, I have to tell you. And your house is being gone over. The furniture can come with you wherever you go, so it'll be more like home for you."

"There's nothing in that house that can implicate anyone in any crime."

"Come on, Jim. There has to be. If Tawny hadn't opened the door for my people, they'd *still* be trying to get through that front door."

"That was for my protection, in case one of my enemies somehow found me."

Tallman looked at him strangely, and Bracken wondered if he'd said too much. Tallman said, softly, "Tawny's in custody, just being questioned at this point. He's not really happy with the way things are going."

"Can you get him here?" One of the officers in the room snickered, and Tallman turned on the man quickly, shut him up with a glance.

"Not just yet," Tallman said. There was a slight tinge of sarcasm in Tallman's tone of voice, the man making fun of him, his mere tone more distasteful to Bracken than the other man's snicker had been.

"After we're satisfied that he's not involved in anything, Jim, we'll ask him what he wants to do. We have to look in the books on this one, I'll be honest with you. We've had wives and girlfriends to deal with before, but never anything like this." Tallman, the pig, smiled.

"But I wouldn't worry, Jim, this is the nineties. The same rules should apply to you as they would to anybody else. But if you want to talk about good faith, Jim . . ." Tallman gave him a suspicious look, his eyes narrowed, thinking he was going to slick Bracken out. "Tell me something else that you wouldn't tell the feds. Tell me why you killed all those people, after all these years of being so careful. Tell me why you wiped out a Don, just to get some pictures, Jim."

Bracken knew that he'd have to be careful here. If he gave an answer that Tallman ever suspected to be less than the truth, they'd move Torelli again, and neither Bracken nor anyone else would ever be able to find him. He didn't know how much of a chance he'd have of ever getting to the man himself, but still, if someone else should find Torelli and kill him, Terri's death would be avenged. So he had to be careful not to give anything away.

What he had to do was throw any and all suspicion away from Torelli, act as if he was hardly aware of who the man was.

It might work, and it might not, but he decided to give it a try. It would be one of the lesser risks that he'd be taking tonight, and if it turned out to be a mistake, well, Bracken didn't believe that he'd be alive long enough to regret it.

One mistake, though, and his credibility would be blown. He forced himself to think: What had he said last night? What were the exact words that he'd said to Pete Papa before he'd killed him? Had he mentioned Torelli by name? He wasn't sure if he had. But he'd spent a lifetime being circumspect, never saying more than he had to. Pap had made the first offer, back in his office behind the candy store. Since leaving the candy store, Bracken was certain, he hadn't spoken Torelli's name. He thought that he'd remember if he had because of the queasy, sick feeling he got whenever he said the name aloud. He would have avoided saying that name at all costs, and besides, Papa had known what pictures Bracken had come for. And, if he remembered correctly, he'd believed that there had only been one single picture. He was sure of that; he'd asked Papa for the *picture* rather than for the *pictures*.

All right, to hell with it, it was time to take a shot.

He set his face, made himself look angry, and when he spoke he gave them the first hint of the long night that he was capable of showing any human emotion.

Bracken said, "That bastard, that dirty bastard Papa. He tried to blackmail me, told me he had a picture of me, a still shot of me killing a man for him, told me he'd had the house wired up, had a picture of me working."

"Wait a minute, you're telling me that you killed him over the *wrong* pictures?" Tallman seemed amazed, he was falling for it. Good.

Bracken said, "Even blinded, even knowing he was about to die, he had to lie, wasn't capable of the truth. All he had were pictures of that fink, that guy who sent him away all those years ago. I saw them, and I wanted to kill Papa again. I took them hoping that someone in his family would know about them, to throw suspicion onto you boys, rather than onto me. See, the mob, they're as paranoid as anyone else. They'd believe it in a minute, that the FBI had killed Papa in order to get those pictures back from him."

Tallman was even slicker now, said, casually, "Do you know what he was going to do with those pictures?"

"How would I know?" Bracken had slipped his mask of indifference back onto his face, and his tone was once again neutral. "Why would I care?"

"I was just wondering."

"Ask Tulio, maybe he'd know. He was closer to Papa than I could ever have been."

"All this for a copy of a picture that never even really existed."

"I thought it did, Mr. Tallman, I sincerely thought he had one. I could see Pete Papa doing it, the way he manipulated people. It was one of the reasons I decided to make a deal, I was sure that you'd find the picture."

"You didn't search the house . . ."

Bracken snorted disdainfully. "Search the house? I'd have been there for days."

Tallman shook his head, as if in awe of the luck that the government had experienced.

Bracken said, "Good faith. It may not mean much to you. But listen to this. If Tawny gets freed, tonight, I can give you someone, someone who's—let's just say a heavy contributor to the other party, to the Democrats." Bracken looked pointedly at the other men in the room, then back at Tallman, signaling that he'd only speak to the man about this face to face.

Tallman rubbed his chin, looked at Bracken quizzically.

Bracken lowered his eyes. "I want my lover. I miss him." He nearly whispered the words, and hid his outrage at Tallman's barely concealed smirk.

"I can give you a heavy political contributor to the Democratic party. Proof that this very rich man had me murder his wife. Very recently. How's that?"

Bracken still had not raised his eyes. He stared at his hands, folded together on the table. The mood in the room was somber, the silence overpowering. Tallman came over to him, turned a chair around and sat down with the chair back protecting his chest. He draped his arms over the back of the chair, a studied, tough guy pose. From the corner of his eye Bracken could see Tallman wave at the stenographer, telling him not to type any of this. He moved his head close to Bracken's, and he whispered, "Staples? You did the Staples thing over at the Plaza Hotel?"

In a lightning maneuver, Bracken made his move. He pushed off the chair and grabbed Tallman by the throat and twisted him around and slammed the back of his head to the table, pinned him there with his right hand while he lifted his left hand high, his fingers twisted into claws, pointing down, then he brought those fingers down at lightning speed, stopped them six inches from Tallman's face.

"Don't move, don't any of you move one fucking inch!" Bracken kept his voice low and steady, and he opened his eyes wide, bared his teeth in a smile.

"Move, and I rip his eyes out. I'll eat them before you shoot me."

Tallman was squirming under his hand, and Bracken squeezed his throat gently and held it that way, giving him just a whiff of the power in his hands.

"Don't move, *Freddy*, or I'll pinch your right ball off your scrotum sac."

"Let him go, Mr. Bracken, there's no way out of here for you." One of the trained monkeys was talking to him, but Bracken did not respond.

"All of you, in front there, you with the machine, on your belly, now." Bracken said, "All of you, now. Take your weapons out slowly, with the tips of your fingers. Slowly!"

The men were looking at him, at their boss, at his red, shaking face, at his bulging eyes, at his mouth, open wide, begging for air.

"I'll choke him!"

Slowly, they began to obey. Tallman was no longer struggling. Bracken could smell him, what he'd done to himself.

"That's right, slowly, boys, drop them to the carpet and take a step back, turn around, that's it. On your bellies now, away from the pistols."

Bracken was smiling now for real, looking at three pistols, shining there on the heavy shag carpet. "Push yourselves away from them lads, that's the way."

As the federal men obeyed, Bracken cajoled them, as if they were children. "A *little* further, lads, that's it, now clasp your hands behind your necks."

The door was unlocked, Bracken knew. But nobody in the hall would be able to hear him talking, unless he screamed. He didn't plan on screaming. Or on shooting off any of the pistols.

He kept his grip firm on Tallman's throat, and pushed the man into a standing position. "Now, *Freddy*, you're going to see what it's like to be on this side." Bracken hit him once, hard, in the stomach. As Tallman fell forward Bracken caught him and pushed him to his knees. He pulled Tallman's tie up around back and dragged him with him around the desk to where the men were lying. The heavy stench filled the room now, Tallman was falling apart, shaking as if in the throes of an acute nervous breakdown. The tie thrummed in Bracken's hand, like a wire pulled tight and flicked with a finger.

"Come along, now," Bracken told him, dragging him. He hauled him gracelessly around the table, walking with great care, the leg irons restricting his movements, Bracken holding tightly to Tallman's tie with one hand, pulling him as if he were a child's wheeled horse toy.

He bent down and used his free hand, grabbed one of the weapons and pushed it across the carpet, to the other end of the room, then did the same with a second pistol. The third one he hung onto. Bracken took the safety off it and pulled the hammer back. Only then did he let go of Tallman's tie.

"Sit down, that's right, go over to the chair and sit your ass down, Freddy." Tallman crawled across the floor, quickly, scurrying as fast as he could. Shaking his fat ass in his haste to please his new master.

Bracken waited until Tallman was in the chair, looking down at the carpet, before he said, "All right, gentlemen, now move your hands behind your back and hold them there, slowly, gently, that's the way. I'm going to cuff you now."

As they inched their hands onto their backs, they exposed the back of their necks, the soft little spot directly behind the ear . . .

"We'll have the cuffs on in a second, boyos," Bracken said.

He silently eased the hammer back down, put the safety back on the pistol and struck quickly, bringing the heavy 9mm pistol in his hand up and down four times, one shot apiece, hitting with precise accuracy. There were no grunts, no yelps of surprise. The men just seemed to relax. They'd be relaxed forever, now. As soon as he was sure that they were dead, Bracken turned to their boss.

Tallman was trying to breathe through his nose, hyperventilating and fighting the urge to scream. Bracken knew that the man wouldn't shout, because Bracken hadn't told him to. Bracken knew he owned him now, that Tallman was his slave. That for maybe the first time in his life, Tallman was finding out what it was like to be dominated by someone who had absolutely no fear of him.

"My God, what they send us to protect us." Bracken said it drily. Tallman's eyes were on him, still bulging, as if Bracken were still cutting off his air. Terror lived in those eyes, Tallman was closer to death than he had ever been before. He was beyond reason, did not need to be threatened. A weak man, shown his mortality, would do whatever he was told.

Bracken sat down across from him, flicked Tallman's tie up at his face, smiled as the man jumped, Tallman whimpering in terror. He took a Pall Mall out of the pack and tapped it on his thumb. He stuck the cigarette in his mouth and lit up, left it in the corner of his mouth as he began to speak.

"Your people are in my house, desecrating it, aren't they. No, don't try to answer, I won't think you impolite. My home is being destroyed, my lover's being terrified. And I can see in your eyes that you want me, you *expect* me to show you mercy. Tell me, Tallman, how much mercy were you planning on showing me?"

Bracken smiled at Tallman, shook his head in melancholy tinged with amusement. He took the cigarette out of his mouth and pursed his lips, raised his eyebrows at the U.S. attorney. When he spoke the hint of bemusement was no longer in his voice. That voice was flat and deadly, quiet, conveying contempt.

"I could skin you alive and make you stay silent, take the flesh off your bones and nobody would know. Hours from now, you'd still be alive and in mortal agony, and I'll bet that FBI man out there won't even stick his head in the door.

"Oh, no, Freddy, because you have them all so terrified of your power. The little bureaucrats with their tin badges and toy guns. You look down on them, but you wish they were in here with you right now, don't you? Your handpicked crew didn't do you much good." Bracken smoked, thinking, the gun on the table between them.

"I could shoot you and then myself, but then where would we be? No, that won't do, unless as a last resort." He twirled the gun around until the barrel was facing Tallman. "I won't go to prison you know, that's not an option. And I won't talk to you anymore, not even if they somehow take me alive. You see, I've lost my respect for you, Freddy."

Tallman was sitting in terror, eyes glued to Bracken's. His hands were free but he kept them by his sides. Bracken smiled at him, acknowledging his cowardice, keeping it their secret.

"You have four houses on this block. Men mowing the lawn, female agents driving in car pools. Belittling hard-trained agents to keep a happy domestic scene in place. Quite a few safeguards, but I'd bet there's a few you didn't tell me about, aren't there. 'Need to know.' Those words are big in your vocabulary, aren't they, Freddy Tallman?"

Tallman had a string of saliva hanging from his mouth. It swung in an arc down to his shirt, down to the second button.

Bracken said, "Shit, spit, what's the difference, eh? Men like you have no pride unless there's someone there to impress with it. Now tell me, Freddy, are these things I don't know? I'll kill you if you don't tell me. Look at your men on the floor, and tell me you don't believe me."

"I—I believe you."

"Good dog," Bracken said.

"There's a way in and out, a tunnel, in case security is breached."

"One would think there would be. It's how all these people came through here without being seen from the street. How they brought me in here, when I was blindfolded. I knew there was something like that! Now tell me, Freddy, just where is this tunnel?"

"I'll take you to it, there's an entrance upstairs and down-stairs, the one we want is two bedrooms down." Tallman's voice was flat, without inflection. He spoke quickly now, begging, trying to gain Bracken's favor.

"There's a stairway there that leads down to the tunnel, inside the walls, we covered an entire bedroom to make the stairway to the tunnel. If anyone ever got in here, was holding the witness hostage, we could get in, with men, from two different vantage points, upstairs and down, storm the place after we knocked out the power."

"And where will this tunnel lead, if there really is one?"

"There is one, I'm being honest with you here. I know what'll happen if I'm not. It goes to the house next door. From the outside, it looks like just another empty house, but the inside's been gutted, we drive cars right into the house, through the attached garage in the alley. The wall between the house and the garage's been knocked out. It's a huge garage, it's basically all the house is. It's locked at all times, and there's a stairway leads right into it."

"Well, aren't you talkative. How many cars are in this garage?"

"We've got seven or eight people here right now, I'd say there's three or four in there right now, counting the car we came in."

Tallman's eyes widened, as if thinking of an obstacle in the way of their escape. Just one of the boys, looking for a way out with his friend.

Tallman said, "We'd have to get by Bittner, he's on the door himself."

"We'd have to, now wouldn't we? He's got the key to my leggings." Bracken picked the gun up from the desk and flicked off the safety, pulled back the hammer, pointed it at Tallman's head and watched the man's face twist. There was blood on the barrel, the blood of his handpicked crew. The blood of three highly trained agents and the poor, sorry stenographer. Tallman was staring at it. A tear rolled down his cheek. He squeezed his eyes shut.

"Please don't. There really is a tunnel."

"You wait until I get behind the door, then you call Agent Bittner in here, Freddy, and your tone had better be calm and convincing. Otherwise, you and me, we'll be marching through the gates of hell together, and which one of us do you think the devil will welcome with open arms?"

MARK SAID, "DEL," and shook the old man's outstretched hand. Around them, in the gym, the early morning workouts stopped as the ex-gangbangers eyed Mark with undisguised anger. He ignored them, looked back at Del. He had an idea as to what would be bothering them, and couldn't think of a way to tell them the truth without making them even more angry.

"Saw you on the news last night." Del shrugged. "You held your hands kind of low. You hadn't hit that guy just right, you'd'a been open for a easy hook." Del spoke in a casual manner, making light of a serious situation, behind Mark in this case and proving it, no matter how he felt about him personally.

"I'll remember that, next time."

The old man's voice softened, and he looked around in that way he had, making sure nobody could hear him.

"Was people calling here all night long. Looking for your ass, wanting your phone number or address. I didn't give them shit. I went into the Rolodexes upstairs and pulled your card out of all of 'em. Somebody gets in there, they can't steal them when our backs are turned. You had all brothers working here, they'd be looking for that kind of shit out of 'em, expecting reporters to fuck 'em around. But those white boys you got working up there would get slicked out, sure as shit. Reporters was looking for you, bangers, cops, shit, that phone was busy. Spent most of the night with the doors open, talking kids out of going out there, rioting over Elmer."

"The same kids who'd make fun of him all day when he would come in here looking for friends."

"I was his friend. You was his friend. He didn't need nobody else."

"Lot of good I did him."

"Don't you talk like that, you shut your mouth right now. You people, the things that make you guilty, and ain't none of you feel guilty over the things you *ought* to feel guilty about." Del shook his head, in disgust at the white man's habits, then glared up at Mark.

"You did that boy good for the time he was here, and you tried to do right by him last night, too. Wasn't your fault the cops kilt him. It's just what they do nowadays, kills them a nigger whenever theys can."

Mark looked at him and nodded. He didn't want to argue. Didn't wanta to be preached to either, but he listened.

"Some of the boys, though, they mad to you, Mark." Del looked Mark in the eye as he spoke. Mark might be able to ignore the men working out in the gym, but Del was demanding an answer, was going to make his case.

"We got boys be knowin' you since they was in they early teens, look at you as sort of a pal, and you don't call on us, don't come up here when you get problems." Del was talking calmly, still, but it was obvious in his tone, Del wanted an answer as badly as the men who were working out in the place. The difference between them being that Del could demand one, could take Mark to task.

"Some of 'em even know where you lives, too, Mark. Was gone go over there last night and find out why you turned your back on us."

"I didn't turn my back on them, or on you, or anybody else. It was my beef, Del, I took care of it my way."

"You sound like some of them boys out there now, as they used to, when they was in the gangs."

"Del, listen to me. There's trouble around me, coming back from my past, and it's only gonna get worse. I'm not going to let any of these kids get hurt over shit that happened fifteen years ago."

Del said, "They's men now, Mark, quit looking down your nose at them. Every one of them old enough to make their own decisions as to who they should stand beside, what they should stand up for." Del's brown eyes were filled with fire.

"Some of these boys waited here through most of the night, figuring you'd come here as soon as you got out of the lockup. Others even went down there, waiting to throw your bail, left when your white lawyer showed up and told them wasn't shit they could do but cause you more grief."

"He didn't tell me anyone was there."

"Why should he? He ain't one of us, and never will be. Shit, he *white*."

Del said, "Was a time, Mark, when you and me did the same for them boys out there, stood beside them when they needed it, and they's only lookin' to pay you back now, do for you for once. You let them down, Mark, and some of them ain't never gonna forget it."

Mark had had enough. There was no amount of explaining he could do that would satisfy Del, not without telling him things that he had never told his wife. He wouldn't disrespect her that way, would not tell Del things that he hadn't trusted Caroline enough to disclose.

Instead, he said, "Who's on the second floor?"

Del looked hurt, then angry. For a second, Mark didn't think that he was going to answer him, then the old man looked away, toward the young men who were working out, hitting punching bags, speed bags, some of them jumping rope. He looked back at Mark, stared at him and spoke in a voice that was cold and all professional. The voice Del used when he was talking to the police.

"Ain't nobody in yet. They was in till late last night, though, talking to everybody, trying to keep the reporters out and the kids under control. I relaxed most of them, made them wait till they talked to you before they went and done something stupid."

"Thanks, Del."

"You got more than outside troubles, Mark, you got plenty of them right here inside the center. The phones didn't *stop* ringing, I could hear them up there, going off all damn night in the offices when they figured out that I was only gonna keep hanging up on them. The politicians, they pissed, wantin' to cut off our funding if you don't come out and change what you said. Or unless you quit." Del looked around, no longer cold, suddenly afraid.

"We lose this place, where's the kids gonna go?"

Mark wondered if Del had any idea where he himself would go without this place.

"We won't lose this place, Del. I won't let that happen."

Del's voice softened. Even as mad as he was, he couldn't see Mark as the Man for very long. They'd been through too much together, had saved too many lives, and even Del couldn't doubt Mark's commitment to the center.

Del said, "Stayed up all night, even after the kids left, with my Louisville Slugger, waitin' for the bastards to come kicking in the door. Be like them, them politicians, to do that, move us out in the middle of the night and change the locks on the door."

"They can't do that, Del."

"Wasn't 'sposed to be able to kill Elmer, neither."

"I'll be upstairs if you need me. You've got men waiting over there need someone to train them, Del, you've got other things to do. Let me handle it, I know what to do."

"And I don't," Del said. "See you, Mark." The little man's eyes were shining.

"This place is gonna make it, Del."

Del looked at him, not missing what Mark had said. He let it pass, did not comment on the fact that Mark had said "this place" rather than "we." Del nodded, disappointed. Del had been there a long time. He'd seen more than one white administrator come and go, most of them having left because they couldn't handle the heat, did not know how real it could get when you truly gave your life to this sort of work. Mark had been different. In spite of his mistrust, Del had tried, at times, to see him as a friend. Mark hadn't missed it either, when Del had said that the lawyer wasn't one of "us."

Mark knew that in a worse case scenario, it would not matter how close they had once been, that if it was a choice between Mark and the youth center, Del would learn to live without him. But if there was a fighting chance that Mark could stay on the job, Del would battle to see him stay. In Del's eyes, now, Mark would look like a quitter.

Del said, "Don't matter none 'bout me. Shit, I'm eighty-two years old. You a young man. They close us down, where the kids gonna go, where the other bosses up there gonna go?" His tone was almost apologetic, Del telling Mark that he was trying to understand what it was that Mark was doing.

Mark nodded again and walked to the steel stairway, began to mount the steps as Del's voice rang in his ears. "Don't you let them close us down . . ."

Mark knew the tough little ex-boxer wouldn't hear him, but he said it anyway: "They won't, Del . . ."

THERE WERE OTHER ways of getting around them, Mark knew that now. He'd come in early on purpose, would have been even earlier if Bella hadn't come by, wanting to convince him that the government was his friend. All the friends that he needed right now were green painted pieces of paper, with pictures of long dead presidents on the front. Mark had a lot of those friends, from fifteen-year-old bank safe deposit boxes that had once been stuffed with cash, that cash long untouched but still there, waiting.

Now Mark closed himself in his office, went and sat behind his desk, picked up the ringing phone and dropped it back in its cradle, then took the phone off the hook, put the receiver on the desk. He slipped a piece of paper in the typewriter and didn't even hesitate, began to tap away.

He'd use that money, it was his emergency fund. He'd live on it, go ten years without a job if he had to, because he knew one thing, was sure of little else: He would not let the youth center go down the tubes because of him.

Enough people had already been hurt, enough hearts already broken. His wife and children were now paying the price for loving him, for trusting him, no one else could be made to suffer because of him. Tommy Torelli, yeah, he'd have fucked anyone over in order to get what he wanted, even if that was only the ego-thrill of doing what he wanted to do and getting away with it, while others tried to get him to bend his will to their own agendas.

But Mark Torrence didn't operate that way. Never had, and it was too late for him to revert to type now, because if he did, the last thirteen years of his life had only been nothing more than a cruel joke.

Mark Torrence wouldn't hurt anyone who didn't have it coming, and this would be, he knew, the last kind thing he did as Mark Torrence.

Some good people would get hurt if he stayed here, if he tried to pretend that nothing had changed after last night. The fact was that everything had changed, including the rules he'd lived by.

Bella had tried to tell him that he was no longer himself, that he was really Torelli, and he'd even thought that himself, that morning and last night, crawling into his old skin and wondering how to play this. It had been so confusing, these last twelve hours. Everything had changed, his entire reality was different.

What he hadn't been aware of until now was how much he hated the man he used to be. And how much he respected the man he had become. And the man he was today would not kowtow to politicians, would not play their game for them either, would not allow them to use Elmer's life and death as pawns in the game they were always ready to play to further their own political ambitions. He'd do this, quit the job, his last official act as the man he so respected. Because his mind was made up, he was no longer confused. Mark Torrence could never survive what would be coming his way, soon.

Mark typed, knowing how the politicians would use last night, and how they'd want him to go along with them. One faction would tell him he was a hero, play to his ego, for photo opportunities. They'd use Elmer's death, use what the cops had done, to win votes in the next election, and Elmer's death would mean nothing more to them than a chance to show that they were truly men of the people.

The others would pretend that he was an enemy of the people, this faction of politician being the hardliners, the ones that Mark already had enough trouble with. More money for problems to help gang youth? Kiss my ass. Tell them that if they break the law they'll go to the joint, and we'll keep building more and more jails until we can finally put them all away, put them where they belong.

There were more of this type than there were of the first, and they were far more dangerous, because they had the people behind them, the people who were sick of being locked in their houses around the clock, afraid to go out in the street or even sit on their porches.

Mark couldn't blame them, that was no way to live. But he knew that things would never get better for them if their only solutions were more jail cells. For every badass gangbanger that went to the pen, there were two standing ready and able to take their place in the street. The hardline politicians could blow all the smoke that they wanted, but anyone who lived out here knew the truth about the neighborhoods: They were only good as the neighbors in it, and three bad kids could wreck an entire city block.

Mark finished typing, took the piece of paper out of the typewriter and put it down on his desk, read it over, then signed it.

The hardliners, he knew, would use last night's hostage drama to cut off what little funding the center got in the first place. They would point out that Elmer was a member of the center, use him as an example of the wasted tax dollars that were sent to the place, of the character of the sort of people the taxpayers were supporting with their hard-earned dollars at the liberal, do-nothing South Loop Youth Center.

Mark couldn't let that happen, not in his lifetime. The place would do fine without him, might even do better, after all the publicity and with him out of the way.

What would they do when the truth came out that the director had once been a federally protected witness? Mark did not know, there was no answer to that question, yet. Nor was it something he could now worry about, he had enough problems, and they were mounting by the minute.

It was just another thing that he would have to refuse to be responsible for.

Mark put the signed letter of resignation on top of his typewriter, sat back and lit a cigarette and threw the match on the hardwood floor.

The door flew open and Mark bolted forward and looked at it, eyes wide and angry, feeling no fear. He took a deep breath and tried to relax as two muscular young black men in suits marched slowly in, took up straight-back, near military positions on either side of the door, their hands folded across their chests, glaring at Mark. He could see the bulge of their weapons underneath their well-cut suit jackets.

EDDIE DOLAN DID not want to get up early, not after having spent all of the night and part of the morning talking to the cop and the civilians who monitored them. He lay in bed, staring at the ceiling, too wide awake to even consider going back to sleep, too exhausted to get out of bed and go and take a shower.

It had been a rough eight hours, worse than the negotiation itself. Every so often a voice would get raised in anger, Dolan or one of the guys who was questioning him getting on each other's nerve and lashing out.

The problem had been the civilian's statement, what he'd hollered out to the community and the reporters, live, his statements running on all three television stations, endlessly replayed on the newsradio stations. It could be Rodney King all over again, only worse; this time, somebody had died. Community leaders were already howling cover-up, demanding investigations, some of them even demanding that they be allowed to conduct their own investigation, naturally at the city's expense.

Dolan would have come out of it in pretty good shape if he had gone totally by the book, had not gone down to talk to Elmer like he had. He'd been raked over the coals for that one, by the brass, and by everyone else. Besides that screw-up, there wasn't much that he could really tell them. Once the civilian snookered them all, Dolan hadn't seen him again until after Lawlor's unit attacked.

His kids had called him at the station, left messages for him that he hadn't returned. They would be local heroes today at their schools, their father a one-night TV star. That or they'd be vilified, attacked for their father's actions.

As his punishment for not going by the rules, Dolan was bounced off of the Hostage-Barricade team, was now just a youth officer again. The brass, they loved you or hated you, depending upon the public's perception of your actions. Now, for a while, they'd hate him, and Dolan could live with that, but being off the unit hurt. He'd loved being part of that, of negotiating with armed, barricaded criminals, matching wits with hostage takers.

The only good news in the entire deal was that the fat son

of a bitch, Lawlor, would probably get canned. Bounced off the force for establishing a green light situation without permission. Elmer should have lived, could have been handled relatively easily. Dolan believed that and had repeated it to everyone who would listen. He was even thinking about calling some reporters he knew and telling them the same thing, if they'd promise to refer to him as only an anonymous source. As far as Dolan was concerned, Lawlor should not only be bounced off the force, he should be charged with a crime; depending on the interpretation of the law, maybe even charged with murder. As far as Eddie was concerned, the man had killed Elmer the same as if he'd pulled the trigger himself.

A senseless death, as a lot of them were these days. This one being aggravated by an impatient civilian, an arrogant SWAT leader, by people not showing up when they should have, not returning their beeps. But who could have guessed that this was going to turn out to be a high profile case? From earliest indications, it was just another West Side black kid, losing his head, going overboard. A call to the station desk would confirm that, and even the desk sergeants would not have taken it too seriously. When a white, employed North Side resident did the very same thing, though, they were all over it, these lazy cops on the Hostage-Barricade team, showing up because they knew that the profile was high and there was a chance that Carol Marin might interview them for the Channel 5 nightly news.

Part of the reason Eddie was awake so early was because of the nightmares, dreams of Elmer, haunting him. Elmer crying, trying not to show it. Elmer with his head on the barrel of the shotgun, twisting his head to look at Eddie with eyes that were so filled with terror they were almost popping out of his head. He'd see the kid in his dreams, but, sleeping, he wasn't upstairs when the kid pulled the trigger. In the dream, he was right there, running at Elmer, shouting for him not to do it, and in the dream Elmer saw him, twisted his head toward Eddie and smiled before pulling the trigger and blowing his head all over the basement, all over Eddie.

The other reason he was awake so early was the bastard who *had* been down there when Elmer had bought it. That guy Torrence, Mark, his name was, who truly had been covered with bits of Elmer's skull, with Elmer's blood and brains. Torrence, who had knocked Dolan on his ass in front of the entire city, captured for all time on videotape. What the man said, what he believed about Dolan, irked him, caused Dolan resentment that couldn't be rationalized away.

He'd tried to tell himself that the guy was just another social worker fool, that he didn't know anything about police work, or about police procedure. That he'd been half-crazed by the torment he'd suffered through, sitting right next to the kid when Elmer pulled the trigger.

He told himself these things, but it didn't do much good. The man had still knocked him on his ass, in front of the entire world. The man had still, after his arrest, threatened Dolan, tried to intimidate him by inviting him into his jail cell.

The worst part had been when they'd run his prints and found out there was a federal hold on them. That could only mean one thing, that the guy was a protected witness, some federal stoolie that had been relocated.

Where did this son of a bitch get off, judging Dolan? That rankled him as much as anything else, the way the guy had criticized Dolan's character, some stoolpigeon judging him, looking down his nose at a working cop.

It wasn't as if it was the first time it happened, Dolan had grown used to it, it had become a part of his life. When he'd been on the street, in a squad car, he'd put up with enough of it, nearly every day, until it had gotten to the point where he either had to learn to let it wash off his hide, or he'd have gone berserk himself.

Every time there was a major crime scene, particularly when a murder had been committed, gossip and rumor would fill a neighborhood, would race through the block like fire throughout the community, until whoever had died had been turned into a saint, or worse, martyred, by the cops themselves.

How many times had he heard it, the shouted curses, the demands that the corpse be removed before the medical examiner had even officially pronounced him dead? Dozens, maybe a hundred times, neighborhood residents demanding dignified treatment for a drug pusher or a gangbanger who'd angered the wrong man. Suddenly, the same sort of people who kept these residents inside their homes, living in terror, were now seen as model citizens, symbols of the class struggle between the community and those who had sworn to protect it.

This wasn't the first time that some ignorant civilian had seen him as the enemy, but for some reason, this one bothered him the most.

In fact, as far as Dolan's career went, his outside dealings with Torrence had been the high point of the night. He'd been complimented on his restraint, on his reserve, unlike a certain other cop on the scene. They'd sat and watched the video, Eddie and a bunch of bosses, the video that showed Dolan being courteous and polite to Torrence, even in the face of an angry crowd, trying to lead Dolan away without any violence, without pulling his piece. The same video that showed Lawlor attacking Torrence from behind, twisting his arm up behind his back, the tape showing the look of agony on Torrence's blood-spattered face as Lawlor manhandled him.

Lawlor, that fat son of a bitch, who'd tried to blame everything on Eddie. Telling the investigators that if Dolan hadn't allowed an unarmed citizen down there with the crazy man, then they wouldn't have had to attack through the windows. Lawlor telling them all that he'd done what he had out of fear for Torrence's life.

Thank God for the grandmother and the two older gentlemen who'd been in the apartment with her. They'd given sworn statements attesting to Lawlor's desire to storm the basement right from the beginning of the situation, had stated, too, that Dolan had personally stopped him, had to talk him into not shooting their baby as soon as he'd arrived on the scene.

Elmer Lee Griffin had been somebody's baby. Well, not anymore. Not ever again.

Dolan got out of bed and took a quick shower, didn't bother to shave, as it was his day off. They might not know who this guy Torrence actually was, and Eddie himself might not be a part of the ongoing investigation, but they knew where he worked, knew what Torrence did. And there was nothing in the regulations that said he couldn't talk to the guy on his day off, if he felt like it.

THE STATE'S ENTIRE law enforcement community would be looking for him now, and Bracken was aware of it, ditched the car and stuck to cabs as soon as he'd gotten to LaGuardia. He wondered what the U.S. attorney would tell them when they found him, wondered how long the man would have his job.

He'd left him a slobbering, blubbering, pitiful mass, locked in the trunk of the car at the airport's long-term lot. Bracken had decided to let him live, and for what he thought was a good reason. He'd left him alive so that the man would suffer, would know true pain for once in his fucking life.

Bracken knew, from long experience, that there were things far worse than death. Tallman would learn that secret now, too, would suffer in the eyes of first his office, then the press, then of his peers and finally, he would suffer in the eyes of an unforgiving public. How could he not, what lie could Tallman possibly tell that would elevate his stature to what it had been before the escape? None, there was nothing he could do, nothing he could say, that would win him back his manhood, the manhood that Bracken had stolen.

Bracken had left two guns with the man, fully loaded, casually stuck down the waistband of Tallman's pants. The message would be impossible to ignore. When they found him they would know that he was nothing but a coward. It would take days, and maybe longer, for Tallman to stop crying, for the man to be able to collect himself enough to be able to start telling lies, to try and cover up his behavior. There was no way that he could pull himself together in time to save his career. He'd been an emotional slave from the moment that Bracken had grabbed his throat, had even Stockholmed with Bracken, had worked with him to cause the death of Agent Bittner. That, he would never be forgiven for. People who had never faced death up close were always prepared to judge how those who had should have acted at the time.

If Tallman had any sense of honor, if he was any kind of a man, he would use one of the weapons on himself, would kill himself now, before his self-image died in front of the entire free world.

Bracken would have bet his freedom that the man wouldn't have the courage to take his own life. He'd dealt with such men before, men who spent their lives building up false beliefs in themselves, in who and what they were, men who then folded the first time somebody showed them the type of worm that they actually were. Tallman would be destroyed, would have to resign or be fired. Would take to living in terror of being recognized, a man who lived for publicity and public acclaim forced to forever shun the spotlight. He'd know what he was, finally. The shit in his pants would be his final evidence. Even Tallman at his egotistical best could never justify his actions of that morning.

It was almost worth giving up what Bracken would now be losing.

Bracken had taken three different cabs, as it was still early morning when he'd abandoned the car, not yet rush hour. One cab into lower Manhattan, another into midtown, a third yet to the upper East Side, the driver dropping him off a few blocks from his destination.

They'd only had him in Jersey City, my God, how stupid could they be? In their arrogance they'd believed that no one could ever escape from their custody, in their impudence they'd underestimated him, thought he'd be like all the rest. Whining and crying and begging to testify, to do whatever they'd demanded of him in order to get a deal.

They'd never dealt with anyone like *him* before, like The Chameleon.

Bracken stood on the corner now, looking up at one of his personal safehouses, scanning the street for any sign of federal agents, for the people who would shoot him down like a rabid dog if they spotted him, as a payback for what he'd done. He'd killed four of them, including an Agent-in-Charge. Was wearing Bittner's suit right now, it fit him a lot better than lardass Tallman's would have. He'd also escaped from a place that they'd thought to be impregnable. If they took him alive, if they somehow managed that, the negotiations would be over, there would be no further discussions, the feds would not want him to testify at any trials. He'd be forced to pay for the men he'd killed, would go away forever, most likely to the federal prison at Marion, Ill., Bracken locked in an underground cell, in a dungeon for the rest of his natural life.

He could never allow that to happen, which was why he'd only left two pistols with Freddy Tallman. He'd kept Bittner's, had it in his pocket right now, his fingers around the butt, the weapon unfamiliar to him, God, how he hated firearms!

Bracken believed that he was safe, that they hadn't yet found out about the safehouses, although he knew that they eventually might. Going inside would be the second to the last risk that he'd ever take in his lifetime, Bracken knew. Once he walked out of there, once he had access to what he'd come for, he'd be forever safe from them. He'd be a new man, an entirely different personality. He'd look different, walk different, be of a different height and weight. His own mother would not be able to recognize the man who would walk out of the apartment house.

And after tonight, by tomorrow at this time, he'd be out of their reach forever, with no trail for them to follow. He would fly away this very night, get on a plane to Switzerland, close out certain accounts there and arrange for the transfers of others. From there, a train to Paris, leisurely and reserved. Bracken would begin a new life there, without any interference from the law. He knew that there were international flights out of O'Hare, nearly hourly. He would be flying out of Chicago, he knew, as once he'd left this country, he would never be coming back. There was unfinished business in Chicago that would have to be attended to, before Bracken could forever abandon the United States of America.

He strode briskly toward the building, picked specifically for its lack of a doorman, inserted his key in the outside door, stepped into the foyer and let the outside door lock shut behind him. Only then did he unlock the door that would lead him to the elevators.

IT TOOK HIM an hour, as he had to clean up a few loose ends. A man who was unrecognizable as Bracken stepped out of the building, carrying a cardboard box that he deposited on the curb at the corner. It wouldn't be there long, he knew. It was filled with Bittner's suit, with other clothing from upstairs. All links to Bracken's past was now broken, no one could learn who he was from its contents, even if the law somehow got their hands on it.

They'd find the apartment eventually, he knew. And the one on the West Side, and he would leave them to be found. They would think that he had escaped the city, had left before they found either place. Bracken had left various identifications hidden around the place, had taken only three with him—the one he was using now, and two spares, in case of emergency—leaving the rest as proof to support their eventual theory that he had escaped from Manhattan without going to either place.

All he'd come for was what he was wearing, and the passports and other documents that were now inside his pockets. And the cash, too, a great many hundred dollar bills that were wrapped around in his belly, secure inside a moneybelt that fastened with Velcro rather than tiny steel snaps. He would take no chance that he would set off any airport metal detectors.

The things he'd left could be replaced in a matter of days, once you knew how to do it, and Bracken had been doing it since he was twenty-one years old. There was nothing in the apartment to show that he'd been there this year, let alone today, the FBI would find the place, and believe that he'd never shown up. Would concentrate their search elsewhere, after they found the car.

Bracken walked two blocks before he lifted his hand and immediately caught a cab, had it drop him off close to the West Side apartment, where he went and got the cash that was inside.

He climbed into another cab, told the driver to take him to Midtown, where he'd catch a limo to the airport and arrive in the sort of style that the cops would not be looking for. They'd be looking for someone acting furtively, and frightened. They wouldn't look twice at the man that Bracken had transformed himself into.

Bracken sat in the back of the cab and ignored the driver's attempt at conversation, the cretin wanting to talk about the Mets, and after a time, the man stopped trying, which was fine, it gave him time to think.

He could blow one ID in Chicago, if he had to. The things he'd need to create two other men could be found at local drugstores and at any medical supply warehouse.

His problem was not identification, he had enough of that. His problem now was one of time, specifically, how much time could he afford to waste hunting down Terri's betrayer? And would he be protected, would the feds be watching him, now that Bracken had escaped, no matter what he'd told Tallman earlier? Important questions, and questions that had to be answered soon, before Bracken arrived in Chicago.

There was something sticky on the armrest, and Bracken moved to the center of the backseat, saw the cabdriver stiffen a bit, check him out in the rearview mirror. He'd see a stocky man, with chubby, ruddy cheeks, a twinkle in blue eyes that were as light as the morning sky. Longish gray hair hung out from the sides and the back of a well worn hat, down onto the shoulders of a cashmere coat. The tie at his throat was wide and out of style, foppish in the way that it had been knotted. Bracken looked like nothing more than an aging boulevardier, a retired entrepreneur who'd fallen on some hard times, but who still thought that things could be turned around, a man who still had faith in himself.

No copper in America would give him a second look.

Bracken caught a quick glimpse of himself in the mirror, secure in the knowledge that he'd make good his escape, would have no problem getting into Chicago.

But what then? What about after he'd landed?

"My good man," Bracken said, and the driver looked at him strangely in the rearview mirror. "I'll get off at the corner, if you don't mind, there's a store back there that I must make a stop in."

"Whatever you want, pal," the driver now surly and superior and cocky, angry at Bracken for not wanting to talk baseball.

He got out at the corner and didn't overtip, slammed the door and walked back down the street until he found the luggage store that he'd spotted from the cab. Although he had credit cards in the name of the man that he changed himself into at the safehouse, he would not use them, would pay cash for a single suitcase. He did not want to leave a trail of bad credit behind him, in case he had to abandon the identity in Chicago. If someone went wrong and he did have to dump it, he didn't want any ties between the man he was pretending to be, and the city of New York. You never knew what the FBI would do with that sort of information, and it wasn't beyond them to check every luggage store in the borough, looking for the names of people who'd bought suitcases that day. They'd been known to pull out all the stops after one of their own had died.

A carry-on was all he needed, and Bracken bought it without bringing any attention to himself. He walked on, until he came to a men's store, and he went inside and bought a few items, put them inside the carry-on and hurried out of the store. He stopped in at the desk of the Hilton on Sixth Avenue, went to the concierge's desk and asked him to order a limo.

"Yes, sir," the man said, and took Bracken's twenty, made it disappear into his pocket and formally nodded his thanks.

*   *   *

MARK SAT BACK in his chair and put the cigarette in his mouth. He took a deep drag on it as their gangleader, Philip X. Jamabatta, walked in.

Two men followed Jamabatta, both of them cut from the same mold as the two who stood by the door, these two walking close behind their leader, taking up positions slightly behind him when he stopped. All four bodyguards were wearing black suits, white shirts with yellow bow ties, their sign of affiliation with the Church of Minister Africaan. All four of them looked like weight-lifters. Mark knew that none of them would smoke, none of them would drink, none of them partook of the poison they so greatly profited from, the crack that was sold on the street, the crack that killed the brothers whom they said they were fighting to save.

Jamabatta was a short man but incredibly wide, with massive shoulders that rivaled those of any of his cadre. His waist, however, was trim, slender. He was not dressed in the uniform of his bodyguards. He wore a black leather jacket with a belt that was cinched close around his narrow waist, tight jeans with brown soft leather half-boots on his feet. His thighs expanded the material of his jeans, threatening to bulge through if he were to squat down. Jamabatta wore a black Kangol hat on his head, Mark knew that was to cover the bald head that was a byproduct of the man's long-term steroid abuse. On his nose were pitch-black wraparound glasses.

Through the open door, Mark could hear the pounding of the punching bags. Del did not come in behind the men. There had been a time, even just yesterday, when Jamabatta would have found himself surrounded by people loyal to Mark. Or at least Mark liked to think so. Maybe none of the men out there had ever really respected him. Maybe they wouldn't have challenged this man, even if their loyalty was still as strong as ever. Maybe they were afraid of Jamabatta. Maybe, to them, Mark had always been just another white man, looking to break their hearts. Someone to be used, when the situation arose, but never trusted, never cared for or even loved.

The bodyguard to the left of the door pushed it shut, then

took his position back up, standing stock still, arms crossed, staring at Mark.

Jamabatta bowed, slightly, nodding his head and barely dipping his shoulders. "Mistah Torrence," Jamabatta said, dragging the words out, slowly. He had a deep voice, and he spoke softly.

Jamabatta was rumored to have had over thirty kills under his belt before he'd reached legal voting age. Mark could see him doing it, killing someone without passion, then standing over him and laughing in deep, rich glee.

Mark nodded, took a drag off the cigarette, dropped it to the floor and looked at it, then stomped it with his shoe.

"Those things'll kill you." Jamabatta was half-smiling, enjoying himself now.

Mark might soon be facing a group of people who would make lung disease seem tame. In fact, he was sitting in the presence of such men—without backup—right now.

"No, they won't," Mark told him, and Jamabatta's smile widened.

"The South Loop Youth Center. Haven for gumps who run from their set, busters ain't man enough to stick it out and get rich."

"Or maybe too smart to want to spend the rest of their lives in prison, don't forget that part of your lifestyle, Philip." The gangleader's smile cracked slightly at the familiarity, but he caught himself quickly, nodded his head at Mark.

"All part of doing business under the white man's domination. He won't be happy till *all* us brothers sitting behind bars, picking cotton on the new jailhouse plantations." The men with Jamabatta grunted their agreement.

"I heard you went political, that the dope you sell was now the white man's tool instead of your own."

Jamabatta shook his head.

"You should see who comes from the suburbs to deal with us, to buy what we have to sell. Ain't many brothers out there in Forest Park, Mistah Torrence." He had a way of saying Mark's name that made it seem like a filthy word.

"And what about the brothers from the city? You turn them down these days, Philip?"

"Some day, Mistah Torrence, we shall have a political discussion, and I'll enlighten your ass as to the evil ways of your people. But today is not that day."

"Then what is it that you want?"

"Don't fear me, if I wanted you dead, you'd be lying on the floor now, bleeding from your eyes." He barked a laugh. "There don't seem to be a whole lot of protection for your type in here, now does there, Mistah Torrence? I mean, look around you, who had the courage to follow us up in here?"

"I asked you, what do you want?"

Jamabatta flexed his muscles without lifting his arms. They bulged at the leather, then relaxed.

"Audacity in a white man sitting by himself is always such a surprise. Usually, when you're around us, you cover, or try to talk like us." His underlings laughed, and Jamabatta stood there basking in it, smiling himself. When they were through laughing, he continued.

"But you, you've always been a different one, ain't you, *Mistah* Torrence? Come in here every day, into the belly of the fuckin' beast, acting like you own the place and trying to tell my people what's good for them."

His face showed his contempt, Jamabatta was snarling now.

"Big badass motherfuckers you got in here, don't cover your ass when we might be in here killing it. I can't imagine how you must be feelin' right now, how scared you must be. You know why I won't imagine it? Cause if five packin' white men walked into *my* den, there'd be a couple of dozen men on their asses, kicking them into the ground."

Mark couldn't let that pass. He said, "You know what I've always thought about weightlifter bodyguards? I always figured they were useless."

Mark shrugged his shoulders, shook his head and smiled. He said, "I see you guys surrounded by them, dope pushers like you, hate-mongers like Minister Africaan, before he got sent to prison again, surrounded by a couple of tons of musclebound glaring fools, and I'd think to myself, What's with all the beef? Me, if I were rich, I'd hire myself just one tiny little woman, but one who had the courage to step in front of a bullet for me if she had to."

Jamabatta smiled, showing filthy, yellow teeth. He nodded his head as his bodyguards glared, Mark having gotten to them, having hurt their pride.

He said, "We ain't here to spar with you, Torrence. I cut you, you cut me, now we even, now we let it drop."

"Third time's a charm," Mark said. "What *are* you here for, Philip?"

"We's here to offer pro*tec*tion."

"Protection?" Mark said. He barked a laugh at the thought. "Protection from *what?* I'm already in as much trouble as I can get into."

The room was coldly silent, the men taking his response as an insult. Their protection, for free, especially given to a white man, was not something they would hand out often, if ever at all. In earlier times, Mark would have felt dread at the prospect of angering such violent, brutal men. It didn't bother him much now, and he suspected that was because he was taking back the characteristics of the man he'd used to be. And that man, Tommy Torelli, would have gladly died before showing his enemies any sign of weakness.

Jamabatta said, "You know about the conspiracy, you ain't worked down here as long as you have without knowing that the Man ain't gonna take what you did sitting down. They gonna kill you, the cops, the same as they killed the retard, Griffin. That retard, he never bothered nobody, I never much cared for crazy people, but he never looked at me wrong, never bothered any of my people."

"Who does?" Mark said, and Jamabatta nodded regally.

"These days, man, you'd be surprised. You got your activist priests out there, they walk right up into your face with a Mini-cam and forty parishioners watching his ass from their cars, recording every move you make, everything you say. The priests, they yell at me, call me names, right in front of everybody. You straighten them out, burn down their church, and along comes the damn local *community activists,* dropping dimes to the po-lice, calling that new eight-hundred number they got to report drug dealers and gun runners. We find out who they are, though, and they don't stay around too long."

Mark sat in wonder, staring at this man. Did he think that they were suddenly friends, that they were somehow bound together? Was the man actually sitting here, telling Mark that he torched churches, thinking that would gain him some form of admiration?

Mark decided that the man hadn't gotten the hints. He decided to be just a little less subtle. He said, "You spit on priests, you burn down churches and the houses of people who see you for what you really are." Mark paused, then spat out, "And *you're* going to protect *me?* You want me to thank you for that offer?"

Jamabatta, Christ, was he dense. He still didn't get it. He said, proudly, "There's nobody gonna mess with you, it's political now, you're under my personal protection. We'll be with you until you testify in court, until justice is done for the dead brother, Griffin." Jamabatta crossed his arms now, and grinned at Mark, waiting for him to express his gratitude. He didn't have to wait very long.

There was no use in saying any more to this man than he already had. Jamabatta seemed so secure in his sense of himself that he was blinded to Mark's insults. He might be so used to people fawning over him, most of them being too terrified to insult him, that he let Mark's comments go totally over his head, or else he was too ignorant to hear what was actually being said to him.

Mark got up out of his chair, dropped the cigarette to the floor, and walked around his desk, slowly, so as not to draw fire from any of the bodyguards. He went over to the door and opened it, was surprised to see Del standing there, Del and maybe twenty other glaring black faces, all of them at least half a century younger than Del was. Mark nodded at Del, did not show his surprise to the old man. Jamabatta, he could insult. Insulting Del was unthinkable.

Mark left the door wide open so the bodyguards could see what they were suddenly up against. He decided to play it as if he'd known that the men had been out there all along.

"These men were offering me *protection*," Mark said, and turned his back on Del, smiled at Jamabatta.

Del said, "He look like he need protection to you, you dope pushin', dumbass, ugly motherfucker?"

Don't sugarcoat it, Del, Mark thought, tell him how you *really* feel. He stared at Jamabatta, saw the fear pass across his face. He had half an impulse to go over there and slap those glasses off Jamabatta's nose, see the eyes that were hidden there, try to see what was in his mind, if he had one.

Del said, "You come stomping onto sacred ground here, youngblood, you defile our center. We got deals with every gang on the West and South sides, includin' yours, and they all know not to come in here, and we can call in five thousand mens we need to, to help us keep that peace."

"Those other gang niggers won't back you, you've never been one of us."

"They know what we do and they respect it. The ancients from all the old-time gangs been behind me since the day these doors opened, and that was when you was still shittin' you panties, when crack was still somethin' you tried to score on Saturday night. Far as we concerned, you done crossed our turf without permission, and that could get your ass killed, you was out on the street. In here, all it get you is an asskicking, you and your musclebound *bitches*, if you don't get out of here in the next thirty seconds."

Mark watched Jamabatta's face harden, then looked down at the man's hands. If he made a move for the inside of his jacket, Mark would jump on him. The bodyguards didn't respond to the insult, to Del's referring to them as bitches. They looked more afraid than angry, their eyes jumping from the crowd out in the hall to their leader, then back to Del. It was a good sign. If Jamabatta picked up on it, he'd have to back down.

Del said, "You come back in here, ever again, I kill you myself, make the world a better place." His voice had no humor in it and he spoke soft and low, as if the two of them were alone and he was telling Jamabatta how things worked. Del's voice, to Mark at least, was having its desired effect. He seemed far more frightening than he'd be if he were shouting.

"You sell your evil shit out there on the street, kill all our young brothers, enslave the ones that live, then waltz on in here like you got a fucking right. Well, you ain't, nigger, and I'm telling you, get out now, or I'll take this baseball bat and do the 'hood a favor."

Jamabatta stood rigid for a moment, his bodyguards stiff with fear. They had their hands open, down by their sides. They knew more than a couple of the men out in the hall, remembered them from their gangbanging eras, and weren't eager to find out what they could do these days.

Would they fight if their leader gave the order, or were they really just there for show? Making money off the asshole and not really willing to die for him. Kill, yeah, they'd do that in a minute, but killing for someone and dying for someone are two entirely different things.

It didn't take long for Jamabatta to make up his mind. He jerked his head toward the door and began to pimp-walk his way out, trying to save face, sneering at Del, his boys falling into line right behind him, single file, walking silently. The bodyguards weren't styling, they had their heads down. Neither Del nor his crew made a sound as the men passed through them, but as soon as the men hit the stairs they began to follow them, and would, Mark knew, until the gangsters hit the street.

All except Del, he stood in the doorway, looking hard at Mark.

"Two minutes on the phone, and look what you got for backup." Del was telling him things, and Mark had to pretend that he was as ignorant as Jamabatta. But it didn't mean that he had to be rude.

"Thanks, Del. It was close there for a second."

"You was gonna throw them out all by yourself, wasn't you? Gonna try to, anyway, get your dumb ass killed."

"I—"

"Yeah, I hear you." Del's voice was tinged with repugnance. "Like you say before, it was your beef, you was gonna handle it your way."

Mark felt embarrassment, did the old man really care that much? He said, "I left my resignation on the desk. I'm quitting." He couldn't think of anything else to say.

Del acted as if he hadn't heard what Mark had said, was squinting up at him, quizzically, as if trying to figure Mark out.

"Well, step aside then," Del said, with conviction, "and let me do the work that God sent me down here to do, without your interference." He looked at Mark with near contempt, snorted through his nose. "I suspect we'll have your replacement workin' before lunchtime."

Mark said, "You have any trouble with those guys, with Jamabatta's gang, you or any of the boys, you beep me, Del, and I'll be down here for you, the way you were for me."

"Don't hold your breath," Del said, "*Mr.* Torrence. I suggest that you go on home and don't hold your breath waitin' for none of us to ever need your white ass around here to help us with nothin'."

Mark looked at him, at the determination on Del's face, and knew that the man just wasn't perturbed with him, knew that this wasn't just another of their frequent clashes of will. Del was disgusted with him, wanted him out of the building, saw him as a traitor, maybe even as the enemy.

What shocked Mark was that Del's feelings didn't disturb him.

In fact, he had to stop himself from smirking at the man. A thought ran through his mind: Who did this little shit think he was? He'd be dead of old age in a year or two, and Mark would still be relatively young.

He stopped himself, made himself think, wondering what the hell had gotten into him. Del was walking away from him, was walking down the steps, and one part of Mark wanted to call him back, wanted to tell him to go to hell, wanted to goad him and his brothers downstairs into a one-on-one battle, winner take all. These same men who'd just now been ready to fight and die for him, he now wanted to alienate, wanted to spur them into combat.

That didn't make sense. Mark couldn't figure it out. What the hell was wrong with him, why was he so angry? These men had quite probably saved his life, and now he resented them, saw them as his rivals.

Fuck them, he decided, they hadn't done anything for him. Anything they'd done, they'd done for Del, not for him, they would not risk that much for him, their behavior had proved that much. Mark was white, not one of them, and all the work he'd done, all the years that he'd spent with them, had been wasted time, beating his head against a wall.

Which meant that he'd been a sucker through all the years that he'd worked there. A bleeding heart dunce, thinking that he could change things. Why had he wasted so much time on people like this? What did he care about them, or about what they did with their lives? Where the hell would they be when the mob was breathing down his neck, coming to kill him?

Shit, he saw what a goof he'd been now, saw it all through eyes that had been closed by fear for the past eleven years. Doing for others when he should have been looking out for himself, getting castrated by some female shrink he'd fancied himself in love with.

As for the kids, so what? Did anyone think that they couldn't live without him? They'd be all right: he'd send them money now and again, if he lived through this.

Mark began to walk down the stairs, his shoulders back, his head up. Through the crowd of black heads below him in the gym, he saw a couple of white hairdos, one blond, one dark. Suits on shoulders, instead of sweat clothes or Starter jackets. His *colleagues*, coming to work, standing around like wide-eyed puppets, wanting to hear all about what had happened just this morning.

How could he ever have felt himself to be a part of them, how could he, with the life he'd lived, ever have felt a kinship with these ignorant little working stiffs? Jesus, a guy could grow lame, after being on the run long enough.

Mark didn't bother returning their greetings, the white men being the only ones who bothered trying, and when he ignored them they stared at him, their mouths open, dumbly. The blacks, too, they were glaring at him now, trying to kick his ass with angry brown eyes, with wrinkled, frowning foreheads, the turn of their lips. After all he'd done for them, this was the way he'd go out.

He hoped that Del would step in his way, so he could bust him one in the face, get this down and real and dirty right away. He was tired of working for nothing, no money, no thanks, just hard feelings coming his way, ego and false-pride his payment from the people that he'd spent over a decade fighting for.

Near the door, a single figure stepped forward, lean, tight-muscled, HardWay blocking Mark's exit.

The kid said, "Mr. Torrence?" confused, HardWay frightened by the look on Mark's face, by the crowd around him that was staring at them, hatefully. HardWay's own face seemed confused, it was twisted into an expression of doubt. The kid looking at him as if he'd never seen him before, as if Mark was some stranger who'd just told him that he was the boy's long lost father.

"Mr. Torrence, where you going, man, you ain't gonna even say *thanks?*"

Mark looked at him, quizzically, and shook his head, fighting a feeling that he was trying to break through his armor, trying to bore through his defenses, that feeling telling him to reach out to the kid, to hug him close, to hold him . . .

NO!

Mark couldn't think that way, not if he was going to survive. There'd been too much confusion in the past night and day, too much hurt and pain and turmoil and suffering. Mark Torrence had to die, right here, once and for all, one way or another.

"Kid," Mark said, "I'm only gonna say this once: get the *fuck* out of my way before I knock you out of it."

For a second, it was touch and go, and Mark felt his hands

ball up into fists. HardWay's face glowered, went crazy, and he took a step toward Mark, and Mark smiled, greedily.

"Come on, kid, come on, show me what you got, I got something for you, too." Mark's voice was an evil whisper, desperately wanting HardWay to jump.

"Get away from that motherfucker, HardWay, shit, he ain't with us no more." Del's voice, giving HardWay a way out, saving face for the kid, saving him an asswhipping, too.

HardWay knew a good thing when he saw one. He stepped to the side, still glowering, and Mark walked by him without looking back, telling the kid that he wasn't important, that Mark wasn't even worrying enough about him to watch his back as he passed him by.

Mark heard the murmuring start before he hit the elevator, black voices raised in outrage, Del's calming influence, telling them to stay where they were. The elevator doors closed on him, and Mark sensed that his metamorphosis was now complete. He got off the elevator on the first floor, and walked quickly over filthy tile to the glass front door of the building. He pushed the handle and gave a shove, and walked through the door, feeling free.

Mark Torrence had walked into the building earlier that morning, but it was Tommy Torelli who walked out, never to return.

BRACKEN GOT OFF the plane at the O'Hare terminal and made his way slowly through the morning crowd. He'd gained an hour, traveling to Chicago. It wasn't even noon yet, and he'd been on the plane for two hours.

He'd rested on the plane, dozed in the first class section, a businessman on the way to Chicago, resting while he could, it had been a long and active night.

He'd felt no eyes on him in either airport, not at Newark, and not here in O'Hare, although he'd seen plenty of federal agents in the airport in New Jersey, at every gate, it seemed, watching for him, for anyone who might look like him or act like or walk like him or sit like Bracken did. They'd be using everything they knew about Bracken to trap him, to recapture him. Bracken did not even think about having a cigarette; they'd be paying close attention to every male who lit a cigarette. So he sat in the non-smoking section of the boarding area, listening to people who knew nothing about him or what he did, shooting off their mouths as if they were experts on the subject.

He was the main topic of conversation in the seats around the boarding gate, people, strangers, asking each other if they'd heard the news, about the madman who'd killed a mob boss and then a bunch of federal agents. Bracken listened to them, even joining in a couple of the conversations, total strangers assuming some bond with each other. *They* weren't killers, *they* had something in common. What they'd done, actually, was mainly show their ignorance. So many of them speaking with authority about something they knew nothing about, telling the man who'd killed the agents how he'd done it, details of the murders, every one of them wrong.

Now, believing himself to be relatively safe, not needing to speak to people for added cover, Bracken followed the directions on the hanging signs that told him where he could find transport to the city, took an escalator down a flight and then stepped onto a people mover.

Was this something? Bracken enjoyed the ride. There were miles of slim and twisted neon lighted tubing above his head, and the airline's theme song played on a Star Wars synthesizer. A voice told him when the mover was coming to an end, and Bracken took the whole thing as an opportunity to look around, touristy, smiling, pretending to be in awe but actually making sure that no one was paying attention to him.

The area was filled with people, men and women in business suits, vacationers in casual clothes, young people with backpacks, children in papooses. He saw no one looking his way, felt no eyes upon him. He believed in his heart that he'd made good his escape.

Now, though, he had a small problem. In order to do the things that he wanted to do, he'd have to rent a car, and get a hotel room in the city. That meant using a credit card. Which wasn't a problem, he had them, in three names. But he knew that if he did, he would have to ditch this disguise before he left, as the FBI would investigate all hotel room check-ins, as soon as Torelli's body was discovered, dead. He should have brought along other disguises, should have taken a suitcase to the safehouse, and filled it with what he'd need.

He could get the things he needed easily enough, but what if he was in a hurry? He should have thought about that before he left, Bracken cursed himself, he was slipping. He'd killed federal agents this time, it was no longer just the wives of millionaires or people who'd crossed some mob. He'd be dealing with men and women who were well-trained in the arts of deception, people who had hunted down many other shrewd fugitives before him, people who would beg to be on the task force that would be searching for James Bracken. People who would see hunting him down as their greatest personal challenge.

He fought a moment of total panic as he remembered buying the airline ticket, remembered reaching into his wallet, pulling out his credit card . . .

They'd have a link, and all the FBI would ever need to solve a crime was a trail. Give them even the smallest shred of evidence, and there was no better police agency in the world than the FBI in tracking down a perpetrator, and they'd have some evidence, that trail, soon, if Bracken didn't start to cover himself with more imagination than he'd been using.

He wondered about it now, what they would have when they put their resources together, after he'd killed Torelli.

They'd have his hotel room, and the name on the plane ticket, the car rental receipts and from those, they'd know he'd done it. It would not take a great leap in imagination for them to put that together. Now, he had asked himself, how much good would that do them? What else would they have? He'd planned to give up one set of ID in Chicago, had two others that would have no connection to Torelli. He could kill him and leave, and as long as he didn't fly out of Chicago again, they would never be able to track him down. They would not know where else to search.

He had to make sure that he had the proper equipment to change identities when he did the murder. And he'd also have to forget how tired he was, tired people made mistakes, and he could not afford any more of those. He'd use caution in approaching Torelli, kill him quick and get out of town, take a flight from a small Downstate airport into a major international airport, go from there to Switzerland.

He would not fly out of Chicago. The feds could check the manifest of every plane that left during any given week, check the backgrounds of every person on those flights in a matter of only a few hours. They could find out about the lives of every human being aboard those planes without the passengers ever knowing that their histories had been checked.

Bracken had histories, backgrounds for all his false identities, but this would be the FBI he was dealing with now—this was not some lazy, fat, private investigator—they would do a thorough search, and would follow up on details that most investigators wouldn't notice.

Damn, he wished he'd brought those disguises!

This was no time for mistakes, he'd already made too many of them. He would have to think each move that he made from this moment on out clearly in advance, well in advance, or they'd hunt him down and kill him; they would no longer lock him away, that was no longer an option for him.

Bracken thought, with self-directed anger, that he should have brought those fucking disguises.

It was a mark of his character that he'd never consider thinking about, the fact that he missed nothing, coveted nothing but his disguises. Since his escape, he hadn't thought once about the house in the Mews, hadn't thought of Tawny, nor of the good, rich life that he was leaving behind forever. All he missed at the moment, and all that mattered to him, was the disguises that would get him out of Chicago, onto a plane for Europe.

Not realizing any of this, angry only at his lack of foresight, Bracken strolled up to the Hertz Rent-A-Car counter and smiled at the female clerk, told her in a deep, unhurried, urbane voice that he'd be needing a car for a day or two, and would she please be kind enough to see that the one he got was a Lincoln?

DOLAN LOOKED AT the names printed behind scratched and faded plastic, at the speaking grille mounted on the security column, found the number of the South Loop Youth Center, and punched it into the keyboard, then waited. After a minute, he did it again. Nobody, it seemed, was going to answer or buzz him in. Or maybe the system was broken.

He looked at it, at the sturdy system mounted on a pole in front of the building. It was easier than looking out at South Wabash, at the wasted husks of humanity whom life had long ago passed by.

He knew that just a couple of days ago, a young man who

lived in the St. James Hotel had been stabbed to death right down on 12th St., less than a block from Police Headquarters. He'd heard about it, listened to the details, and had read a small paragraph about the death in the paper the next day. The only reason such a mundane murder had even been reported was because it had occurred so close to the headquarters building. What the reporter wouldn't write—because she didn't know—was about the embarrassment that damned murder had caused the commander, how much heat he'd put on the local cops for allowing it to occur.

In the last few days and nights, there'd been a crackdown in the area, everyone spotted loitering, anyone who was just standing around, had been rousted, put up against the wall and searched, their ID checked. Frenzied complaints of harassment had been reported, often, and the cops had been told to back off, had been chewed out by the same commander who'd gone berserk over the killing in the first place. It wasn't easy, being a cop these days. You had too many conflicting signals always being sent your way.

A young man with a lot of red hair, wearing an Army jacket and carrying a small sculpture, was heading toward the door, from inside the building. Mark watched him, decided not to pull his badge. There was no sense in advertising who and what he was. The young man pushed the door open and brushed by Mark without a word, and Mark held the door open, stepped into the building and closed it behind him. He walked the fifteen feet to the elevator, got in and pushed the button for the fourth floor.

Once he got upstairs and saw what was going on, he almost turned around and left without even asking for Mark Torrence.

MARK PULLED HIS car to the curb in front of his house and got out without even checking out the street. If the mob were going to kill him today, he'd never see them coming, and if the cops were there, the Marshals or the FBI, there was nothing he could do. He would not go to the newspapers, as he'd threatened. All he wanted to do now was get the hell out.

He'd gotten his money out of his bank lockboxes, had it all in a suitcase that he held tightly in his left hand. He would pack a few things, get into the car and run, head somewhere, change who he was and start all over again. He knew how to do it, it would not be that hard. He'd do it himself, too, would not ask Bella for a thing. He never intended to ask a cop for a favor again in his lifetime, no matter how long or short that lifetime happened to be. He was sure, thought that he would have a longer life if he got the hell out of Chicago, and right away.

What was there to keep him? Some crap about honor or love? He'd been shown what that was worth. He'd loved his wife more than he'd loved his own life, and she'd left him, as soon as the heat began. Had known about it for months and she'd stayed, but as soon as it looked like he might need her to back him up, wham, she was gone, back to live with daddy. And honor, what about that? Could you eat it, could you spend it? He'd thought that he'd given his all to the center, and he'd seen today how much they appreciated him. He hadn't come crawling to them for help when he was in trouble, and they took it personally, the way they had when they were in some gang.

No, there was nothing here to keep him. Life was all there was. Nothing more. You come in alone and you go out alone, and the time in between is spent in a state of extreme self-deception, years, decades, scores of your life consumed in your search to not be alone. Did it stop you from lying in a hospital bed someday, all by yourself, dying? Could any spouse or child really and truly go through that with you? No, nor would they trade places with you if they were given the opportunity. You had life, and it would end someday. That was all that you could be sure of in this world. Anything else was bullshit. Mark knew that, now.

He saw that ignorant son of a bitch, Tomczak, looking out his screen door at him, the maniac with his personal video recorder, standing there pointing it at Mark, capturing the moment. Tomczak stepped onto his porch, and lowered the camera, shouted at Mark, in outrage.

"I've spent the morning talking to the FBI, Torrence! They wanted to question me about *you*, wanted to harass me because I live next door to you, you son of a bitch."

Mark stopped, on the sidewalk, and looked at the man, more curious than anything. How could he have ever gotten mad at such an inconsequential little piece of shit like this? How could he have been so egotistical as to have ever allowed a punk like this to get under his skin, to anger him?

It wouldn't happen now, that was for sure. He was nothing,

an insect, could not harm Mark in any way. All Mark was interested in was the visit by the FBI. They would have come about the pictures, the pictures Bella had told him about. Did they tell this little man that, or question him about taking them? Mark would bet that they hadn't. They would have laid a trap, and if Tomczak was guilty of something, he would have walked right into it, without even smelling the cheese.

He said, calmly, "Did you film them going into my house?" and Tomczak seemed taken aback. His face fell a little, as if surprised that Mark was being so kind. He took a slight step forward, perhaps wondering if he'd somehow been wrong, had unfairly judged his neighbor. He was a man that didn't seem used to being treated with kindness, or respect. Mark figured that was because he couldn't command those things from people.

When he spoke his voice was tentative—like most bullies who'd been backed into a corner—letting his adversary set the tone of the conversation.

"No, they didn't go in there. I watched after they left, after I told them I wouldn't speak to them until they had a warrant, and then I'd want my lawyer with me before I'd say a word."

"This is important, Tomczak, bigger than you know. Did they mention any pictures that you'd taken, that you'd sold or given to the wrong people, maybe even had stolen?"

That got to him, hard. Tomczak jerked as if Mark had slapped him.

"Pictures?" His voice was high, and it creaked. "What do *you* know about my pictures?"

"You'd better call that lawyer, Tomczak," Mark said to him, solemnly. "You're going to be needing him."

He was walking toward his house now, hurrying, wanting to get out. "They'll charge you soon, with a federal crime. They'll say you were part of a conspiracy, that you helped set me up to be killed."

"Killed?!" Tomczak leaped down his stairs, was running toward Mark across the lawn, the recorder hanging loose in his hand, his tool of torment now forgotten. "Who's going to kill you? I had nothing to do with that!"

Mark turned, looked at Tomczak. "Go in your house and write your story, get it all down on paper, then mail it to someone you trust. They'll be coming for you, soon, and they might not let you live."

Tomczak was blubbering, and Mark looked at him, soberly, inwardly pleased. Finally, after all this time, he'd truly gotten to this son of a bitch.

Tomczak surprised him, he stood his ground and swallowed. This time when he spoke, his voice seemed determined, nearly courageous.

"Tell me all about it, Torrence, give me the story and let me put it in the *Leader*."

Mark pretended to think about it for a minute, scanning the street while he did so. He looked back at Tomczak.

"Tomorrow. We'll sit down tomorrow and discuss it. I'll tell you everything then, and you put it on the front page. It might save both of our lives, Lloyd."

Tomczak looked at him for a second, then decisively held out his hand. "Bury the hatchet?"

Mark shook his hand.

"Tomorrow Lloyd. You'd better write up your report now, though, there's no telling when they'll be coming back."

"Tomorrow." Tomczak began to walk back to his house, a spring in his step, a man with a mission.

By tomorrow, Mark planned to be in LA, or as close as his car would get him by then.

Tomczak stopped at the edge of his property, turned and called to Mark by his first name. Mark turned, his key in the lock, raised his eyebrows in question.

"You *didn't* steal my pictures then, did you?"

"No, I didn't."

Tomczak nodded, and turned, and began to march toward his house. Mark turned the key in the lock and went in, shaking his head and smiling at the man's stupidity, and knew before he'd even closed the door behind him that he wasn't alone in the house.

ANDI WAS FEELING better, Bella could tell. He could smell her cooking something, fussing around in the kitchen, acting as if she wasn't concerned about the calls he was making on the living room phone. He was through making them now. Now he was waiting for a call to be returned.

Andi's uncle the Senator should be calling, any minute now,

with the information that Bella had requested. The information he'd demanded.

All of a sudden, things had changed. He'd seen it on the television, now that the word was out. The pictures of Bracken, taken just last night, and the breathless reports about what he'd done, about his daring escape from captivity. Not even the FBI could keep a news blackout in effect when something of this magnitude was going on. Bella had reported to his supervisors then gone to the television room, had stood with the other marshals and two judges, all of them enthralled as they watched the television news, the reporters breaking into regular daytime programming. They'd heard Tom Brokaw going on about the search for the man who'd killed four federal agents and who'd wiped out the country's most powerful mobster. At the moment, Fred Tallman was missing, and the federal spokesman didn't think that he would be found alive.

It was then that Bella had left the building, had come home to make calls.

Not that the privacy had done him any good. Nobody in Washington, New York, or anywhere else was saying much of anything, at least not to him. All he could get out of them were cryptic statements, the gist of which was that he should mind his own business, back out of this, right now. Which was why he'd called the Senator. The Senator could get his questions answered, no one short of the President himself ever ignored the Senator when he was looking for information.

Right now, on the screen, on CNN, the debate was raging: Why had the government allowed such a dangerous man to escape? Bernard Shaw was going nuts with the few details that he had, on a split screen, glaring at some guy in a three-piece suit and a red power tie, Shaw demanding that a spokesman in Washington tell him how the government could ever offer refuge to a psychopathic killer. The guy, he was vacillating, wanting to know where Shaw got off saying that the killer was being offered refuge. As far as he knew, to the best of his knowledge, the suspect had escaped while being questioned by Fred Tallman. The spokesman was young, maybe fresh out of college, he was no match for Shaw, who was eating him up alive. Bella was leaning forward to watch the lion eat the lamb when the phone rang and he shut off the TV, took a deep breath and answered it.

"Senator."

"Bella, how's my little girl?" Christ, Bella hated talking to this man.

"She's fine, sir, same as she was a half an hour ago when you asked. She's still relaxing, Senator, taking a little nap." Bella wouldn't dare tell the man that she was in the kitchen, cooking. He was one of the four people alive outside of her prayer group who knew that Andi was ill, and if it had been up to him, he'd have 24-hour nurses in the house, a doctor living on the premises. Bella could not have lived with that charity.

"You tell her I love her, that I'll be talking to her soon."

"Yes, sir, Senator, now, as to what I called you about?"

"Get off it, let it alone. It's an FBI matter now, they're on top of it, I just hung up with the director himself." The Senator had a deep, low voice, an affected Southern accent that he used to his advantage. He always spoke as if he knew exactly what he was talking about, knew more than you did, even when what he was saying was bullshit. Still, it was rumored that women loved his voice. Bella thought they might be attracted to his power as well.

"Are they going to protect my man out here?"

"*What* man, you keep saying that, but as far as they're concerned, your *man* is only a ghost."

"*What!*"

"Someone who dropped out of the relocation program thirteen years ago is not a top priority within the federal government just now."

"They're hanging him out to dry. Either using him as bait, or they're going to sacrifice him." The Senator chuckled. There he went again, knowing things nobody else did and letting his tone of voice tell you all about it.

"You've always been paranoid, you know that, boy?" Bella bit his tongue. The Senator was doing him a favor by calling him at all. "For the sake of my adopted daughter, I'll tell you what's going on."

"Please . . ."

"We have him, or soon will. Your *man*, as you call him, is safer than he's ever been since he went into custody. The mob's running for its life, and this Bracken fella, we're onto him. He boarded a plane bound for Germany at ten-oh-nine this morning, out of Kennedy. We have a positive ID from a boarding agent, and the pilot has confirmed it, took a walk through the cabin for us. Get this, his name was Bracken? The alias is *Bratton.* They've got witnesses told him he ran to the gate, wearing an ill-fitting suit, and paid with a credit card that had an edge so sharp it cut the clerk's finger. It goes along with what they've found in this Bracken's house. Credit cards that had been sharpened, all kinds of sharp-edged weapons, shit, get this, son, hidden in a desk drawer was a picture of him with some old boyfriend. This fella, this guy who's got you shittin' your pants and raising hell all over the Beltway, he's as queer as a three-dollar bill."

"Uh, Senator? About the ID by the pilot, sir?"

"Oh, yeah, he took a walk through the cabin for his government. Like Bracken, this man's bald, with a scalp bleeding in a couple places, he obviously nicked himself shaving the rest of his hair off his head. Rest of the description's precise. Pilot's been ordered to treat him the same as anyone else, not to tell even the stewardesses who our man really is." The Senator chortled.

"He's in First Class, drinking one glass of wine after another. Only fags drink wine when they're wanting to get drunk."

"I take it we've got people in place in Frankfurt?"

"Well, not FBI, but there's people there, if you catch my drift . . ."

CIA. Just as well. Still, it didn't seem right to Bella, it just didn't make any sense.

"What they'll do, Dan," the Senator said, "is grab him as he's coming off the plane, have the Germans take him into custody with our backup, until the extradition papers are drawn up and we can send our boys in without creating a damn international incident. It's damage control, and you and me, son, we never had this conversation, but what they're gonna do, is, they're gonna come out of this smelling like a rose. It's why they've held off telling anyone anything, including their own people, such as you. It'll be a publicity coup, and make everyone forget about the dead federal men. Can you see it? The FBI got their man, the second he tried to leave the country. It'll be worth five or six lives to the folks at Justice, reinforce the mystique of the FBI. It'll be as if old John Edgar is still alive."

"Be worth it to everyone except the dead men's families."

"They're's casualties in wars, son, and those boys, rest their souls, they fucked up royal. Letting an unarmed man disarm them and kill them all? Hell, wherever they're at, they're *glad* they're dead. They'd never live this down."

Bella couldn't see a way to respond that wouldn't offend the Senator, so he decided to change the subject.

"Will they give him back to us? We have the death penalty here, and they don't."

"Oh, I wouldn't worry about that. What with the New World Order, with what we've done in Europe, I believe we can get him back without much of a problem."

The smugness in the Senator's voice bothered Bella as much as what he was saying. He seemed so *sure*. Bella sure wasn't.

Would a professional killer who'd evaded arrest for over twenty years be so careless? He wouldn't be a man to fold easily under any kind of pressure, or he'd have been captured or killed a long time ago.

"Senator, thank you for your time and the courtesy of the call."

"Don't make a habit of it, son, you've used up your quota for a time to come." The Senator paused, and when he spoke now, he seemed almost a human being instead of the embodiment of the political animal.

"I thought, when you called—"

"I know what you thought, Senator." Bella's voice was dry, the man had been about to articulate the unthinkable.

"Well, give Andrea my love, and tell her to call me, soon."

"I'll be doing that—" Bella began, before he realized that the man had hung up on him.

He sat looking at the phone, unsure of what he'd been told. He hung up, softly, thinking, and went in to tell Andi, and naturally, she had the solution to the problem.

If the man on the plane was Bracken, then there was really nothing to worry about. If it wasn't Bracken, Andrea said, then there could be a problem, and Mark could get killed. So Dan had to go and get Mark Torrence and bring him back here for a visit, right away, and that would solve everything, or so she thought.

Dan didn't tell her that he didn't know exactly how to get him here, what he would have to do. He looked at her, at the pale, thin hair, hanging off her scalp in unhealthy patches, at the white, doughy face, and he kept his opinions to himself.

He grabbed his keys and kissed her goodbye, told her he'd see her in a little while.

SAFE HARBOR

*   *   *

THERE WERE A bunch of muscular black guys standing in what looked like a boxing gym, angrily shouting at two white men in the middle of the room who were talking loudly, waving their arms, trying to calm them down. A tiny old black man was at the edge of the crowd, his arms crossed, looking defiant. Looking pleased, too. More than anything, to Dolan, he looked like an instigator. Eddie walked up to him, politely, and waited until the man took notice of him.

"What you want," the black man said, and Eddie forced himself calm. It would do no good to respond in kind, he might get hurt in here. The place seemed like a riot zone.

"I'm looking for someone, please, could you help me, sir?"

"How the hell I know if I can help you if you don't tell me who it is you looking for?"

Oh, this guy, he was asking for it. Marsha would be proud of him, if she could see the way he was acting.

"His name's Torrence, Mark Torrence," Eddie said, and the guy went hard.

"Torrence don't work here no more. Motherfucker quit. This whole shit in here about just that, cop." The old man looked at him wisely, and Dolan steeled himself; he knew that he was about to be insulted, could tell by the look on the man's face.

"We don't want no more white motherfuckers in here, tellin' us how to run our own center. We can't trust them, none of them. Your Mark Torrence proved that to us, consortin' with 'bangsters, treatin' us like dirt. Now go on, get your ass out of here."

What could he do? He didn't want to incite a riot or overextend his authority. The man was within his rights, and there was no law against being a bigot. Dolan knew from long and sad experience that there was no reasoning with such people once they decided to hate you. Anything he said now would only make matters worse, reinforce the stereotypes that had been long set in the old man's mind. Dolan realized, with a small twinge of shame, that the man probably had many years of observation—and hard, hands-on, practical personal experience—to back up his feelings.

So he said, "Thank you," and started to walk out of there,

fast, was waiting for the elevator when the old man came out into the hall.

"You want Torrence? Here his address, his phone number, whatever you need, officer." The man was holding a Rolodex card out to Eddie. Dolan could see that it had been ripped out of the holder. Why was he doing this? His eyes held intimate confidential knowledge that Dolan knew he would never share with Eddie, but he had his reasons, that was obvious. And from the look of the man his reasons weren't to close the gap between the youth center and the law.

"Thank you," Dolan said. The elevator came.

"What I said, in there?" the old man said. Dolan stepped into the elevator, held the door from closing with his left hand, and nodded.

"Mark was a good man, once. If we couldn't trust him, we couldn't trust no one. I met a good white man once or twice in my life." The man smiled as Eddie pulled his hand back, and the doors closed before he could figure out if the old man had been kidding him or if he'd really meant what he'd said.

THERE WAS NOBODY watching the house, of that, Bracken was certain. He drove around it slowly, four times, the Lincoln nearly driving itself. It was like driving his living room sofa, with a steering wheel attached. Maybe in Europe, in France, he'd purchase one. That or a Mercedes, he was through with Jaguars. The FBI would be looking for that, for someone buying a Jag, looking for him to replace the car that he'd driven at home, and they'd use Interpol and the Suirette to help them, they wouldn't rest until Bracken was brought to justice.

He would have to think like that for the rest of his life, he knew. Would have to stay more than a step ahead of them, would have to stay a mile ahead if he planned to die of natural causes. No, he couldn't think that way; if he was going to *live*.

So what was he doing here? A place where they were nearly certain to eventually look, if they hadn't already? For Terri, that's why he was here. Here and unarmed, having only his wits and his superior strength as his weapons. He hadn't even had time to sharpen his new credit cards. But he would not worry about it, Torelli couldn't possibly be in the sort of shape that he himself was in. And when would be the last time Torelli had killed another human being? Bracken had killed a bunch of them, just last night. Outwitted armed men and then killed them, many times over.

He'd rented a room downtown—more to reapply his cosmetics than to rest in; he didn't plan on spending much time in Chicago. He'd stopped and bought the things he'd need to become the man he'd want to be after he ditched this disguise, the man who would go on to Europe. Those things were back in the hotel, locked in his carry-on, the carry-on checked with the well-tipped bell captain. The passports and IDs were strapped to his chest with surgical tape, the money, every dollar of it, secure in his moneybelt, the canvas belt cinched tightly around his waist. He had left nothing in the hotel safe, he could afford to take no chances; the only way he would lose his tickets to future freedom was if they killed him, shot him down in the street. He knew that he would not allow himself to be taken alive, even if he had to pretend that he had a weapon; after last night, all he'd have to do was reach into his inner jacket pocket, and they'd take him down without hesitation.

He drove by the house again, and this time he openly stared at the place. The FBI would have the pictures he'd taken from Papa, and by now they would have spoken to this man, to this Lloyd Tomczak person. Or maybe they hadn't, maybe they didn't care. If Torelli had dropped out of the witness protection program, maybe they couldn't find him, they might not know where he was, might even be frantically searching for him.

Looking in order to set a trap for him. Bracken would have to be extremely careful.

Last night had been the first time in his adult life that he'd ever done a murder without extreme planning, done one impulsively, and look how that had turned out. There was a manhunt on for him. He had gone from an anonymous, unknown subject to public enemy in the short space of twelve hours, and now he was planning on doing it again, to commit murder without meticulous planning, without his usual precise, orderly procedure that would leave no room for error, and no margin for failure. But back then, even yesterday, he'd had things to lose. Today, right now, all that was left was his life itself, what he'd been was gone, he had to entirely reinvent himself. Today, nothing much mattered but his desire to avenge his Terri.

The smart move, Bracken knew, the right move, would be to run away, right now, and wait until the heat was off. If they *were* laying a trap, they wouldn't guard Torelli forever, if they were guarding him at all. But he knew that once he left, he'd never come back to this country. He'd retire to his beloved Paris, drink his wine and take a lover, grow fat and old with his memories.

No, he had to do this, and do this now, or Terri had died in vain. Bracken could never enjoy a moment of his life if he became a coward at this point, if he didn't avenge his beloved Terri. He'd waited too long for this moment, spent too much time, money and blood to walk away from it now, now that he was so close. Torelli would die, and if Bracken went down with him, Terri, he knew, would be on the other side to help him, extending his hand and smiling, helping Bracken through those terrible initial moments of eternity. That, or there'd be nothing. Either way, Bracken didn't fear death. They only thing he feared was facing it without honor. That, and prison, he feared prison, too. Would rather burn in hell forever than spend a single week in a jail cell like a common, petty killer. It would be good to kill Torelli, and proper, this close to the anniversary of his Terri's death. The man had it coming, had been skating now for fifteen years. It was about time that reality caught up with him.

He parked at the curb, down the street, got out and looked up at the house numbers curiously, as if he were lost, did not know which address he wanted. Bracken began to slowly shuffle away toward the house over there, next to the one with the big backyard fence. Something about that fence seemed so familiar to him . . .

He mounted the stairs and rang the doorbell, waited, then rang it again, heard a small dog yapping, then a frightened voice shouting: "Don't open that, I'll get it," at the same moment that a beaten-up-looking little Oriental woman pulled the door open and looked out at him, the look on her face begging him to take her away from this, please, get her out of here. A black and white mutt was jumping at the screen, Bracken could see little holes in it, right about at the spot where the animal's paws would reach if it was standing up and scratching at it.

Bracken said, "I'm looking for Mr. Lloyd Tomczak, please?" raising his eyebrows and smiling, and the same voice that had moments ago been filled with terror was now speaking at him in a superior, in-control manner; the short, bald man who pushed the Oriental woman out of his way looked out at him and demanded to know if he was the cops, or what?

"HELLO, MARK," CAROLINE said, and for a moment, he almost lost it, but he managed to stay cold inside. He put the briefcase with all his money in it down on the carpet beside him and just looked at her, remotely, as if he didn't recognize her. Caroline was smiling slightly, seeming disconcerted, something she wasn't used to being. Shy and maybe even slightly remorseful, Caroline not knowing what to do with her hands, rubbing them at first, then putting them behind her back, then finally letting them fall to her sides after giving a little shrug. He hoped she wasn't waiting for him to open his arms up to her, so she could run into them and hug him. He wasn't the sort of man who would do such things anymore.

He said, "Call me Tommy," coldly, and saw the hurt cross over her face. Still, she tried again.

"My father, you know what he said when I told him?" Mark didn't bother to answer or raise his eyebrows, he honestly didn't care. Caroline continued as if he'd wanted to know and had asked her what her father had said to her.

"He said, 'That poor, sorry son of a bitch.' "

Mark grunted. "I don't need his pity, or yours."

"He wasn't pitying you. And I'm certainly not. What he was doing was empathizing with what you've gone through all these years. He told me he couldn't imagine how hard it was on you all this time, keeping that terrible secret. He told me, too, that you did it for me, and for the kids."

"Fuck him, what does he know about hard? He never had it hard a day in his life, and neither have you."

The phone rang and he went to it. He hadn't answered the phone since Elmer had died, but he stormed toward it now, to get away from her. The sight of her, it was breaking what was left of his heart. How could that happen to him? He'd walked away from the youth center, from Del and HardWay and all the others without even a backward glance, and now the sight of her was killing him.

"Yeah."

"Torrence?"

"Who wants him?"

"This is Sergeant Dolan."

"What the fuck do *you* want?"

"I want to talk to you, face to face, right now. I'm at the 7-Eleven on Ewing Avenue, I was just calling to make sure you were home."

"Go fuck yourself, cop," Mark said, feeling strong as he said it. Hoping that the anger would carry over into his conversation with his wife; he'd need it. He hung up the phone, turned, and there was Caroline, who continued as if he'd never cut her off.

"Mark, it's normal what you're feeling, believe me, I *know*. It's what I do for a living."

"Don't you psychoanalyze me." He said it coldly, without anger, warning her of potential violence more than looking for an argument.

"I'm not, goddamnit! What I'm doing is telling you a fact, that's all. I left and you were hurt, and now I'm back and you're going to try and push me away. You think it's for my own sake. Lord, I know how you are, you want me out of danger, now that you've had a chance to think about it."

"You believe that?" Mark dismissed her, reached down, picked up his briefcase and began walking to the staircase. "You believe that you know how I *am*?" Mark half-laughed. "Jesus Christ."

"Mark?" Caroline called after him, he could hear her starting to follow him. He stopped and turned, looked at her, and she stopped where she was, staring at him strangely. Good.

"You go away now, Caroline. You don't want to be here anymore. I'll be out of your house in a half hour, and if you have any sense, you'll put it up for sale. Out in Arizona, nobody'll hurt you, nobody'll come after you. You move back in, I can't say that'll be the case. If you don't believe me, you can ask your daddy. If you move back in here, you get him to send some of his boys over to cover those kids. You can pick my replacement out from one of them."

"How dare you." Caroline's voice was low and deadly, she was staring at him, venomously.

"Just leave me alone for a half an hour, and I'll be out of your hair for good."

"Don't you even try to think that I'm that easy to get rid of."

"And don't you flatter yourself into thinking that I give a shit about your fucking hypocritical, outraged resolve to stay with me after your daddy talked you into it. I needed you yesterday, more than anything on earth. I don't need you today. It's over, I'm gone. I'll pack a few things and be on my way. In the meantime, get the hell away from me, I've got enough problems."

Caroline slapped at her thighs in exasperation.

"I was *wrong*, all right! Imagine how I felt, can you imagine that? You've always been reasonable, Mark, always sensitive. OK, I understand you're mad, but you can't just run off like this!"

"You did."

"But I came back!"

"I," Mark said, turning his back on her and starting up the steps, "won't make that mistake. It's a woman's mistake, it's emotional, weak." He saw her eyes narrow and he smiled. He'd scored.

Mark said, "You made the wrong move, Caroline, first in leaving, then in coming back. I've had too much time to think, too much time to look at what I really need. This marriage, this life, it was a bad move for you, for me, for everyone." He was nearly at the top of the stairs now, and he could hear her behind him, coming up fast after him, shit.

The last thing he wanted was to get into it with her, as he didn't know how much longer he could last. He was fighting the urge to grab her, hold her close, cry into her hair, wipe his tears on her shoulder.

Goddamnit. No!

He couldn't do that, that was Mark Torrence's act, not his. The man he was, the man he'd always really been, couldn't afford weakness, and he had proof to back that up; look where his weakness had gotten him, look how he'd wound up. College educated and making nearly nothing, his getaway money being the dough he'd stolen when he'd been just a kid. No, he couldn't afford to love her, couldn't afford to give in.

He walked quickly into their bedroom, and took a deep breath before she came in behind him, Mark determined not to think of her on that bed, of the years they'd slept together, the times he'd awakened in the middle of the night and had just lain there looking at her, watching her in her sleep . . .

He shut his eyes tightly, shook his head to clear it. He went to the bed and dropped the briefcase on it, walked over to the closet and opened it, took a suitcase off the shelf and tossed it on the bed.

He felt Caroline watching him, kept his back to her. He could do this, he had to do this. Once he was out of this ghost-filled house, he'd be all right, he knew it. He just had to get through this, had to be strong for a few more minutes.

"Get it through your head, lady, 'cause I'm only gonna say this once." Mark was pleased to hear the sound of his voice, the biting harshness in his tone. "I don't need a wife, I don't need any kids, I don't need anything but the cash in that briefcase. Money was the only thing I ever fucking needed." He paused to light a cigarette, saw that his fingers were shaking. He kept his back to Caroline so that she wouldn't notice, blew out the first drag and grabbed some shirts off their hangers.

"You were right before you left, Caroline, it was all a scam to me. From the beginning, you, the house, the kids, the job, everything. It was all nothing to me, never was anything more than a goddamn masquerade. I didn't realize that until three o'clock this morning, but now I know it's true."

"You expect me to *believe* that? I don't. And what the hell are you trying to prove by smoking? You can't believe it makes you more of a man. You can convince yourself of that, and that it's all a masquerade; if you tell it to yourself long enough, and if you're disturbed enough, you'll believe it. But I know better, and so do you, Mark."

"You don't know *shit*, Caroline, you suspect; that's what shrinks do. They suspect things about you, then they give you dope to make you think the way they believe you should."

"Mark, come on, it's not playing well, your voice is giving you away."

He pulled open a drawer and grabbed a handful of underwear, shoved it into the suitcase and went back to get his socks.

"Leave me alone, Caroline, I'm telling you." He was moving quickly now, because she was sharp, she'd seen him wavering.

"Look at you, your hands are trembling." She was observing him, clinically, her voice no longer loud, her tone no longer full of hurt. "You're falling apart, Mark."

"I'm fine."

"For how long? Wait until you wake up hung over tomorrow or the next day, wait until you think about what you did to me, to your kids. Within a month you'll kill yourself, or put yourself into a position where somebody else will. You'll walk into a casino or some other place where you know they'll recognize you. What's the plan, Mark, to go back to Little Italy and hang out at a coffee shop? I've got your number. You think you're so unique? My God, I've seen hundreds like you."

Hundreds like him? That got to him, and he was grateful to her, she'd made him mad, angry enough where he felt secure that he could speak without breaking down and begging her forgiveness.

"Work for the government, now, do you? See a lot of protected witnesses?"

"I've only had to see one, Mark, to figure out his game."

"Go away, Caroline, I'm warning you . . ."

"Warning me? Yes, that's what Torelli would do. He was primitive, you know. He'd threaten anyone who got in his way, who made him feel at all uncomfortable. He'd push people out of his way if they didn't listen to his first warning. He'd maybe even kill them, if they kept on pushing him, if they didn't back down. Tommy Torelli would never understand about things like loving your wife and children, like saving gang kids from living the sort of life that he himself had. He wouldn't understand things like mowing the lawn and paying taxes and staying up all night at the kids' bedside when they're running a small fever. Torelli would see those things as being for suckers, wouldn't he, Mark? Sure he would." She paused and then spat out, "But *you* wouldn't, *you* know better, don't you, Mark?"

He wouldn't let himself be drawn into that contest, wouldn't be dumb enough to try and play any mindgames with a shrink. He was almost done packing, he'd be out of there soon enough. As long as he didn't look at her, he thought that he'd be all right.

He went into the bathroom and threw the cigarette butt into the commode, flushed it and watched it swirl down and away, taking deep breaths, preparing himself for whatever her final onslaught might be. He shoved his toiletries into a travel kit from under the sink, so she'd think that he was still packing in here, so she wouldn't think that she had him going.

Mark made fists and loosened them, looked into the mirror and did not like what he saw. He looked at himself, posed and set his face, the same way that he'd once done in hotel rooms around the country, did that until he managed to make his face an impassive shield. Keep your guard up, Tommy. She'll be out of your life in ten more minutes. He walked out of the bathroom and back to the closet, got the hanging suitcase out, and hung it up by its hook on the closet door. As he was reaching for one of his suits, Caroline started in again.

"You think you can walk away, Mark, but you're not Torelli anymore. You weren't the man you thought you were even when you *were* Torelli. You were molded by your experiences, the same as we all are. You processed what was there for you to see and then you decided on a route for yourself. But even then, Mark, even in your worst day, you couldn't pull it off, could you? Even then you were racked with guilt, you hated what you were, hated yourself even worse, didn't you? As a matter of fact, until Mario came along, you thought that you were more of an animal than a man, didn't you, Mark? And now you say you want to go back to that life." She snorted. "Lots of luck."

He could feel her eyes boring into the back of his head, Caroline always having that knack; he could always tell when she was mad at him, could always feel her eyes on him, could even sense the part of his body that she was looking at, Caroline's glare making it shrivel up and itch.

What was wrong with him? His hands couldn't pull the hangers off the closet pole. They were shaking worse than a junkie in detox, and Mark grabbed at the suit fabric, squeezed it, hard, tried to control the shake. He leaned against the doorjamb for a minute, just for a second, until he could think again.

Why wouldn't she shut up? It would be so much easier if she'd just shut up. But she wouldn't, and she wouldn't even raise her voice at him now, either. She just kept talking, in her quiet, shrink voice, telling him things she had no right to know, Caroline right on target, though, never missing a trick.

"You know how I found out? Mario came to me, Mark, your son, last winter. He'd been having terrible nightmares, and he came to me in confidence, for help. Naturally, I couldn't work with him, but guess what? I knew someone who could. Mario never worked on Monday and Wednesday afternoons, Mark, he didn't go to his job on those days, on those days, he was in therapy. After a month, when, at his request, I began to go with him, after he told us everything, I knew how that boy had suffered, what he'd been through in those first, important six years of his life.

"He didn't have the same kind of life that Kenny and Elaine

had, did he, Mark? He grew up with strangers around him, with federal marshals instead of a family."

Mark wanted to tell her that he'd done the best he could, but he couldn't open his mouth, it was twisted, his lips now quivering. He lowered his head now, still squeezing the suits, leaning against the doorway, shaking his head from side to side. He closed his eyes, tightly. Wished that he could do the same with his ears.

"That boy worships you, Mark. You're all he's talked about since we left this house. Not school, not work, not his therapy, not Diane. You, Mark, he's worried to death about you. He wanted to come back with me, but I wouldn't let him. Elaine and Kenny, they're upset, but Mario might have a breakdown before this whole thing is over."

When Caroline spoke now her voice was filled with disbelieving awe.

"You testified against your friends for him, Mark. Went on to college and made something out of yourself. Married me and we had our children, and now you're actually trying to tell me that it was all part of some plan, that you don't love any of us anymore? You're going to try and make me believe that you don't wish Elaine was here right now, with her arms around your belly, comforting you? That you don't wish Kenny was downstairs with you right now, pretending he's strong enough to pull weights off your chest if you drop them? You're going to tell me that all those years, all those noble things you did, were just to keep a charade going? Leave me if you want, but don't insult my intelligence. A lobotomy couldn't turn you back into Tommy Torelli, Mark."

He didn't want her to shut up now, he wanted to hear her talking. Needed something to concentrate on, Christ, he was losing his strength. What was wrong with him, how could she get to him like this? He was acting weak when he had to be strong. Torrence was weak, Tommy Torelli was never weak, except one time, one lousy time when he'd forgotten to look out for himself first and decided to look out for Mario, and look how that had wound up; what it had cost him.

His mental strategy did not work. He felt himself weakening, felt himself slipping back into the personality that he'd carried for so many years. This was not Del, this was not HardWay, this was not anyone who could go on happily without him. This was

Caroline, and he was Mark Torrence, and after all these years, there was no way that he could change that.

Mark pulled the suit off the hanger, lost his balance and slipped off the doorframe. Mark fell to his knees, the suit jacket in his hands, tearing at it, pulling at it until it ripped apart between his fingers. He pushed the pieces at his face, wiped at the tears on his cheeks. He staggered to a crouch, turned to face his wife, and when he spoke his words came out of his mouth slowly, driven from his heart with shattering force, each word almost a sentence in itself, each syllable dragged out, his tears dripping off every shattered, bitter word.

"All I ever wanted was a safe harbor, Caroline. I spent my entire fucking *life* looking for that; was that too much to ask for, was that more than I deserved . . ."

He saw her, Caroline blurry, walking hurriedly toward him, taking him in her arms and holding him. There could not, he knew, be a man on earth who'd ever so desperately needed to be held like that; no other woman who had ever made a man feel so safe with merely her touch.

"That's too much for me to ask, though, isn't it, Caroline? I don't have that coming, I never had that coming."

"You've found it, you've always had it with us. *We're* your safe harbor, Mark, we'll always keep you sheltered." She pushed him away and looked at him, tears pouring down her cheeks. But when she spoke, her voice was strong.

"We'll go to Arizona, stay there with my dad. We'll sit down and figure a way out of this, Mark. We're together and we're too smart for them, we'll out-think the bastards."

Mark squeezed her tightly, feeling his strength returning, suddenly realizing that she *was* his strength, and always had been, and that knowledge made him secure.

"Don't leave me, Caroline, stay with me, please, stay with me."

"Try and get rid of me, buddy," Caroline said, and before she could say anything more, the kitchen doorbell rang.

DOLAN COULD NOT believe the balls on this son of a bitch, and for a second, he saw red, had to fight the urge to call him back, but what would be the point? The guy would only hang up on him again. Who the fuck did he think he was? God? A two-bit federal stoolpigeon, hanging up on him. He should have just listened long enough to make sure the guy was home, and then hung up himself and gone on over there. It was easy to talk tough, on the phone, from the safety of your home. He'd go over there now and see how tough this Torrence was when the cameras weren't rolling, when the two of them were face to face.

Did Torrence have a wife? Kids? The kids would be in school, unless they were toddlers. A wife could screw things up; at the moment, Eddie was only thinking about revenge, about going in and busting the guy up. Yes, he did have a wife, someone had said that his father-in-law was a copper. Last night, when they'd been searching for information on the guy. Someone had remembered that this Torrence had been married to some captain's kid, the guy had even been at their wedding, back when he'd been a rookie. Someone else had called the retired boss, but as far as Dolan knew, they hadn't gotten far with him.

He got back in his car and made himself calm down. He'd already been bounced off the negotiating team, and he had to calmly consider what it was that he was getting himself into here. He could see the headlines in his mind's eye: REVENGE-SEEKING COPPER ASSAULTS CITIZEN WHO'D KNOCKED HIM ON HIS ASS IN FRONT OF THE TV CAMERAS. He'd get suspended, for sure, maybe even canned. He and Lawlor, shoulder to shoulder at the Unemployment Office, or, more likely, the welfare line. Or, worse yet, waiting in line for his commissary, over at the County Jail, standing next to Jonah and his homeboys, trying to not act like a cop.

If he had a brain in his head, he'd turn around and go home. Right now, before he let his temper override his better judgment. It wouldn't be the first time, Dolan had once had a reputation as a cowboy; back when he'd ridden in the squadcar, back when he'd still been married, back when he'd still been drinking and popping pills and thinking that nobody had him figured out.

But he wasn't in a squadcar anymore, nor was he drinking, taking pills, or cheating on his wife. He was a sergeant, plain-clothes, a youth officer, and hurting. There were things he felt he had to resolve, and investigators would be into Torrence soon, if the legal department hadn't already warned them off. Once Torrence had talked to them, once he'd given them a detailed statement, it would be hands off for anyone else in the department. The brass would can him in a minute if they found him talking to the guy after the headhunters had debriefed him; Torrence could make a bundle in a harassment lawsuit if what he'd said hadn't pleased the IAD guys.

Shit, the choices he had to make in his life.

When he'd still been partying, he'd had a certain practice that ensured him the opportunity to continue feeding his habits. Dolan would get into his car after work, and let it drive him wherever it wanted to go. If it turned into the bar, so be it, he'd drink; if it turned toward home, he'd head on in for the night. Unless he was broke, he knew where the car would turn, and often it would turn into a tavern anyway, even when he was flat out busted. The credit of a man with a badge and gun is good in any tavern in the city, particularly the type of places to which Dolan had once been drawn. It would be, for the bartender, like having a personal bodyguard.

Dolan would once again let his car decide now, let it take him where it wanted to go. If it wanted to head home, fine, he'd go get some sleep. He was feeling pretty woozy now, he hadn't had much sleep. If it wanted to head over to Torrence's house, well, he wouldn't try to stop it. He turned the key and fired the car up, put it in reserve and backed out of the 7-Eleven parking space.

HE WASN'T CRYING anymore, and his eyes had quickly dried. Caroline was here with him, standing beside him, and he couldn't be weak now, he had to be strong. This was how they'd come, he knew, when the sun was shining; through the back door—but would they bother to ring the bell?

Mark was holding a baseball bat in his hand, stepping carefully toward the back door, through the kitchen, gliding along the wall with his back to it. He motioned for Caroline to stay where she was, by the connecting dining room door. The back door was half-glass, but the curtains were pulled, so all he could see was a figure, standing on the back stoop. The curtains on the small window three or four feet to the left of the door were open, and he couldn't see anyone standing out there near it. It appeared that what he had was one person, all alone.

Mark stepped away from the wall, holding the bat in his right hand. He reached for the curtain with his left, pulled it back an inch, and saw Tomczak standing there, biting his thumb, his head hanging down.

What the hell was wrong with this son of a bitch! In disgust, Mark made a spitting sound, grabbed the doorknob and threw the door open. He shook the baseball bat in Tomczak's face.

"What in the name of Christ are you—"

Out of the corner of his eye he saw the man come into view, from where he'd been standing against the brick wall, between the window and the door, the man holding a gun, stepping fast behind Tomczak and pointing the pistol at Mark.

"Drop the bat, Torelli," the man with the gun said, and Mark did, stepped back, and watched helplessly as the man, pushing Tomczak in front of him, entered his house and kicked the door closed behind him.

Up close like this, Mark could tell, Tomczak had reverted to his childhood; his eyes were glazed and he was crying, and he wasn't biting his thumb, he was sucking it.

BELLA PULLED TO the curb and studied the street, seeing something he didn't like; a rental car, a few doors up. That might be the way they'd do it with a man that they knew might be watching for them. There were no telephone or cable trucks, no electric company vans parked in the area. If that Lincoln was the FBI though, where were its occupants? It was probably just an out of town visitor; Bella's years as a pariah had made him grow paranoid, looking into every seam in the fabric, always expecting to discover a hidden enemy. If it was the FBI, Bella knew that he'd be out on his ass. He'd been directly ordered to lay off this case, to back off and let the FBI handle it on their own. Even the Senator couldn't help him then, and, knowing the Senator, he might not want to help, even if he could. He, too, had told Bella to stay out of it, to leave it alone.

The phone at the Youth Center hadn't been answered, so Dan had figured that they were closed, that the board had met and decided to stay out of the public eye until Mark Torrence was officially yesterday's news. That, or they'd fire him. But if they had, wouldn't someone have answered the phone when he'd called?

Bella had come down 112th St. and stopped at the house to see if Mark might be home. Dan had no idea as to what taverns Mark hung out in, if any; if he hadn't been home, Bella would have had a problem. But his car was parked at the curb in front of his house, and Bella was relieved. He wouldn't dare go home without at least talking to the man, or Andi would see him as a coward, might even insist that Dan drive her out here so she could speak with Mark personally and convince him to come home with them.

Dan still hadn't figured out how he'd approach the man. Mark wouldn't be happy to see him, either, not after the way they'd parted company that morning. Could he get him to come with him, convince him that he'd be safe in their home? His wife and kids were gone, he'd told Dan that, there was no reason for him to hang around, moping in his house. Nothing but pride could keep him here, or, perhaps, a death wish.

God, he loved his wife, Bella thought that as he got out of the car. Dying—there, he'd thought it again, that filthy word was out in the open, right in the front of his mind now, no longer hiding in the dark recesses—and she still thought of others first. How she must care for Mark, to allow him—to want him—to see her, as sick—*dying*—as she was. He could picture her, mothering him, maybe five years older than Mark was, tops, but fussing over him as if he were Danny grown and raised, cooking him soup. Mark would take one look at her and be too ashamed not to accept their hospitality. He'd always been compassionate, Bella always saw it, no matter how tough he tried to act. All you had to do was see him one time with his kid . . .

Bella locked the car and absently pulled on the handle, double checking, then began to walk toward the house, trying to think of what he would say to the man.

"I BELIEVE I'LL let you live," the man said, and Mark cringed because he knew what the man was really saying. Caroline didn't, that was obvious from the look that passed across her face as this guy spoke the words.

"There's been enough death, already. You should see the mess next door. Maybe just—" he looked pointedly at Caroline—"one more. And then I'll come back, fourteen years from now, and see how you've managed since today."

Caroline was close to being in a state of shock, Mark could see that from where he was sitting on the living room floor, tied hand and foot with telephone cord, the wire wrapped around many times, all the way to his elbows, his knees. Good knots, too, Tomczak had tied, before the man had hit him on the top of his head with the gun; when Mark tried to force them, the cords just cut into his muscles. Not that that stopped him from trying, which seemed to amuse the man.

Caroline was standing a couple of feet away, halfway between the man and the fireplace, Caroline unbound, the man pointing the gun at her, knowing what he was doing. He wouldn't need to fire the weapon to kill either one of them; he'd proved that with Tomczak, who was lying on the floor with blood oozing out of a large gash on the very top of his head. Tomczak didn't appear to be breathing, and from the sound the heavy pistol made when the man had hit him, Mark thought that he was more than likely dead.

"No, Tommy, I think I'll let you live."

Who the hell had sent him? Mark didn't know. His voice had no accent, and Mark had never met a New York wiseguy who didn't speak as if he'd come from Brooklyn, no matter where he'd been born. He looked to be in his fifties, had a thin face but a heavy, soft-looking midsection, from what Mark could see through the man's topcoat. He wore thin gloves on his hands, and he was now taking the right one off, a finger at a time, chewing it off his hand, the left holding the gun, pointing straight at Caroline.

"It's funny, getting old, isn't it, Tommy?" the man, now his confidant, said to him. "I looked at pictures of you, many of them, saw the same fence over and over again, and yet this little thing on the ground here had to tell me this was your house." He sighed, sadly.

"Twenty years ago, I wouldn't have needed his help. Then again, it was he who told me, very convincingly, that the police weren't guarding you. He was most willing to share information with me."

The man didn't look especially professional, or like a crazed mob killer. If he had been sent by the mob to kill them, Mark knew, they'd already be dead by now. A professional hit man would have done the job and escaped as quickly as possible. What this man appeared to be doing, more than anything, was enjoying himself.

Like now, smiling down at Mark, the glove hanging out of his mouth. He let it drop to the floor, and Mark watched, fascinated, as a saliva string followed it down, as if the glove were a hand-shaped yo-yo. The man wiped his smiling lips.

"You've waited fifteen years for me to come, haven't you, Tommy? It's probably a relief to you, to see me now, to think that I'll end your suffering. And I gotta tell you, I really was looking forward to killing you, but I've changed my mind, I'm going to let you live."

Dear God, let Caroline keep her mouth shut. If she tries psyching *this* guy out, he'd draw it out, make her suffer. Mark strained against the telephone cord, but it was pulled too tight around him, he couldn't get any play to work with. Still, he kept trying, not answering the guy, trying to keep from looking at Caroline.

"*Her* now, she might have to go. Like Terri, only slower, remember him?"

"Who?" Mark said.

"Terri!" The man's face got ugly, his eyes squinting, and he spat the name out, harshly, then said it again, in an evil whisper: "Terri, you son of a bitch, don't try and tell me you don't remember him."

Mark could only hope to anger the man enough so that he'd kill him. He couldn't bear the thought of seeing Caroline die before him. Maybe if the man killed him, he would spare her, would no longer feel the need to take her life without Mark there to suffer. There wasn't much chance of that though, Mark knew. The best that he could reasonably hope for was that he might kill Caroline quickly.

"I never heard of him," Mark said.

The man glared at him for a second, then his face broke into a smile. He walked slowly toward Mark, his eyes now gentle, squatted down next to Mark and spoke softly, with conviction.

"*Do* try to remember," the man said, and brushed his fingers against Mark's neck. Caroline cried out, and the man turned to her, the gun unwavering.

"Shut up," said softly, almost to himself. "Your turn's coming."

Mark felt wetness seeping down into his shirt, the man had somehow cut him. With what? Mark looked at his hand, saw blood on the man's fingernails. He'd cut him with fingernails? No wonder he'd worn gloves, his hands were slender and shaped strangely, they appeared to be misshapen, the edges were fatter than they should be, callused. He was some sort of karate freak, with strong or fake, sharp fingernails. How badly was he cut? There was no way for Mark to tell.

He lunged forward, off the wall, and butted the man in the chest with his head and the man slapped at Mark's head with the pistol as he staggered back, Mark seeing stars as the man caught his balance and got gracefully to his feet.

"*I* would have used my teeth," the man said. "I'd have gone for the neck, trying to chew out a vein." Mark sat back and closed his eyes, waiting for the pain to go away. He could feel the side of his head swelling. When at last he opened his eyes, the vision in the right eye was partially impaired. It must be closed near shut.

Caroline was glaring at the man, but he ignored her, the man focused on Mark, looking at him lovingly.

"I've waited so long for this, you'll never know how long." He shook his head, a kid at Christmas. "Terri died because of you."

"I'm Torelli, I won't deny it, but I don't know any Terri. And she," Mark twitched his head toward Caroline, "doesn't even know that I'm Torelli. I never told her anything, I used her as a cover, that's all."

"And now I'm supposed to let her go, is that where you're taking this?" The man shook his head and laughed. "Dear God, you're even more stupid than I thought." He said, "Pay attention now, and don't you dare close your eyes. If you do, I'll cut your eyelids off." The man began to walk toward Caroline, slowly.

"Tell me you remember Terri, and maybe I'll show her mercy." Caroline was moving along the wall, away from Mark, and Mark rolled to his side, flexing his muscles as hard as he could. Thousands and thousands of hours of lifting weights, and he couldn't even break a bunch of goddamned telephone wire.

"Come on, sweetums, don't make it harder on yourself." The man was moving toward Caroline, cutting off her space. He put the gun in his coat pocket, waved his arms out in front of his body as if he had knives in both hands. "Come to papa, come on, come to papa, sweetums."

Papa. Pete Papa. And Terri. Terri, the blond kid, who'd been out with him, the last time Mark had invaded a civilian's home.

He said, "Terri, Terri DeLayne!"

"That's right." The man had turned to him, still smiling, delighted now. "I *knew* you'd remember! Just had to jog your memory!" He shook his head though, having a secret he couldn't wait to share. His eyes shone with psychosis; Caroline would have spotted that long before Mark noticed. He bit his bottom lip and giggled.

"I lied, though, I have to tell you that, Tommy, I lied. I'm not going to show her mercy!" he shouted gleefully, then jumped, grabbed Caroline by the hair before she was able to move out of the way, threw her to the floor and stood over her, not even breathing hard, no longer smiling. Now his lips were turned down in disgust, and he kicked Caroline once, not hard, just a man out at the used car lot, testing a tire, experimenting.

"I'm going to take my time with her, Tommy, and I'm going to make you watch. Every time she screams, I want you to apologize to Terri. And you sweetums," he kicked her again, the same way as before. "I want you to be thinking of your loverboy over there, I want you to know that it's all his fault." He studied her for a minute, as Mark struggled to a sitting position, trying to find a way to get to his feet.

"I believe I'll start with her eyes . . ." the man said, just before someone began pounding on the front door.

"Who's that!" the man demanded, his hand going to his pocket. He pulled out the pistol and he pointed it at Caroline's head. "Tell me or I kill her."

"It's the cops," Mark said. "I called them from the upstairs bedroom, I saw you standing out there."

"Liar!"

He grabbed Caroline's hair and yanked her to her feet. The pounding began again at the front door, officious, without regard for the occupants. A cop's knock, it sounded like, and Mark could see that the man was wavering.

"Get out the back door, before they get back there."

"I've got a better idea." The man tapped Caroline on the side of her head with the pistol and let her fall to the floor, at Mark's side. He tore the other glove from his left hand and leaned down and grabbed the one he'd spat out. He shoved them both in

Mark's mouth, used his fingers to push them far down into Mark's throat.

"Insurance policy," the man said. "If it is the cops, you'll die of suffocation before they can get to you." He reached out fast with the barrel of the pistol, and Mark felt an explosion on the left side of his head, right under the ear. He closed his eyes and let himself fall limp, barely conscious, but nevertheless conscious. As if through a tunnel, he heard the man walk out of the room at the same time that he heard Dan Bella's muffled voice shouting through the front door. Mark suddenly realized that the gloves were blocking his windpipe.

"Mark, come on, Mark, I know you're in there! Open the goddamn door, or I'll kick it in!"

Mark felt himself swimming in a sea of red and black, tried to shake his head to clear it, but the second he moved it, the pain assaulted him. Jesus, he had to be bleeding in there. Caroline! He fought the pain and opened his eyes, feeling mucous draining out of his nose, Mark unable to breathe, his throat constricting now, Mark about to vomit. If he did, he knew, he'd die.

He pushed at the gloves with his tongue, blew air out of his lungs, trying to dislodge the gloves. He forgot about Caroline as the terror engulfed him, as his oxygen-starved lungs fought to breathe in air that the gloves wouldn't let him have. He was trying desperately to take breaths in through his nose, but the gloves were blocking his breathing passage, he couldn't get any air into his lungs, and he panicked.

Mark fought at the bonds, fought the gloves with his tongue and his throat, tried to inch them forward with his teeth, felt fabric moving and fought harder, trying to force himself to relax. His head and lungs were on fire, and, as if under water, he heard the pounding again at his front door, heard Bella's voice, but couldn't understand what the man was saying. He worked his jaws madly, seeing black dots in front of his eyes, the dots growing larger, swimming in his vision, threatening to block out all of Mark's vision entirely.

He felt one glove fall free, felt the other clear out of his windpipe. Mark drew in large grateful lungsful of breath as he fought at the second glove with his teeth and tongue, finally felt it fall past his lips and down onto his chest.

He tried to scream a warning to Bella, but no sound would escape his lips. His throat burned. He took a deep, painful breath, let it out in a wheezing gasp, then another, Mark's face twisted in agony and concentration, and when he let the breath out this time, the words he was trying to form came with it.

BELLA POUNDED ON the door, put his hands up against the glass and tried to see in, but that glass in the top half of the front door was that stupid cloudy stuff with little etchings all over it, and all he could make out was a figure moving toward him from inside the house. Torrence, you son of a bitch. He pounded on the door harder, kicked it twice in anger.

"I see you in there, goddamn you, do I have to come back with a warrant?" There, let him worry about his neighbor hearing *that*. Speaking of the guy, where had he been? Maybe he was working, or the feds had him in custody. He hadn't been shooting videotape out of his front window, Bella had checked.

He heard a car pull to the curb behind his own, but didn't look around to see who it was. He leaned against the glass again, his hands cupped around his eyes, and saw Torrence reaching for the door. Good. He pounded it again a couple of times, just for good measure.

As it flew open he said, "What the hell's wrong with you—" got that much out before the incredibly strong hand grabbed his shirtfront and dragged him into the house.

EDDIE SAW THE man pounding on the door of the house that should be Torrence's, and there was no doubt in his mind, right from the start, that the man at the door was a veteran cop. He had that look about him, impossible to miss. There was a car with federal license plates parked right in front of his. Shit, the feds had got there first.

Dolan sat in his car, his anger fading, fast. He wasn't about to beef with the feds, he shouldn't even have come here. He sat in his car at the curb, and wondered why the guy was kicking at the door like that, why was he pounding so hard? Did he need backup? What should Dolan do?

He saw the door open quickly and caught a mere glimpse of a hand reaching out and grabbing the fed, dragging him inside.

That arrogant son of a bitch, he was assaulting a federal officer. If nothing else, Dolan knew he had probable cause to kick in the door and help the guy out.

Before the door slammed shut again, Dolan was out of the car and rushing toward the concrete staircase.

AS HE WAS being pulled inside, Bella heard Mark's strangled voice shout to him: "Bella, run!" but it was too late for that. The man who had him was remarkably strong, dragged him in and whirled him around, threw him against the wall. Bella bounced off the wall and let himself fall to the floor, and as he hit he rolled, reaching for his pistol, and felt something sting his side as he cleared his weapon, and man, out of a clear blue sky, that little two-pound regulation .38 suddenly weighed about a half a ton. He looked at it, at the hand that couldn't lift it, Bella puzzled, then felt another sting in his chest, a sting that had some kick to it, it rolled him over onto his back.

Wood was crashing somewhere in the distance, far away, he could hear it. Glass breaking, lumber cracking, trees falling: *Timber!* If a tree falls in the woods and nobody's around to hear it . . .

Oh dear God he'd been shot. Bella figured that out as the pain hit him, came onto him like open flames blown into his side and chest, shocking him out of his fantasies, Bella seeing things clearly now, how they were, what was happening to him.

He'd die before his Andi. There were blessings in this life. He heard wild scuffling somewhere to his left, a terrible pained scream. Somebody was fighting. He hoped that the bastard that had shot him got his ass kicked. All that really mattered to him now was that he was going to die before his wife. Which meant there was a God.

God? What? Was Mark back there, fighting a man with a gun?

It was bad, and Bella knew it. He would not make it, could feel the life draining out of him, making him weak, helpless. It wasn't so bad. He certainly wasn't scared. Andi? A stab of pain gave him a moment of lucidity, and he realized that his friend, Mark, was back there, about to get shot. It had to be Mark, fighting the man who'd shot him, who else could it be?

With a massive effort, Bella rolled over, onto the side that had been shot. The pain itself was enough to kill him, but he welcomed it, it made him sharp. He had to use every ounce of strength left in his body, and all his concentration. And he'd have to close one eye, as he knew that if he could pull this miracle off at all, he would only get one chance.

God, steady my hand, Bella thought, and with an incredible effort of will, he started to lift his gun hand.

DOLAN HEARD THE gunshots before he got to the door, and there he was, in street clothes, a youth officer who felt pretentious carrying a pistol around juveniles. Still, he couldn't go back home for one now, or back to the 7-Eleven to use the outside pay-phone. A fellow cop was in there, maybe dying from a gunshot. An asshole fed, yeah, but still, a fellow cop.

Eddie reared back and kicked the door at the lock, felt it shatter under his foot, and he was leaping through the door as soon as his kicking foot hit the ground.

The man with the gun was standing maybe ten feet from the downed fed, Eddie took this in in a fraction of a second, running, as the man turned, Eddie banging into him before he could bring the gun around and shoot him. Eddie hit him with his right fist, aiming for his throat, the punch missing its mark but landing, still a good shot, in the man's upper chest. He reached for the gun hand and got a grip on the man's wrist, and the bastard, he was punching Eddie in the head with his free hand, heavy blows that hurt him. Eddie leaned his head down and bit the man's wrist as hard as he could, tore at the flesh like a Pit bull biting a rat, and he heard the man scream in his ear at the same time that the gun fell out of his hand. Eddie let him go and turned to face him now, one on one, himself against this short, fat, middle-aged out of shape motherfucker, who suddenly shot out a foot and damn near took Eddie's kneecap off.

"MARK?" CAROLINE'S VOICE was pained and soft, as if she was com-ing out of a nightmare and calling out to him at dawn. "*Mark!*" Urgent now, Caroline seeking him, feeling him, pushing herself up and then nearly falling over in pain.

"Mark, talk to me, Mark . . ." There was terror in her voice, and through his own terror and exhaustion, he managed to speak her name.

"Caroline."

"Mark, Mark what happened?"

"Caroline, if you can, get to the kitchen, get a knife out of the drawer and come back in here; you've got to cut this shit off me."

"What's going on? Where's that man?"

"Out in the living room. He's fighting with Bella—a federal agent. Caroline, you have to cut me loose."

"I'd have to go through the dining room to get to the kitchen."

"We can't stay here, when Bella loses, we're dead."

Caroline looked around, then stood hurriedly, swayed on her feet and grabbed the wall, groaning. She didn't waste any time on the pain, though, just pushed herself away from the wall and staggered to the fireplace. She took a poker out of the stand and began to walk toward the door.

"Caroline, don't! Come over here and use that thing to pry this cord off me!"

She didn't pay him any attention, just kept walking toward the dining room.

Bella lost it as the barrel of the pistol was steady on the back of the man who had once had a gun, but now didn't. Was it him, or was it Mark that the pistol was pointing at? Bella couldn't tell. He couldn't shoot Mark. Mark was his friend. Thinking about this, he lost his strength, and his hands fell to the floor, the gun flopping out, onto the carpet. Bang. No shot, although he'd expected one. He'd had the hammer back, ready to go. But still, there was nothing. Or maybe it had gone off and he was too far gone to hear it.

Dan Bella, with three years to go before his retirement from the federal marshal's service, died on the floor in the dining room of the house where Mark Torrence had spent ten happy years living with his wife and children. His last conscious thought was of how glad he was to go out knowing that his daughters would have the chance to finish college.

WHAT WAS WITH this bastard? Dolan couldn't figure him out. He was losing the fight, getting beat bad, and he was breathing like a freight train while this guy in front of him, the son of a bitch, had yet to break a sweat.

Eugene Izzi

It was all he could do just to stay away from the man now, far enough back so that some of the steady stream of kicks and chops wouldn't hurt him. The man was advancing though, and it was just a matter of time until he backed Dolan against a wall and maybe then he would not even bother to go after the gun, maybe he'd just beat Dolan to death with his bare hands.

He'd almost done it already. A couple of hard kicks and a punch to the ribs had hurt him, bad, and his left arm was numb from some kind of karate chop. It was no good offensively, all Dolan could use it for was to cover his ribs from attack. There was blood dripping off his forehead into his eyes, making him blink rapidly, the guy doing some kind of shit with his fingers, flicking them at Eddie's face and every time Eddie would duck his head, trying to save his eyeballs, the fingertips would slice through his forehead, and the guy'd do a swivel kick and tag him one in the belly.

The guy, he was playing with Eddie now, toying with his ass. Coming in for the kill, and there wasn't anything Dolan could do about it except hold his ribs and wait for the end.

He'd managed to kick the gun a couple of times, though, away from them, when he'd still thought that there was a chance that he could win the fight on his own. That was over now, he was no longer under any such delusions. He was scared, but he could handle it, the guy was in no hurry. Maybe the neighbors had heard the gunshots and had dialed 911. If he could just get one damn solid punch in, if only the man wasn't so fast . . .

He danced backward yet some more and felt his back hit the wall, shit. What now? Here he came, smiling that deadly smile, whistling through his teeth, and suddenly, Eddie Dolan understood horror.

The maniac slashed out at Dolan with his fingers again, and this time Dolan didn't get his hands up in time, wasn't able to bow his head. He felt a terrible pain in his left eye, saw a red and white flash, and he fell to his knees, shrieking, forgetting about defending himself, this bastard had popped out his eyeball; he could feel it, dangling, in the palm of his hand.

Where was the bastard, why wasn't he coming in for the kill? Eddie couldn't see, but he could hear, and he heard a woman's grunt, again and again and again, and the sound of a baseball bag hitting a melon, and he realized that he'd been saved.

He let himself fall to the carpet, on his ass, both hands holding

338

his eye. He tried looking through the other one, lifted his head just an inch, saw a woman standing over the guy, something slim but heavy in her hand. He had no depth perception, so he didn't know how far away she was, it looked as if she were right on top of him, and that was okay with Eddie. The sight of her, standing there, chest heaving, a determined, warrior look on her face, looking down at the body of the man on the floor, let him know that in her presence, Eddie Dolan was safe.

"Miss?" Dolan said, but she didn't look at him, never took her eyes off what was left of the man on the carpet. Dolan could feel part of him, spread across his toes. "Ma'am?" Dolan said, his voice shaking, knowing he was going into shock and needed help, fast. She looked up this time, squinted at him, and her expression changed as she shook her head and took a staggering step backward.

"Please, lady, call an ambulance, will you?" Dolan said.

"GREATER LOVER HATH no man, than he lay down his life for another . . ." The priest's voice was deep and booming, falling gently across the open space surrounding Bella's grave, and Caroline tuned him out; she didn't believe what he was saying, or to whom he was saying it to. Not today, maybe not anymore, forever.

It was raining, the way it was supposed to at funerals. The sky was dark and heavy with black clouds, the rain falling gently at the moment, but Caroline knew that it was about to burst forth at any second, a soaking, cleansing rain. She stood next to her husband, holding his arm, Mark tall and strong, wearing dark glasses even in the gloom. The gravesight was filled with men in dark suits, wearing shades. Mark was just another of them, but even a passerby could tell, he was not of them.

He had made that clear earlier, at the funeral parlor, Mark freezing out these hypocrites who had come up to him with their hands out, as friends. She'd never been more proud of him, of the way he'd acted, than then. Mark glaring at them, then staring down at their hands. After a short while, the others had caught on, but when those two or three had tried, it had been a beautiful sight.

A once-protected witness shaming them, using them to his

own advantage and at his own pleasure. It was usually, with such men, Caroline knew, the other way around. But Mark hadn't insisted on coming here just to insult the men who had once been his keepers. Mark's main concern, and Caroline's, was the woman, Andrea, the widow.

Caroline looked around at the dozens of floral arrangements, at the people gathered at graveside. Her eldest son, Mario—*her* eldest son as well as Mark's—stood quietly at his father's side, his hair combed, in his suit. Looking so much like a man.

Andrea's daughters were at their mother's side, holding themselves together as best they could, for their mother's sake. They were lovely young girls, and in them, Caroline could see the beauty that the illness had stolen from Andrea, could see what she'd once been. Now, seeing her like this, everyone knew that Andrea would shortly be joining her husband. Now, the beauty was gone, there was only the wait for death. She hoped, when their time came, that she herself would die before Mark.

Mark touched her elbow and leaned down, whispered in her ear.

"Are you all right?"

"Yes, I am." She said it quietly, with reserve, while she'd wanted to shout it out. You're damn right she was all right, even with Mark thinking she wasn't, waiting for some delayed reaction. Caroline was hurt more by the stinging lump still under her ear than she was by the remembrance of what she'd done to the killer.

What Mark didn't know, what she hadn't told him yet, was that she was glad that she'd done what she'd done, would do it again if she had to, a hundred times over. That bastard had broken into their *home,* had been prepared to kill them both and smile at them as he did so. She felt no grief, no remorse, no burden or sense of guilt. Mark would feel those things for her, because he was blaming himself.

But that wouldn't work with Caroline, she knew a little more about things than Mark could ever guess. That man had come into their lives of his own free will, not because of Mark, not because of anything except his twisted need to kill, his sick desire to avenge a crime that he'd committed himself, many years ago.

What she'd done, as far as she was concerned, was to perform surgery without a license. Cut out a cancer, that was all she'd done. It surprised her that she felt this way, but it also made her glad.

The priest was winding down now as the rain began to pour upon them, fat droplets soaking them, matting down the widow's sparse hair under the thin black lace veil that was perched on top of her head. Caroline could see the white skull sticking out, around the patches of hair. Andrea's daughters were helping her to her feet, and as she staggered, a group of marshals stepped forward, but she glared at them and waved them away with her purse. As weak as she was, look at her courage.

Andrea looked around, until she spotted Mark. With a weak half-wave she beckoned to him, and Mark and their son went forward. Mark took Andrea's left arm, while Mario took her right. Mark's eye was multi-colored, and there was a slash mark above the eye. He had a lumpy surgical bandage covering the side of his head, where Bracken had hit him with Tomczak's pistol. The cut on the side of his neck was visible above the collar of his shirt. Mark and Mario, what a reunion they'd had; and only a day before it, the man had tried to tell her that he didn't need anyone.

Her husband and her son walked the widow to the casket and steadied her as she dropped a rose into the casket that held the mortal remains of her husband, then they escorted her away, holding her up as she sobbed, her daughters walking behind her, falling apart, but no marshal had the courage to step forward and try and comfort them.

The twins were still with grandpa, safe and far away, and the three of them would be joining the rest of the clan, as soon as this funeral ended. The madman, the killer, he'd already been buried, in a pine box, better than he deserved. She'd wanted to go to that burial, too, but Mark hadn't thought it wise. Some of his enemies might show up there, he said. What he didn't seem to understand, yet, was, his enemies were her enemies, and she'd sent a signal to them in the form of the corpse of the killer, Bracken. She didn't think the others would accept any of her future invitations.

Caroline tossed a rose onto the casket before she went to catch up with her family, wearing a dark veil over her own face, more to hide the contempt she felt for the federal bastards attending the funeral than to conceal her personal grief. Although she felt it, strongly, that grief.

She'd never met Dan Bella, but he'd died for her husband, and that was all that counted. Her husband, right over there, waiting for her by the family limo. She went to him and leaned into the limo, kissed Andrea on the cheek and heard Andrea ask God to bless her, and she thanked her, stepped back, as her husband closed the door.

They watched the limo drive off, the three of them, standing close and touching. Mark looked down at her, love in his eyes, concern, too; Mark was worried.

Behind Mark, she could see Ed Dolan standing cautiously next to their car, his head on a swivel, watching the crowd. He'd told her to call him Eddie, but she had trouble referring to a full-grown man in that manner. The poor man with the bandage over his left eye, acting as if it didn't matter to him. It would be a few weeks before he would know if he'd lose the sight in it. He'd get them to the airport and would keep his mouth shut. He was beholden to Caroline, she knew, thought that she'd saved his life, and she had, but only in the process of saving her own, and her husband's.

"Let's go home," Mark said, found his wife's hand and squeezed it.

"To our safe harbor," Caroline said, and tried her best to smile.